Birthday Wishes

BIRTHDAY Wishes

ELAINE CORUM STRAWN

Other books written by Elaine Corum Strawn

Everytime I See You Falling
Strokewaves
Kiddie & the Major
Going on a Bear Hunt
Lessons Learned in a Primary Classroom

Other books from Off & Running

Ornithomancy by Mollie Jackman
Crooked Lines by Dyarl Lewis
Edgewood Village by Linda Koenig
Warren's Hill by Linda Koenig
Olive You! by Charlotte Brumfield
My Name is Annabella by Beverly Miles
There's a Snake Down There by RGO Books

*"The more you praise and celebrate your life,
the more there is in life to celebrate."*
—Oprah Winfrey

*This book is dedicated to all our loved ones we've
lost too soon. We miss you, we love you, and we
will do our best to find ways to make every day
count, not just on our birthdays.*

(If you're suffering a loss and need counseling
support, call or text 988.)

PROLOGUE

He stood watching her sleep in the padded chaise lounge chair, taking in her birthday tiara and her floral dress pulled around her legs that she had tucked up under her. Having worked to casually ignore his best friend's kid sister for years now, he was startled to realize she was growing into a young woman. A beautiful young woman. He shook his head, quick to dismiss his inappropriate thoughts. He went to find a dry towel to cover her as the cool night air descended upon the remnants of a teenager's typical pool party. Gently he covered her with the oversized towel he had shook out.

She jumped when he tucked it around her shoulders, her eyes flying open wildly as she searched to make sense of where she was. He could see relief flood her face as her eyes met his.

"Oh it's just you Billy." she said, settling back into her chaise. "You startled me. Why are you and Jordy crashing my party?"

He sat down on the chaise beside her, taking in her unruly dark curly hair, her light blue eyes still sleepy. "Why would two grown men crash a little girl's birthday party?" he teased her.

"Ha! Gown men, you wish! I'm sure my party was equal to whatever lame thing you two were doing tonight. And this just in, I'm not a little girl anymore, in case you haven't noticed. Where's Jordy?" she asked as she moved the towel off herself, stretching her long tanned legs out in front of her, oblivious to his stare.

"Headed to bed. I was just cutting through your backyard to head to my house. It's late. Shouldn't you be getting to bed too?" he asked.

She reached for her phone, checking the time. Realizing it was just after midnight she jumped up as she yelled, "Woohoo! It's official! I'm seventeen!"

He watched her curiously as she stood watching her phone, her pointer finger held out to him, putting him on pause to hold that thought. Eyeing him with a shy smile, she closed her eyes and mumbled something to herself before opening them and sitting down beside him.

"What just happened?" he asked.

"I just made my birthday wish for the year. I decided making my wish at the time I was born is more significant than with the cake and candles. But it can't hurt to double down either!" she added with a wicked grin. She neglected to tell him she was wishing for her first romantic kiss to sweep her off her feet.

As Taylor Swift suddenly popped up on her blue tooth speaker she used her phone to turn up *Blank Space*. "Yes! I love this song!" She sang animatedly into her pretend microphone while dancing around him.

Amused, Billy sat back in his chair, taking in all that was seventeen year old Sam. He raised his eyebrows at her as she emphasized the words about being young and reckless. Listening to her sing, he had no doubt the boys in her future were in big trouble. It surprised him to realize he found himself a little jealous of who might one day be her forever. Regrettably it was hard to know what the future held for either of them, but for the present, he was going to enjoy this unexpected night with Sam. How could he not?

HOW
IT
STARTED

CHAPTER ONE

Sam's birthday, three years ago

Despite the burning in her chest, she kept going, as always running a fine line between pushing or punishing herself. Every year on her birthday she used her run to measure where she was with her health, both physically and mentally. As Jordan's favorite song came through her earbuds, she was grateful for the shades that kept her emotions shielded, letting Imagine Dragon's words fill her head, the beat slowing her pace. As the song finished, she paused in one of her favorite spots in Chelsea Park to catch her breath and hydrate.

It was a decent day for August and the park was crowded as people in the surrounding neighborhoods came out to enjoy it. She could hear the cheering of the crowd at the ballpark close by, letting the familiar sound wash over her and restore her equilibrium. Taking one last swig from her water bottle, she popped her earbuds back in, glancing around her as she prepared to head back the way she had come. Noticing the same man she had seen when she first started her run, she paused to wonder if he was following her. It occurred to her, she had noticed him on her runs before. She watched him for a minute, taking him in before shaking her head to dismiss him, working to keep her insecurities at bay.

Headed home, she knew she would need to maintain her brisk pace to ensure she had enough time to shower and get to her parents house for her birthday dinner, another annual tradition that could at times be equally as painful. As she ran, the conversation with her mom yesterday replayed in her head. Today was the day she had to face the fact her mom was ready to clean out Jordan's room and move their family another step forward in their healing process. She dreaded going into his room, the emotional slam of choosing any sentimental mementos causing her chest to hurt. She understood her mom's point, but she didn't have to like it.

It had been three years since her brother's car had exploded when he started it. According to the experts, the battery had been under the right conditions to cause it to explode, debris hitting Jordan in the head, his wound traumatic enough to kill him. It had seemed like a flimsy explanation, but regardless, it seemed her family had no choice but to accept it. The freak accident had devastated her tight knit family, a rude awakening for her twenty something self who had only experienced the sudden loss of her grandfather when she was in the seventh grade.

Turning the corner onto her street she sprinted the last little bit, focused on her ragged breathing rather than the guilt she struggled with over her brother's death. She paused in front of her building, her hands on her hips, catching her breath before she climbed the stairs to her loft. Drinking greedily from her water bottle she noticed the man again out of the corner of her eye. Quickly she went inside, moving discreetly to the side of a window to see if he would walk by, her heart pounding loudly as she waited. When no one did, she shook her head, mentally telling herself she should know better after binge watching episodes of Castle so late last night.

Castle had always been her and Jordan's favorite show to watch on Monday nights. Her big brother had been one of her best friends, their relationship built on good natured barbs and lots of time centered around sports. Letting the hot water of her shower wash over her, she thought of the first time she and Jordan had gone for a run. She had resisted at first, giving him a hundred other better things she could be doing. Like she always did, she had caved and they eventually headed out together one day, listening to his shared playlist, giving her thumbs up along the way, reminding her to just stop running when she needed to.

It turned out she had been a natural and she had ended up running track all through high school. As she grew into an adult, running had become her lifeline whether she was struggling or celebrating, although there had been a lot more struggling than celebrating since they lost Jordan. Pulling a simple blue cotton dress from her closet, she was determined to make today a good day. After all it was her birthday and Sam loved celebrating her birthday.

Pulling into her parent's driveway, she was thankful it wasn't a milestone birthday like last year. It had been painful to watch everyone bend over backwards to make sure turning "flirty and thirty" was nothing but a good time. Thirty-one was a lot less pressure. Having arrived before her sister and her family, the quiet of the house felt almost deafening. She greeted her mom with a warm hug, accepting her happy birthday with a smile before letting her take her by the hand and lead her into Jordan's room.

"It's time Sam. We will always remember Jordan with love and laughter, but the hard truth is he's gone and we're still here. It's time to start living our lives again with all the light and joy we can find." She said it quietly, her arm around Sam's waist.

Sam nodded, forcing herself to keep her emotions in check. "What do you want to do with the room now?" she asked, her voice sounding strange.

"It's going to be a bunk room for the grandkids. They're getting bigger and need a space to play and sleep when they stay with us."

Nodding, Sam could only agree. "Jordan would like that."

"I'll leave you to it. Dinner will be ready in thirty so take your time. I left a box on the bed if you need it." Her mother leaned into her, squeezing her in a side hug before leaving the room.

Still standing by the door, she let her gaze slowly sweep the room, noting how neat and clean it was, not a dirty sock or stinky pair of shorts to be found. She thought of her mom having to eventually come in and pick up Jordan's dirty clothes, make his bed, and dust around all the trophies and knickknacks on his shelves over his desk. Her brother had been a great guy but a terrible slob. She had learned the hard way her mom was one of the strongest women she knew and she took a deep breath, embracing her strength as she moved to do as she was asked.

Going to his bookshelf first she touched the backs of some of their favorites the two of them had read together, pulling a few out to add to her own collection. She grimaced at finding *Lord of the Flies*, the only book they had ever disagreed on, Jordan loving it and Sam hating it. He had loved debating a variety of topics with her, from books to the best place to get ice cream to whether computers would someday take over the world. Jordan was always a tech geek, often touting that *The Jetsons* technology had not been that far off almost sixty years ago. Her brother was smart, graduating with a degree in computer science from Columbia, his dream job to be in cybersecurity.

Suddenly she switched gears and went to the middle top drawer of his dresser, pulling it out expecting to see Jordan's sock collection in a crazy disarray. Instead they were in tight little balls, neatly arranged by color. Sam's heart hurt to think of her mom going through them all, remembering with a painful smile how Jordan had referred to his socks as his signature accessory, believing himself to be somewhat of a trendsetter for high-school boys everywhere. Choosing two, she stuffed them into her dress pocket, before noticing a notebook at the bottom of the shallow drawer. Flipping through it she could see it was Jordan's journal, mostly notes about technology stuff and drawings to go with them. Pausing, she realized a page had been torn out near the back. Shrugging, she dismissed it before tucking the journal into her oversized bag laying on the bed.

Wandering over to his desk, she untacked a photo of Jordan with his best friend Billy, their arms around each other's necks, their tanned faces and big smiles radiating all the joy of being twelve and carefree during the summer. Feeling a warmth to her cheeks and regret in her heart, she wondered what had ever happened to Billy, remembering Jordan announcing he was going into the Navy just a few days after her seventeenth birthday. She wondered if Billy knew Jordan was gone.

Tacking the photo back up, she noticed another one of her and her brother, a first place medal hanging beside it on his board. She recognized it was for swimming at state, remembering that meet with all the feels, the smell of chlorine and hearing the splash of the water as swimmers moved their arms and legs with all the urgency their bodies could muster. Three years in a row Jordan had lost first place in the backstroke to his nemesis, but his senior year he had pushed himself hard to train for a win when he went to state for the last time. Her small twelve year old self had sat on his back as he did push ups, the number he could do improving weekly. When his final state meet had finally come to pass, she had been the loudest to cheer him to a victory, her eyes stinging with pride when he won. Tucking the photo and the medal into her other pocket, it wasn't the first time she thought about how much of an influence Jordan had been on her, cheering her on to her own state titles when she finally made it to high school.

Moving to the closet, she took a deep breath before she slid the door open. Front and center hung Jordan's letterman's jacket, his pride and joy, the red and white as vivid as the last time she had seen him wear it. She smiled remembering him hanging it up in the back of his closet one day, explaining gloomily to Sam that freshman girls at Columbia were not impressed with boys still living out their high school glory days. Pulling it off the hanger, she hesitated briefly before putting it on. Going to the mirror, she appreciated the style of it even over her summer dress. Should she take it with her?

"Sam! Dinner's ready! Come on down, birthday girl!" her mom called from the bottom of the stairs.

Grabbing her bag before heading down, she left the jacket on, wanting to make sure it was okay for her to take something so important to Jordan. The talking at the table came to an abrupt halt as she walked into her family's dining room. Glancing from face to face, she shifted uncomfortably before asking, "Does this look weird on me?"

It was her mom who got up and came to her. "Of course not Peanut. Jordan would love for you to have his jacket."

Looking from her dad to her sister Riley, she asked, 'Are you guys good with me taking this?' Her dad was a little misty as he nodded approval while Riley got up to hug her. "Mom's right. Jordan would love to see someone making his jacket look good again. Happy birthday Sami!"

Suddenly two littles were at her side. "Happy birthday Auntie Sami!" Bending down, she scooped her sister's two year old twins up, one in each arm. "Thanks luvs. Who's ready for birthday cake?!"

"Me! Me!" They both cheered eagerly.

Taking one twin from her to put back in his chair, Riley announced with a cheerful smile, "But first we're eating birthday dinner Nana worked hard on. Aren't we Auntie Sami?"

Placing the other twin back in her chair, Sam nodded in agreement. "Pasta and breadsticks for everyone! Yay! Then cake *after* we all eat a good dinner." she added hastily upon seeing Riley's face.

It wasn't long before her dad was lighting the candles on her cake, her mom hurrying to get small plates. She felt her cheeks go pink when her sister teased her, telling Sam she needed to wish for a handsome man to come and sweep her away from her safe, boring life. With a great sense of satisfaction her foot connected under the table, causing her sister to howl in surprised pain, Riley's husband not the least bit surprised by this sisterly exchange. Regretfully, she knew that Riley did have a point, having already made a wish similar to that just after midnight, her birthday wish that she knew counted.

On her sixteenth birthday Sam had learned at family dinner the exact time she'd been born, weeks premature and the reason she had ended up with the nickname Peanut. It had been her seventeenth birthday the first time she made a wish just after midnight. She didn't advertise making her wish knowing it probably sounded dumb, but still it became a tradition for her to make her wish every year at the time of her birth, cake and candles not required. Years later, it delighted her to know she had mostly a winning record when it came to her wishes coming true.

She could only hope this year would lean to another win, somewhere in her very near future.

Will Shaw was one of the first clients to walk through her newly opened door at *Paws for a Cause*, arriving early one morning, just a few days after her birthday. His rugged good looks immediately caught her attention, but she quickly realized his detached demeanor left much to be desired. Walking in with a handsome German Shepherd, Sam had been happy to greet them both. Accustomed to seeing a wagging tail to signify her gentle pets were more than welcome, she was curious when the dog merely sat stoically beside his owner, his ears alert, his eyes on her every move.

When she turned her attention back to the man she was quick to notice he seemed weathered, a growth of whiskers hovering between a beard and needing a shave just covering his strong jawline. Realizing he somehow seemed familiar, she wondered why. "Welcome to *Paws for a Cause*. How can I help you today?" she asked with a smile.

Introducing himself as Will Shaw, he then turned to introduce her to Prince, informing her that Prince was a working dog. His attitude was just short of condescending as he launched into his needs and expectations if she were to care for his dog. She watched him thoughtfully as he droned on before she interrupted him to ask, "I'm sorry, but have we met?"

His face froze, before shaking his head no. "I don't think so."

As he continued, she interrupted again. "I'm sorry, but you seem familiar. Do you live around here?"

She could see he was choosing his words carefully. "I live between here and Chelsea Park." She noticed his look became guarded, still paused to see if she was ready to let it go.

"That must be it. I run from here to the park at least once a week." she said, her tone friendly, her look still thinking about it.

He nodded before saying, "I run in the neighborhood too."

Satisfied she was done interrupting, he got down to the business of what he was looking for, not only a groomer, but also a place to board Prince when he was away. He had noted in her ad that she took a holistic approach to her grooming services and offered massage therapy as well, informing her that Prince would be in need of that on a regular basis.

Assuming she had passed his quick assessment of her credentials, she suddenly cut him off again, acknowledging that German Shepherds are prone to hip dysplasia and massage would be helpful for relieving his pain. His arched brow, however brief, signified a point for her. He soon requested the necessary paperwork to fill out before signing his name on the line of her electronic pad.

He was on his way out the door when he turned back to share a handful of commands he used with Prince while she mentally made a grocery list. Realizing he was finished and staring at her expectantly, she commented innocently she was surprised he didn't have a special whistle for her to use too. He stared at her hard, before finally taking his leave. Leaving Prince with her for his first grooming, she watched him walk down the street, before kneeling down to him. "Don't worry Prince. My house, my rules. You can relax when you're with me."

Quickly becoming one of her regulars, she grew fond of Prince and was always happy to show him some love, rubbing behind his ears and under his chin. She could tell it pained Will to see this display of affection and she found it amusing when he took it upon himself one day to remind her Prince was a working dog and didn't need the attention. With a slight smile, she reminded him she had never met a male who didn't enjoy being rubbed in just the right way. Seeing his eyebrows arch, she felt compelled to amend her statement, but let it go instead, smiling to herself.

It had taken at least a good six months, but slowly they began to establish a mutually respectful relationship on behalf of Prince. Will became even more attractive as he became less condescending, eventually realizing Sam's expertise regarding dogs and acknowledging out loud that he could see Prince moved more with ease, her regular massages helping his dysplasia. Sam came to realize that despite Will seeing Prince as a work dog, he truly did care about him and wanted only the best for him. To Prince's credit he learned to keep it in check until Will was long gone before allowing himself to bask in the attention Sam bestowed upon him. When he stayed over, it made Sam smile to see he always chose to sleep on the floor at the side of her bed, his protection undeniable. It felt nice to have a man in the house, even if he was four legged.

CHAPTER TWO

Today, after closing early, Sam found herself headed to Charlie's, her favorite neighborhood bar where her friend was planning to meet her when she got her littles to bed. Her heels clicked as she walked, the bar just a few blocks from her loft. As she approached the door, a man standing close by said with a leer, "Well look at you sweetheart. I bet you taste as good on the inside as you look on the outside." Ignoring him and his repulsive comment, she turned her face to stone as she pulled the door open and went inside.

She paused for a beat, shaking off his comment before heading to the bar where she was greeted heartily by Frankie, the owner and her friend. Scanning the bar, she was surprised to see her client Will sitting not that far from the stool she had just pulled out for herself. Their relationship, while albeit a professional one, had definitely grown over the months and she reminded herself he wasn't just one of her clients, but *the* client that always had her full attention despite his aloof manner. She lived for an opportunity to provoke him, feeling the need for him to engage in a real conversation with her.

Unknowingly Frankie pushed a glass of wine to Sam at the same time she pushed a beer over to Will. In unison they thanked her, their eyes flickering to each other. Sam raised her glass to him before taking her first sip, the cold pinot just what she needed. Not waiting for an invitation, she moved down the three seats to sit beside him, ignoring Frankie's obvious surprise to see her make such a bold move.

"I don't think I've seen you in here before." Sam offered casually.

"It's my first time here," he replied in a less friendly voice.

Ignoring his attitude like usual, Sam tilted her head at him before teasing him, "I'm not sure you recognize me in a dress."

He paused to sip his beer making her wait for his response. She all but blushed as he pointedly looked her over from head to toe. "You groom my dog Prince. Clearly you're a master of your craft."

Sam felt a slow burn rise from her chest to her brain and come out her mouth. "You're too kind." she said, her sarcasm obvious. She added a biting afterthought. "Some things done with expertise can look easier said than done while other things, like being an asshole, some people pull off without even having to think about it."

She was even more annoyed when she saw him give a slight smile. "Touche!" he said. As she made a move to go back to her original bar stool, he put his hand on her arm to stop her. "I'm sorry for that. I don't get out much let alone sit in the company of a pretty woman. Please stay and I'll behave myself. Promise."

She eyed him warily before settling back onto the barstool next to him. "Don't let your pendulum swing too far the other way. That's annoying too."

This time he gave a soft laugh before raising his glass to her. "To be able to always say it like you see it." After a few minutes of sipping their drinks, he moved to safer ground, asking her to tell him how she came to start her grooming business.

Hesitating, she knew small talk could be a struggle for some and as such was curious as to the sincerity of his interest. "My grandmother passed away and left me her brownstone. I was working as a dog groomer for someone else and walking dogs to pay my bills. It was a no brainer when I realized she had given me such a generous opportunity. She ran an art studio in the lower part of the building for decades. I learned a lot about running a business from her. She was well loved in the neighborhood as her customers were always the bottom line." Sam finished, her cheeks pink, knowing she had over shared. She loved to talk about her grandmother even to Will.

"She must have been very special. You still miss her." he said softly.

Sam nodded, not able to meet his eyes. "Every day. I owe so much to her and she's not here to see it."

Sam was taken aback when Will gently lifted her chin up, forcing her eyes to meet his. "She sees you. I have no doubt she is very proud of you."

Sam was touched by his sentiment but his hand on her face was giving her a different kind of slow burn. "Thank you." she said softly.

Remembering where they were, Will quickly dropped his hand, moving the conversation along. "It seems unusual to include massage therapy in grooming services. How did that come about?"

She took another sip of wine before answering, needing a minute to store that last bit where she could retrieve it later. "Once upon a time I was in Vet School. A semester before graduation, I dropped out, but I knew dogs were my passion. When I opened my own grooming salon I knew I wanted to offer a holistic approach. I wanted to take care of the whole dog and not just make sure they look good. Sounds indulgent I'm sure."

Will was quick to dismiss her last comment. "Not at all. You're most definitely prolonging and enhancing Prince's life and for that I'm grateful. He's the closest thing I have to a family. He's worked hard and as he gets older, I want him to stay healthy and live as long a life as possible. I have no worries about him when he's with you. "

Sam took in what Will was saying, surprised by his openness but appreciative of what he said. Somewhere along the way people had come to treat their dogs more like their children than just a pet. It made her feel good to think that what she did could make a difference. Her parents didn't always see it that way, but she knew Will was right, Gram would have approved.

"Thank you for saying that. Prince is a special dog for sure. I always enjoy it when he's around."

Eyeing her curiously, he asked, "Why did you quit vet school?"

Taking a minute to absorb his question, she answered best she could. "I couldn't handle the down side of being a vet. When animals are in so much pain with little to zero chance of recovery and you have to put them down. Telling the families was just as hard. I didn't have what it took to do that so I quit."

She avoided looking at him, focused instead on sipping her wine, keeping her trauma she's experienced to herself. She was relieved when he changed the subject abruptly, asking Frankie for a menu. As he perused it, he asked Sam what she would recommend before ordering her personal favorite, the pimento cheeseburger and fries. When Frankie looked at Sam expectantly, she nodded telling her to make it two. It wasn't long before they were enjoying their juicy burgers in companionable silence.

Feeling her phone buzz beside her, she quickly checked it for the message. "Shoot!" she said abruptly.

They both turned to her expectantly. "What's up?" Frankie asked.

"Jen just canceled on me! Her kids were playing with Rachel's and now all the kids are throwing up. She won't be able to meet me either."

Winking at her, Frankie announced, "Well looks like you're in good hands here. I'll bring you another glass of wine anyway."

Another hour quickly passed as Sam and Will chatted about any and everything that could constitute a casual conversation. She noticed how comfortable she felt around him, making their conversation easy. Having finished her glass of wine, Sam decided it was time to call it a night. She said her good-byes and headed out, declining Will's offer to walk her out. Pulling her jacket tighter around her, she was startled to see the offensive man was still standing close by smoking a cigarette. She had forgotten all about the incident, but was hesitant to walk out the door to face him alone. It made her uncomfortable that he was still there hours later and couldn't help but wonder if he was actually waiting for her.

She turned as Will walked up, her phone in his hand. "You left your phone on the bar." Handing it to her, he noticed her expression and quickly asked, "What's wrong?"

She took a deep breath wanting to shake off the feeling in her gut. "It's nothing." Seeing his look of doubt, she went on. "When I came in tonight there was a man who made a lewd comment to me and now I see he's still out there. But I'm sure it's nothing." Her heart pounded in her chest as she worked to get up her courage to walk out the door.

She was astonished when he told her sharply to stay put, watching him walk back to the bar before returning to her in no time. He held his arm out for her to take as he returned to her. "Frankie is going to call the police and let them handle it, but in the meantime, I can take you home. Ready?"

Nodding, she took his arm, letting him guide her out the door. On instinct she turned towards home before realizing Will thought he was taking her to her car. "Actually I walked here." She finally managed to get out once they were safely past the offensive man, his eyes on them unnerving.

Will paused to confirm. "You walked here?"

She nodded to him. "Yeah sorry, but I walk pretty much everywhere I go. I don't own a car."

He studied her for a moment before making a decision. "No worries. I'll walk you home."

As they turned a corner, they paused briefly to watch as a police car pulled up to Frankie's. Releasing a long deep breath, she turned to Will with a quiet "Thank you."

Turning to follow her, Will decided to lighten the mood. "I know Prince is your favorite, but tell me about some of your other favorite clients."

As she searched for the right thing to say, Sam knew that explained a lot about Will's aloof manner. She stared into her wine glass, suddenly filled with her own feelings of loss for family members.

"I see why Prince is so important to you." was all she could think to say as she looked up at him, her eyes full of compassion.

Suddenly Will got up and went to the bookshelf, picking up a picture of a little girl sitting behind a birthday cake, her mouth in the middle of blowing out five candles, her eyes aglow. "Is this you?"

Sam sighed before answering. "It is. Gram took that picture years ago and that's where it has sat ever since. I asked her about it when I was older. She told me she loved that picture because of the pure joy on my face. She always told me to celebrate my birthday and find the joy in living a good life, knowing that not everyone gets as many birthdays as they should." She realized Will knew this as well as she did.

Seeing her getting emotional, Will gave her a minute. When she got up and took her empty wine glass to the sink, he followed, rinsing his coffee cup out before placing it beside her wine glass.

They stood close by the sink, facing each other, both of them reluctant to end the night, but knowing it was time. Unexpectedly Will put his hands on her shoulders, his eyes dark and focused on her lips. His hands were warm and she felt her pulse quicken as she wondered if he was going to kiss her. Instead he pulled her into a warm hug, his scent intoxicating, his strong arms more than comforting. "Thank you for a really nice night Miss Cooper." he said into her hair. She pulled away ready to thank him for walking her home when he added, "I'll see you soon."

She looked at him quizzically, wondering if he was going to ask her out. Seeing her expression, he clarified. "You said Prince could stay with you the next couple of days. Is that still good?"

She nodded before moving away from him to head to her door, ready to walk him out. "Of course. And thanks again for walking me home."

"Anytime. Take care." he said.

She locked her door, her thoughts whirling as she got ready for bed, realizing her birthday wish was in full swing and she couldn't wait to see where it would lead her in the near future.

Walking the few blocks to his own brownstone, Will mentally berated himself, shaking off the thought of his lips on Sam's, his tongue exploring her from head to toe. Damn she was the whole package for him. He found her dark wavy hair and light blue eyes stunning, but also appreciated how she had tackled her burger and fries. She was funny too, her sense of humor dry, much as his would be, if he had one. He knew she must be smart to make it through vet school, and he really did appreciate how she looked after Prince for him when he was out of town.

Of course, Prince had been the best way to get to know her and her habits. Thinking back to the day they met, he remembered how he had panicked when she thought she recognized him, not expecting her to make a connection to him this early. He had kicked himself when he realized she had noticed him during their parallel runs, annoyed with his own naivety that she wouldn't. He reminded himself of his task to keep her safe while at the same time wrapping up unfinished business that was long overdue.

And personal, very personal. Only someone like him would be OCD enough not to be able to let this go, even after all the dead ends, the near misses, the dangerous run-ins he had had to extract himself from over the years. This mission had started long ago and his commitment to following it through to the end was not for the faint of heart. The more he got to know Sam, the more he regretted the possibility of her becoming a pawn in this life or death game, a game that he could only hope wouldn't become deadly. For either of them.

CHAPTER THREE

Standing at her window, she watched Will and Prince head back to their brownstone as long as she could. She was trying not to let her emotions get the best of her, but talking about Gram and her family had triggered her, making that easier said than done. She couldn't stop thinking about Will, focused on the fact that there had always been something about him that drew her to him, something more than a physical attraction. It annoyed her that she couldn't put her finger on what it was.

Locking herself into her loft for the night, she kicked her shoes off and went to sit on her couch as she checked her phone for texts. Ignoring how late it was, she moved on to her playlists, scrolling nearly to the bottom to find an old one titled *Bro's Jams*, bracing herself for the emotional rollercoaster she had willing just stepped onto. Closing her eyes, she could easily picture her brother Jordan and her sister Riley in so many great moments growing up together. She was more than grateful her parents had given them a perfect childhood.

Impulsively she got up to go to her closet, moving clothes on the rod until she found what she was looking for. Pulling out his letterman's jacket, she appreciated that her family had let her have it with their blessing. She hugged it to her, smelling it, trying to see if it still smelled like Jordan's classic woodsy scent. She put it on, letting his playlist and memories wash over her.

Going back to her closet, she worked to move things out so she could retrieve a large box stashed deep at the back of it. She was suddenly desperate to see all the little mementos she had collected over the years, painful as it might be. She was grateful her mom had insisted she take it with her when she moved into her loft, hoping someday she would be ready for it.

An hour later Sam surveyed the many cherished keepsakes from the box scattered all over her bed. She stood up and stretched, before moving to her couch with a photo album she had found tucked at the bottom of the box. Her mom had always loved scrapbooking and again she found herself grateful she had literally created the story of her childhood. As the youngest in her family of five, all the pictures of her included her siblings as the three of them smiled cheesy grins together for the camera. There were trips to the zoo, lake life, and summer vacations to the beach. There were the holiday photos taken around Christmas trees, in Halloween costumes, and 4th of July sparklers held in little hands.

Noticing the shift as they all got older, there were more and more pictures taken with her and her friends as she went through her different sports and extracurricular activities such as dance, track, and summer swim teams. She noticed her mom had always included a picture with her siblings as they gathered around her and her birthday cake, posed and ready to make a wish before blowing out the candles.

Pausing abruptly, she went back to take another look at one picture in particular. She read her mom's writing "Happy 12th Sami!" She was startled to see her brother's best friend Billy had been included in this particular picture, his eyes on her rather than the camera. Using her cell phone, she took a picture of the pic, quickly zooming in on Billy's face. She thought about how Billy had become a fixture around their house after his parents had died suddenly, leaving him to be raised by his grandmother or granny as he referred to her. *I don't have one.* Sam sat focused, giving her mind time to search for why this face seemed so familiar to her.

Suddenly she froze as it hit her. It was him! Muttering to herself WTF, she didn't have to scroll far in her messages to find his number. Her text was short. *I need you. Now.* In no time her phone lit up. *On my way.*

Pacing the loft while she waited for his arrival, she tried to organize her chaotic thoughts running rampant around her brain. Studying the picture more, she noted what a scrawny seventeen year old he had been, his hair long and curly, his face tanned from long summer days spent outside. She knew Jordan had always considered Billy his best friend and after his parents had died tragically, her mom had taken him under her wing too. Despite how often he was around, she realized she had never paid much attention to him, the two boys always off playing video games or teasing her about something. Innocent at seventeen, she had never been kissed or had a drink until Billy had changed everything that night for her, his kiss leaving her breathless and waking up her young teenage heart. She had spent countless hours overthinking the situation, wondering if it had just been the tequila or there had been an attraction between them. Or maybe it had been some of both.

More than a decade later he was far from scrawny, his frame having filled out into a man quite nicely. His face was weathered, his hair much shorter and flipped back when it wasn't under a hat. He had facial hair now, a little bit of gray already starting to creep in, but a look that worked well for him. It would be hard to deny their attraction to each other now and she wondered if it was strong enough to move them out of the client zone.

It wasn't long before she heard him call her name from the stairwell. Surprised he had got to her so quickly, she went to open the door, still unsure where to start. She was mad, but why? Had she really been that oblivious to him all those years ago to not know him when he stood before her today? The realization took some of the steam out of her as she watched him move up the last few steps, Prince trailing behind him.

"How did you get here so fast?" she asked, feeling almost guilty she had demanded he come. Seeing him stare at her, he looked like he'd seen a ghost and she realized she still had Jordan's jacket on.

Pulling himself together, he answered her, his breathing ragged. "I thought you were in danger. That guy. I thought something had happened. You said you need me. Now." His voice had an edge to it, fueling her words as she finally knew where to start.

"Yes Will, I do need you, to talk to you *now*." She paused dramatically before adding sarcastically, "Or should I call you Billy?"

She was rewarded with a flicker of surprise in his eyes before he averted his gaze, quickly scanning her loft before coming to rest on her bed, her mementos strewn about. He took a deep breath, his hand going to the back of his head, clearly choosing his response carefully. "So you figured it out."

She wasn't sure what she had expected him to say, but his flip tone annoyed her. "So you figured it out?" she repeated back to him. When he shrugged at her, she pushed the photo into his chest, her eyes flashing angrily. "Yes Will, no thanks to you! Why didn't you say something? *My* name hasn't changed. You had to know who I was! Why wouldn't you say something the first time you came into *Pause for a Cause* with Prince? And tonight, when you saw that picture of my family! A family who you spent lots of time with because my brother was *your best friend!*"

She watched the emotion on his face as he studied the photo, before he brought down his shield, his eyes now guarded. Handing it back to her, he finally responded. "Lots of people have the same names. I didn't recognize you in the beginning. You're not a teenager anymore. You're a beautiful grown woman and it's been a long time since we were those kids." He was playing it cool, but she could hear it in his voice.

Knowing he made some valid points, and calling her beautiful, disarmed her a bit, but still she stuck to her guns. "Bullshit! I want the truth Will! Billy! Or whoever the flip you are!" she said heatedly. She watched incredulously as he went to her bar and poured two shots of Casamigos, handing a shot to her before tapping his to hers. Suddenly she had a flashback to her seventeenth birthday, a young man standing before her offering her a tequila shot, squeezing the lime into it before handing it to her with a grin, knowing she had never drank before.

'Cheers." she whispered before throwing it back, the burn barely registering with her. She couldn't take her eyes off of his as she said quietly, "We've done this before."

"Yes." He said simply.

"It was my seventeenth birthday. Everyone had left and we were out by the pool." Her cheeks turned pink as she remembered singing and dancing to a Taylor Swift song, him laughing with her. "We did some shots. We slow danced together. You kissed me, then you left me standing there." He could see the memory flooding her face. In a whisper she asked, "Why did you leave like that? I felt like some stupid school girl."

He had come to stand so close to her she could feel the heat of him. He was torn with how much truth he should tell her. It didn't seem necessary for her to know he had looked up to see Jordan watching them, his disapproval obvious. She didn't need to know that he and her brother, her hero, had had a heated disagreement before he found her sleeping on the chaise lounge chair. How could he tell her that night had been a fork in the road for him, neither of them knowing it would be so many years before he looked into her face again.

Suddenly he took the shot glass from her and walked the glasses to her sink, leaning against it, the distance between them helping him to think more clearly. "You were so excited to be seventeen that night Sam. You had so much life ahead of you. I was done with college but going nowhere. It was time for me to make a serious change in my life."

It was all coming back to her. "You joined the Navy and then you were gone in a week. You didn't even say good-bye to me. I haven't seen you since that night by the pool." Sensing her anguish, Prince gave a small whine and came to stand in front of her. She bent down to pet him, rubbing his ears the way she knew he liked, while remembering all the little details she had shoved so far away after Jordan died.

Turning back to Will, she found his eyes locked on her. "I didn't realize you and I were that close. I said my good-byes to the people who would miss me." His look challenged her to deny his statement.

She flinched knowing that was fair, but remembering how much his kiss had meant to her. Assuming it hadn't been a big deal to him, she tried to take a different route. Returning his gaze she corrected him. "You were part of our family. Jordan was lost without his best friend around." Unable to let it go, she added her own truth. "I blamed myself that you left. I thought you were embarrassed to come around any more. That you regretted kissing me. "

Narrowing his eyes, he shook his head before denying it. "You're wrong Sam. That kiss was part of the reason I left, but because of me, not you. I realized I had nothing to offer a girl like you and I knew you deserved the world Sam. I realized it was time for me to grow up. The real world was calling and hard as it was, Jordan and I both knew it was time to move on, time for us to become the men we were meant to be."

Silent tears ran down her cheeks as she buried her face in Prince's furry neck. It wasn't what she expected to hear, but she focused on her brother. She suddenly wondered if Will knew Jordan was gone. Still holding onto Prince, her voice quivered as she tried to ask, "Do you know, do you know. . ."

He nodded, not making her finish the sentence. She stood up swiftly, her voice now bitter. "Then why didn't you come? We waited for you to come. When Jordan died, we thought you would come back. To say good-bye. But you didn't!" She challenged him to deny that too.

"Actually, I was there Sam." He said it so softly she almost missed it. "I was devastated we lost Jordan. My heart ached for all of you. For us. I had to keep myself removed, but I was there, I promise." His face mirrored her own pain and she believed him.

She was having another flashback of her broken family sitting around the dinner table, pushing their food around on their plates, a poor attempt to have some normalcy in their lives. She could see her dad coming in from the garage perplexed. He had gone to take the trash out, only to find it already on the curb. She thought of all the little jobs around the house that had mysteriously gotten taken care of in those first few months. Her mother always said there was a guardian angel watching over them during this time when they were struggling so much just to take care of themselves.

Her eyes searched his face. "It was you. You were doing all the chores that had always been Jordan's." When he didn't answer her, she pressed on. "You took out the trash. You cleaned the gutters. When a storm blew down a tree, you hauled it away. Why? Why would you do all that and not come to see us?"

He closed the gap between them, his voice ragged with emotion. "I couldn't face your family Sam. They were always so good to me and it was hard enough to leave the first time. When Jordan died, I wondered if I had been there, if things would be different now. It took me a long time to let my guilt go."

"You!" she exclaimed, pushing away from him. "It wasn't you, it was me! There are things you don't know because you left. I'm the reason why Jordan was getting into his car that night!"

Seeing her face contorted into so much pain nearly broke his heart all over again. He had to make her see. "I know why he was in the car, Sam. It was his choice to go. He had something to take care of."

She looked at him shocked. Did he know? Had they remained friends and Jordan never shared about it. "You know about Spencer? How? And what things?"

"Jordan and I didn't communicate often, but we had an unspoken understanding we would always be there for each other. We checked in with each other every so often. He told me about your college boyfriend. He worried he was bad for you, that he was going to hurt you.

He found out things about him that you didn't know." Will shared the news tentatively, not sure how Sam would take it.

Staring at him dumbfounded, she asked the obvious question. "Why didn't he tell me those things?"

Calling her on it, he reminded her gently. "He did, but you couldn't hear it because you were in love with this guy. He decided to take things into his own hands. He did what he needed to do to protect you, to make sure you were safe."

Sam shook her head as she cried out, "I knew it was my fault! You just said so! I should have listened to him and broke it off. I was never in love with Spencer. He was just a distraction, like they all were. Why didn't I listen to him!"

Will took in this news, relieved she hadn't been in love, but understanding it made her loss feel even more devastatingly pointless. "It wasn't your fault Sam. It was an accident. It was Jordan's time to go and things happened the way they were meant too. Bad things happen to good people."

Suddenly she was exhausted, the long day catching up to her. She didn't resist when Will pulled her to him, leaning her head on his shoulder, soaking up the warmth and strength of him. She thought about how far they had both come over the years, living separate lives, only to reconnect with each other now. What would her family say about this crazy turn of events, that Will had come back into their lives after all this time.

She turned to look up at him before moving away. "My mom always worried about you. You became like one of her own you know. None of us would have ever blamed you for what happened. We knew how much Jordan meant to you. We just all missed you." Sam shared quietly.

"I know." Will took a deep breath, pushing the honesty train just a little further. Seeing her quizzical look, he shared how he knew.

"Your mom came home in the middle of the day and found me cleaning up the tree. She didn't seem surprised to see me. Just hugged me and brought me inside for one of her famous talks at the kitchen table."

This made Sam smile, easily able to picture the scenario he described. "Knowing Mom, I'm sure she tried to feed you too."

Will smiled too as he continued. "She did. We talked and cried and laughed. I told her I was there anytime your family needed me. I made sure she had my number and then she helped me finish loading up the tree. I felt better, but I still couldn't face you."

Nodding her head, she acknowledged her family could be a lot, even during times of grief. He didn't correct her, that it wasn't her family he hadn't been able to face, but her and knowing that he had a crush on her. He would never have been able to leave if he'd seen her. And no one knew better than him, it was up to him to finish what Jordan had started, and more importantly, to make sure his family was protected and safe. He wondered if knowing who he really was would change their current relationship. He still had things to take care of. He still needed to keep her at arms length, but now that she knew who he was, he couldn't deny it was a game changer. He had to admit, he wasn't mad about it.

CHAPTER FOUR

Sam's birthday, two years ago

Checking her backpack one more time, Sam decided to add a disposable rain poncho just in case the weatherman actually got the forecast right for tonight. She was in good shape walking there, but who knew what the weather could be hours from now. Satisfied she had everything, she headed out the door. Dressed in an oatmeal linen vest and matching shorts with her white sneaks, she headed north, having several blocks to walk before she got into Bryant Park.

Fondly glancing up at the Empire State Building, she never tired of its iconic presence, always finding it reassuring. She loved her Chelsea neighborhood, knowing it by heart as she had several routes she ran regularly. Besides her market down the street, she frequented Charlie's often as well as The Empire Diner where she could get great food any time of day. Bryant park was also one of her favorite destinations to walk or run to, often joining a crowd in the park on Thursday nights for their martial arts classes.

Tonight Sam was headed there to meet her sister Riley and her family. It was her birthday eve and concerts in the park were one of their favorites to enjoy during the summer months. Her family had been attending the concerts ever since she could remember and it always promised a fun evening ahead.

It didn't take long for Sam to spot Riley and her crew among all the other families laying out blankets and claiming their green space for the evening. With loud shrieks, she was delighted when her niece and nephew ran to her with open arms. Scooping them both up with a laugh, she headed back to their blanket, dropping them and her backpack onto the quilt laid out. It was a family heirloom and Sam loved that Riley used it regularly, believing it had been made to be enjoyed and not just stored away. Eagerly they watched Auntie Sami open her backpack knowing she would have some kind of sweet treat for them. Tonight she had brought Nutella Biscuits, the hazelnut spread on the shortbread one of her personal favorites as well.

"Sam! We talked about bringing fruit tonight, remember? They'll have birthday cake tomorrow night!" Riley said, her protests only half-hearted.

Shrugging mischievously while her niece and nephew watched anxiously, Sam answered back. "Okay, you heard your mom kiddos. You can only have one. At a time. When she's not watching!"

While Riley rolled her eyes, her husband Scott added his own two cents. "And make sure you get Auntie Sami when you want to go run your sugar off."

Giving them all a thumbs up, she nodded her agreement. "Yep, who wants to go run right now?" Taking a little's hand in each of hers, Sam looked back over her shoulder at their parents before adding, "Enjoy the peace and quiet! You're welcome!"

Having walked for a good twenty minutes around the park, they came back to find paper plates with a finger friendly dinner and juice boxes laid out for the littles. The music was just starting as everyone settled in and they all turned their attention to the stage. It wasn't long before Sam noticed Scott nudge Riley, pointing to a bank of dark clouds off in the distance. She waved him off, telling him not to be such a worrywart.

Always the proud aunt, she looked over to watch Riley and Scott, each with a little on their laps enjoying their family time. She loved that they were teaching their kids an appreciation for music at such a young age, much as her own parents had done for her. She was happy to be included, but at the same time nostalgic for days gone by when she would climb into her own daddy's lap. Quietly she got out her phone and snapped a candid shot of the happy family.

Suddenly the first ominous rumble of thunder rippled in the distance, causing some families to start packing it in. As lightning streaked the sky, the music stopped abruptly and it was announced the concert was over due to a severe storm headed their way. Sam helped Riley get everything packed up while Scott corralled the littles, their faces anxious as the thunder grew louder, the early dusk hastened by the threatening bank of clouds headed their way.

"Sam let us take you home. You can't walk home in this." Riley demanded as Sam was already getting out her rain poncho.

Pulling it over her head, she waved Riley's concern off. "I'll grab a bird scooter and beat it home. Don't worry about me. Get your littles home! Go!"

Hugging her quickly, Riley pulled the wagon behind her, running to catch up to Scott and their kids. She paused briefly to yell back, "Be safe and text me when you get home!"

"Don't worry! I'll be fine! Love you too!" she yelled back to her before breaking out into a run, dodging all the other park goers also hustling to get home before the storm hit. As she jogged along the street she kept an eye out for a scooter. Finally spotting one lonely one sitting at the corner ahead, she picked up her pace. She watched in annoyance as someone reached it just before she could.

Suddenly a crack of thunder hit so loud above her, she nearly dropped to her knees. Standing there trying to decide what to do, she was startled again when a motorcycle pulled up alongside her.

"Sam, get on!" he said. Seeing her pause, he pulled his helmet off, holding it out to her. Realizing it was Will she quickly grabbed it and hopped onto his motorcycle, relieved to be moving towards home at a faster pace. With one more crack of thunder, the rain started to fall, big fat drops at first before quickly becoming sheets of horizontal rain. She wrapped her arms around Will even tighter, leaning into him and closing her eyes.

As the motorcycle slowed down, she realized he was headed into the parking garage under his building. Just like that the rain stopped, the thunder less deafening. As he pulled into his parking spot she released her death grip on him before jumping off his bike. Handing him his helmet, she was struck by how good he looked even with water dripping down his face, his wet clothes seeming to cling to every muscle in his body.

Taking his helmet from her, he gave a small laugh. Realizing her poncho hood was still up, she pulled it down smiling ruefully. "I'm sure I look a fright, but thanks for the rescue. Clearly I needed it."

He smiled at her before leaning away from her to shake the water from his dark hair. "I'm sure I look a *fright* too. And you're welcome."

She quickly followed him as he headed to the stairwell. Taking the steps two at a time, he apologized for bringing her to his apartment, informing her that Prince really hated thunderstorms, especially when they were as intense as this one. She nodded, completely understanding his concern for him.

Opening his door to her, he swore softly when he got no reaction to flipping on his lights. "Looks like the powers out," he announced as he knelt down to greet Prince, reassuring him he was okay before closing the door behind her. She watched as he went to a closet and pulled out a couple of camping lanterns.

Handing one to her, he headed to his bedroom telling her he would be right back, Prince following closely on his heels. She took off her wet shoes and socks and poncho trying to keep the wet area to a minimum. Suddenly he was back, handing her a pair of joggers and a hoodie.

"I know these will be big on you, but you need to get out of your wet clothes. The bathroom is down the hall and to the left." Noticing her bare feet he nodded, "I'll get you dry socks too."

Thanking him, she headed to the bathroom. It wasn't long before they sat on the couch together, thankful to be in dry clothes, the lanterns giving the room a soft glow as the rain continued to pour outside his large window.

Breaking their awkward silence, he asked, "So why were you out in this weather? Were you at the park?"

Nodding she clarified. "With my sister Riley and her family. We were there for a concert." She gasped, suddenly realizing she hadn't texted Riley she was home.

Picking up her phone, she added, "My family used to go every summer when we were kids and now she has her own littles to take." Hearing her phone buzz, she read her sister's text before turning her attention back to Will.

"Summer days were the best. All the good stuff happened then."

"Summer was sweet. As you know our family lived by the pool. I'm sure you remember plenty of Marco Polo. And baseball games." She added fondly."

"As I remember, you were die-hard Yankee fans," he said.

She paused, still finding it hard to believe Will was Billy. "Yep, we still are although we rarely make it to games anymore." Watching his face, Sam thought about Will not having a family, his granny passing years ago. "We should go sometime!" she said brightly. "Who do you root for? Or do you even like baseball?" she asked.

"This is New York, who doesn't like baseball?" he asked, teasing her. "I would go with you if you find a good game to go to."

"Great! It's a date!" Realizing what she had said, she added, "I mean a plan. We'll do it." Desperate to change the subject, she asked, "I didn't know you had a motorcycle. How did you get into riding?"

Shrugging, he kept his answer vague. "It's a cheap, easy way to get around town."

Pulling his phone out, he checked the Yankees schedule, ready to hold her to their plan. "How about tomorrow?" he asked. "They play the Phillies."

She hesitated to overshare and then decided why not. "Actually tomorrow's my birthday and I'm having dinner with my family. How about a raincheck? Or you could come with me?"

Seeing him raise an eyebrow she asked cautiously, "What?"

"I didn't know families still celebrate birthdays together. At your age I mean. Don't tell me you still have cake with candles for you to blow out too?" She couldn't tell if he was mocking her or just teasing.

Nevertheless, she felt the heat in her cheeks, not sure she appreciated his comment. "What's wrong with spending time with your family?"

Smiling, he said. "Nothing. Aren't you a little old to be making birthday wishes? Aren't you like thirty something? A little old for kids stuff."

Knowing Will didn't have a family, she tried to give him the benefit of the doubt, keeping her rude retaliation to herself. Shrugging, she played him off. "Yep, thirty something and still making birthday wishes. You found me out." Looking out the window, she was relieved to realize the rain had finally blown itself out and had downgraded to sprinkles.

Getting off the couch, she went to collect her things. "Thanks again for the rescue. I owe ya one." she said lightly.

Coming to stand in front of her, Will leaned in, his eyes dark. "I didn't mean to offend you. It's cute you do stuff like that."

Trying not to feel annoyed, she walked to open the door as he added. "Hold on, Prince and I will walk you home. It's getting late."

Prince, hearing his name, came to stand beside them, wagging his tail in anticipation. Bending down to him, she focused her attention on him, rubbing his ears. "Thank you Prince. I would be happy to let you walk me home, but I wouldn't want you to think I was trying to be cute!"

Grabbing Prince's leash from a nearby hook, he responded dryly. "Noted. Cute is offensive, but nothing wrong with letting us walk you home."

Headed home, she walked quickly, ready to be rid of Will and his condescending attitude. Being the baby of three, she had learned a long time ago that cute wasn't a compliment, but an excuse to patronize her or exclude her. Starting high school she quickly learned cute meant not pretty or beautiful enough to date. Realizing it was her baggage not his, she tried to dismiss her annoyance.

Grabbing her arm, he pulled on her to slow down. "Hey, where's the fire?"

Working hard to ignore the fire his hand on her arm was causing, she let her sarcasm roll off her tongue. "I'm sure you're not used to babysitting, so I'm trying to keep this short and sweet for you."

Having reached her building, he let her go. Her voice was tight, but she kept her words light. "Here we are. Thanks again for walking me home."

"Are you mad about that too? I care about you Sam and just want to make sure you're safe." he said, his eyes intent on hers.

She was taken aback to hear him say he cared about her and decided to take the high road. "I'm not mad, just tired." Still feeling annoyed, she couldn't resist pushing back just a bit. "I'm lucky to have a friend like you."

Stepping right up to her, she wondered if he felt the heat between them or if it was just her. She was shocked when he took her face in his hands and kissed her, long and deep. "And just so you know, I can be a really good friend."

Abruptly he turned, heading Prince back the way they had come. They hadn't gone far when he turned and yelled back to her, "And tonight's escort services are on the house. My pleasure! Night Sam!" he said.

Huffing with annoyance, she headed into her loft trying to tell herself she was reading too much into his harmless banter. She didn't want to be *cute* when she had so many inappropriate thoughts about him. But if he saw her as cute, why had he so thoroughly kissed her just now? Was he playing with her? She suddenly had the same feelings she'd had at seventeen, but this time her teenage insecurities were taking over her adult brain. His kiss left her weak in the knees, stumbling up the stairs to get her door unlocked, having felt his kiss all the way down to her toes, her libido dusting itself off and going on high alert. Hanging her clothes up to dry, she had to wonder just how old he thought she was, surely knowing she was early in her thirties. Climbing into bed she couldn't stop thinking of how annoying Will could be and decided she was actually mad afterall.

Headed to the park in nothing more than shorts and a cropped tank top, Sam knew her body would soon be sweating as she got into her workout. Pleased to see a good crowd for tonight's martial arts class, she waved to a few girls, happy to see some people she knew. Tonight's class was dedicated to sparring with a partner and she was about to head over to join them when someone else caught her attention. She watched curiously as he gave her a casual wave, clearly headed in her direction.

When he reached her she asked, "Are you lost? What are you doing here Will?"

Looking around, feigning interest, he informed her he was there to take the class. "I heard tonight is for sparring and decided I could use a refresher. Want to be my partner?" he asked with a grin.

Glancing at the girls first, she paused before deciding why not? They had only seen each other once in the last month when Will had brought Prince by for a massage, neither of them choosing to mention his killer kiss he had laid on her in her own doorway. Shaking it off, she chose to focus on being called cute, having no doubt he would under-estimate her skills. Nothing annoyed her more than when someone underestimated her.

"Why not? And since you said refresher, I'm going to assume you have experience with the martial arts?" Not waiting for his reply, she added smugly, "But just in case, the safe word is Uncle."

"Good to know, thanks." he said with a bigger grin.

As the instructor got the class underway, she reminded them to be respectful and remain in control while they sparred as they would be "fighting" a friend, not foe. After getting everyone warmed up with some basic kicks and jabs, she set the timer before blowing her whistle to signal it was time to begin. Turning to face her unexpected partner, Sam focused on the expert kicks she was about to reign down on him, not knowing Will was prepared to go easy on her.

Quickly she had Will's attention as her kicks, punches, and blocks proved her a worthy adversary. Sam also quickly learned, Will had moves of his own and they were both breathing hard when the whis-tle blew.

"I see you're serious about your martial arts." Will said after guz-zling from his water bottle.

Setting her own bottle down, she smiled sweetly before answering him. "I am. Isn't it cute!"

As they moved into round two, it became apparent to anyone who might be watching, they seemed to be well matched although Sam was naive not to realize how much self-control Will was actually using.

It was their final round and Sam was feeling pretty good about her performance, exhausting as it was. They were only a few minutes into the round, when suddenly Sam found herself pinned to the ground, Will looming over her, his hands warm on her arms. His eyes glowed as he challenged her what she would do now. Finding herself distracted by the heat between them, she found herself focused on his mouth, remembering their kiss on her doorstep not that many weeks ago.

"All out of moves Sam?" he asked softly.

"We don't pin each other when we're sparring. You're cheating." she said, her voice breathless.

"And you're forgetting to be respectful. I'm not the enemy Sam." Quickly he released her, then held out his hand to help her up. Ignoring him, she came to a stand. "See ya round." he said, flipping his towel over his shoulder before heading off.

She jumped when her instructor walked up beside her to ask, "Are you okay? I take it you two know each other?"

Picking up her own towel, she nodded, her eyes following him as he walked to his motorcycle, donning his helmet before throwing his leg over the seat. "Yeah, I know him. Thanks for the class." she said, glancing at her instructor. "See you next week."

She put her earbuds in, choosing a brisk walk over a run. She could already feel her tired muscles, letting her know Will had given her quite the workout. She was easily within a block of her building when she flipped her water bottle open to drink the end of her water.

As she flipped it closed, she felt her toe hit concrete, propelling her to the ground. In a flash of sharp pain, she felt her shoulder pop. Cussing like a sailor, she sat up, holding her shoulder, worried she had dislocated it. Fighting off the wave of nausea overcoming her, she struggled to get up, oblivious to someone calling her name.

Suddenly a strong pair of hands were carefully helping her to her feet, his voice soothing. "I've got you. Easy does it Sam." Seeing the color drain from her face with the movement, he quickly offered her a drink from his water bottle. Greedily she drank from it, hoping it would wash away her nausea.

Unable to look into the stranger's face, she could only murmur thank you as the pain came in another wave. As it finally registered with her it was Will, she allowed him to lead her to a brick wall close by, gently helping her to take a seat.

"Can you move your arm?" he asked her, his face concerned.

Trying unsuccessfully, she said, "I need an Uber to get myself to the hospital. Thanks for your help." she said, attempting to dismiss him.

Pulling his phone out, he nodded in agreement. "I'll go with you."

Sharply she shook her head no, crying out as it provoked another wave of sharp pain.

His tone became annoyed as he informed her, "It's okay to let someone help you Sam, even if it's me."

Closing her eyes she informed him back, "I've been taking care of myself ever since. . ." She stopped abruptly as she waited for the pain to subside. Looking up at him she finished with, "long enough. I'll be fine."

Will shook his head in annoyance, refusing to argue with her. He could only think to say, "Then you're way overdue and you're going to let me help you."

"I can still manage an Uber." she said through gritted teeth.

Turning his attention to the street, he announced their Uber was only a minute away before adding dryly. "You'll just have to humor me then because I'm coming with you."

Not in much of a position to argue, Sam let him have his way, actually relieved to have someone there to help her, even if it had to be Will.

The doctors told her that she was lucky, the damage to her shoulder was minimal, her recovery three to four weeks give or take. As promised Will had helped her through it all, including getting her home and making sure she took her first pain pill. Gently he got her into bed, removing her shoes and covering her with a blanket, propping her pillows behind her to support her shoulder. She watched him as he hovered over her, grateful the pain pill was soon doing its job. She realized he was holding her water bottle out to her, but it seemed neither of her arms were currently working. He scooped his arm behind her to help her sit up, holding the water bottle up for her to drink from.

Feeling her eyes getting heavy, she could hear herself ask him if he would stay. Seeing him nod, she finally let her eyes close, mumbling a thank you. Thinking she was asleep, Will sat on the edge of her bed, watching her, taking in her fragility even as he remembered her kicking his butt just hours ago. She was tough, this one, and somehow it made his attraction to her just that much deeper.

Feeling him move off the bed, her eyes flew open. "Where are you going?" she mumbled.

Moving back to her side, he answered, "I'm just checking my phone. I'll stay but you need to get some sleep."

He was taken aback by her intense gaze when she asked softly, "Why are you doing all this?"

Sitting back down, he reminded her, "I told you the other night, I care about you Sam."

"Right. You care about me. As a friend." she asked, her words slightly slurred from her pain medicine.

Nodding, he agreed with her. "Yes. As a friend."

Struggling to keep her eyes focused on him she asked, "So do you kiss all your friends like the other night Will? Or am I just one of a few lucky ones?"

Doubtful she would remember their conversation in the morning, he took the easy way out. "So you enjoyed that, did you?"

Letting her eyes close, a slight smile on her face, she murmured, "Most definitely. I've been waiting for a kiss like that since my seventeenth birthday."

Her words hit him hard and it suddenly seemed in both their best interests for him to use Sam's phone and text her sister Riley to let her know what had happened, emphasizing that she would need tending too. He didn't trust himself or Sam, particularly while she was under the influence of her pain meds and her thoughts flowed so freely. Staying until he knew Riley was almost there, he confirmed she had a key to let herself in before reluctantly sharing his cell leaving no name, but wanting her to know he was available if Sam needed anything.

Her words still rang in his ears, his head spinning at the implication of her declaration about their recent kiss and one that had happened over a decade ago. He had to wonder if it had been her first kiss and that's why it had seemed so memorable to Sam. Or maybe, he could only hope, she had kissed a lot of toads through high school and college. Regardless, her words were a double-edged sword, feeling a ray of hope that his kiss had an impact like that while telling himself no good could come of starting a physical relationship with her. He didn't need to be a relationship expert to know that someone's heart most likely could get broken and it shook him to admit to himself it might be his.

Besides, he wasn't here for romance. He had a job to do and knew people were keeping tabs on both of them, their eyes and ears everywhere. It was easy to justify spending time with her as part of the job he was tasked with. However, keeping it plutonic was going to prove more of a challenge than he could have ever had expected, but to be honest, had hoped for.

CHAPTER FIVE

Sam had been grateful to her family for taking care of her, their love and attention just what she needed during that first week of recovery. She had tried not to think about Will, dismissing feelings of being abandoned by him a bit dramatic. She knew he was busy and due to go out of town as Prince was on her schedule in the next few days. Forcing herself to pack her bag, she used her good arm to carry it downstairs, ready to convince her mom she was ready to go home. She had even called an Uber to ensure there would be no prolonged discussion.

Finally headed back to her loft, Sam texted Riley to thank her for rescuing her and taking her home to her parents. Overly independent, she had resisted being made to slow down and let her mom and dad do things for her. It was hard to be in the house without her siblings, but also nice to have some downtime to catch up on her reading, napping, and long talks with her parents.

Arriving back at her loft, she was surprised to find Will there waiting for her. "What are you doing here?" she asked, not bothering to hide her surprised annoyance very well.

"Your sister texted me and let me know the little chick had flown the coop." he said, his voice amused.

Indignantly she demanded, "Riley better not have sent you to check on me! I'm quite capable of taking care of myself!"

Taking her bag from her, Will agreed. "And don't we all know it. I don't think it was a tag, you're it kind of thing, but more like an fyi. I was in the neighborhood anyway and just thought I would drop by to make sure you're all good. And see if Prince could stay with you starting tonight instead of tomorrow?"

Using her good arm, she unlocked her door, holding her hand out to take her bag from Will. "Sure. I'm all good and I always love to have Prince. What time tonight do you want to drop him by?"

Realizing she was not inviting him in, he sat her bag by her door and headed out, saying over his shoulder. "Thanks! I'll text you later and let you know."

I t was her first day back to work at *Paws for a Cause* and it had been long and grueling. Thankfully Will had brought her some groceries and some of her favorites from Empire Diner when he had dropped off Prince last night. She was starving but needed to check her calendar for tomorrow, before heading upstairs.

She turned to Prince with a sigh. "Too bad you can't help me get my pups up on the table." she said tiredly. Having had to close her business for the past week, it was important to her and her clients to get back to grooming as usual. She had finagled her schedule today for her smaller pups, feeling confident she could manage even with one good arm, but it had been a struggle and not her best work.

"What I need is to hire someone. Just temporarily to help me for a few weeks." she said, still talking to Prince. She toyed with the idea of asking her mom, a retired nurse, but she really needed someone who could deal with her telling them what to do all day. Not her mom. Heading to the door to lock up, she was startled when a young man opened the door first.

Stepping back she announced, "Sorry, I was just closing."

Grinning at her sheepishly, he responded. "Sorry to bother you, but I'm new in the area and trying to find a job. I don't suppose you know of anyone around here hiring?"

Sam glanced down at Prince, who had come to stand beside her, his wariness of the stranger unmistakable. Patting him on the head, she wondered if her prayers had just been answered.

"How do you feel about dogs?" she asked hopefully.

Keeping an eye on Prince, he was quick to answer. "I love dogs! My family has two back home."

Smiling at Prince's low growl, it occurred to her he didn't seem to believe the stranger. Proceeding cautiously she asked, "And where's home, if you don't mind me asking."

"I just moved here from San Marino. It's a small country inside of Italy." he said, his gaze on her warm.

Intrigued, Sam began an informal interview. "I suppose you have references? Have you worked anywhere in the states?"

"I attended university in Rome, but I did not work. I've been helping my family run their winery since I finished my classes. I'm good with the customer and have a head for business. If that helps?" he asked hopefully.

Sam stood there, sizing him up and thinking about what to do. Was it crazy to hire this complete stranger? Or was it fate he had walked in just when she had finally admitted she needed some help. The bottom line was that it was cheaper to pay him to help her rather than close her doors for another three weeks and lose money and possibly, even customers.

"I'm only looking for someone to help me for the next three weeks." she said, pointing to her arm in a sling. "I wouldn't be able to pay you much though." she added hastily.

With a big smile he nodded, accepting her terms. "I trust you to pay me what you think is fair."

Sealing the deal, she asked. "Can you start tomorrow?"

"Volentieri!" he said excitedly. Seeing her confusion, he added, "With pleasure."

Taking in his brown eyes and dark curly hair, it was hard to deny how handsome he was and wondered just how old he was. Younger than her for sure.

"Great! I'll see you tomorrow at eight am sharp. And wear grungy clothes. This job is a lot of dog hair and keeping it all under control." Sam said with a laugh.

Holding out his hand to shake hers, his appreciation was apparent. "I will see you in the morning, Miss?" he said, his look suddenly concerned.

"You can call me Sam." she said laughing. "And you are?"

"Marco Moretti, at your service Miss Sam." he said proudly, his hand on his chest.

Locking the door behind him, she turned to see Prince watching her. "I know what you're thinking, but it's only temporary and I need the help!" Besides, who didn't enjoy a little eye candy to make a day pass faster she thought to herself? It was all going to be fine, just fine.

Sam found out quickly what a hard worker Marco was. He did everything she asked of him and he did it with charm and confidence, his first week passing by quickly while Prince kept a watchful eye on him. He had even met Riley, who had popped by to check on her, quickly assuming he was the mystery man who had texted her about Sam's accident a few weeks ago. She had not believed Sam's denials, until she had been forced to confess Will's name to Riley, laughing when she had shown Sam his text, identified in her phone as 'Sam's mystery man.'

That had opened another whole can of worms as Sam played off her relationship with Will, stressing it was a professional relationship, their low grade friendship built around Prince. It didn't hurt any that Prince lay close by, always watchful and most definitely keeper of the gate. Riley had reluctantly let it go for now, teasing Sam that maybe Marco would turn out to be more than a professional relationship.

It was Friday night and she was desperate to shower and head to Charlie's for dinner and a glass of wine, more than ready to start her weekend. She had paid Marco for his work for the week after wishing him a good weekend. Standing at the door, having just locked up, she was surprised by a short knock on her door. Assuming it was Marco, she unlocked the door, opening it with a smile and a "What did you forget Marco?"

She caught her breath at the sight of Will standing there, his aviators making him even more attractive than she remembered. "Who's Marco?" he asked, following her into *Paws for a Cause.*

"Well hello to you too. I thought you were getting back tomorrow?" she said, moving to her desk, ignoring his question.

Bending down to greet Prince, Will stood up, taking her in. "Something came up that brought me back early. Who's Marco?" he asked again, his eyes narrowed at her.

"I decided I needed some help with my bad shoulder and Marco is my new associate. He's working out beautifully." she said airily.

Turning to look at her door, Will asked, "Is that the guy who was just leaving?"

Deciding this really was none of his concern, Sam answered him with some irritation. "It is, not that it's any of your business. Now if you don't mind, do you want me to bill you or would you like to run your card now? I'm in need of a hot shower and would like to call it a day."

Walking over to pay her, he pulled out his card before asking. "Got a hot date or is your shoulder still bothering you?"

Handing him her pad to swipe his card, she rolled her eyes. "Again, none of your business. But yes, I've got a date with a burger and a glass of pinot and a hot shower helps loosen my shoulder up after a long day." Handing him his receipt, she added dryly, "Thanks for your concern."

Taking the leash from her, he nodded to Sam before taking his leave with Prince. "Thanks for taking care of Prince." he said briskly.

Disappointed this was their encounter after not seeing each other in a week, she called out lamely as the door closed behind him. "You're welcome!'

Walking into Charlie's, she immediately noticed Marco at the bar already sitting in her spot. She paused for a moment to collect her thoughts and decide how she wanted to play this. Should she pretend to not see him? He was doing a great job and handsome as hell, but she was ready for some down time, her mental bandwidth only able to handle small talk with Frankie and her glass of wine. Realizing she had been spotted, she moved to the bar to greet him with a smile. She was surprised to see a glass of pinot grigio already poured, waiting for her like the trophy she deserved after such a long week.

"Marco! I didn't know you come here." she said.

"It's my first time. I was telling your friend Frankie here that I'm working at *Paws for a Cause*–temporarily of course–and she told me you always drink wine." He smiled graciously as he handed the glass to her, clearly quite pleased with himself. She had to admit he really was hard to resist.

"Thank you Marco, that's so thoughtful of you." she said before raising her glass to Frankie who stood by watching her with amusement.

"The pleasure is all mine. Cincin!" he said, holding his frosted mug of beer out to her. Suddenly he jumped up, pulling out the barstool beside him, offering it to her. "Please, you'll join me, si?"

Hesitating just briefly, Sam sat down. "I'm not staying long. I just came in for a glass of wine and some dinner." With that she motioned to Frankie, mouthing cheeseburger and fries to her.

Marco held up the menu laying on the bar in front of him. "What do you recommend? I'm starving."

Having a definite sense of deja vu, Sam sighed inwardly. How long had it been since she and Will had had this very conversation and look how well that was working out. "The pimento cheeseburger is my favorite. The fries are good too." she shared, reminding herself Marco was not Will. Both were very handsome albeit in different ways, but Marco was much more open and friendly. And younger.

They made small talk as two people who don't know each other well are forced to do, something they had been doing all week in-between her four legged clients.

Suddenly Marco turned to her, his face earnest. "Sam, I hope you don't mind my forwardness, but I would love to take you out to dinner. A nice dinner."

Sam nervously ran her fingers along the stem of her glass. "Do you mean like a date?" she asked, not looking him in the face.

Taking her hand, he squeezed it. "Yes, like a date. You're a beautiful woman and I would love to get to know you better. If you'll let me? Please?"

Turning to look him in the face, she was caught off guard by the intensity in his eyes. Was he attracted to her? "How old are you Marco?" she asked, answering his question with a question of her own.

He laughed at her openly, "You do not need to worry. I'm old enough." Running his finger along her arm, he added, "We can just go out as friends. But I should warn you, to know me is to love me." His expression challenged her to say no.

She laughed, suddenly realizing Will was walking toward them. Giving Marco her most radiant smile she surrendered to his charm. "Alright, it's a date!"

"Excellent!" he said, smiling provocatively before boasting, "You won't regret it." Picking up her hand, he kissed it, giving her his best smile. Where did she know that smile from she asked herself for the hundredth time this week. As he turned back to his beer triumphantly, he also noticed Will headed their way.

Abruptly he stood up, his demeanor doing a fast three sixty. She watched as he pretended to check his phone before announcing he needed to take a call and then he was gone.

"Your new friend seems in a big hurry to get out of here." someone said in her ear.

She didn't need to look to know it was Will. She shrugged it off as best she could. "That tracks." was all she said.

"What does?" he asked, throwing his leg over the newly empty bar stool.

"That you know a deserter when you see one." she said.

"Ahhh. So you're mad about me calling your sister?" he asked, signaling Frankie for his usual beer.

"I know I was doped up, but you definitely promised you would stay with me. You should have just told me if you needed to go. I didn't appreciate you calling a babysitter for me." Sam said scornfully.

Putting his hand on her arm, Will tried to make her understand. "Sam you were really hurting and needed someone to be there for you around the clock. I knew I couldn't do that so I texted Riley. Someone else who cares about you. You're lucky to have a family who shows up for you. Not everyone does you know." He finished with his gaze averted, ready to move on to their next topic of conversation.

Feeling her indignation deflate, she hated to admit he was right. "I guess you have a point. And thank you for getting me to the hospital and staying with me until Riley was close by."

"You're welcome. How are you feeling? Are you taking it easy so you can heal?" he asked, his look serious.

"It's getting better and I'm off my pain pills. Hiring Marco has been a life saver." she said, immediately regretting sharing about her new assistant.

"So tell me more about how you came to hire Marco. How did you post and interview so quickly?" he asked.

"Actually it was a happy coincidence. He walked in looking for a job and I just happened to be needing someone. On a temporary basis of course." she stated it all matter of factly, hoping to shut down any further questions.

"That didn't seem like a red flag that he just happened to be so readily available at the precise time you needed some help? Tell me you at least called his references." Will said, his eyes narrowed, daring her to deny it.

"Of course! I would be stupid not to!" she said, picking up her glass.

"You're a terrible liar! I'm glad you had Prince there to keep an eye on him." His voice was hard, not able to let her spontaneous hire go.

"It was nice to have Prince there, playing back up for me. But I've gotten to know Marco better this week and it's a good fit. He's a hard worker and will only be there another two weeks. So shut your radar down and relax! You're not my keeper Will." she finished crossly, the conversation well past annoying. She cringed at the thought of telling him she had agreed to go on a date with him. With any luck there would be no reason for him to even know.

Thankfully Frankie showed up at that moment with two plates of food. Upon seeing Will sitting there instead of Marco, she paused. "This seems familiar, but different. Did we lose someone?"

Shrugging, Will reached for the second burger and fries. "I'll be happy to take it off your hands. Just put both burgers on my tab."

Wanting to argue Marco could still be coming back, Sam decided to let it go. If he returned, they could always reorder his food. She hated to admit it, but she was curious about his demeanor changing at the sight of Will. What was that about and why did he leave so abruptly?

In between mouthfuls, Will wanted to play catch up, having not really spent any time with Sam over the past two weeks. "So how was spending a week with Riley and her family?"

Pausing between fries, Sam was shaking her head. "Oh no, she took me to my parents' home. I appreciate you texting her, but man did you open a can of worms."

Will smiled. "See, you're a handful. How was staying with your parents?"

Thinking through her answer, she took a sip of her wine. "It's hard to be the only kid in the house. We're all adults and have our own routines. And you know I hate needing people to help me. But we all survived and I was able to escape after a week. By the way, you're now on Riley's phone as 'Sam's mystery man.' Congrats! You're thrilled I'm sure. "

Will nodded, having realized that when she texted him the chick had flown the coop. "What's Riley's deal? Why is she holding onto my number?"

"Oh Riley has high hopes for me finding a man and getting laid anytime in the near future. She's convinced you could be the lucky one." she said wickedly.

Feeling a certain sense of satisfaction as Will practically choked on his beer, Sam patted him on the back helpfully. "You okay?"

She continued blatantly. "Of course when she met Marco, she thought he was my mystery man. When I corrected her, she was beside herself to think I had two possibilities up for grabs." Sam knew she really should stop, but she couldn't seem to help herself.

Brushing his hands off with his napkin, Will pushed his plate away as he turned to face Sam head on. "I'm game if you are. I don't mind doing my part to keep the family peace." There was no way in hell Marco would be laying his hands on her ever if it were up to him.

It was Sam's turn to choke on her fry. Using her wine to wash it down, she searched for the comeback she wanted. "Don't make promises you aren't willing to deliver on Will." She tried her best to look like she didn't believe him.

He watched as she finished her burger and pushed her plate away too. "Looks like the dinner hour is over." He leaned into her, saying softly into her ear. "Time for dessert." His breath was warm, his voice suggestive and she felt her whole body go on high alert.

Downing the end of her wine, she turned to face him with a smile. "Fabulous. But you should know, I'm currently injured and will need you to do all the work." She was smug as she called his bluff.

Pushing his bar stool back, he threw some cash down before holding his hand out to her. "It's your lucky night. I'm up for the challenge."

She faltered, glancing at Frankie who was trying to decipher the exchange happening between the two of them. Suddenly she could hear Riley in her head, *go on Sam! You've been wanting this!* Hopping off her bar stool and sticking her phone in her jeans pocket, Sam took his hand.

"See ya later Frankie!" and they were out.

As they walked to her loft, she was curious if Will would try to back out, her libido firing on all cylinders and ready to hold him to his promise. The small talk was painful, the anticipation distracting. They paused as one of their cell phones buzzed. Realizing it was hers, Sam checked the caller id, dismissing it when she realized it was Riley.

Seeing Will's questioning look, she told him, "It's Riley. I'll call her back later. After you've had your way with me. She'll want all the details anyway."

They were standing outside her building, Sam catching her breath at the look Will was giving her. Still holding her phone in her hand, he pulled her to him. Placing a hand at the back of her neck and using the other one to tip her head back, he thoroughly kissed her, his tongue gentle at first before his sense of urgency nearly swept her off her feet.

"We should take this inside." she said shakily, searching for her key in her crossover.

Walking up to her door, she suddenly paused. Sensing her swift change in demeanor, Will moved to stand beside her. He didn't have to ask, he could see the door had been jimmied. Instantly he was moving her behind him, pulling a small pistol from the back of his jeans. She stood watching, unsure which was more alarming, her door or the gun he was carrying.

Turning to her, he mouthed, "Stay close." She nodded mutely.

Being that her loft was an open floor plan and relatively small, it didn't take long to ascertain it was empty. Still, she was devastated by what she did see. Her loft had been destroyed, books and vinyls all over the floor, her clothes drug out of the closet and strewn about.

Her first reaction was anger. "What the fuck!" she bellowed.

Will stood beside her, his face grim. "This is my fault." He was kicking himself, knowing he had taken his eyes off the ball.

"I don't need a martyr Will, I need to know what the hell happened here and why!" She was shaking, her anger temporarily immobilizing her.

"I guess we should call the police."

Looking around, Will suggested trying to figure out what or if anything had been taken first. Throwing her hands up, Sam asked heatedly, "And where do I even start?"

Putting his hand on her back, he turned her to face him, forcing her to look at him. "Take a deep breath. You're okay Sam. We don't have to deal with this right now if you want to go back to my place. We can face this in the morning in the daylight, if that's better. Either way, I'm here for you."

Doing as he said, she did the breathing technique she had learned in therapy. "I'm okay. It's just a shock to see all my things ransacked like this. I need to stay. I'm not going to let whatever asshole did this win."

He nodded, not surprised by her answer. "I'm going to run home and get Prince so we can stay with you tonight. I'll be back in ten. I want you to lock the door and sit tight. Got it?"

She nodded numbly, locking the door behind him. Slowly she slid down to the floor, her back against the door. She knew her Chelsea neighborhood was safe and never in the sixty years her family had occupied this building had there ever been a break in. What freaked her out more than her stuff strewn about was the fact it seemed like she had been targeted, the intruder clearly looking for something. Suddenly her brother Jordan popped into her head. Frantically she ran to her closet, looking for his letterman's jacket. Not finding it anywhere, she yelled, "No, no, no!"

She stopped, forcing herself to breathe. Where had she left it last?

Think Sam, think. Glancing at the chair beside her bed, she realized it had been left untouched, the random pile of clothes covering it seeming innocuous. Sighing with relief, she found it at the bottom of the pile. Quickly she put it on, feeling Jordan's presence and letting it calm her. Looking around her loft, it occurred to her she didn't see her computer. Hoping she had left it downstairs in *Paws for a Cause*, she decided to head that way. Aware she was in the middle of a crime scene, she went to get her fanny pack first, securing it around her before pulling out her pepper spray.

Cautiously heading down the backstairs, she was unaware Prince and Will were coming up the hall stairs. She jumped hearing him call her name, his voice booming apprehensively. Seeing her computer, she quickly snatched it up, taking note her business was untouched. Turning to head back to her loft, she nearly collided with Will.

"What the hell are you doing down here? I told you to stay put!" his tone was harsh, his eyes raking over her angrily.

Narrowing her own eyes at him, she matched his tone with her own anger. "I'm not a child Will and I don't need *you* to tell me what to do! I just needed to make sure I still had my computer." She held it up to him to prove her point.

"How do you know your intruder wasn't down here? How do you know he wasn't waiting to attack you? You need to think. . ."

Her voice rose an octave as she cut him off furiously. "Shut up Will! Don't YOU dare tell me how to take care of myself! I don't need a man to tell me how a woman needs to be aware of her surroundings at all times and that men are dicks looking for the weak to prey on. I told you,

I've been taking care of myself a long time and my stuff being in disarray is nothing. Now get the fuck out of my way before I pepper spray your ass and you're the one crying like a baby!" She watched him move aside, letting her pass, vaguely aware angry tears were running down her face, which pissed her off even more.

He stood watching her as she crammed her pepper spray back into her fanny pack, alongside her brass knuckles and poop bags. Setting it on her bar, she turned to him, finally letting him take her into his arms.

"I'm sorry I yelled. When I couldn't find you, it scared me. And you should know I don't scare easily. I know how strong you are Sam, but tonight you have me to lean on. What can I do to help?" He asked gently.

They both smiled as Prince lay down at their feet with a big sigh, resting his head on his paws, clearly relieved mom and dad were done fighting.

She was heartbroken to see her beloved vinyls dumped out of their covers and all over her hardwood floor. "Could you put the albums back and I'll do the books." she asked, relieved when he nodded.

Walking around her loft she turned on every lamp she had and even her light over her sink. The books had mostly been her grandmother's collection and less personal and as she struggled to remember in what order they had been in, she realized it didn't really matter. She was relieved none of her picture frames had been broken as she put them back where they belonged. She paused suddenly realizing Will was putting an album on.

"I thought you're not a fan of music?" she asked with a smile.

Looking at her with a shrug he acknowledged with his own smile. "You've actually got great taste in music minus this Spice Girls album."

As the Eagles played on her Victrola, she sang softly, focusing on the task at hand. Within an hour her apartment appeared back to normal, everything put back in its rightful place. Standing with her hands on her hips, Sam surveyed her loft, the stench of being violated still weighing her down. Decisively she went to light the candles around the room, spraying some Febreeze here and there to move the process along faster. Exhausted physically and mentally, she collapsed on her couch.

Will went to turn off some of the lights before pouring each of them a shot of tequila. Squeezing a lime into hers, he handed it to her. She thanked him for it, clinking hers to his before throwing it back. Coming to sit beside her, he was torn between wanting to pull her to him and letting her come to him. Putting his arm along the back of the couch, he didn't touch her. He could see her exhaustion, but knew sleep would be hard to come by tonight. Jordan's jacket rustled as he was finally rewarded when she slid closer to him, laying her head on his shoulder. Only then did he put his arms around her, holding her to him tightly.

"It's getting late Sam. What do you want to do now? He asked.

"I'm not sleeping in my bed, you can sleep there and I'll take the couch. I'm going to need some Castle first though." she said quietly.

She moved away from him as he got up from the couch. She watched him as he refilled her water bottle, brought pillows from her bed, and pulled the oversized velour blanket off the back of the couch before bringing her the remotes. Seeing her face, he hastily said. "Just let me help and say thank you. Please." She gave a small laugh when Prince gave a small whine, sensing Will's tension.

"Thank you. Sorry I lost it earlier. My adrenaline was flowing and I really do hate being told what to do." she said ruefully.

He smiled at her, his eyes growing dark. "Tell me about it."

They settled in for the night, her head on a pillow in his lap, his feet up on her coffee table with a pillow behind his own head. Snuggled into her blanket, he gave her the couch to stretch out on, keeping her bad shoulder up, Prince laying at their feet. Stroking her hair, Will played over the night in his head, all the what ifs eating him alive. He was fairly certain he had an idea of what they were looking for, but as all slime is, his suspects were slippery to catch and always one step ahead of him.

Thinking she was almost asleep, he was startled when she suddenly popped up excitedly. "We didn't check our crime scene for clues!"

When he looked at her blankly, she clarified for him. "I've been asking myself what would Beckett do and she would check for clues to who the perp was. We never checked!"

He watched her as she turned on her phone flashlight and started scouring the floor while still talking to him. "It would be fantastic if we could find some prints somewhere." She paused, turning to Will. "Or do you think they were smart enough to wear gloves?"

Feeling like he should get up and help, he sat and took in all that Sam was, a woman who was not going to lay down and be a victim. He felt guilty he had talked her out of calling the cops, but if she found something, he would reassure her he had his own people he could send it to.

She moved methodically around the perimeter of her loft, starting with her sink before moving to her albums, her book shelves, and finally to her closet, her bed last. He went to her when she gave a shriek. "I found something!" Running to her bathroom, she came back with tweezers, using them to pick up a well used tissue, adamant it wasn't hers when he asked.

She held it up delicately as she went to her kitchen pointing to a drawer and asking Will to get her a baggie. Triumphantly she dropped it into the baggie he held open for her.

Smiling at her, he gave her the props she was looking for. "Well done Sam. Beckett and Castle would be proud. I have a guy I can send this to in the morning and we can maybe get a name from his DNA."

She nodded. "Thank you."

Placing the prized baggie on her bar, she headed back to the couch, her exhaustion making her emotional. "I need to know who this guy is so I can understand what he was looking for." she said wearily.

Keeping his own voice even keel, Will asked gently. "What do you think he could be looking for?"

She shook her head vehemently before dismissing his question. "How should I know! Does this maggot even need a reason to enter and destroy?"

He studied her for a minute, realizing she wasn't ready to face the reality that was brewing, but knowing it would catch up to them sooner or later. He could only assume they were watching her, choosing to come into her loft knowing she was otherwise occupied at Charlie's. He had to admit he had been impressed when she had found the tissue under the edge of her bed. Not willing to burst her bubble, he let her rest in the false sense of having some control. One thing was certain, he was as anxious as she was to have some answers.

And he knew with certainty he was going to need to be more focused in keeping an eye on her. He needed back up, knowing he would be traveling again soon. Hearing her finally snoring softly, he turned the tv off, letting his eyes adjust to the complete darkness, her nightlight from the bathroom the only illumination of the room. After years of walking a fine line between light and darkness in the name of national security, Will had resources he trusted explicitly, but knew they were nothing compared to what he was up against. Feeling his own exhaustion, he closed his eyes, finding Sam's presence comforting, he was asleep in no time.

CHAPTER SIX

He noticed her walking long before he would be able to greet her. He knew Prince had seen her too, feeling him pick up the pace of their walk. He smiled to himself knowing he was as crazy about Sam as he was, free to return her love and devotion unconditionally as any dog would. Who could blame him? As he got closer to her, he felt like something was wrong, her body language withdrawn. Realizing she hadn't seen him, he toyed with the idea of letting her pass, but his need to check on her won out.

"Hey Sam. You good?" he asked, touching her arm.

She looked up then, her shades unable to hide she'd been crying. Taking her earbuds out, she bent down to hug Prince before turning to Will. "I'm just out getting dinner from the diner. See ya." Abruptly she turned, heading up the stairs of her brownstone.

Reaching for her hand, he stopped her. "What's wrong?"

"I'm okay, but thanks for asking." She turned again, but he wasn't going to let it go.

"Talk to me. What's the problem? I can see you've been crying." Suddenly his eyes narrowed, his voice becoming hard. "Did Marco do something?" He had moved up the step to her, his hand now on her back.

Sighing, Sam mumbled to him, "Why don't you just come in."

Watching her take her things to the kitchen and casually pour herself a glass of wine, his patience was wearing thin. "What is it Sam? What happened?"

Her eyes filled with tears as she went to sit on the couch, her voice emotional as she shared. "One of my clients has had cancer for the past couple of months and we thought he was doing better. But he passed away this afternoon. I just found out an hour ago. Dumb to be this upset over a dog I know. He was, he was just such a sweet boy and his family loved him so much. It gets to me, you know?"

Joining her on the couch, Will pulled her to him. "That's not dumb. I would be devastated if that was Prince." Hearing his name and sensing her distress, Prince came and inserted himself between the two of them, laying his head in her lap, his big brown eyes trying to convey comfort to her.

"Speaking of sweet boys. Thank you Prince, I'll be okay" she said, stroking the top of his head. Turning to Will she added, "It was just such a shock. I taught them how to do touch therapy and use massage to help with his pain management. Chemo can only do so much. We all thought he was getting better. Rest in peace Rocky." she added the end softly, brushing away more tears.

Squeezing her hand, Will nodded. "I'm sure they were grateful for all you did to help make him suffer less." Feeling at a loss as to help her feel better he asked gently, "What are you doing tonight? Can we stay and keep you company?"

Waving him off, she went to take her food out of the bag. "I'll do what I always do when my heart gets broken. Pig out on my comfort foods and watch my favorite movie."

He went to stand beside her, taking in the mac and cheese, chicken sandwich, and chocolate chip cookies. She turned to him shrugging. "I'll never eat all this if you want some. But I don't think you'll like my movie choice."

He raised an eyebrow at her. "What is it? You never know."

"Pretty Woman." She said, waiting for his reaction. She laughed when he shook his head.

"Yeah, I don't think I've seen that one. Isn't it really old?" he asked.

She frowned before turning to pull two plates off the shelf over her stove. "Careful. It's actually older than me."

"I've already had dinner, thanks anyway."

Putting a plate away, she dug into the creamy mac and cheese before cutting the chicken sandwich in half. "Just in case you need a snack later."

"What, no popcorn?" he said as he followed her back to her couch. She took a sip of her wine, still thinking about the loss of her client.

"Excuse me. I just need to wash my face." she said, heading to her bathroom. He nodded, understanding she needed a minute to collect herself. Wanting to do something to help, he googled to see where the movie was streaming before pulling it up for her on Disney+.

When Sam came back she seemed calmer, her face freshly washed, the smeared mascara wiped away. Seeing that the movie was queued up, she gave Will a grateful smile. "So I take it, you're going to stay and watch?"

"I have no plans tonight. How bad can it be?" he asked, clearly teasing her.

Smacking him on the arm, she acted offended. "Hey! I'll have you know Pretty Woman is *the* best romantic comedy ever!"

"Really?" he asked, his skepticism clear. "I thought rom-coms are a dime a dozen?"

She studied him for a minute before answering. "You'll just have to watch and see." Pushing play, she picked up her plate of food and settled in, arranging her favorite blanket around her.

The two hours flew by as Will watched Sam go through a gamut of emotions. She had gushed over Vivian's red dress, informed him horses were her spirit animal during the Polo match and cussed Phillip like a sailor when he hit on Vivian. He had been mesmerized watching her face glow when Edward showed up in his limo, climbing Vivian's fire escape to rescue her, smiling as she breathed out the words "she rescues him right back" as if they were magical.

The room grew dim when she turned the tv off, sighing loudly as she turned to him. "Well? What's the verdict?"

Giving her a vague smile, he hedged. "It was fine, but you tell me your thoughts."

"Come *on*!" she said, rolling her eyes at him. "It's about hope and that love can find anyone, anywhere, any time. It doesn't matter where you've been and the crap life dealt you that got you there because we all deserve a second chance. It's about where you're going and that we all have the possibility of a happily ever after. And who doesn't want that?" She felt breathless, the look he was giving her lighting her up like the fourth of July, realizing how much she wanted that, possibly even with this man sitting across from her.

"Anwhere, anytime? Is that what you want Sam? A happily ever after?" he asked.

She caught her breath, wondering which way he was wanting her to play this. "Of course. Everyone does. Even if you have to wait a while like Vivian and Edward did."

His eyes were dark and she could feel the heat between them, his eyes becoming focused on her lips. "And what about kissing some toads while you wait for your prince to come along? Or are you saving yourself?"

She shrugged, not wanting him to know he was getting to her. "I'm not into one night stands if that's what you're asking, but I'm very much for team kissing. If it's the right situation."

He stood up holding his hand out to her. When she hesitated, he said softly "Let's see if this is the right situation."

Taking his hand she stood up, her anticipation causing her skin to tingle as she thought about the other kisses he had bestowed on her. With both hands, he took her face, turning it to the angle he wanted, his eyes glowing in anticipation as he slowly descended his lips to hers. Gently he kissed her before parting her lips, his tongue hungry and taking what it wanted, making it clear he could rule her if he wanted to.

She wasn't sure if they stood there for five minutes or five hours, time seeming to stand still. Her arms were around his waist, holding on for dear life as he wrecked her with his mouth, his hands warm on her face.

Pulling back from her he asked, "What's the verdict? Is this the right situation?"

All she could do was nod, letting him go and trying to come back to her senses. "Night Sam. I'll call you tomorrow." Kissing her forehead, he moved away, Prince following him to her door. "Don't forget to lock up."

Still dazed, she did as she was told before heading to bed. Laying between the sheets, she was grateful for the coolness of her crisp cotton percale, the heat slowly leaving her body. Turning onto her side, she picked up her phone to send a text. *Thanks for keeping me company tonight.* Hitting send, she closed her eyes, hoping there might be a happily ever after out there for her after all.

Hurrying Prince along the couple of blocks to his apartment, he could feel the tightness in his jeans, hopeful no one would notice the predicament he had put himself in. As he closed and locked his door behind him, he felt his phone buzz. Quickly he responded to her text. *No problem. I'm always here for you. Sweet dreams Sam.*

CHAPTER SEVEN

Tonight was the night Sam had agreed to go out to dinner with Marco, despite the epic kiss between her and Will a week ago. She saw it merely as dinner between friends and a way to thank him for all he had done to help her at *Paws for a Cause* in the last three weeks. He was due to pick her up in less than twenty minutes and she scrambled to finish getting her makeup done before she shimmied into her dress. She jumped when there was a knock at the door, swearing softly when she smeared her mascara. Checking the time on her phone, she could only assume Marco was early.

Seeing him through her peep hole, she swore again, but opened her door to him with a big smile. "Hi! You're a little early, but I'm almost ready I promise!" she said, taking in the beautiful bouquet of flowers.

Presenting them to her with a flourish, he came in and headed to her kitchen sink. "Go ahead and finish getting ready. I can find something to put these lovelies in for you."

"You spoil me Marco. They are absolutely stunning!" Sam gushed, appreciating his thoughtful gesture. "There's a vase under the sink."

Her loft had little privacy, but she grabbed her dress off the bed and headed to the bathroom for a quick change from her bathrobe to ready for a night out. Flipping her hair one more time, she assessed herself in the mirror. She comforted herself with the fact that Marco was used to seeing her in jeans and t-shirts and this was definitely a step up, especially for her.

As she opened the door, it was Marco's turn to gush. "Bella! You are stunning Sam. I will be lucky to have you on my arm tonight!" he said, kissing her on the cheek before holding his arm out to her. "Shall we?"

She hadn't really thought about how they would get to dinner, but she was surprised to see an expensive black sports car parked outside her brownstone. Gallantly he opened the door for her before running to the other side and climbing in beside her.

He gave her side-eye with a smile. "What do you think of your chariot?"

Without missing a beat, Sam bantered back. "I think I've way over paid you for the last three weeks or you have a fairy godmother you neglected to tell me about."

Laughing at her comment, he enlightened her. "Actually I have a father who is very generous with his money."

"Lucky you!" she said simply.

"Lucky for both of us tonight." he said, running his finger down the side of her arm.

Sam had to give him credit, not only was he handsome to look at, he knew how to choose a nice place for dinner and make a girl feel special. They feasted on wagyu steaks and drank champagne while he kept their small talk moving, sharing stories of his family's winery and growing up in San Marino, the jewels of Italy always close by. Sam never shared that her grandmother had been born in Italy, always hesitant to share personal information.

Their plates had just been cleared away when he leaned into her and took her hand. "You are too quiet. Tell me about your family. Do you have sisters or brothers? Did you grow up in New York?"

Startled by the swift change of topic, she replied quickly, her answers somewhat flip. "Yes, yes and yes."

Seeing his look of dismay she hastily added, "Yes, I grew up in New York, yes, I have one sister and yes, I had one brother. He passed away a few years ago."

His look made her cringe, prompting her to reach for her champagne and down what was left. "Is there more champagne?" She could only hope he would take the hint and leave her statement alone. It had been a lovely evening but Sam was ready to head home and spend some quality time with her couch and the new book she had started earlier in the week.

Taking her cue, Marco signaled for the check. "I have a surprise for you! We have reservations at a rooftop club on the lower east side. You're going to love it. Their spicy margarita is superb!"

Sam bit her lip, choosing her words carefully. "That is so thoughtful of you Marco, but I wasn't planning on being out late tonight."

His smile suddenly seemed a little less sincere as he leaned over to say into her ear, "You shouldn't have worn a dress like that if you didn't come to party Sam."

With a firm grip on her elbow, he walked her to his car. Once inside, she attempted to decline again. "Dinner was lovely Marco and the flowers were so thoughtful, but my shoulder is throbbing and I would appreciate it if you would take me home. Please."

Turning to face her, he stroked her cheek with his finger. "Sweet Sam. You're going to love it." Leaning into her, he kissed her, his lips possessive. "Now be a good little girl and let's have some fun."

Sam's heart started pounding in her chest as she suddenly realized why Marco had seemed familiar from the moment they met. She had a flashback to an old boyfriend who had told her that once when she had challenged plans he had made without asking. She didn't like being told what to do, but she felt a little apprehensive thinking about what could happen if she didn't go along with his plans. For now. Thinking about how she was going to play the situation, she rubbed her throbbing lips.

They were soon seated at the rooftop bar, surrounded by large lush foliage, a glimpse of the Manhattan skyline peeking out near the Williamsburg Bridge. The music was loud and the dance floor packed.

As the waitress sat down their drinks, Sam immediately took a sip, deciding she would make him think she was all in for drinks and dancing.

"This place is cool. How did you hear about it?" she asked.

He smiled, picking up her hand and giving it a squeeze. "That's my girl. A friend told me about it. I knew you would love it. Cincin!" he said, raising his spicy margarita to hers. "Did you see the skyline behind you?" He asked.

Turning in her chair, Sam cringed, fearful that he was putting something in her drink. Turning back nonchalantly, she said, "It's not Italy but it's a pretty cool view."

Suddenly she jumped up and grabbed his hand. "I love this song! Let's go dance!"

Squeezing in among all the people, Sam felt a little less panicked. It would be hard for him to do anything with all these witnesses around. It turned out Marco loved dancing and they were in two or three songs deep when the band started up a slow dance song. "Grab your lover's kids and let's get busy!" one of the band members announced.

As she turned to head back to their table, Marco snaked his arm around her waist and pulled her close. "One more dance and then we can go sit down." She tried not to recoil from his touch as his hands started at her waist before moving down to her ass.

Having suffered through the song, she was relieved to be back at their table, her plan mentally in place. When a server passed by, Sam snagged her. "Excuse me, can I get an angel shot please?'

"Sure hon. On the rocks or with a twist?" she asked.

"She has a drink, we're fine thanks." Marco said sourly.

Giving him a withering look, she turned back to Sam, her pen ready.

Ignoring him, Sam requested "On the rocks please and thank you." Handing her spicy marg to her, she had one more request. "I think this drink might have been made with an old mixer. It tastes funny."

"I'm so sorry about that. I'll make sure it gets taken off your tab." she said, glancing at Marco.

As she walked away, she could see Marco was angry with her. "Why did you send your drink away? Those aren't free, you know."

Ignoring his anger, she looked surprised. "Marco you know I couldn't drink that!"

Narrowing his eyes at her, he growled, "Why the hell not?"

"I thought you saw him too. Some guy came and put something in my drink while we were dancing. I can't be sure, but maybe in yours too. Besides, she said she would make sure it came off your tab." Sam said, fingers crossed he would buy her story.

"What guy?" he asked, looking around.

Randomly she pointed, trying to buy herself some time. She almost did a double take when she noticed Will standing to the far side of the room talking to a cop, a young man in handcuffs standing between them. Her heart soared to realize if she couldn't get herself out of this, Will was close by.

"Which guy? Be more specific!" he growled again.

Suddenly a man with an apron walked up to them, his gaze focused on her. "I'm sorry to bother you, but you have a phone call at the bar. She says it's a family emergency."

Feigning surprised concern, Sam answered, "Oh my gosh, thank you for letting me know! Can you please show me where I can take the call?"

As she moved to get up, Marco grabbed her wrist to stop her. "Hold up. No one calls a landline anymore. Why wouldn't she just call your cell?" he asked suspiciously.

Clutching for straws, Sam reasoned with him. "I'm sure it's my sister and she probably did but my phone is in my purse and I didn't answer."

"How did she know you were here? You didn't know we were coming here until an hour ago." He was definitely not letting this go.

Thinking quickly, Sam told a half truth. "She tracks me through my phone when she knows I'm on a date. She's an overprotective big sister that way." Sam said, rolling her eyes.

"Miss, right this way and I can show you where you can take the call." the bartender said firmly, leaving her no choice but to come with him.

Glancing in the direction she had last seen Will, she could see he was making his way to her. Making eye contact with him, she saw him pause and realized he had read her right. Looking in the same direction she was, Marco suddenly jumped up, almost overturning their high top.

"Fuck! Why is he here?" he bellowed before sprinting off.

Seeing him flee, Will mouthed "Stay with him!" pointing to the bartender, before moving into his own sprint after Marco. Sam watched until the two of them had disappeared from sight.

"Miss? Why don't you come join me at the bar?" he asked, his tone comforting. "I'm Tony by the way." he added as she walked beside him, her relief to be free of Marco palatable.

"I'm Sam. I really appreciate your help back there. And your server too. She didn't miss a beat when I asked for an angel shot." He led her to the far end of his bar, a little less busy and not so conspicuous.

"Kudos to you that you knew to ask for it. All of our servers are trained to act quickly when we're faced with that request. Not everyone knows we take that as a sign a customer is in distress and needs our help." Sam nodded, a small lump in her throat. She wasn't good at asking for help, but now hadn't seemed like the time to take chances.

"Thank you. I wasn't sure if it was a real thing or an urban legend." she said.

"No worries. We get all kinds in here. When they need some muscle, they come get me. I've done all kinds of security and dealt with all kinds of dirtbags like your date."

"Really?" Sam asked.

"Yep. Military, TSA officer, a bouncer, you name it, I've done it."

Curious, she asked. "So do you know Will?"

His smile got broader. "Oh yeah, I know Will. Great guy, especially when you're in trouble."

She was about to ask for some details, when his next comment took her breath away. "I knew your brother Jordan too. Another great guy."

Struggling to breath, Sam echoed him. "You knew Jordan? How? And how did you know he's my brother?" Her head was spinning.

"We played football together in high school. Jordan was the first friend I made when my family moved to Brooklyn my sophomore year. He made sure I felt included. I was the tall awkward kid that would randomly show up at your house sometimes."

Sam stared, trying to remember him. Jordan's football games were some of her best memories of him. Tony continued while he washed glasses. "I remember you up in the stands yelling your heart out. Jordan always called you his biggest fan, even with your mom and dad sitting beside you." His grin started to fade as he realized Sam was getting emotional.

"Hey! I'm sorry. I didn't mean to upset you. It tore us all up when we heard what happened to him. I can imagine how devastated your family must have been. Let me get you a drink. On the house!" he said, his look concerned.

It had been a long time since someone had mentioned Jordan's name to her and while it had been startling, it was a sweet memory of being in the stands under the Friday night lights, cheering the home team on, but mostly remembering Jordan. He had been fast and the quarterback could always count on him to run the ball down the middle or go deep and complete the pass. He had scored numerous touchdowns over his high school career, but didn't play in college, focused instead on his education in computer science.

Giving a small smile to Tony, she agreed with him. "Jordan really did love football. And I really was his biggest fan. Those were some of our family's favorite Friday nights during the fall. Thanks for saying something. And I'll take you up on that offer. An espresso martini would be fantastic, thank you."

Setting the drink down in front of her, Tony leaned toward her, his elbows on the bar. "Jordan would have been proud of you tonight. Figuring out how to save yourself. We checked the drink you sent back and it had been roofied too by the way. How did you get mixed up with that guy?"

It was startling to hear what she suspected was true, but nonetheless, Sam shrugged. "He was in the right place at the right time and I needed help running my business. He seemed like a nice guy. And he worked really hard. He definitely made my life easier the past couple of weeks."

"Until he didn't," said Tony.

Raising her glass to him, Sam could only say, "Touche'! Will tried to warn me. I can't wait for his, I told you so!" She said, sipping her martini.

Chuckling, Tony could only say, "Yep, you're due for sure. Can't blame the guy though. He's very protective of his people."

Setting her glass down, Sam pretended this wasn't news to her. What did Tony mean by his people? Had they talked about her or was he going on their past history which included Jordan.

"Speaking of Will. I think I'm going to Uber home. It's getting late. Can you let him know for me please?" Sam said.

Shaking his head, Tony informed her, "Will texted me you need to sit tight until he can personally take you home." Checking his watch, he added, "It should be any minute now though."

Another man telling her what to do. "I appreciate that, but I'm ready to go now. You can let him know for me, right?"

Laughing at her, he shook his head. "You really are Jordan's sister. He didn't like being told what to do either."

Luckily for everyone, Will suddenly appeared. Sam was immediately struck by how tired he looked. Finishing her martini, she jumped off her barstool. "It was great to meet you Tony. And to talk about Jordan. Will are you ready?" she asked, turning to him.

Nodding at both of them, he said, "Yep. Thanks Tony. I'll see ya round."

Walking out into the cool night air, Sam gave an involuntary shiver, her sleeveless dress not covering much of her upper body. Immediately Will took off his jacket and helped her into it before handing her his helmet to wear. Discreetly she hiked her dress up before climbing onto the back of his motorcycle behind him, instinctively wrapping her arms around his waist and laying her head on his back, grateful to be there, warm and safe. She didn't like being told what to do, but it did feel good to let Will take over.

Before she knew it, they were outside Will's apartment. "Are we walking from here?" she asked him, handing his helmet back to him.

"Sorry, but I need to talk to you about Marco. And I think you should stay here tonight, just in case." Will said, unlocking his door and moving aside for her to go in, Prince greeting them both sleepily.

Turning to face him, she said, "I cannot think any more about Marco tonight. I'm exhausted and I just want to go to sleep."

Surprised she wasn't going to argue with him, he nodded to her. "Sure. You're welcome to stay here. Take my bed. I'll sleep on the couch."

She was already headed to his room, but turned to look back at him. "No Will. We're both exhausted. Come to bed. I promise to be good." Kicking her shoes off, she pulled back the covers and crawled into Will's bed.

"Do you want a t-shirt to sleep in?" he asked.

Waving him off, her eyes were already closed. Standing on the other side of the bed he hesitated briefly before taking off his jeans and pulling his t-shirt over his head. Sighing he went to pull on some gym shorts before crawling in beside her. He was exhausted too, but even in the dark, he could see her in her dress, clinging to all her curves and revealing all he longed to touch. Laying on his back, he stared at the ceiling, trying to focus on something other than Sam.

He wasn't sure how long it had been, before he heard her say "Will?" in a small voice.

He turned to look at her. "Yeah?"

"Can you hold me? Please?" she asked, her voice emotional.

He wasted no time pulling her to him, embracing that her head rested on his shoulder, her legs pulled up alongside his.

"I was so stupid. I can't believe I put myself in that position. Thank you for being there. And for holding me." she said, her voice nasally.

He could feel her tears on his chest, realizing how scared she must have been. When she had sent him that beseeching look across the bar, it had taken all his will power not to rip that punk apart when he finally caught up to him.

"And thanks for not saying I told you so." she added. She could feel the rumble in his chest as he contained his laugh.

"No problem. There will be plenty of time for that tomorrow." he said.

Sighing heavily, Sam snuggled deeper into him. "What now?" he asked softly.

"I'm tired but I can't go to sleep." she said, her voice muffled in his chest.

His hesitation was brief before rolling her onto her back and cupping her face. "If you're awake, I have some ideas." he said, his eyes glittering in the darkness.

"I'm open to suggestions." she said, tracing his lip with her finger.

Turning his body to face her full on, he kissed her, his lips soft on hers before his tongue searched her mouth urgently, his hand on her hipbone.

"You might be more comfortable out of this dress. Can I help you with that?" he asked softly.

Nodding, she felt her skin light on fire as he pulled it off her shoulders, kissing each of them gently before moving it further down her. Reaching her arms around his neck, she arched toward him, wanting more. Shifting to straddle her, he shimmied her completely out of her dress, her nakedness bringing him to his knees. He had imagined this in so many ways, he was going to make the most of it.

As his lips and tongue worked their way down, he took his sweet time to explore every inch of her, wreaking havoc as he discovered her sweet spots. Her eyes were glued to his as he hovered over her, finally rewarded as he moved inside her slowly at first before the pace became more frenzied. Moaning her name, he dropped his face into her hair, suddenly pushing deep, feeling her climax at the same time he did.

They were both breathing heavily as he rolled off of her, pulling her to him once again. Even with her head on his chest, she hated that her thoughts turned back to Marco.

Snuggling deeper into him, she sighed heavily, hating to admit it. "I'm going to need to know more about Marco Will."

Kissing the top of her head, he said quietly. "I know. Tomorrow Sam. Let it go tonight and try to get some sleep."

She focused on his nakedness beneath her, the warmth of his skin, the dark curly hairs on his chest soft, knowing he was everything she had imagined he would be and more. She knew he was right. There would be time tomorrow to sort it out. Closing her eyes, she pictured him hovering over her, her downstairs starting to stir again at the thought of him inside her.

"What?" he asked.

"I know you're right, but. . ." her voice trailed off as she took his shaft in her hand. Feeling him grow hard again, she moved under the sheet, rewarded as it was her turn to drive him crazy. They might both be exhausted, but they had been waiting to be together way too long and they both knew one and done wasn't going to cut it. Tonight was their night and tomorrow could just wait its turn.

The sun was streaming through as Sam focused to remember where she was. Quickly realizing she was alone in Will's bed and still naked, she sat up and called out to him. Waiting for him to answer her, she noticed he had left her a t-shirt at the end of the bed. Slipping it on, she went to his bathroom to make herself presentable. Pausing only briefly she picked up his toothbrush and added toothpaste. After where their tongues had been last night, it seemed like a reasonable transition and quite necessary to rid herself of her morning breath.

Feeling refreshed she wandered out to greet Prince and see if there was any coffee. Instead she found a note. *Went to get breakfast at the diner, be back asap.* Moving to the couch, she started her usual morning routine, doing Wordle on her phone before checking for any pertinent emails. She was grateful it was Saturday and nothing could be too urgent. Nothing but dissecting her Marco debacle.

She was still shook to wonder if Marco was actually Spencer's brother, although at no time had Spencer ever mentioned his family let alone growing up in San Marino. It seemed crazy to think they were related, but then again their looks and similar mannerisms made it hard to believe they weren't. Or was she just being paranoid again, triggered by five little words. She also had to ask herself, was it an incredible coincidence Marco had walked into *Paws for a Cause* or had she been targeted? But what could possibly be the reason for that? Curiosity?

None of it was setting well with her, but she was hesitant to share her concerns with Will. Saying it all out loud would make it seem even more preposterous. Or was it more real? Sitting on the fence about how much to tell Will, she wondered if it would compound the problem or bring clarity? She decided to hold her tongue until she heard what he had to say.

She was quickly distracted when Will walked in, two sacks in tow. Seeing her sitting there in his t-shirt, her bare legs pulled up under her, made him smile.

"Morning. I thought you might be hungry." he said, offering her a cup of coffee and then a small bag of hot food. His smile grew as she took it from him, greedily opening it.

"Did you get me their breakfast sandwich? With potatoes?" she asked, the thought of their egg, cheese, and sausage making her mouth water.

He nodded. "You're welcome. And I brought you some clothes from your loft so you don't have to do the walk of shame for two blocks."

Immediately she froze. "You have a key to my loft?" she asked, looking at him suspiciously.

"Nooo, I used your key I found in your purse." he said, watching her closely, before holding them up and making a show of putting them back in her purse.

Immediately she relaxed, refocusing on her sandwich. "Of course. Thanks for that and breakfast. I am starved!"

Sitting beside her, he sipped his coffee, his eyes smirking at her over the rim. "I bet. You were a busy girl last night."

"Yeah, well I'd been saving up for that for way too long." she said after swallowing her mouthful of food.

He laughed at her candor. "Touche!" he said, raising his cup to her. "You know there's no rush for you to go home. I mean if you have anything else saved up you care to share?" he asked, his gaze focused on her mouth.

Sipping on her own coffee, her look turned serious. "I think we have other things on our agenda this morning. Tell me what you know about Marco."

"You first." Will said.

Not in the mood to argue, she shared what she knew. "Not much. He said he's from San Marino, went to university in Rome, his family owns a winery and they seem to have money. Seemed like he hadn't been in the states that long." Her gaze was steady, preparing herself for the worst.

Sighing, Will chose his words carefully. "You're right, he hasn't been in the U.S. that long, but that's because he's been a very busy boy in Europe participating in espionage." He watched her as she took it in.

Putting her sandwich down, she said quietly. "I see. Do you think he targeted me or just happened to wander in randomly?"

"What do you think?" he countered.

"I asked you first. Clearly I'm not a good judge of character. I want to know what you think." she said, her look earnest.

"Why would he target you?" he countered, his voice quiet.

Abruptly coming to a stand, she started pacing. "I don't know Will! Why would he? It seems like it worked out randomly, that he was new to New York and looking for a job and I was just stupid enough to offer him one on the spot! The only thing I know for certain is I got lucky I'm no worse for wear." Her voice was loud, her nerves still raw.

"If he didn't target me, who would he be after?" She paused her pacing. "You?" she asked, her look concerned.

Shaking his head no, he said, "Think harder Sam."

"One of my clients?" she asked, the thought occurring to her as it came out of her mouth. "He's had free reign with whoever's been on the schedule for the past three weeks."

As her pacing continued, Will thought about that. It was a possibility, but who and why? Moving to stand in front of her and corral her pacing, Will put his hands on her shoulders. "You don't need to worry about him coming back. He's been on the FBI's most wanted list for a while now and he will be locked up for a long time."

Sam nodded at him. "What was he wanted for?"

"Cyber espionage. Compromising the national security of several countries including ours. Can you think of any of your clients who are computer programmers?" he asked, staring her down.

Swallowing hard, she still wondered how much to share with Will. Off the top of her head, the first person she thought of was Jordan. However, she had built quite a list of clients in the few short years she had been open and there was a small possibility there could be a connection. She shook her head. "I can go over my files and see if anything pops up though."

Moving away, he wondered if he should offer to do it for her. "I can help you with that if you like. Also, you should know I swept your apartment for bugs while I was there. Where did the flowers come from?" Will asked, his scrutiny intense.

Quickly realizing why he asked, she told him what he already knew. "From Marco."

Nodding he informed her, "That's where I found the first one. The other was on the back of your mirror near the bed. Do you have any idea why he would want to listen in on your private conversations?"

Her brain was whirling. Of course she didn't. The truth was, no one came to her loft. Well no one but Will and to be fair, that was not that often.

"I don't know." she whispered, suddenly remembering her intruder a few weeks ago destroying her loft. Will had told her they had picked the guy up, his wrap sheet growing as he was convicted of numerous offenses.

Reading her face, he pulled her close to him and hugged her tight. "It's all good. You're all good. Neither one of those scumbags is coming back for a long, long time."

Pulling away from him, she looked into his face, her demeanor deflated. "Thank you for taking care of all this, for your help last night." Moving away from him, she went to pick up the other sack he had walked in with. "I guess I should go get dressed and head home."

Watching her walk past his window, it was hard to let her go. He was curious if she had realized Marco was Spencer's brother, but chose to save that conversation for another day. The two men were too similar for the thought not to have occurred to her. It made him insane to think about either one of them touching her in any way. He assumed she had made the connection, but then again, it had taken her a while to recognize him.

To be fair he had always played the side lines, passing through to get a snack, being in the car when Jordan dropped her somewhere, rarely spending any time in her presence except for the occasional family birthdays. He had treated her like he should, as Jordan's kid sister, until that night by the pool on her birthday. That night had changed his life forever, his thoughts of Sam well beyond the kid sister zone. Now, in real time, he was trying his damnedest to keep her in the friend zone, but last night had been a game changer. Having been inside her, having her naked under him, he knew he was failing miserably. He was wrecked that he hadn't put the kibosh on Marco, but reminded himself Sam was independent and did what she wanted. Lucky for him, he was what she had wanted last night and he had been more than happy to take her up on it. In the stark daylight, he realized he would need to resist more of that in their future, but then again, he would do whatever he needed to for Sam.

CHAPTER EIGHT

Sam's birthday, one year ago

Checking herself in the floor length mirror one last time, Sam smiled at her reflection, satisfied she got it right, the boho dress perfect for her mood tonight. It was her birthday and her friends had promised her a big night at Charlie's. She was never one to enjoy shopping, but had come across this gem in a thrift shop a few weeks ago and bought it without even trying it on. She loved the rust and beige paisley print, the sweet puffy sleeves in contrast to the low v-neckline, her lariat necklace dropping into her cleavage. Impulsively she had put on her cowgirl boots, her leg currently peeking out from the side slit as she posed in the mirror.

Tonight she wasn't just wishing for a man to come into her life, she was wishing for one in particular to show up and just for the night, give his damn self-control a rest. It had been a frustrating four months since the Marco debacle and they had reestablished a delicate professional relationship which revolved around Prince. He was a logical reason for Sam and Will to see each other nearly every week as Will traveled often and Prince would keep Sam company during his trips.

When he was in town, they would somehow both end up at Charlie's for the night, sometimes sharing drinks and maybe even cheeseburgers and fries. They kept their conversations easy breezy, although she had come to realize if she stayed late enough, Will could not help himself and would insist on walking her home. She was happy to let him, although she had learned the hard way not to get her hopes up anything would happen.

Knowing she would be making her birthday wish just after midnight, she set her alarm on her phone accordingly. She was setting her sights high tonight, expecting gratification in the early morning hours of her birthday. Heading out the door, she was oblivious that her boots gave her a different sway as she sashayed the couple of blocks to Charlie's.

Frankie had booked a country music band to play for the night, saying she was way overdue for a show that might bring in more than her regulars. Sam had been happy to hear Frankie make a point to invite Will, letting him know the band would be good, the beer extra cold. He in turn had been noncommittal, giving her a simple "good to know." She could only hope he would show, knowing he was who she had dressed for tonight.

As she headed into the bar she was greeted loudly by Jen and Rachel, already seated at a table. They had chosen one strategically placed between the bar and the stage, front and center of the parquet dance floor that had been laid for the night.

"Oh my god Sam you look incredible!" Rachel gushed, reaching her first and taking her hand to twirl her. Jen, not far behind, added her own thoughts as she handed a flute of champagne to her.

Frankie came to join them as they settled into their table, Sam taking in the beautifully decorated cake and small gift bag beside it. She watched as Rachel poured Frankie a glass of champagne as well, handing it to her as the three of them turned to toast the birthday girl.

Her smile was big as Jen did the honors. "To our beautiful birthday girl! May all your wishes come true tonight and every day! We love you Sam! Cheers!"

The girls were all dressed in their country chic, their expectations for the band and their evening ahead set high. They noticed Frankie wore her own big smile as she made her way back to the bar, the lines growing as people made their way in. Having ordered her favorite for dinner, Sam scarfed down her pimento cheeseburger and fries hoping it would soak up her champagne. The band was just starting to play as someone cleared their table and brought a new bottle of champagne. Rachel was the first one to notice a handsome young man dressed in jeans and a white t-shirt eyeing her friend.

"Don't look now, but I think your first admirer for the evening is about to make his move." she said playfully to Sam. She turned just as he reached their table, his handsome boyish face hopeful yet confident at the same time.

"Evening ladies. Everybody ready for a good time tonight?" he asked, his white teeth flashing in his tanned face.

Jen quickly jumped in. "Of course! How about you?" she asked.

He focused his attention on Sam. "Absolutely! I'm Sam." he said as he put out his hand to her, introducing himself. Rachel and Jen giggled, causing Sam to glare at her champagne riddled friends.

"Nice to meet you Sam. I'm sure we'll see you round." Her tone was friendly, but dismissive.

Turning back to her friends, she picked up her champagne flute, avoiding his fallen face as he walked away. She held her hand up to silence their protests before they could even get them out. "Don't say it! I'm looking for a man tonight, not a boy, even one as cute as him! And for sure not one named Sam!"

They all burst out laughing just as the band started to play Shania Twain's *"Feel Like a Woman!"* With a scream they all headed to the dance floor, feeling their champagne and embracing Shania's sassy lyrics. As they shimmied and sang to the music, Sam couldn't help but check the bar for one handsome face in particular. Pushing away her disappointment, she turned back to her friends, determined to enjoy her night with or without him. The night was young and there were plenty of cowboys out on the dance floor tonight.

From the outside, the evening had been a success, Sam's friends keeping her flute full, her birthday cake all but demolished, her new bracelet sparkling on her wrist. She might not have a lot of friends, but the ones she had were the best. They had all taken turns dancing with the variety of men that were brave enough to come to their table, although they deferred the majority of the dances to Sam. Having given up on Will, Sam eventually became focused on one man in particular who had clearly singled her out. She liked his look, his beard and mustache scruffy, his brown eyes warm on hers as he moved her around the dance floor. She ignored how much he resembled someone else as they danced to some of her favorite country songs, hopeful Will might be jealous if he ever did show. Knowing it was almost midnight, she resigned herself to the fact he was going to be a no show and tried to keep herself in the moment with her new friend Lucas. Maybe he would be the one to get her out of this dress tonight, her birthday wish about to go out to the universe.

She felt herself stiffen as the band announced they were going to slow it down a bit and to find your special someone for the next song. She fanned herself with her hand to signal to Lucas she was hot, leaning into him to say she needed some water. As the keyboard played Sheriff's distinct opening to *"When I'm With You,"* Lucas grabbed her by the hand, pulling her into him.

"Don't leave me hanging Sam." he said in her ear. Feeling her stiffness, he added, "Relax! I won't bite."

She closed her eyes, imagining a different someone else holding her close. Her back was to him when he walked up and surprised them both, tapping Lucas on the shoulder before saying, "Sorry buddy, but I gotta cut in. This birthday girl is taken."

Lucas was so startled he didn't notice Sam scowl at the man, as he relinquished his hold on her to Will. Failing to resist as he pulled her into him, she focused on glaring up at him. "A little late to the party aren't you? Just who do you think you are to cut in like that?"

Will pulled her even tighter into him, his breath warm in her ear, sending a shiver down her spine as he spoke, "You can yell at me later Sam. I want to enjoy this song with you." He had pulled away to look at her, his eyes dark. She could feel the heat between them as his eyes dropped to her lips before following her necklace down into her dress.

Glancing at her table, she noticed Jen holding her phone up and pointing to it. She could see her alarm going off and realized it was time to make a wish. They were both smiling broadly at her, giving her thumbs up. Will moved her slowly around the dance floor while she listened to the words of the song, wondering why he had jumped in for this song in particular. Deciding to let herself enjoy the moment, she rested her head on his shoulder and closed her eyes, putting this year's birthday wish out there with all her heart. She felt her heartbeat quicken as she realized Will was softly saying the words to the song in her ear. *I never cared for nobody like I care for you. And I never wanted to share the things I want to share with you.*

Too soon, the song finished, Will releasing her abruptly. "I'll let you get back to your dance partner. Happy birthday Sam." he said before he kissed her on the cheek.

She stood there, shocked to watch him walk away from her, realizing he was headed back to his usual spot at the bar. Walking back to her friends, she found their excited faces annoying as they quizzed her. "Who was *that*? I can't believe he cut in on you like that! Did you make your wish? Does it include him?"

Taking a deep breath, Sam reached for her champagne and pasted a smile on her face. "You know this birthday girl doesn't wish and tell!"

She was relieved to see Jen check her phone for the time before finishing off her flute of champagne. "Sorry to be a party pooper girls, but this mama needs to get home before her kids are up in six hours!"

Rachel nodded in agreement and Sam quickly downed the rest of her champagne as well. "I'm ready too, no worries. Thank you for the best birthday! I love you and appreciate the cake and this beautiful bracelet." she said, standing up to hug them both.

"Why don't you catch a ride with us in our Uber? She'll be here in three minutes." Jen suggested.

Collecting her things before pouring herself the end of the champagne, she decided she had some unfinished business before she headed out. "No, I'm good. But don't worry, I'm not walking home, I'll Uber too."

One more round of hugs and they were out the door. Sam headed to the table Lucas still sat at with his buddies. When he turned to her, she quickly jumped in. "Sorry about that earlier. He's just a friend. And this birthday girl is most definitely not taken. Yet." Her smile was big, her voice light.

"No worries. It was nice to meet you. Hope you enjoy the rest of your birthday." His voice was equally light, but she could see the coolness in his eyes.

Mentally cursing Will, she made one more attempt to reconnect with him, touching his arm to regain his attention."How about the next round of drinks is on me? What are you boys drinking?" She swept the table with her question, but kept her gaze on him steady, hoping he couldn't hear her nerves in her voice.

"I think you've got the wrong cowboy. Your *friend* made his point and I got it." It annoyed her his rejection stung more than she expected. "You should go to him. I watched you together and I know when to cut my losses. Take care Sam." With that he got up and headed to a nearby table, making his point with a big smile to some new girl.

Downing her champagne swiftly, she sat the empty glass on the table, giving the other two men a nod before she turned and headed out the door. She could feel anger replacing her hurt feelings as she pulled out her phone to get an Uber. Feeling tears sting at the back of her eyes, her Uber app became blurry, challenging her ability to connect.

Deciding it wasn't that late and noting the number of people milling outside the bar, she threw her phone into her clutch and decided she would walk after all. She had gone only a few steps when someone grabbed her by the arm.

"Where do you think you're going?" he asked, his eyes glinting darkly.

Seeing Will with his hand on her, quickly inspired her biting retaliation. "I'm headed home early thanks to your cock block. And alone!" she added vehemently.

"You don't need to be walking alone at this time of night. Especially not dressed like that." he said, his eyes sweeping her from head to toe before coming back to her stormy expression.

"Like what Will? What are you worried about?" she asked icily.

He paused before answering. "I'm worried about you walking home in those boots after all the champagne you've had tonight."

"Bullshit!" she said. "You have no idea how much champagne I've had tonight, but you do know I look damn good and for some reason you're running overtime in the friendship zone trying to take care of me. Back the hell off! I'm a big girl and I can take care of myself!"

She turned abruptly, headed home, her boots thudding loudly as she stomped down the sidewalk. Suddenly a car horn blared as she stepped out to cross the street, failing to look either way.

She felt Will's hand grab her arm to pull her back to safety. As she tried to shake him off, he walked her across the street before relaxing his grip and moving his hand to her elbow.

Annoyed, she kept moving forward, choosing to ignore him and the small fire that was starting to blaze where his hand touched her skin.

When they finally reached her building, she turned to him, her expression still stormy. "There! You've done your due diligence and can go home now with a clear conscience!"

His eyes narrowed as he responded. "I'm coming up with you and it's pointless to argue about it." Ignoring her glare, he took her clutch to dig out her keys. Her protests fell on deaf ears as he unlocked the door before following her inside and up the stairs where he unlocked her loft door and ushered her in.

She immediately went to her couch, angrily pulling off her boots, her eyes blazing as she scolded him. "I think you've forgotten we are just friends and what you did tonight overstepped those boundaries. How dare you! Lucas was a nice guy and we were having a great night until you. . you. ."

"Cock blocked I believe is what you called it." he said helpfully. "Tsk, tsk, such language from a lady."

"I'm serious Will! Why would you bother to go to the trouble to do that when we are *just* friends?" She stood up and came to stand in front of him, jabbing her angry finger into his chest to better make her point. "I want to know now!"

He grabbed her finger before pulling her to him, closing the small gap between them. "Is that really what you want, birthday girl?"

His voice was husky, his eyes deep pools and focused on her lips. "I'm sorry if I ruined your birthday Sam. Is there anything I can do to make it up to you?"

Taken aback, she wondered if he could hear her heart beating loudly in her chest. He watched as confusion flitted across her face. "What is happening here? What are you doing?" she asked, holding her breath.

"What do you want to happen here? When you made your birthday wish, did you wish for me Sam?" he asked, his finger lightly tracing the neckline of her dress.

Surprised to hear him suggest that, she let her champagne get the better of her. "How did you know I made a wish?"

His lips curled in a slight smile. "Lucky guess, but here I am Sam. What do you want from me?"

She studied him for a minute, her voice was shaky when she told him. "I want you to take me out of this dress and. . .and to feel your skin on mine."

Pulling his shirt over his head, his eyes met hers. She gasped as he slowly unsnapped the top of her dress, rewarded to have her fully exposed to him. Pulling her up against him, she could hear the lust in his voice. "Just my skin seems like such a waste when there's so much more I could do for you."

Pulling her face to his, he kissed her, his lips soft and sweet at first before wreaking havoc and lighting her on fire, his kisses dipping lower. Pulling away he asked her "What about what my lips could do for you."

Slowly his finger traced what was left of the neckline of her dress, lingering in the dip where her cleavage begged him for more. "Do you remember my touch on you Sam?"

Playing along, she whispered "I forget. Show me."

His eyes glittered as he answered her challenge. "With pleasure."

Stepping back from him, she finished unsnapping her dress, enjoying his eyes taking every inch of her in. Letting it fall to the floor, she told him. "Let the pleasuring begin."

His lips found hers, quickly escalating into deep and passionate kisses, his tongue eagerly embracing hers. Pressing herself into him, she could feel his hardness beneath his jeans. She moaned his name as his lips once again moved down her neck, before following her necklace into her cleavage.

His voice was soft as he took her in. "You're so beautiful Sam. You can't imagine how consumed I am with you. All I can think about is being with you."

Imagining she had a pretty good idea, she moved to unbuckle his belt, pulling his jeans down to the floor. She yelped when he picked her up and carried her to the bed, relieving them both of what little still stood between them.

She embraced the feel of his lips moving down her, taking his time to rediscover every inch of her from top to bottom. She gasped as his lips moved from her inner thigh to between her legs, his intention clearly to drive her wild, the heat of it making her desperate to feel him inside her.

Grabbing his head with both her hands, she pulled him up to her, her eyes on his as he loomed over her, anticipating what was to come next. Finding the sweet rhythm she had been waiting for, she relished in feeling his skin on hers and having him inside her again. She was torn between the pleasure of making it last forever and her desperation for satisfaction right now. Either way, she realized blissfully her birthday wish had worked out even better than she could have imagined, happy to have this man's skin on hers anytime, anywhere, as often as possible.

CHAPTER NINE

She had been disappointed but not surprised Will hadn't reached out to her since their night of passion. She had no regrets, but found her thoughts turning to that night often, remembering the feel of Will's skin on hers, his lips putting her entire body in overdrive. She had awoken in the wee hours of the morning to find him gone. In the light of morning she had discovered a post-it sitting by her Keurig with a simple "Happy Birthday Sam" on it. That had been a week ago.

Having checked her appointment book last night, she knew Will would be bringing Prince in today. She had agonized over what to wear, her emotions a rollercoaster at the thought of facing him. As always, Prince was her first appointment for the day and she was grateful there would be no other clients to witness the awkwardness of seeing him again, not sure of what she would say to him. She didn't want to seem needy, but could not believe they were in this position again. It was annoying as hell, but she decided she would follow his lead, waiting to see how he handled it.

She didn't have to wait long after unlocking her door to *Paws for a Cause* before she noticed Prince and Will walking briskly towards her. Quickly she moved to her counter where she welcomed her clients and kept track of business for the day.

Keeping her voice light she greeted them with "Good morning boys!"

Will briefly arched his brow at her before returning with his more subdued greeting. "Morning Sam. I hate to impose but is there any way Prince could stay with you for the next couple of days? I have some urgent business to take care of or I wouldn't ask."

Sam's face looked concerned as she quickly responded with "Of course. You know I love having Prince around. Is everything okay?" She couldn't help but wonder if it had anything to do with Marco.

He waved her concern off with "It's work related. I appreciate it. We've had a busy week and Prince will need an extra long massage." Before turning the leash over to her, Will bent down and rubbed Prince's ears before leaning in to say something quietly into his ear.

As he stood up, he turned back to her. "Take care, Sam. You know how to reach me if you need me." With that he was gone, leaving her standing there to stare after him.

She looked down at Prince when he gave a small whine. Bending down to him, she rubbed his ears too, knowing it was his favorite. "Don't worry Prince. He'll be back soon and then we'll figure this out." She hated to admit it, but even she wasn't sure of what she wanted from Will. Actually that wasn't true. She knew she most definitely needed more of him in between her sheets and she would be really disappointed if Will didn't feel the same way.

After a long day of corralling dogs, Sam was restless to go for a run. Buckled into her fanny pack, she headed down the stairs and out into the night, the air cool on her skin. When Prince stayed with her, she loved going for night runs, feeling her safety was a given. Knowing Will should be back tomorrow, she had saved her long run for their last night together, giving Prince time to recover from his work week. Finding her playlist, she laughed when Prince headed them in the direction of Will's apartment, causing her thoughts to turn to him. She often wished Prince could answer her many questions about Will, regretful that she could count on one hand the few things she did know about him.

Hearing Prince give a low growl, she paused her music, straining to see ahead of her what he was seeing. Suddenly Prince lunged into a true run, dragging Sam behind him. Realizing there were men up ahead having a skirmish, she tried to reign the dog in, but he was desperate to get to them. Worried she was going to go down, she let go of his leash, hoping it was the right thing to do. When she saw one of the men go down, she yelled "HEY!" with all the bravado she could muster. As one of the men raised his foot to kick the fallen man, Prince jumped onto his back, his teeth taking hold as the man became frantic to fling him off.

Instinctively Sam kept yelling, telling them police were on their way, waving her phone in her hand, pepper spray in the other. She called Prince's name as the man and his friend ran off, the dog still on his back as he screamed hysterically for him to get off. Suddenly she could hear Will in her head and yelled "Prince release!"

Immediately the dog dropped down before rushing to the man that lay on the sidewalk. Sam also rushed to his side, gently turning him over, telling him he was going to be okay, the men were gone. She was shocked as Prince started to lick his hand, whining frantically. Looking from Prince to the man, she drew in a sharp breath as she realized it was Will.

"Will! Oh my god! I'm going to get help, don't worry!" she said as she moved to call 911.

She paused, leaning into him as he struggled to speak. "No police."

Shaking her head, she disagreed. "I need to report those men. They could have killed you! You need medical attention."

"NO!" he said, the effort to speak evident.

She studied him, his face bleeding and already bruising. "Fine. I'll call an Uber to get you to the hospital. You need a doctor."

Suddenly he was trying to sit up, reaching for her to help him. "Sam, no hospital. I can't do hospitals. I just need help getting inside. I have everything I need. Will you help me?" His breathing was labored, the effort to talk evident.

When Prince whined, she looked from him back to Will before realizing the two men had jumped him in front of his apartment. Was he serious about this? She had no idea how to move him, let alone get him inside. Feeling his hand on hers tighten, he added one last plea. "Please Sam."

"Okay, I'll help you, but I don't know how we will get you up your steps. Can you even walk?" she asked, trying to keep the desperation out of her voice.

She watched in amazement as he said softly, "Prince assist." Immediately the dog moved under Will's arm, leaning into him. Turning to Sam, he held his other arm out to her. Not sure how it was going to work, she got under his other arm, bracing herself as Will leaned heavily on her to pull himself up between her and Prince. He moaned profanities softly as he struggled greatly to come to a stand.

"Just tell me what to do." Her voice was trembling, her face concerned for the pain that moving caused him.

Gritting his teeth, he moved forward slowly, but they were finally inside his apartment, his body laid out on his bed. Frantically Sam searched his hall closet for the first aid kit he had promised her. She was shocked to see professional grade triage supplies when she opened it, including heavy duty pain killers, antiseptic to clean wounds and bandages in a variety of sizes.

Gently she started cleaning his face, using warm water and a washcloth to remove the blood. He laid there stoically, his eyes watching her. Once she felt the area was clean, she got q-tips to apply the antibiotic ointment to his cuts. Realizing she was still shaking, she took a deep breath.

He reached out to her, taking her hand. "I'm going to be okay Sam. Thanks to you."

Collecting herself she told him, "I need to go to the kitchen for an ice pack and water for you to take some pain medicine. I'll be right back."

When she came back she was surprised to see him trying to sit up. Quickly she moved to position his pillows for support behind him, before handing him some pain pills and his glass of water.

"Usually I take these with a shot of bourbon." he said as he handed the water back to her.

She moved off the bed again, "I can get you a shot."

She was back in no time with a short glass filled with three fingers of bourbon. He smiled weakly at her. "I was kidding, but I'll take it." Raising it to his lips, he took a healthy swig of the rich amber liquid, letting the burn of the whiskey fill him with that familiar warmth. "You drink the rest." he said, handing it back to her.

Without giving it a second thought, she slammed it back, hoping it would calm her nerves, making a face as it went down.

"There's one more thing I need you to do." he said softly.

"What?" she asked in alarm.

"I'm going to have to get this shirt off so you can check my ribs. There should be a rib brace at the bottom of the first aid kit, but first I need to know if you think they're broken or just bruised." His eyes were intent on hers as he spoke.

Holding his gaze, she said softly, "Okay. Ready when you are."

Prince let out a whine hearing Will's expletives as she gently wiggled him out of his t-shirt. He lay back into his pillows again, his effort exhausting him.

Not convinced they weren't broken, she touched him gently while observing the severity of the swelling. He tensed under her touch, only relaxing when she finished, announcing they didn't seem to be broken, just severely bruised. Wrapping an ice pack, she applied it to the side where he had taken the most abuse.

"How do you know about ribs?" he asked, his eyes closing, his pain medication kicking in.

She smiled weakly at him before answering. "Don't worry about it. We can ice them for twenty minutes and then get your rib vest on so you can get some sleep. I'll sleep on the couch, but Prince is on the floor beside you."

Thirty minutes later, she was relieved for both of them, having secured him into his rib vest before covering him with a blanket she found in the hall closet. Standing over him, her heart swelled, thankful he was going to be okay. She shuddered to think what might have happened if she and Prince had not come along when they did.

Turning away from him, she paused when he opened his eyes. "Stay with me Sam."

"I'm not going home, I'll be on the couch. I'm here for you." Her voice was soft as she said it.

He patted the bed beside him. "No Sam. I want you to stay with me. Here. Please."

Shaking her head, she reminded him she didn't want to disturb his bruised body, but she would keep checking on him.

"I want you right next to me Sam. Please. Can you do that for me?"

"Alright." she agreed, her heart in her throat. "'But I gotta warn you, no funny stuff tonight. I'm exhausted."

He smiled weakly at her. "Okay, got it. No funny stuff. Tonight." he said softly.

She laughed, happy to hear him return her banter. Realizing he was out, she bent down and gently kissed him on his forehead. "Good night Will." she said softly before she went to the other side of his bed, kicking her shoes off and laying on her side to face him. She had so many questions, but knew there would be no answers tonight. Tonight she would just lay beside him, grateful to be there.

Up with the sun, Will was filled with a gamut of emotions when he turned to see Sam sleeping beside him, her hands tucked under her chin. His body screamed out at him as he tried to turn and face her, wanting to caress her face. He was lucky she and Prince had come by when they did or Marco's goons would have done a lot more damage than he was currently enduring. Still, if they had wanted him dead it would have been handled swiftly from the street leaving little possibility of a witness that could be a loose end later. They were definitely trying to make a point and he needed to make sure Sam didn't get caught in the crossfire. He hated like hell he would be challenged to protect her in his current condition and had already reached out to Tony for backup in keeping an eye out while he healed over the next couple of days.

After the trashing at her place not that long ago, he wanted to keep Sam with him as much as possible. He knew she would need to work during the day, but nights were more concerning to him. Struggling to get up, he swore under his breath while trying not to wake her as he headed to the bathroom. To see himself in the mirror made him grimace, but reality was he'd look worse over much less.

As he opened the bathroom door, his sleeping beauty popped up.

"What are you doing out of bed?" She asked, rubbing her eyes.

"Sorry to wake you, but nature called." he said.

Jumping up, she came around to his side of the bed to rearrange his pillows behind him. "Please, wake me. I'm here to help." As her phone alarm buzzed, she went to get Will another round of pain pills.

Taking the pills from her, he shared a thought, his look focused on her lips. "I have some ideas."

Rolling her eyes, she bantered back. "I'm sure you do."

Will soon convinced her he needed to be on the couch, his bedroom quickly becoming claustrophobic in the daylight. He had a front row seat when the Uber eats girl brought four bags of food to the door from the diner. Knowing he didn't eat breakfast, she brought him black coffee and a breakfast sandwich for herself. Sitting in the chair opposite him to eat, she noticed his bruises were quickly becoming the star attraction. It hurt her to see the devastation to his handsome face or hear him grimace in pain when he needed to move.

As his latest pain pill kicked in, Sam announced she was going to run home to shower and pack a few things. He insisted on her taking Prince with her and told her to do what she needed, he would be fine.

Heading out his door, she promised over her shoulder she would be back in an hour. Letting himself drift off, he had a smile on his face thinking of her in bed beside him.

It had been a week since Will's attack and they were both basically back to their normal routines. That first weekend, Sam had stuck around to take care of him knowing work would be a good reality check come Monday morning. She had gone to the market to stock his kitchen with foods he could eat with little to no preparation. By Sunday afternoon she knew Will was going to be just fine as he tortured her by insisting on a shower. She had run the water, relieved there was a built-in bench for him to sit on. After helping him to the bathroom, she quickly fled as he started peeling his shorts off, but waited anxiously outside the closed door, ready and willing to go in to help him if he needed her. Her senses had gone into overdrive to see him freshly showered, his wet hair wild and unruly, his loose fit joggers hitting him low on his torso. As she helped him into a t-shirt, she tried to be discreet as she rewrapped him into his rib vest, taking in his clean smell, his soap and shampoo a deadly combination for her senses.

Back in bed, propped up on his pillows, he studied her, a small smile on his face. "I smell pretty good huh?" he teased. "You could probably use a shower yourself. Feel free to jump into mine. I promise not to peek. It won't be hard to lay here and picture you naked and wet under the water."

Her cheeks were warm as she waved him off. "Okay, that's my cue to go home and give you some space. You should have everything you need for the night."

"When will you be back?" he asked, his eyes intent on her.

"I'll come by tomorrow after my last client and make you dinner. Does that work?" She asked, having moved to stand beside his bed.

He nodded, but grabbed her hand as she turned to go, his look serious. "Thank you for everything Sam. I'm used to taking care of myself, but I've really appreciated you being here. We both know you don't have to be." His voice was husky, his emotions evident.

Squeezing his hand she simply said "You're welcome." before hustling herself to the door, afraid she wouldn't make it out after all.

Her week had gone fast balancing her four legged clients during the day and then caring for Will at night. She had to admit there were worse ways to spend an evening and Will didn't protest that she brought take out as often as she cooked. It was finally Friday night and she was in his kitchen making pasta, the garlic and onions cooking making his apartment smell divine. She brought breadsticks and caesar salad for sides and a bottle of Chianti to share. Seated on his couch together, they used his coffee table as their makeshift table. She had found a playlist to play from her phone, choosing one with old seventies hits, the music casual background noise.

It made her smile to see Will enjoying her pasta, reminding him there was more if he needed it. Slurping up his last noodle, he asked "Where did you learn to cook like this?"

Putting her plate down, she picked up her glass of wine to buy some time before answering. "Let's play a game. I answer one of your questions and then you answer one of mine."

He frowned, his guard suddenly up. "I don't play games. It seems like a simple enough question to answer."

Watching her take another sip of her wine, he realized it actually was a tough question for her. "When my grandmother's cancer started to get the best of her, I moved in with her. I was there to help her with anything I could and along the way she taught me how to cook. She was born in Italy and moved here when she was just a little girl. She grew up making everything from scratch. We soon discovered cooking doesn't come naturally to me, but she was patient with me and eventually I mastered some of her favorite dishes. The best lesson she taught me was that your family will eat almost whatever you put on the table as long as you always remember the most important ingredient." She paused, her face lost in a cherished memory.

"What's the most important ingredient?" Will asked gently.

Her eyes were bright as she answered simply. "Love."

His eyes locked on hers before he responded. "I'm glad you have those memories Sam. When we lose someone we love, that's what we hold onto. I didn't know your grandmother was from Italy."

Seeing his empty plate, she stood up abruptly, picking it up as she did. "Yep. I'm saving money, hoping to go there some day. Looks like you could use a little more. I'll get it for you."

Moving slowly he followed her to the kitchen bringing her empty plate. "It was a fantastic meal Sam, but I'm good." He took his plate from her, putting both plates in the sink before turning back to her. Gingerly he pulled her to him, his strong arms engulfing her as she pressed her face to his chest.

She closed her eyes, taking in his scent and the warmth of him. She wished she could stay in his arms forever, but instead she pulled away to ask her own question. "Why did you ghost me again Will? After my birthday?"

He stiffened ever so slightly before releasing her. "I didn't ghost you. Things came up. That's why I needed Prince to stay with you." His eyes were warm as he added softly, "I care about you way too much to ever ghost you Sam. My turn for a question. How do you know so much about ribs?"

She watched as he poured her more wine while his glass sat untouched. She resumed her spot on the couch, taking a sip before she responded. "From all the hits Jordan took playing football in high school. You can imagine he got hit hard a lot. You know my mom was a nurse and she always let me assist her when she would tend to his wounds, major or minor." Sam shrugged, trying to be casual.

"Jordan did love to play. He was the toughest guy I knew."

Nodding, Sam moved on. "My turn to ask a question. Why didn't you report those men to the police? What if they come back and try to finish what they started?" Her face was earnest, her concern evident.

He looked away, choosing his words carefully before he turned back to her. "If I thought they were going to come back I wouldn't have you here with me. But I know they won't come back because they weren't trying to kill me, they were warning me. If they had wanted to kill me, I would have already been dead when you and Prince came down the street."

She shivered at the thought of his last comment, not sure she felt any better after his answer. "What were they warning you about? Did you know them?" she asked, pushing harder.

Shaking his head at her, he queried back. "Nope, my turn to ask the question. Why don't you ever talk about Jordan?"

Her face was stony as she grinded out her answer. "Jordan was your best friend. Why don't you ever talk about him?"

She could see her answer startled him, but she quickly moved on. "I would really like to make sure you don't end up like Jordan. Now tell me about those men!"

He studied her hard for a minute, realizing she wasn't going to back down, but after all she had done for him, her question seemed reasonable. "I don't know them, but I know *who* they are and that they didn't like that I brought their friend in even though he's a criminal and skipped his bail." It was his turn to shrug, trying to seem nonchalant about it all.

Watching his face, she thought about what he had just said. Having checked his employment status on his application on day one, she had been under the impression he was doing safety management. Being blunt, she came right out and asked. "Do you mean skipping bail as in you're a bounty hunter?" He nodded at her, watching her reaction.

He could see she was not happy to hear this news. "Seems like a dangerous job."

"It can be. Depends on the job and who I'm trying to bring in. And who their friends are." he answered solemnly.

Needing to process this information, Sam got up to pace around, realizing it actually explained a lot. Prince, who had been sleeping on the floor near them, popped his head up to watch her. She stopped in front of him before turning back to Will.

"So is Prince for your protection? Or does he work with you?"

Keeping his gaze steady, he answered her. "Some of both, but not all my jobs are dangerous."

He watched her face as she thought about it. "Is that why you were in the bar that night I was with Marco? You were working?"

He nodded. "College students love to go there and it's easy money."

Sitting down with a thud on the couch, she picked up her wine glass distractedly, trying to wrap her head around this news. She looked up when Will gingerly moved closer to sit beside her.

"I don't usually talk about what I do for a living because a, it's no one's business and b, it freaks people out. Are you going to be okay? Are we done here?" he asked, his eyes narrowed at her.

Turning to him, she nodded before taking a deep breath. "I guess I just assumed safety management meant going into factories and making sure work conditions were up to code. It seems like a pretty big jump from that to a bounty hunter."

Finishing her wine, she moved to take her glass to the kitchen sink. As she started to run the hot water and open the dishwasher, Will joined her.

"I'll get those later. Come back to the couch." he said, turning the water off.

Drying her hands on a nearby towel, she looked into his face. "I think it's time for me to head home. It's been a long week." Her face was passive as she moved past him to find her backpack she had brought with her.

Standing at his door, she turned back to him when he came to stand in front of her, his voice serious. "I hope you understand I trust you not to share what I told you with anyone. It's crucial to my job to be able to move under the radar."

Giving him a small smile, she nodded. "I understand. Thank you for trusting me. Good night Will."

Moving to leave, he took her by the arm to stop her. "I appreciate your discretion, but what I really want to know is *do you trust me?*"

She could feel the heat of his touch on her arm, wanting nothing more than to lean into him and let him hold her again. Instead she kept her gaze steady on his as she answered truthfully. "I don't know Will. It depends on if you're hiding anything else from me."

Abruptly he released her, his response curt. "Got it. Good night Sam."

He hated like hell they were both in this position. She knew there was more to the story, that he was holding out on her, but technically was that hiding something? Why did it have to be so complicated? He just wanted to spend the rest of his life making sure she was safe and happy, but their reality was there were a lot of loose ends standing between them and a happily ever after. Was it time to come clean? Would knowing the story behind the story put her in danger or help them close this case up once and for all.

Laying in bed, he only had to close his eyes to picture her there. It hurt him that it hurt her to talk about Jordan, knowing she still desperately missed him. There had to be a way for them to do it together, to help each other over the loss. He thought about when his parents had died and how his granny had talked about them all the time. *Your momma always said this, your daddy always liked that.* Eventually he had realized it had been her way to help him keep them alive and understand they would always be a part of him in his mind and heart. It hurt to think he had no family, missing granny's sage advice and her stories about his parents.

He missed Jordan like hell too. He thought about when they were young boys, how they loved to play spies in the backyard, each of them with a walkie talkie and a homemade weapon of choice. As they thought about college, they got more serious about saving the world and how to make it a better place. College had been a given for both of them, Jordan's focus on cyber security and his on international relationships. It had been hard to leave, but after his granny had died, it was hard to stay too. He needed a new chapter and felt like the Navy would give him the opportunities his restless soul craved.

As Will prepared to start boot camp, Jordan had found his dream job working in cyber security. Everything about it warned Will it would be dangerous for Jordan, but he was craving his own adventures and dismissed Will's concerns. Agreeing to disagree, Jordan had taken him to the airport, parting ways after bear hugs, vowing to be brothers forever.

He really hadn't counted on kissing Sam the night of her seventeenth birthday, an unexpected gift with incredibly bad timing. He grimaced to think that's where they were now. His feelings for Sam ran deep, way past their physical attraction. His fear of her rejection was another reason to keep her at arms length. Still, maybe there was something else he could do to help both of them. Sighing, he knew now was as good a time as any.

CHAPTER TEN

She had purposefully left all her lights off, having only her little battery operated lamp to prevent her from sitting alone in the dark. She had come home in a funky mood, vacillating between wondering what Will was not telling her and why didn't she talk about her brother. Why didn't *they* talk about Jordan? If any two people had stories to tell about him, it was the two of them. She went to the chair by her bed and uncovered Jordan's letterman's jacket. Putting it on she walked over to the window, the familiarity of her neighborhood calming as always. Leaning her head against the window, she stuck her hands into the pockets, closing her eyes to just breathe.

Slowly she pulled back, having realized something was in the pocket of Jordan's jacket. Curious, she opened up a piece of paper, finding eleven digits on it, assuming it was a phone number. Quickly she checked Will's number but it wasn't a match. It didn't seem like it belonged to anyone she knew. Whose number could it be? Or was it not a phone number? Her phone was still in her hand when it buzzed. *I'm coming up.*

Quickly she shoved the piece of paper back where she found it and went to get the door. Why would Will come to see her, especially in his current condition? "What are you doing here? You shouldn't be out!" She chastised him, her tone a little cross as she opened the door to him and Prince.

He paused seeing her in Jordan's jacket. Closing the door behind him, he jumped in. "We need to talk."

Sam felt her heart start to pound. Was she up for more tonight? "About what?' Nervously she turned on a small lamp as she headed for her couch.

Taking a deep breath, he jumped in. "We need to talk about Jordan. We both knew him better than anyone else. We both loved him and miss him. We know all the best stories about him and we should be sharing them with each other. He deserves to be remembered."

Stunned, she knew he was right, but needed a minute to process. Deflecting, she asked "What's in the bag?"

His grin was a little sheepish as he pulled out a bottle of tequila. "I thought we could start with a toast to Jordan."

She was nodding. "I think that's a great idea." Standing up, she headed to her kitchen for limes and shot glasses. Bringing them to the couch, she patted it beside her, beckoning him to join her.

Neither of them spoke as she cut a lime and Will poured them both a hefty shot. Squeezing her lime into hers, she turned to him, tapping her glass to his. Together they said, "Cheers to Jordan." Embracing the burn, she leaned back on the couch, sticking her hands in her pockets.

Seeing him watching her she asked, "Is it weird to see me in his jacket?"

He nodded. "Yeah, a little bit. He thought he was cool shit in that jacket. Was convinced it was his ticket in with the ladies."

Sam believed him. "Yeah, I don't need the gory details of his love life, but I can imagine. I was there when he finally retired it to his closet. He was quite disappointed that the college girls didn't give a rat's ass about his high school glory days."

She was rewarded with a smile from Will. This time she poured the shots, not quite as generous. Lime, tap, cheers, throw it back. It was awkward at first, but the tequila did help loosen them both up. A couple of hours flew by while they shared some of their favorite stories about a great brother and a best friend. They both agreed he had been the smartest when it came to the books, but also the best at charming his way out of a number of situations, some of them quite embarrassing Sam discovered thanks to Will's recollections.

Laying her head on his shoulder, Sam sighed heavily. "I still miss him. Almost everyday something happens that I wish I could tell him about."

Kissing the top of her head, Will agreed. "Same. But I like to think he's up there watching out for us and that makes it less lonely." Pouring one last shot, he handed hers to her. "Team Jordan forever."

"Team Jordan forever." she repeated softly. Setting her glass down, she gave Will some side-eye. "This was good. We needed it. I *thought* you were coming over to tell me something you've been holding out on me."

She always knew just what to say to get his attention. He looked at her. "Like what? Why are you worried about that?"

Sizing him up, she switched gears, surprising them both when she asked. "Do you really believe Jordan's car blowing up was an accident Will?"

Giving himself away, he rubbed the back of his head, a tell tell sign he was choosing his words carefully. "Isn't that common knowledge?"

She stared at him, unflinching. "You're not answering the question."

"Why would you think otherwise?" he asked, his own gaze steady.

She shook her head impatiently. "Answer the fucking question Will! Do you believe Jordan's car blowing up was an accident?"

He cringed to think of the can of worms he was opening. "No. I don't."

He watched her face, her emotions there for him to see. "Neither do I." she whispered. Finally she could say it and not be dismissed or destroy her family's closure they had desperately clung to when the report came, hard as it had been to believe.

They sat together on her couch, both of them lost in their own thoughts for who knew how long. Suddenly Sam took a deep breath and pulled away from Will to look at him. "There's one more thing Will. I should have told you sooner, but I think Marco could be Spencer's brother. I'm not sure if or why, but it could be Marco targeted me for that reason."

She felt a load lift as she shared this news with him, completely unprepared for his response. Picking up her hand, he kissed it and simply said, "I know."

"What do you mean, you know?" she asked suspiciously. "You mean you already know they're brothers? How?"

He kept his answer brief, not needing her to know more than what was necessary. "When you were dating Spencer, Jordan sent me a photo of him. He knew I had a buddy who was in a position to dig deeper into his background, anything that could convince you to break up with him. From their rap sheets, they seemed to be running in the same criminal circles."

He could see her processing what he said, a variety of emotions moving across her face. "Is Tony that buddy?"

When Will nodded, she went to her window, her face a mask. "I tried to break up with Spencer once, after an. . .an incident between us. He scared me, but he promised it would never happen again. He acted desperate for me to stay with him. He was always so attentive, made me feel like a princess, and he was fun to hang with. I knew he wasn't your typical college boy, but he knew how to show me a good time."

She hung her head, her face miserable. "I should have followed my gut, but when Jordan demanded we break up, it just made me dig in deeper. I haven't heard from him since Jordan died."

He came up behind her, wrapping his arms around her waist and pulling her into him. "We've been down this rabbit hole already. Things work out the way they do."

Feeling a sob escape her, he turned her to him and held her tight, asking the last thing he needed to know. "Did Spencer ever hurt you Sam?"

Getting control of her emotions, she pulled away and shook her head. "Not really. We had a disagreement one night about going out. He was always making plans for us, meeting up with his cronies and one night I didn't feel like going out. I'd been up all night cramming for a test. When I told him I didn't want to go, he became threatening, telling me it wasn't my choice. He pulled out a dress for me to wear and. . .and. . .put me in it. It was humiliating. Then he sent me to the bathroom to fix my face. He told me to be a good little girl and everything would be fine. I never realized how much he called me that until that night."

Breaking Will's embrace, she turned back to the window, sharing how she had put it all together.

"When I declined to go with Marco to the bar, he responded in a similar way, using the same line with me. It gave me chills to realize that's why he seemed so familiar to me. Since that night I've been racking my brain trying to decide if it was a freak coincidence or if he knew it was me and was just fucking with me." Her voice trailed off, her bitterness apparent.

He answered her with what he hoped would be comforting to her. "It's a small world especially in New York City and most likely a coincidence." She nodded, letting him pacify her.

It was very late and they were both exhausted mentally and emotionally. She found it surprising to know Will already knew about Spencer, the information bittersweet that Jordan had shared his concerns with his best friend regardless of how many miles apart they were. She had been even more surprised to know he knew Marco and Spencer were most likely brothers. She felt guilty she hadn't shared this information a month ago, but in the big picture it didn't seem to matter. What really shook her was to know Will thought Jordan could have been murdered too.

Murdered was such an ugly word. What in the world could Jordan have done to cause someone to take such a drastic action? She had often wondered if there could be any way Spencer was responsible, their dislike for each other apparent the few times he had joined her family for dinner. Still, lots of families didn't like boyfriends, but that didn't get anyone blown up. It didn't make sense, but she was way too tired to figure it out tonight.

Dejected, she could feel her sadness was about to overtake her. "I'm going to go take a shower."

"Do you want us to leave?" he asked quietly.

Shaking her head no, she added over her shoulder, "Make yourself comfortable. I'll be out soon."

Knowing she needed some time to process all that had come to light, he gave her thirty minutes before he went to check on her, knocking on her bathroom door tentatively.

He called out to her. "Sam? Are you okay in there?" The shower was running, but she didn't answer him back. "Sam? If you don't answer me, I'm coming in. Are you okay?" When there was still no answer he turned the knob and entered.

She was sitting on the tile floor of her shower, the water raining down on her, her head on her arms which were across her knees. "Sam?" he said softly. When she looked up at him he could see her face was red and blotchy, her eyes full of tears.

"I'm here, baby girl. Let's get you out of there." he said, trying to keep his own face neutral. Never could he have imagined how much her pain could become his pain.

Grabbing a towel, he opened the shower door and turned the water off. Pulling her to a stand, he wrapped the towel around her, trying to be discreet as he dried her off. She stood letting him do what he needed, her eyes not able to meet his. Noticing an oversized t-shirt hanging on the back of her bathroom door, he picked it up, pulling it gently over her head before releasing her towel.

Her makeup was smeared and her hair limp and wet hanging down her back, but he was suddenly struck by the fact he was madly in love with Sam. Despite all his best efforts to avoid it, despite how dangerous it could be for the two of them, it hit him hard and fast, realizing he would go to any lengths to protect her. Grimacing with pain, he picked her up and carried her to the couch, her arms and legs wrapped around him, her head in his neck. Reluctant to break their connection, he sat down, keeping her wrapped around him.

"Let it out Sam. You don't have to be so strong around me." he said, kissing the top of her head, his hands moving gently up and down her back. Feeling her burrow even deeper into him, he wished desperately for a way to ease her pain, to know the right words he could say to help her feel better.

He wasn't sure how long they sat like that on her couch, but he was relieved when she pulled away from him. He took her face in his hands, searching her face. "Is there anything I can do Sam?"

Smiling, she shook her head. "I'm okay. It was just. . .just a lot to hear it all out in the open. It made it all seem so real."

Nodding, he agreed with her. "I get that. It is a lot, but everything's going to be alright. I'm going to make sure you're going to be alright."

Her gaze was direct as she said fiercely. "I want to find out who killed Jordan. I want them punished to the ends of earth and then to burn in hell."

He worked hard to keep his expression neutral, knowing he couldn't agree with her more. "It was a long time ago Sam. It would be hard to go back."

"But not impossible. Cold cases are solved all the time." she persisted.

Taking her hands in his, he knew he needed to put the brakes on her. "You're talking about opening a Pandora's box. A box that could put a target on your head. It's not worth the risk."

She shook her head, "It is worth the risk! I need to know if it was Spencer!"

He squeezed her hands tightly, facing her head on. "And then what? No Sam. This isn't an episode of Castle that can be wrapped up in an hour. Whoever did that plays for keeps. They know what they're doing. And you know your family would not survive another loss."

She studied him for a minute, thinking about what he said. "Did you ever open Pandora's box Will? After Jordan died?" she asked quietly.

He hesitated before answering her. "I did. And I came up empty handed." He resisted adding *so far*.

"Did you feel like a target was put on your head?" she asked.

Nodding, he simply said yes, leaving out the unsettling details.

Not able to let it go, she asked another question. "Is that why you keep your distance from me? Why we do this two steps forward, one step back?"

Again her directness caught him off guard, but he nodded. "Partly."

Her eyes narrowed ever so slightly as she asked her final question. "Do you feel like it's your job to watch over me? Do we hang out because I'm Jordan's little sister and you have some misguided bro code?"

He laughed before making a face, his bruised ribs reminding him to take it easy. "Hardly." he answered, the tip of his finger caressing her jaw line before landing on her bottom lip. "If I was in better shape I would throw you on your bed and show you all the reasons we hang out."

He could feel her relax and finally she smiled. "Given your condition, I will have to trust what you say to be true and not make you prove your point. Tonight. Can you and Prince spend the night?"

He pulled her face to his with both hands and kissed her tenderly. "We can. It's been a long day. Ready to call it?" he asked.

Climbing off of him as carefully as possible she nodded, before holding her hand out to him. They were under the covers in no time, her head on his chest, careful not to jostle him.

"Will?" she said so quietly he almost didn't hear her.

"Yeah?" he asked.

"Can you hurry up and get this target off your back? Please?" she said, turning to look up at him, her free hand cupping his face.

Kissing the top of her head, he answered with a sigh. "I'm working on it. I promise."

THE
BIRTHDAY
TO END
ALL
BIRTHDAYS

CHAPTER ELEVEN

One week before Sam's birthday.

Sam stood on the doorstep, feeling the sweat trickle down her back. Despite hustling the three or four blocks from her brownstone, she knew she was late even if only by a few minutes. Glancing up at the number over the door, she double-checked she had the right address as she waited. This was the last place she wanted to be and she was annoyed she had let her sister talk her into it like she had so many other things over the years.

Abruptly the door swung open, a well dressed older woman catching Sam off guard. "Yes?" she asked kindly, making Sam announce herself.

"I'm. . .I'm here to see Athena. I'm Sam Cooper." She said, clearing her throat, annoyed she sounded so tentative.

"I'm Athena. Can I help you?" she asked.

Sam had to physically force herself not to roll her eyes as she said the words. "I'm here to have my fortune read. I believe you're the person to help me with that?" Having found her voice, she worked to subdue the edge to her tone.

"Of course." the woman said as she graciously moved aside to let her in, waving her hand to indicate where she should head. As they took their designated seats at her table, Athena asked, "What took you so long?"

Sam was apologetic. "I'm sorry, but the pedestrian traffic is fierce today and walking here took me longer than I anticipated."

The woman gave her a discerning look before correcting her. "No, why have you taken so long to come and see me? It's been almost a year since your birthday."

Sam caught herself, quick to remember she had given the woman her basic information when she made her appointment. Of course the woman would use any nugget she had to try and reel her in.

"I've been busy." Sam answered coolly, keeping 'living in the real world' to herself.

"Aahhh. Your dog grooming business." she said matter-of-factly.

"Among other things." Sam said as she shrugged.

The woman tilted her head at her before firing off her next question. "You seem skeptical about your sister's gift. You said you're here to get your fortune read, but tarot cards are much more than that."

"I'm sure." Sam murmured dryly.

Not phased by her doubt, Athena added one more thought. "Many people use a reading as a way to self-reflect, consider where they've been as well as where they're going." When Sam could only stare at her, she moved on. "Did you bring your personal item?"

Reaching deep into the pocket of her jacket, she retrieved her necklace, gently handing it to Athena without saying a word.

Taking it from Sam, her eyes lit up as she took in the less common pink sea shell that was carved into a cameo which hung beautifully from an eighteen carat gold chain.

"Your grandmother had exquisite taste. This is absolutely lovely." the woman said softly.

Sam was surprised to feel her emotions rise to the surface and yet felt annoyed to have the woman tell her something she already knew. She had hesitated to bring her most valuable possession, a wedding gift from her grandfather to her grandmother years ago. Nodding wordlessly she waited for her to say something less obvious.

She watched as the woman closed her eyes, gently rubbing her thumb over the cameo. She had never had her fortune read before and was curious to know if this was common practice or more Athena's personal style. She spoke in a quiet voice to Sam when she opened her eyes.

"Your grandmother was very close to you. Someone you still miss a great deal." Athena said, her gaze unwavering, pleased to see Sam return it, finally having Sam's attention. "How would your grandmother feel about the life you're living?"

Quickly masking her surprise, Sam answered her question with her own question. "What do you mean?"

"Did your grandmother live life playing it safe or did she get out there and take chances? Would she want this cautionary tale you're living?" As Sam sat there unresponsive, she pushed harder.

Focused on the cameo the woman still held in her hand, she could hear Gram's voice in her head. *If you want your ship to come in Sam, you're going to have to make waves.*

Barely audible, the woman threw the final punch. "And your brother? What would he think of your walls?" Sam's soft gasp gave her away knowing that most definitely had not been on her application.

The woman handed the necklace back to Sam before taking both her hands to hold gently, her eyes kind and warm. "Your sister gifted you this session because she wants you to start living your life, not hiding behind it."

Sam gave a quick sigh of relief. Of course, her sister would have been the one to overshare while purchasing the gift card, even sacred family details like the traumatic death of their brother.

"Can you just please get on with it? You can skip the digging and cut to the chase. I suppose I have a knight in shining armor in my future? I'm destined for a large money drop any day now? Please, do tell." Failing to conceal her sarcasm, it was clear her patience was wearing thin.

Abruptly the woman pulled out her deck of Tarot cards followed with "As you wish."

Sam watched as Athena shuffled the cards, her anxiety for the situation starting to root in her stomach.

Laying three cards out, Athena flipped the first card, nodding sagely. "Just as I thought." Seeing Sam's quizzical look, she explained. "This card is the III of Swords and is your past. I see the deep heartache you've experienced. How you continue to carry your grief from your losses with you."

Sam jutted her chin defensively. "Everyone has experienced heartache of some sort. Many of us are carrying around grief for one reason or another." She waited for a lecture but Athena moved on.

Watching the woman flip the second card, she was surprised to see the woman's eyes light up ever so briefly. "This card is your present. The Lover's card represents a relationship, someone you feel passion for."

Immediately Sam pictured him, his dark hair combed back, his stubble ever present, his eyes always intent on whatever she was saying. Athena watched as her thoughts flitted across her face, noting her blush slightly, assuming she was thinking of her certain someone.

Shaking her head, she denied the card. "Sorry, but no relationship for me. I'm passionate about my four legged clients."

Raising an eyebrow at Sam, Athena shook her own head. "Awww yes, your safety net. You can deny it, but it will not serve you to do so. You're in a relationship and you should allow yourself to embrace the feelings you have for this man. Take a chance."

Sam scooted her chair back, ready to leave. "I am in a relationship, but one that's stuck in the friend zone. I don't always get to choose the way that life works out for me." She shrugged at the end, wanting to seem more nonchalant and less bitter.

"You can tell yourself what you want, but the Lover's card does not lie. Have you told him how you feel? Have you showed him how you feel?" Her all knowing look annoyed Sam, knowing that being naked under him was her version of showing him. She focused on the third and final card, desperate to be finished with the charade.

Athena's flinch was unmistakable as she turned the final card. Learning forward, Sam read The Tower at the bottom before noting the drawing of a man and a woman falling from a burning tower that seemed to have been struck by lightning. She gave a nervous laugh before she murmured, "That doesn't look like the money drop I was hoping for."

"This card symbolizes an upheaval or a disaster in your future, one that will lead you to a chaotic revelation. While it may be difficult, it will provide you with a release or an insight you seem to desperately need." The woman's gaze was unfaltering, her words heavy in the small space between them.

Abruptly Sam stood up, her heart pounding in her chest. "Okay, well thank you for the heads up. I'll keep an eye out for any nearby disasters I can't seem to avoid. Who knows, maybe my lover will save me." she said flippantly.

She knew she was being rude and wondered how other clients responded upon hearing news such as hers. Or maybe she was just special enough to be the only one to get The Tower card. As she turned to go, Athena stopped her, once again taking Sam's hands in her own, her look intense as she shared her final thoughts with her.

"My dear child, as hard as it might be, embrace your future and let it set you free. You're right, we all have a past, but that doesn't mean we have to live there. Let your pain go and live for today. Let your future set you free." The woman's words were earnest and rang true in her ears.

"I'll try to remember that. Thank you for your time." With that Sam fled, hurrying down the street and as far away as possible.

Angrily she rounded a corner, letting out a cry as she crashed into a stranger, feeling strong hands grab her by the arms to keep her from falling as she bounced off of him.

"I am so sorry!" she exclaimed to the stranger as she regained her balance. "I was. . " Her voice trailed off as she looked into the face of the stranger, The Lover card immediately coming to mind.

"Will!" she exclaimed. "What are you doing here?" she asked crossly.

"Usually people just say thank you when I've just saved them from a nasty fall. Would you like to try that again?" he asked, his eyes narrowed.

Taking note of his demeanor, Sam adjusted her attitude. "You're right. I'm sorry for crashing into you and thank you for saving me from a nasty fall. I just. . .I just." her voice trailed off as her emotions got the better of her.

Taking her elbow, he headed her down the street a short distance before opening the door to Charlie's. As they walked to sit down at the far end of the bar, he nodded to the bartender. Within seconds a cold beer and a glass of pinot grigio sat before them. He let her take a sip before pressing her for details.

"Okay Sam, spill. What's wrong? You look like you've seen a ghost." he asked her, his eyes searching her face.

Stalling, she picked up her glass of wine again, choosing her words carefully. She could see Gram nodding to her with a big smile, *Time to get messy.* Even after all they had been through together, she and Will continued to stay in the friend zone, Will's self-control annoying as hell. They saw each other regularly, but she was tired of him keeping her at arm's length. She told herself it was for both their sakes knowing he was working to figure out who had killed Jordan, even if it was starting to wear thin.

Taking a deep breath, she jumped in. "Last year for my birthday my sister got me a gift card to go see a fortune teller and today was the day I finally made myself go because she has harassed me endlessly for the past few weeks refusing to let it go until I did."

She saw his eyebrow arch the way he did when he wanted more information. Without realizing it, Sam reached into her pocket and squeezed the cameo. "She knew very personal things about me before she flipped my three cards so I found the cards somewhat unnerving."

Thinking about her words, Will asked, "Why?"

Hesitating briefly, she continued. "Because there are things she knew that I don't know how she knew and that made the cards seem more likely to come true." Sam was annoyed with herself, knowing she was being foolish to buy into the woman's cards. It was exactly what she had feared most, walking in as a logical person and coming out emotionally distraught because of a small piece of decorated cardstock.

"What kinds of things did she know?" Will prompted.

Jordan's face popped into her head, his challenging look painfully familiar, but also encouraging.

"She knew about Gram and how much I miss her."

Will nodded at her. "And? What else?" He noticed her hands were shaking slightly as she sipped from her glass looking for some liquid courage.

"She knew about Jordan." she said into her glass of wine, her voice low. "She wanted to know what he and Gram would think about how I'm living my life. Seems like people think I'm living life with one foot in and one foot out." Glancing at Will, she had a sudden revelation of her own. "You would know something about that, wouldn't you?"

Taking a sip of his own beverage, Will shook his head. "This isn't about me. This is about you. What did the cards say?"

She skimmed over the highlights of the three cards, trying to keep her voice nonchalant. Giving her side eye, he asked her, "So are you worried about the lovers card or a disaster happening in your future?"

Watching him pick at the label on his beer bottle, she had to wonder if it was her impending disaster or the relationship card that bothered him more. She sighed deeply, knowing it had all been triggering. Sensing her reluctance to share, Will nudged her. "What is it? Do you have a lover I don't know about?"

She could tell by his voice, he was teasing her, but she didn't laugh. "It's my birthday next week. I'm supposed to be taking my big trip to Italy, but now I'm wondering how crazy I was to think I could travel abroad alone. So that should answer your question. The role of lover appears to be up for grabs."

Ignoring her flip response, Will wasn't sure if he should reassure her or add his own flip response. He decided to play the middle. "Lots of women travel alone, but you're part of a big tour group right? Who knows, maybe your lover will be waiting for you in Italy."

Sam focused on her wine. "I'm sure. And maybe he will know Marco and Spencer too." she said dryly.

Putting his hand on her shoulder, Will gave her a gentle shake. "Hey. What's really going on? Are you really that worried about this card reading?"

Keeping her eyes on her glass, she struggled to find the words. "I don't know if you remember that mine and Jordan's birthdays were a few weeks apart. This year I'm turning the same age Jordan was when he died. My rational side knows this is all a dumb coincidence, but my irrational side is a little freaked out."

He was startled by her statement and kicked himself inwardly for having not realized this information on his own. Standing up, Will went to put his arm around her shoulders, pulling her to him. "I can see why you would worry about that, but you're not Jordan. You know Jordan and your Gram are up in heaven watching over you, keeping you safe and cheering you on."

It killed him to see the anguish on her face, her pain still very real even after the six years it had been since Jordan died. Before he thought better of it, he announced helpfully, "I could go with you."

Her eyes darted to his face, checking to see if he was serious. Assuming he wasn't, she replied with the first thing that popped into her head. "What? As my lover?"

His eyes were glowing, sending heat throughout her, the first thing to truly distract her. "It wouldn't be that big a stretch would it?" Seeing his gaze focus on her mouth, she ached for him to bend down and kiss her. As long as she was fantasizing, how about he just picked her up and carried her out of the bar, straight to her bed.

Shaking his head slowly with a smile, he brought her crashing back to reality. "But no, as your friend."

His words hit her hard. Right. She told Athena there were no lovers for her. Quickly she hopped off her barstool, heading for the door before he could see her face. Over her shoulder she mumbled back to him, "Don't bother. I'll figure it out." Then she was gone.

Instinctively Sam headed for Bryant Park, needing to walk her familiar loop and figure some things out to help her pull herself together. It was a beautiful summer day and she embraced the sun on her face, thankful for her shades to hide her inner turmoil.

Of course Will only wanted to go as her friend. Why was he so damn frustrating? Clearly she was wanting, even needing more of a relationship with him than he seemed up for, but she had been in the dating world long enough to know when a man wanted her. If they needed to be just friends with benefits, then so be it. Her head told her she was ready, able, and consenting, but her heart told her she was in love with Will and that would make it easier said than done. Looking back she now realized when he had kissed her by the pool on her seventeenth birthday, he had set the bar high for any other man to kiss her.

She knew her sister and Athena weren't that far off the mark, that she kept her heart guarded, but to be fair, she had never met a man that had given her a good reason not to. When Will had walked away from her that night, she had been devastated, prompting her to believe she wasn't pretty enough to stick around for let alone continue kissing. She had muddled through high school, never at a loss for dates but settling for boys that were safe that she wasn't really interested in. College had been a new beginning and like any red blooded teenager with lots of freedom, she had embraced all the escapades. She ended up in loose relationships, knowing it would never be serious, smart enough to know the boys were just out for the adventure as much as she was.

She had been in Vet School when she met Spencer and it seemed like almost immediately they had become serious. He was attentive and sweet and great in bed and she bought into the idea that maybe, just maybe this one could be a serious relationship. Her family had been lukewarm in their acceptance of him and she dismissed it to the fact that she had brought home a lot of boys over the years. The incident she had shared with Will had put a temporary damper on their relationship, but Spencer had bent over backwards to make it up to her.

A serious rift had started to fester between her and Jordan when he had started telling her vague stories that Spencer wasn't the guy she thought he was. As Spencer's actions seemed more secretive at times, she dug in deeper, resentful that Jordan was creating scenarios that jeopardized her trust in her first serious boyfriend.

The night Jordan's car had exploded in front of their house had brought their relationship to a screeching halt and in her grief, it had never even dawned on Sam that Spencer had seemed to evaporate into thin air himself. Her grief and guilt knotted tightly into the pit of her stomach had left her inconsolable for days. It had been an endless parade of family and friends that brought food and checked in on them that first year, her family going through the motions of living, snatching at the brief moments of happiness that would occasionally grace their day to keep moving them forward one day at a time. Sam had spent a lot of time with her grandmother, needing the distraction and embracing her nurturance without the sympathy. It had been a devastating blow to learn her grandmother had breast cancer only a couple of years later, their fragile existence once again shattered.

The realization of who Will actually was had been a game changer for Sam. While they kept it in the friend zone, they had begun to hang out more regularly. It had started innocently enough with nights spent together over dinner and drinks at Charlie's, the coincidence of their habits quickly turning into unspoken routines. They actually had gone to a baseball game together and he had been quite amused, albeit not surprised, to see her competitive side come out as she cheered on the Yankees to a win. Her favorite activity to do with Will though had become motorcycle rides around the city on Saturday afternoons. She always left their destination up to him, just content to sit on the back of his bike with her arms wrapped around him, her body pressed into his, hanging onto him more tightly than was necessary. She could only hope it was as good for him as it was for her.

What Sam cherished the most with Will though were their continued conversations about Jordan. Having realized he was a big part of who she was, she knew it was important to keep him alive in her thoughts and stories, which was in a way keeping a part of herself alive. She knew they would both always miss him, but new and happy memories were slowly growing around the hole he had left in their hearts, healing them both.

It annoyed her that the card reading had shaken her like this, but she had to give herself some grace and acknowledge she had valid reasons to feel the way she did. She thought about what Riley and Athena were pushing her to realize, that it was time to live life beyond her daily routines and make some memories that would last a lifetime. While her feelings for Will were strong, if he wasn't going to act on them, should she make herself move on? Before she walked away though, should she lay her cards on the table and tell him how she felt? She realized one thing was certain, she was going on this trip, ready or not for what adventures lay ahead, with or without Will. It wouldn't hurt her feelings if he joined her, if not as her lover, then as her friend, but preferably a friend with benefits.

CHAPTER TWELVE

He checked his phone for the hundredth time, wondering where in the hell she could possibly be. He had been keeping her stoop warm for almost an hour, unable to resist his urge to check in on her. He knew she had been upset when she left the bar, but to be fair, she had walked in upset and he could see why the cards had shook her. He had dismissed the lover card, unable to go there regardless of how much he wanted to. He had other things to focus on such as the likelihood of a disaster in her near future actually becoming a reality.

He had used the possibility of her being in danger to justify popping up regularly in her day to day routines, using the bar as a way to keep it casual. They had spent enough time together for him to realize she did have feelings for him, but it was hard to dismiss the possibility that something could go wrong for either one of them at any given minute if he took his eye off the ball. He debated with himself often if he should come clean with her or if that could potentially make the situation even more dangerous. Unbeknownst to her, the players involved were closing in and he worried who they would go for first.

Realizing she was finally heading his way, he stood up to greet her. "Where the hell have you been?" he asked, failing to keep his annoyance to himself.

"I've been out for a walk. And I stopped by Empire to get some dinner." She held up her bag as if to prove her point before pulling her keys out. "I'm glad you're here."

He caught himself, surprised to hear her say that. "So you went for a walk to clear your head? Did it help?" he asked hopefully.

"It did. I'm going to Italy. It's silly to think one little card can predict my future when everyone knows the future is unpredictable. Besides, it's not like I have a target on *my* back. Right?" she asked him.

He knew her question was rhetorical but it still made him uncomfortable to think about the answer to it. "Sure. I'm glad you're going. You'll love Italy."

She met his gaze square on, before brushing past him, her key posed and ready to unlock her door. "Good. I'm glad you're glad." Pushing her door open she turned back to look at him, keeping her voice light as she added one more nugget. "And if you *were* serious about going with me, feel free. As a lover or my friend, your choice either way. Good night Will." Closing the door behind her, she was relieved he had no time to respond.

She sat up in bed with a start, calling out Jordan's name. Her voice turned into a sob as she realized it had been a dream and she was alone. She had been dreaming of him, the two of them out by the pool having one of their heart to heart conversations that had helped get her through so much over the years. Suddenly there was an explosion and Jordan was gone in an instant. Shaking off her dream, she sat in bed in the dark, desperate to absorb the feel of his presence, having no doubt he really was close by. Pushing the covers off, she put on her robe, pulling it tight around her before going to stand at the window. She embraced the moonlight streaming in brightly, the peace of her neighborhood washing over her. She took a deep breath as Jordan's words rang in her ears. *I didn't lose my life for you not to go out and live yours.*

She felt the loneliness overcome her, another sob coming from deep within before the tears began to flow. She went to retrieve her phone, noting it was well past two in the morning. Not thinking it through, she quickly texted Will, knowing that more than anything she needed to be with him tonight. She kept it simple, *I need you,* hitting send before she could think too much about it.

Staring out her window she thought about the last time she had texted him that. He had come quickly, surprised but not surprised when she confronted him with what she had figured out for herself. It had been an emotional night for sure. She was suddenly consumed with how tired she was of always trying to be strong and take care of herself. She was blessed to have her family and close friends, but sometimes she needed support and love in a different way. She couldn't explain it, but more than anything she needed someone who could take care of her in all the ways. She knew he didn't realize it, but that's what Will had been doing for her this past year. And tonight she needed to not feel alone, to let someone else be strong.

Wondering if Will ever felt like that, she realized he had been taking care of himself much longer than she had. Of course, taking care of yourself was part of being an adult, but he had been just a kid when he lost his parents. Her heart caught as her phone lit up in her hand. *On my way* was all he had typed in, but it was enough.

Hearing a knock at the door, she checked the key hole before letting him in. She hadn't turned on any lights, the moonlight filling the small loft.

"You came." she said, her voice emotional.

"You said you needed me. So I'm here." He could see she was struggling to keep her composure, and it took all his will power not to just pull her into his arms. He wanted to hear from her exactly what he was doing there.

"I can't be alone tonight. I just need. . . I need you to hold me. To be strong for me." Her voice became a whisper. "Just for tonight."

In a flash he was in front of her, scooping her up into his arms and carrying her to the couch, holding her in his lap like she was a delicate bundle he loved more than anything in the world. She nuzzled into his shoulder, her face tucked under his chin, grateful for his strong arms around her. He wasn't even sure how long they sat like that, her body limp, ragged breaths coming from deep within her.

Finally, she pushed herself off of him, her voice stronger when she spoke again. "Jordan visited me tonight." Seeing his expression she quickly added, "In my dream I mean. We were having a long talk by the pool."

Will smiled before saying, "A lot of good things happened around your family's pool." His voice was light, but his eyes had grown dark and intense.

Returning his gaze, Sam shared. "Jordan told me he didn't lose his life for me not to go out and live mine."

Will briefly closed his eyes, feeling the enormity of the situation, the loss for all of them. "Jordan always did know just the right thing to say. What does that mean to you?"

Climbing out of his lap, Sam stood up and looked down on him. "It means I'm going to start living my life and do things that make me happy. Turns out my happy includes you." She said, her invitation obvious.

Standing up, he took her face into his hands, his mouth finding hers, his tongue gently exploring before becoming more urgent. Moving his hands under her bum, he lifted her up, feeling her legs wrap around him as he carried her to her bed. Gently he sat her down before pulling her t-shirt over her head. She returned the favor, her nether region already throbbing just at the sight of him. She could see his hardness and he moaned as she released him to her moving her from a slow burn to fully ignited.

Slowly, ever so slowly he moved up her, using his hands and mouth to explore every inch of her. She moaned with pleasure, realizing that wherever his hands had been, his mouth would follow. She pulled him to her tightly when he entered her, the rhythm of him leaving her speechless.

She whimpered when he suddenly stopped, moving her hair away from her face, his breath hot in her ear as he whispered, "I'm taking my time Sam. It's been awhile and I'm going to make it last as long as we can."

An hour later she lay curled up beside him, her head resting on his shoulder, the intimacy of their nakedness all she could ever want in life.

She was first to break the silence. "God that was good."

Will laughed but was quick to agree. Pulling her even closer to him, he kissed the top of her head, smiling as she threw her leg over him. It felt possessive, but he didn't mind in the least.

"Will." she said tentatively.

"Hmmm." he responded lazily.

"Thank you." She turned her head to look at him, her chin on his chest. She watched as he opened his eyes to look at her.

Caressing her cheek, he nodded. "The pleasure was all mine."

He loved to see her smile as she deferred his statement. "Well, not *all* yours, but I meant thank you for coming. For being here for me when I needed you."

Despite how it seemed like she had made a booty call, he realized it had been much deeper than that, the intimacy between them part of their healing process. Pulling her closer, he said softly, "I will always be here for you Sam. Reach for me anytime you need to and I'll come running."

CHAPTER THIRTEEN

Six days until Sam's birthday

She could smell the coffee before she even opened her eyes. Stretching out under her blanket, she paused to take in the sun streaming through her tall windows. She checked her phone for the time, surprised to find a short text from Will. *I'll be back at 7 with coffee and bagels.*

According to her phone she had just missed him. She wondered why he hadn't woken her. It had been impulsive to reach out to him, but she didn't regret it. She was grateful that he had stayed with her until she eventually fell asleep, knowing it had to be almost daybreak when he had slipped out.

She got up and went to retrieve her coffee and bagel. She smiled to find a post-it stuck to the sack. *Wherever you are, wherever I am, I'm always here for you Sam. You are not alone.* She felt a flood of warmth in her chest, the sudden rush of tremendous feelings she had for him something she had never felt before. She sat on the couch in her white t-shirt she had found on the floor, a blanket draped over her knees, coffee in one hand, her bagel in the other. She might look like crap today, her face dry and tight, her eyes still red and swollen, but she had to admit she felt lighter.

Her phone buzzed beside her, a picture of her sister Riley popping onto her screen. She grimaced as she realized she had never called her and shared about her visit with Athena yesterday. Tempted to let it go to voicemail, she paused only briefly before answering.

"Good morning Riley!" she said breezily.

"Is it a good morning Sam? You didn't go up in flames yesterday with the fortune teller? You survived and have lived to tell me all about it?" Riley's voice was light, but she could feel the dig.

"I did. Actually it was remarkable how she brought it all together. I'm sure the information you fed her made it seem more authentic, even to a naysayer like me." Sam tried to seem generous with her appreciation. She realized her sister worried about her and in her own way was trying to help.

"Excellent! I'm so happy to hear you say that and can't wait to hear every detail at lunch today. But just to clarify Sam the only information I gave her was my credit card number and your name. I'll see you at 1:00 for lunch! Can't wait!" Just like that Riley was gone.

Sam felt her heart pounding loudly in her chest. If Riley hadn't told her anything, how did Athena know so much about her. She picked up her phone and quickly googled her name. Everything out there was about her business, *Paws for a Cause*. She googled her sister's name and found even less. She shook her head, letting it go, knowing it was way past time for a shower and damage control for her face. Her first client for the day was due to arrive in less than an hour.

Freshly showered, she was ready for her day, knowing without looking at her calendar, it was fully loaded. It was a small price to pay to close her business for ten days while she was in Italy, a present to herself for her birthday. Despite her tight schedule, she was happy to have lunch with Riley so she could share all the details of her card reading and get her take on it. When she arrived right on time, bringing her lunch, she quickly locked her door before hanging up her closed sign and taking her upstairs..

Riley hung on every detail she shared, promising Sam she had not told Athena anything personal about her. Much like Sam, Riley had experienced a range of emotions as she shared the three cards that had revealed her past, present, and future. She had teased her if the Lover card was Sam's mystery man she had greeted a few weeks ago as they walked somewhere together. Thankfully he had been walking Prince and she accepted Sam's casual reply to who's that. She had been equally dismayed to hear about her Tower card, before choosing to dismiss it as two out of three cards wasn't bad.

For the past month, Sam had sat on the fence about telling Riley about Will, aka Billy. She decided today was as good a time as any. Sipping the end of her tea, she cleared her throat in anticipation, not quite meeting Riley's gaze.

"So there's more news I've been meaning to share with you." Her sister stared at her expectantly, nodding for her to go on. "There actually is a man in my life."

Before she could elaborate, Riley broke out into a broad smile. "I knew it! You've had this glow about you. For awhile now actually, but I've been very patient, per mom's request, waiting for you to share in your own time. So is it serious?"

Recovering from Riley's outburst, she shook her head. "Actually we're just friends. We've been hanging out a lot, but we're just friends."

"Yeah right! With a glow like yours, you're in love! Who is he? Tell me everything!" Riley announced excitedly.

She stared at Riley, her statement causing some alarm. "No, you're wrong. Will and I are just friends."

"Oh, I see, friends with benefits. Very modern of you Sami." Riley was clearly not going to let it go.

Clearing her throat again, she jumped in. "You actually know Will too." Seeing Riley's curiosity, she kept going. "Only you knew him as Billy. Our family knew him as Billy, Jordan's best friend."

Riley stood up, clearly flabbergasted. "What? Are you serious?"

Sam nodded, letting the bomb she had just dropped sink in. She watched the wheels turn as Riley processed. Finally deciding where to start, she had questions. "So what's he like? Is he still scrawny with his hair a wild mess? How did you meet? And why haven't you said anything before now?"

Laughing nervously Sam shared. "We met here, Prince is his dog. And actually, he's grown into his manhood quite nicely."

Giving her an incredulous look, Riley exclaimed "Oh my god! You've slept with him!"

Sam could feel herself blushing furiously and answered with a pained expression. "Not as often as I would like, but yes a couple of times. Just to clarify though, we are just friends!"

She could see Riley was truly astonished by her news, giving her a shrug as she finished her tea, popping it into the waste basket close by.

"I see. Have you two talked about Jordan? Where the hell was he when our family was struggling to stay out of the abyss?"

Sam's expression immediately softened. She nodded and launched into how he had been around, but had worried their family would have held him responsible for having not been around for Jordan, possibly changing his destiny.

Shaking her head, Riley's emotions flitted across her face. "So much guilt and wasted emotion keeping us all from healing. We all worried about you so much Sam." Her voice wasn't bitter, but the sadness was evident.

Taking her sister's hand, Sam leaned into her, eyeing her earnestly. "I know and I'm sorry I was part of the problem. Will helped me see it wasn't my fault. We've had some really good trips down memory lane remembering Jordan."

Squeezing her hand, Riley said. "I'm glad to hear you finally listened to someone. We all tried to tell you that, but you refused to believe us. Stuff happens and when it's your time, nothing can change that."

Reaching over to her big sister, Sam hugged her. "I know. I love you Riley."

Fanning her face to relieve her emotions, she asked Sam one more question. "So, are you still going to Italy?"

Nodding with a big grin, Sam answered. "Yep. I didn't believe in Taurot cards when I walked in there. Why would I believe in them now?"

Riley returned her sister's big grin. "Aww my little sister is growing up! Getting laid and finally believing in herself!"

CHAPTER FOURTEEN

Four days before Sam's birthday

Closing and locking the door, she paused her closed sign as she again noticed a car sitting across the street in the same spot it had been this morning when she opened, the driver clearly evident. She shook it off, pushing her paranoia away, choosing to let it go. Having shampooed, clipped, trimmed, and loved on her four legged friends all day, she was now ready for some adult time. She knew she should start packing, but instead she had made plans to meet her friends Rachel and Jen for prebirthday drinks. Realizing she wanted to be at Charlie's in less than an hour, she bounded up the stairs to her loft to shower and get dressed in something not covered in dog hair.

It wasn't long before she was sitting at her usual spot at the bar, enjoying a cold glass of pinot grigio while she waited for her friends to join her. She had arrived early, needing to decompress some before starting the birthday shenanigans for the evening. She could already feel her wine kicking in, making her realize she had never had lunch.

While her wine was taking the edge off her day, her mind shifted to Will, knowing he was a regular at Charlie's now as much as she was. Despite their night of passion a few nights ago, she hadn't really talked to Will again about her open invitation to join her in Italy. She could only assume he was not interested and she did her best to brush it off.

She knew Prince was on her schedule first thing tomorrow morning and she stared into her wine glass wondering what she would say to him. Annoyed with how familiar this felt, she decided it seemed best to let it go and act like they had never had the conversation. But still, she thought he was a schmuck for not reaching out to her even if it was in a text. How hard could it be?

As her phone buzzed she saw her A-team had texted to tell her they were getting out of their Uber. Finishing her glass of wine, she swung around on her stool ready to go get a table for the three of them. She found herself apologizing as her legs crashed into someone standing behind her, before realizing it was Will.

"Where's the fire? Leaving so soon?" he asked with an easy smile.

"No fire. Jen and Rachel are coming in and we're having dinner. See ya." she said as she slid off her bar stool. "The bar stool is all yours." She added airily.

"Enjoy your birthday dinner." He said as she sashayed to choose a table as far away from the bar as possible.

"Oh I plan too!" she announced over her shoulder, needing to have the last word.

The three old friends greeted and hugged each other before sitting down to a table. They chatted nonstop until their server came to take their orders, briefly interrupting their conversation about work, kids, husbands, and the latest shows they were hoping to stream soon. Annoyed to find herself seated with an unobstructed view of the bar, Sam found herself glancing over to where Will sat perched on her abandoned bar stool.

"So what do you think Sam? Should Rachel dye her hair pink or purple?" Jen asked, a big grin on her face.

Realizing the conversation had stopped, Sam turned her attention back to her friends. "What?" she asked, oblivious to their question.

Laughing they pointed Will out before asking, "So what's the latest with your cowboy over there?"

Scowling, Sam was quick to fire back. "He's not my cowboy. We're just friends. Next topic."

Exchanging glances with Jen, Rachel did as was requested. "When do you leave for Italy? Are you getting excited?"

Looking into their expectant faces, Sam couldn't fake excitement for them. Quickly Rachel scooted her chair around to block Sam's view of Will at the bar. "Hey, what's wrong? Did your trip get cancelled?"

Taking a deep breath, she jumped into her long story starting with realizing that Will was once her brother's best friend a lifetime ago to all the time they had been spending together emphasizing that they were *just friends.* Ignoring their knowing looks she moved onto her Tarot reading and her three cards to her dream about Jordan and ending with her invitation for Will to go with her to Italy.

The girls sat speechless as they processed all Sam had shared, watching her as she downed the end of her glass of wine. Flagging down their nearby server, Rachel ordered another round of drinks. Sam was relieved when their food arrived a few minutes later, a welcome distraction from all the drama she had inflicted on her besties.

"I have a few questions, Sam." Jen said as she picked up her salmon wrap. "If that's okay!" she added hastily.

Rachel was nodding beside her. "So do I but you go first."

Sam sighed, knowing their conversation about Will was way overdue. "Will's the one you slow danced with on your birthday last year right? Are you in love with him?" she asked, their expectant expressions on her.

"Riley thinks I am, but what would be the point? He just wants to be friends." she said, her eyes on her food, jabbing her fries repeatedly into her sriracha aioli.

"Hmm. Have you slept with him?" Rachel asked knowingly.

Giving up on her fries, Sam threw them down on her plate, nodding without being able to look either of them in the face.

"A few times." she mumbled.

"Well this is just my opinion, but we all remember what a hard road Billy aka Will had growing up. He doesn't seem like he would sleep with you if he didn't care about you. Have you told him how you feel?" Rachel asked gently.

Shaking her head, she nodded to the server as he offered to take her plate of food, most of it now laying hidden under her napkin. "I know he's attracted to me, that's not the problem. It's all his damn self-control that's so annoying. And we all know there's a difference between an attraction and being in love with someone." Sam said.

Her friends nodded sympathetically, choosing their words carefully. "So maybe he's waiting for you to tell him how you feel?"

Thinking they sounded like Athena, Sam shook her head before answering. "It would be pointless. I'm ready to take some risks, but that one could cost me a lot. I would rather have Will as a friend than not in my life at all." She shrugged before adding, "Beggars can't be chosers."

"Girl you are no beggar! He would be damn lucky to have you!" said Jen, her hand reaching out to hers across their small table.

They all looked up as someone walked up to them, interrupting their conversation abruptly. They had similar responses to see it was Will. "Ladies. How's the birthday celebration going?"

Without waiting for Sam to respond, Rachel jumped in. "Great! It's always our pleasure celebrating our girl Sam!"

Sam met Will's eyes, remembering the last time she had heard that word pleasure. She could feel her cheeks getting pink and could only hope no one else noticed.

She didn't need a map to read Will's expression, his smirk directed at her. "I can agree with that. No better way to spend an evening than doing something that brings you pleasure."

As her cheeks went from pink to red, Sam struggled to find a witty comeback. Luckily, her friends had her back. "To Sam! And how we love to root for her happiness!" As they raised their glasses, she found herself moving in slow motion as Will reached to tap his beer to her glass of wine, failing to give any attention to the other two women at the table.

"Touche.' Let me know when you're ready and I'll walk you home Sam." he said, his eyes dark.

"Oh that won't be necessary. She's going to Uber with us and we will make sure she gets home. But thanks! That's sooo thoughtful of you!" Jen said sagely.

"Got it. Enjoy ladies." he said before walking away.

All three of them watched as he walked back to the bar and reclaimed his barstool.

"Oh girl! What was *that?* Clearly he's got a thing for you too!" said Rachel knowingly.

Sam shook her head, finally finding her voice. "Oh I know he finds it difficult to resist *all this!*" she said, her hand moving down her body. "But what guy isn't willing to sleep with a cute girl? I'm ready for a real relationship, girls. I want what you two have!"

Once again Sam was staring into her wine glass, her look dismal. "Well that's ironic as we are always talking about how we wish we had the freedom and adventures you have." Even as Rachel said it, she knew it fell flat.

Checking her watch, Jen declared it was time to get an Uber and head home. Walking out together, they all put on a show of having a great time, laughing like only three old friends can. Rachel couldn't help but notice, Will was watching even if he was trying hard not too.

Struggling to juggle unlocking her door with her buzzing phone, Sam paused for a moment to check her latest text. *Can we talk?* She froze for a moment realizing it was from Will.

It's late. I'll see you and Prince in the morning. She kept her text short and sweet, torn between going to bed and hoping he would come by anyway. She sighed heavily as she opened the door, mentally kicking herself for being a glutton for punishment. *I'll make it quick,* his text insisting he come by. Turning on a small lamp, it was only minutes before she heard him knock on her door. Opening it to him, she moved aside as he entered, the sight of him instantly putting her on high alert.

"It's late Will. What couldn't wait until the morning?" she asked.

Turning to her, he studied her a minute before answering. "I wanted to get back to you about your invitation to go to Italy. If it still stands, I would love to join you. But no labels. It's your first time in Italy and your birthday and I want to make sure you have a memorable trip."

Turning this information over, Sam found her heart beating a little faster. No labels could be promising. "That sounds good. Thanks." She was working hard to appear nonchalant, not wanting to do something stupid.

Raising his eyebrow, Will asked. "Sounds good? I thought you would be a little more excited than that."

Taking it as an invitation, Sam decided to take him up on it. Her voice was husky as she moved closer to him. "You're right." Moving to stand in front of him she reached up on tiptoe to kiss him on the cheek before adding softly, "I need a memorable birthday. I can't wait for you to show me a good time in Italy." Heading to her door, she opened it for him. "Goodnight Will." It felt good to have the last word, his face disappointed as he walked out.

Three days before Sam's birthday

Struggling to get out of bed, Sam wanted to lay there and relish in the thought they would be going to Italy together, looking forward to the endless possibilities. It was going to be a helluva birthday and she couldn't wait. As the Tower card popped into her brain, she quickly dismissed it, not willing to give it a second thought. Finally throwing her sheets off, she pulled on her favorite jeans and a t-shirt, knowing it was going to be a long day and she had a lot to do. After pulling her largest suitcase out of the closet, she unzipped it and threw it open before she started searching for clothes to fill it with. Realizing she wouldn't be hanging out with senior citizens on her trip after all was a game changer. Staring at her closet in despair, she knew exactly who she needed to help her. Going to her phone she texted Riley, *Will is going to Italy with me! I have nothing to wear!* The response she was hoping for quickly popped up. *I got you. I'll see you at 1:00 for lunch.*

Taking her coffee to her window, she was startled to realize the same mysterious car was parked across the street from her brownstone for yet another day. The driver was clearly visible and her gut instincts told her he was watching and waiting for something, but for what she had no idea. Her photographic memory knew everything she would need to report the car to the police, including knowing it was expensive despite its compact size. It wasn't parked illegally, but it seemed suspect to park your car and sit in it for hours on end. From her loft it was easy to discreetly observe the driver noting his pulled down cap and shades. While her practical side dismissed her concerns, her gut told her that her suspicions were justified.

Knowing Will and Prince would be in soon, she secured her ponytail before adding minimal makeup. Checking herself in the mirror, she shrugged at her reflection before heading downstairs to open her business for another day. As she headed to the door to unlock it, she paused when she noticed Will and Prince already coming down the walk, a good twenty minutes early.

Astonished, she watched as they crossed the street and went to the car, her jaw dropping as the driver got out, seemingly familiar to Will. She could tell from Will's body language he was not happy to see him and as she continued to watch the show, a part of her told her she should walk away. She gasped as the driver took off his hat and swept his hair back in a nervous gesture, making her realize that he was actually a she. She ducked back to the safety of the wall as Will glanced in her direction.

As Will moved on down the street, Sam stood there trying to decide how to take this newest development. Had the driver just been waiting for two days to see Will, knowing he would show up here sooner or later? And what could be so important to go to that much trouble? Sam was a mix of curiosity and suspicion all wrapped into one. Thoughtfully she moved on to finish her morning routine before clients started arriving.

At eight o'clock Will and Prince walked in. She was so focused on his face she failed to realize he was carrying a bag from her favorite diner.

"Thought you might need some food to start your long day."

After greeting Prince with some good back scratches, the bag finally registered with her. Cocking her head to one side she smiled at Will. "That's very thoughtful of you. Thank you."

Nodding he handed her Prince's leash, his hand pausing deliberately as it brushed hers. "I'll see you two later this afternoon. Have a good day." And with that he was gone, leaving her holding her favorite breakfast sandwich and a leash.

As she stood watching him walk down the walk, Prince gave a little whine. Turning to him, she said, "If only you could tell me who *she* was?" As Prince stared up at her, she shrugged, knowing she had no time to worry about it now. "Alright, let's get this day started." Following her to the back, Prince was eager for his morning run followed by his massage that he knew would soon be coming.

Her door chimed nonstop as clients came and went, their pups just as happy to leave as they had been to come in and see her. She looked up with a smile as Riley walked in, her arms full of an assortment of bags. Hurrying over to help her, she asked, "What's all this?"

Pausing only briefly, she exclaimed, "All for you little sister! But can we go upstairs so I can lay it all out? Away from all the dog hair, no offense."

Going to lock the door and put up her closed sign, she knew she had an hour until her next client was due. Patting her leg for Prince to follow, the group headed upstairs, Sam eager to see what Riley had brought for her.

Dropping the bags on the floor at the end of Sam's bed, she reached into a large Nordstrom bag, pulling out an assortment of dresses before reaching into another sack and pulling out a straw fedora with a white ribbon tied around it. "I know you might not like all of my choices, but consider this your early birthday present from me and the fam. Whatever you don't like, I can return, no worries."

Sam was all smiles, exclaiming, "Aww thanks, but how did you do all this since I texted you this morning?"

Taking Sam by her shoulders, Riley admonished her. "I got your S.O.S. loud and clear and you know I am always here for you Sami! And I can't *wait* for you to have this trip!"

Laughing at her excitement, Sam sat down to watch as Riley started shaking out clothes waiting to hear her yays or nays. There were easy cotton dresses, wrap skirts and blouses, a colorful floral scarf, white shorts, and a new pair of sandals. Picking up the scarf, she turned to Riley to ask "How do I wear this?"

With a big grin, Riley took it from her, pulling her sunglasses off the top of her head before wrapping the scarf around her neck loosely before pulling it up over the back of her head. "The fedora is casual, but this is for blending in, but also letting people know you're here for a serious Italian adventure!"

Hands on her hips, Sam took in her big sister. "I gotta say this is a big step up from a Tarot card reading!" She laughed as Riley pulled down her shades to roll her eyes at her.

"You're welcome!" Getting back to business, she went to Sam's closet pulling out some of her own clothes to make sure she had everything she might need. Going back to the scarf, she pointed out two outfits, letting her know she could add it to her ponytail or tie it like a belt to dress up shorts and a blouse.

Suddenly Sam groaned as her phone alarm buzzed, knowing she had ten minutes before her next four legged client arrived. She looked at Riley ruefully. "That's my cue back to business so I can pay for this trip. Thank you so much for all this." she said, her hand sweeping the bed. "You're the best! Just leave it all there and I'll pack later."

Riley waved her off, announcing, "I've got an hour until I get the kids from preschool. I'll get you all packed!" Suddenly she picked up one small bag and handed it to Sam. "I almost forgot your lunch! Quick! Go eat and enjoy your last American food for a while."

"I forgot about lunch, thank you!" Giving her sis a big hug, Prince followed her as they headed downstairs, leaving Riley to work her magic.

The afternoon flew by in a flash and before she knew it, she was locking up and ready to finish packing knowing they had an early flight out of JFK in the morning. Pausing at the door, she checked her phone again for any texts from Will, sighing as she texted him once more, *All good? Text me when you get this.* Prince stood watching her at the door, voicing his own worry with a whine. She was trying hard to keep her little wiggle of worry from becoming full fledged apprehension.

"Don't worry Prince. I'm sure he'll be here any minute." she said, impulsively bending down to hug him. Shaking it off, Sam headed upstairs to see how much Riley had actually got done. She was shocked to see her suitcase locked and loaded sitting by the door. Her black carryon still sat on her bed where she found Riley had her travel size items neatly arranged in a smaller clear bag. She caught her breath as she noticed her poster laying nearby. Riley had left a note on top of it, her handwriting unmistakable. *What the hell is this? Throw this away and move on Sam. Have a great time in Italy and we will celebrate your birthday when you're back! XOXO*

Sighing heavily, she picked up the poster and studied it, regretful Riley had found it in her closet while helping to get her packed. It was her evidence board she had created after Jordan's death, inspired by all her episodes of watching Castle over the years and her need to figure out what had really happened to her big brother. She touched the photo of Jordan before looking at her meager bits of evidence. She had a photo of Spencer from their days of dating, and had added a photo of Marco and then the note she had found in the pocket of Jordan's letterman jacket. She had tried to trace the number numerous ways but had always come up empty handed. She had made a few notes under each picture, having few facts about anything. Under Jordan's photo she had written *cyber security.* He had shared with her that he wanted to create a program to protect the world, but she didn't really know if he had ever done so let alone even started. Getting up, she tucked it discreetly back into her closet, where it belonged.

Checking her phone frequently, Sam went through the motions of getting ready to be gone, giving her apartment a light cleaning, putting clothes away that hadn't made the cut, and finishing up with packing most of her toiletries. Prince followed her everywhere, making her even more nervous that he seemed to sense something wasn't right too. Finally feeling she was ready for her trip, she turned to Prince to announce if they hadn't heard from Will in the next ten minutes, she would need to take action. Sighing heavily, she went to sit on her couch, her phone in her hand to watch the ten minute timer or even better, see a text from Will. As her timer ticked down, she heard in her head on repeat, *where the hell are you?*

Sam was oblivious as she sipped her coffee, the dark liquid both cold and vile, failing to register with any part of her. For the hundredth time she got up to pace the police station, holding onto her cup like it was the lifeline she was desperate for. As darkness fell upon the city, she had Ubered to the station, convinced something had happened to Will. Something bad. On her way she had called the surrounding hospitals to see if he had been admitted anywhere, for any reason. Not able to keep her anxiety to herself any longer, she went to the front desk to inquire how much longer one more time. Noting she seemed to be coming unhinged, the clerk took pity on her and made a call, finally ushering her into the mysterious back offices to actually talk to someone who could help.

"Sorry for your wait Miss Cooper. How can we help you?" The officer was breezy, a pen and paper sitting in front of him, indicating he was prepared to take notes.

"I need to report a missing person. Will Shaw." Sam responded, trying to keep herself calm.

"I see. When did he go missing and where did you last see him?" The officer picked up his pen, ready to write down her information.

"I saw him this morning at eight o'clock when he dropped his dog off at my grooming business *Paws for a Cause.* We were expecting him to return this afternoon, but we haven't heard from him. At all. Despite my numerous texts." Sam forced herself to keep her voice steady.

The officer paused his writing in mid-air. "We?" he asked.

Nodding she stammered out, "His dog Prince and I."

Putting the pen down, the officer leaned back into his chair before asking, "I see. Is this a professional or personal relationship Miss Cooper?"

Biting her trembling bottom lip, she answered. "It's both. I groom his dog but we're also friends."

He eyed her with sympathy. "I see. Are you friends that sleep together?"

Feeling her cheeks grow pink, Sam became defensive. "This isn't about our relationship. This is about the fact that Will hasn't checked in since eight o'clock this morning and that's very unusual. Besides, he would never leave his dog Prince high and dry!" She heard her voice crack, hearing it out loud making it a hard reality.

"Do you take good care of Prince? Has he ever left Prince with you overnight before?" the officer asked gently.

Sam nodded, unable to speak.

"Maybe something came up that he's unable to contact you, but he knows Prince is in good hands and will check in when he can." he said kindly, assuming his voice of reason would help her feel better.

Shaking her head, Sam would not be put off. "I can feel something isn't right. Can you please put out an APB for him to your officers?"

He smiled then. "If you know how to use APB, I'm going to bet you know our hands are tied until he's been missing for twenty-four hours. You can come back tomorrow and we can make a list of who else might have heard from him or know where he could be."

Like a punch in the gut, she realized she had no idea who else was in Will's life and no idea where to start looking. Suddenly she pictured the girl take off her hat, letting her hair fall around her shoulders. Was this about her? Still she needed the officer to take her seriously.

"Will would never desert his dog!" she said firmly.

The officer frowned at her. "Is leaving him with you, deserting the dog?"

"Prince is his family. They mean everything to each other!" she said, staring the officer down.

Getting up, he came to her side of his desk. "Look Miss. You seem like a nice lady and I want to help you, but when people are loners, eighty percent of the time they choose to disappear and reinvent their lives somewhere else."

Her look became hard yet earnest at the same time. "And what about the other twenty percent of the time? How do we start looking for them?"

He admired her tenacity, well aware of how she was struggling to keep her emotions in check. "You can always call the hosp."

She cut him off, not the least bit apologetic. "I already did."

Starting to lose his patience with her, he added one more nugget to think about. "Are you sure you even have his real name?"

Seeing her eyes flicker ever so briefly, he was now even more curious about the missing man. Sam stood up, realizing she was not going to be able to get anywhere tonight. "Thank you for your time Officer. I'll come back tomorrow after your required twenty-four hours."

He nodded sagely. "You do that. And good luck Miss."

As she walked out of the station, she was quick to get her phone out to get an Uber, needing to get out of the area before she seriously lost her shit. She hated to admit it, but the officer had brought up some good points. Should she call hospitals and ask for Billy Shaw? It didn't seem likely he would use that name. But it was a hard pill to swallow to realize that she didn't really know much of anything about Will. He'd had a hard life growing up, had served time in the Navy and she knew somewhere along the way he had become a bounty hunter. It hadn't been that long ago that she had realized it could be dangerous work depending on the fugitive he was trying to bring in. Should she have told Officer Brooks he was a bounty hunter?

As her Uber got her back into her neighborhood, she suddenly gave the driver Will's address, wanting to see for herself that he wasn't there. She was reminded of the time she and Prince had been out for a run and had come across two men beating him up. Her heart beat faster, the thought of it elevating her anxiety to just under a panic attack. Thanking the driver, she got out of the car, noting his apartment was dark. Pulling out the key he had given her months ago, she paused only briefly, saying a small prayer before she entered.

Instinct told her to leave the lights off, using only the light of her phone to look around. She quickly realized it was in complete shambles, someone clearly having been through it and seemingly searching for something in the process. Moving through each room, she realized it was foolish to be there, but she was desperate to make sure Will's body wasn't laying on the floor anywhere.

Suddenly she froze as she heard men's voices in the hallway, stopped outside Will's door. Frantically she glanced around the small apartment searching for a place to hide before she quickly stepped into the coat closet near his front door. She held her breath as they picked the lock and entered, praying they wouldn't hear her heart trying to beat out of her chest. Stuffing her phone inside the side pocket of her leggings, she focused on their conversation, mentally preparing herself to be discovered at any second.

It didn't take long for her to realize they were not happy to see someone else had already been there. The two men argued if it was worth their time to go through the apartment again, one of them trying to convince the other the first intruder may not have found what they were looking for, the other concerned it was too risky if Shaw came back and found them.

Taking hold of the door knob, Sam knew they were coming closer to her, the closet an obvious place to check. As one of them reached for the door knob, she used both hands to hold tight with all her might, before taking a deep breath and slamming it as hard as she could into whoever was on the other side. She was rewarded with loud cursing as the man fell and landed on the ground holding his face. Quickly she darted from the closet to the front door, jerking it open and getting to the street as fast she could.

Running down the deserted street, she could hear them coming behind her and searched frantically for a place to hide. It was all residential between Will's place and hers and it was well after midnight, their neighborhood dark and peaceful. Would someone notice if she screamed? Suddenly she stopped as one of the men jumped in front of her his arms outstretched to tackle her. She jumped from side to side trying to get around him, but he was just as quick. As he moved to tackle her she kicked him as hard as she could in the groin and then again in the leg, relieved to see him go down howling.

She glanced behind her to check how close the other man was, but there was only an empty street. She was close to her brownstone, but was suddenly fearful of leading them there. She thought of Prince knowing he would defend her, but wasn't sure she could get to him in time. Finding large bushes near the wall of a driveway, she crouched down between the two, trying to catch her breath and figure out a plan.

Hearing a twig snap she whirled around to find the other man behind her. "Think you're a bad ass little bitch? We'll see how tough you are when I get a hold of you!" The menace in his voice and the sneer on his face made her cringe, but she bravely stood her ground.

Realizing this man was much larger than his partner, she knew her strikes and kicks would be challenged to have any impact. As she made a move to dart back to the street, she tripped over a root and fell back into the wall. When he came close to her, she instinctively kicked as hard as she could for the groin, crying out in pain when he caught her foot and twisted her leg, forcing her to fall back against the wall.

Releasing her foot, he quickly maneuvered her into a choke hold. Feeling his offensive hot breath on her face, she struggled to tuck her chin as she unsuccessfully attempted to break his grip. His hateful eyes gloated with the power he had over her as she desperately tried to kick at his mammoth tree-like legs, but they would not budge. Her arms were useless as the weight of him kept her pinned against the wall. She could feel herself starting to lose consciousness and closed her eyes. From a distance she heard a scream as she felt herself falling, going down in slow motion.

She was out cold as Will carried her to her apartment, having clubbed the goon from behind as Prince's death grip on his leg distracted him with pain. Seeing Sam at the mercy of that goon had taken all his will power not to club the bastard to death, but instead he focused on getting Sam to safety as quickly as possible. He waited anxiously for her to come too after he laid her on the couch and placed a pillow under her head before taking her hand in his.

"Sam." he said, shaking her gently. "Wake up Sam. Come back to me Sam. Please!" Hearing the crack in his own voice, he realized his worst fears were coming true. As he took her hand to his face and gently kissed it, he finally felt her start to stir.

Opening her eyes, she slowly pulled Will's face into focus. "Will? You're here?" she mumbled.

"I'm here. And you're safe. You're at home."

She closed her eyes again, letting it all sink in. "Where were you? Prince and I were worried." Hearing his name, Prince squeezed in between Will and the couch, licking Sam's hand.

Smiling, Will asked, "Prince was worried?"

Opening her eyes she studied Will before answering him with a grimace. "The officer thought that was funny too, but we both know Prince is very smart. He knew." Instinctively she put her hand to her throat, wondering if there would be bruising.

Will froze hearing this last comment. "You talked to a police officer?"

Hearing the edge in his voice, Sam stared at him. "I told you we were worried about you. You said you would see us in the afternoon. You weren't returning my texts. It felt like something was wrong."

Moving to help her as she struggled to sit up, he was taken aback when she shook him off before demanding, "So where the fuck were you?"

She watched as he rubbed the back of his head, his tell when he was choosing his words carefully, one of the few things she did know about him.

"Some things are going down and it wasn't safe to come to you. I couldn't text you because they were tracking my phone. I'm so sorry you got caught in the middle of this. It's the last thing I wanted." Seeing his anxious face, she relented.

"They trashed your apartment. But the goons chasing me weren't the first ones there." she said, watching him closely.

"Why were you at my apartment? And how did you come across those goons?" He asked, his eyes narrowed.

It was her turn to pause. "I was in your apartment looking for you when they broke in."

His look was sharp. "Why would you go to my apartment? At this time of night?" He asked again.

Her voice rose as she finally let her emotions get the best of her. "I told you I was worried about you! The police were no help and I had to see for myself you weren't hurt or dead lying on the floor of your apartment! If anything happened to you I don't know what I would do!" She ended with a sob, her eyes filling with tears.

Pulling her to him, he shushed her, knowing exactly how awful that felt. He hadn't been sure she wasn't dead when he had picked her up off the ground. He let her cry into his shoulder, kissing the top of her head and apologizing over and over. He was relieved when she quickly pulled herself together.

"Who were those men? What do they think you have?" her look was intent.

Moving away from her, Will faced her head on, knowing it was time to give her some real answers, even if they were only partial truths.

"A case I took on has a lot more to it than I realized. I found out too late and now I'm working to get to the bottom of it and make sure justice happens." He seemed sincere, but she wasn't sure she believed him.

"Does this have anything to do with my loft getting trashed a while back? Or you getting a target off your back?"

He hesitated, always taken aback by her directness. "Possibly." was the best he could do.

Thinking it over, Sam's eyes rested on her suitcase sitting by the door. She smiled slightly seeing a black duffle bag on the floor beside it. "I guess it's a good time to get out of the country. Or do you need to stay for your case?" she asked, her look turning anxious at the thought of it.

Shaking his head, he answered with a smile. "Nothing is going to get in the way of your birthday trip to Italy."

She smiled, turning her face up to him, happy to have the light kiss he bestowed on her. Her thoughts were a jumbled up mess, but she chose to focus on her trip, knowing it would be the best birthday yet. Picking up her phone, she went to set an alarm to make sure she made her birthday wish even if it was still a few days away. She kept her alarm in her own time zone, knowing it would be early in the morning in Italy. Seeing his curious expression as he watched her, she blushed to explain what she was doing. "I'm setting an alarm to remember to make my birthday wish."

He couldn't help but ask, "I can see that, but why is it so important to you?"

"Because!" When he raised his eyebrow, she explained. "All the wishes I've made regarding you the universe has graciously given to me."

He could not resist the look she was giving him and taking her face in both his hands, kissed her gently before taking her mouth hostage and leaving her breathless.

"You don't need to make a birthday wish for me to kiss you Sam." he said softly.

Suddenly she grabbed his watch, gasping to see the time. "Oh my gosh! We need to leave for the airport in five hours! I need to shower and maybe we should get some sleep?"

Pulling her to him, his hands on her hips, he asked playfully. "Is that for my information or an invitation to join you in the shower? I could use a quick rinse."

Laughing she pushed him away, taking her clothes off as she headed to her bathroom. "Sorry, but gotta make this last scrub a good one before I land in Italy."

Disappointed he followed her, catching her bra as she threw it behind her. "I get it, girl stuff. That's fine, I need to make a quick phone call anyway."

"I'll be quick!" she called back.

Hearing the water start, he pulled out his phone. Not realizing she was listening at the door, he kept his call brief. "Is everything in place? Good. I've got everything under control here. It will need to be done quickly before they realize what's happening. See you soon."

Sam popped into her shower, pulling her lavender soap from the alcove and lathering herself quickly. She was curious about what had been said on the other end, but more importantly wondered who *they* were and *what* exactly would need to be done quickly? Seemed like she would be finding out soon.

CHAPTER SIXTEEN

Two days before Sam's birthday

They had made it to JFK International, past security, her big black suitcase checked, the two of them sipping their Starbucks. A few days ago Will had informed her Prince would be going with them much to Sam's delight and the man who had taken her suitcase had taken Prince as well. Despite her quick cat nap after her shower, she could feel herself running on fumes and was more than ready to board their plane and take a very long power nap.

Dressed comfortably for the long flight, she had on black flowy pants with a black tank tucked in under her cropped jean jacket. She had been bemoaning the bags under her eyes and was surprised when Will paused at a kiosk to buy her a NYC hat, ripping the tag off before placing it on her head.

"You look beautiful to me, but this may help," he said casually.

She had just finished texting her family they were about to board when Will stood up, holding his hand out to her. "Ready?" Noticing his gaze kept sweeping the airport, she appreciated his vigilance that nothing else was going to happen before they were in the air, mentally agreeing that after last night it seemed more than necessary.

Throwing her bag over her shoulder, she stood up and took his hand, suddenly feeling him imperceptibly stiffen beside her. Following his gaze she didn't notice anything threatening about. Quickly he led her to their gate, smiling briefly at the girl who scanned the tickets on their phones before wishing them a good flight. Sam had already noticed they would be walking outside to the tarmac to board the plane, a first for her. She allowed Will to lead her, following him to the first set of airstairs at the front of the plane.

Once they boarded, Will leaned down to say quietly in her ear. "Keep your bag and don't stop. We're going out the back."

Confused, she kept moving but not before she noticed two men just boarding, one of which was the one she kicked in the groin just hours ago. She didn't protest when Will took the hat from her and threw it on an empty seat. With a sense of urgency they headed to the back of the plane, needing no encouragement when Will grabbed her by the hand and hustled her around the tail of the plane, before breaking into a brisk walk.

Suddenly he froze when someone yelled at them, "Hey! You two can't be out here!" Quickly he pulled out an id and flashed it at the young man, who nodded and waved them on. "My apologies Mr. Shaw. Have a good flight!"

Feeling even more confused, Sam wondered where they could possibly be going. And how did that man know Will? What kind of badge had he just flashed? They walked briskly for a few minutes before Will led her to another set of airstairs, this one clearly attached to a private jet.

For the first time she balked, pulling him to a stop. "What is happening here?"

Glancing behind him, Will faced her. "I need you to trust me. I was concerned this might happen and I arranged for a private jet so we will be safe. Do you trust me Sam?"

Searching his face, she had some serious questions, none of which he seemed to have time to answer for her right this minute. "I'll answer all your questions after we get in the air." he said, squeezing her hand and reading her mind.

Nodding she could feel his relief as they boarded the plane, the captain greeting Will before he said, "Wheels up asap Tom."

As she followed him into the jet, she was relieved to find Prince already on board, her oversized luggage sitting in a rack nearby. Stunned by the luxuriousness of it, she was speechless as Will handed her a glass of champagne, chilled and freshly poured.

"Cheers to a great time in Italy for our birthday girl." Will toasted.

Clinking her glass to his, she watched him as she took a sip. "You're just full of surprises aren't you?"

Taking a sip, they both took their seats as the captain came over the intercom asking them to buckle up as they had been cleared for take off.

His eyes rested on her, his expression warm. "Once we're in the air and get the all clear you can stretch out and take a nap. I'm sure you're exhausted."

As the plane taxied to the runway, Sam set her glass down, her expression serious. "So tell me about those men. And what badge did you flash that kid? And who's jet is this?"

Will's look was serious as he faced her questions. "Those men want something they think I have but I don't. My badge is from my days as a Federal Air Marshal. After leaving the Navy, I served with the TSA. When they're short staffed they still reach out to me for assistance. A while back I was brought in to help investigate a particular group of terrorists and those men are most likely doing the dirty work for men higher on the chain of command. Last, this jet belongs to a friend of mine who let me borrow it when I explained the situation."

"The situation? You mean those two men following us? One of which was in your apartment and followed me last night!" Sam announced, putting her own spin on the situation.

Will's expression briefly darkened upon hearing her news, but he recovered quickly to reassure her. "No. That a very special girl I know is having a birthday and making her first trip to Italy. He lives in Naples and has invited us to join him and his family for dinner one evening."

His eyes never left her face and she felt like he was hedging his bets, feeding her information, but still not telling her the whole story.

As the jet taxied to take off, Sam could feel her exhaustion taking over her mentally and physically. She decided at this point she had no other choice but to trust Will and let this adventure begin. Sipping her champagne, she focused on the ground getting smaller and smaller out her window, finding themselves cruising at a safe altitude in no time.

As soon as they received the all clear, Will unbuckled and came to her side, pulling out a pillow and blanket, showing her how to recline her seat into basically a bed. "Sweet dreams Sam. We'll be in Italy before you know it." Gently he kissed the top of her head before going back to his own seat. Much to his relief, she was out within minutes.

Pulling out his laptop he was quick to get to work, needing to track the two clowns that had followed them onto the commercial plane. Quickly he pulled up the manifest of the plane they had deboarded, searching for the names he was sure he would find. Grimly he glanced at Sam, realizing they had dodged a serious bullet. Twice. So far. He wanted this trip to Italy to be everything for Sam, but realized it would be a delicate balance of enjoying Naples and keeping her safe. The truth was shit was about to hit the fan and his days of protecting Sam were about to kick into high gear. He was going to try his damnedest to give her the trip of her dreams, having spent a few hours arranging some things he thought she would enjoy. He smiled when Prince left his side, moving to lay on the floor beside Sam. He looked up at Will as if to reassure him he was on the job too. Reaching over, he patted him fondly on his head. "What would I do without you ole boy?" he asked softly. Looking at Sam he added, "Either of you."

Exhausted, she slept soundly on the plane, but quickly shook off her grogginess when Will woke her hours later to show her Naples from the air. The sea sparkled in the sunshine, the hills dotted with homes. Arriving at their hotel, Sam delighted in its charm and traditional architecture from the outside, yet modern and simplistic luxury on the inside. Coming into their suite, she immediately went to their french doors, catching her breath as she went out onto their veranda. She took it all in, appreciating the large potted plants and plush chaise lounges provided to enhance their enjoyment of their beautiful view of the Gulf of Naples.

She turned to Will with a big smile. "This is so beautiful Will. Thank you for taking care of it." Placing her hand on his arm, she reached up to kiss him on the cheek.

"Just wait, birthday girl. There's much more to come." Pulling her to him, his hand caressed her face while his lips descended on hers. "So much more." he said gruffly before letting her go only to answer the discreet knock at their door.

Opening the door revealed a beautiful cart of breakfast foods. Eagerly she surveyed her choices of yogurt with fruit, bread with jam and butter, and frittatas made with sausage and mushrooms. Generously filling her plate, she realized she had no idea when she had eaten last. Taking their plates back to the veranda, she quickly shed her jacket in the noonday heat, realizing Naples weather felt much like what they had left in Chelsea.

Seeing her plate empty. Will encouraged her to get more. Shaking her head she announced what she really needed was a hot shower and a change of clothes. Seeing him grin at her expectantly, she was quick to say, "Still for your information, not an invitation!" Going back to the doorway, she turned back to add, "This time."

Feeling the sun on his face, Will closed his eyes momentarily. He could see how happy she was and was surprised to realize he was experiencing some happiness himself. He thought about their conversation after watching Pretty Woman and for the first time wondered if Sam was his second chance. It was time to make a professional change and move into the slow lane. As long as he and Prince had Sam to come home to, he would be happy to sell life insurance door to door if that kept them all safely together. Sighing, he regretfully told himself, first things first.

It had been a fabulous afternoon strolling along the Lungomare Caracciolo, a waterfront promenade well known in Naples to both tourists and the locals alike. Looking out over the rock wall along the bay, it was hard not to be drawn to the sight of Mount Vesuvius or Castel deli'Ovo as they stood majestically in the distance. Sam embraced the feel of being in Italy, the many restaurants and cafes welcoming with their colorful outdoor seating and intriguing menus. Italy's reputation for having the best pizza in the world, made pizza a no-brainer for lunch and Sam was happy Antonio & Antonio did not disappoint. Sitting along the promenade with Will had been relaxing and Sam reluctantly agreed to head back to their hotel.

Standing in their hotel lobby, waiting for the elevator, Sam took in the shiny floors reflecting the light from gorgeous chandeliers, appreciating the feel of luxury. Having suggested they head to their room to freshen up, Sam checked herself in the mirror, pleased that her blue sundress and hat kept her cool and stylish. Will's eyes were warm on her as they moved to their veranda to sit for a minute.

"I have a surprise for you." he said, a smile on his face. "I've arranged for you to have a cooking lesson with a friend of mine and make some authentic pasta this afternoon. The car will pick us up in thirty minutes."

Shading her eyes from the midday sun, she studied him. "I would love to do that. Tell me about your friend. Is she Italian?"

Nodding, he shared more details. "She and her husband are and live in one of the most beautiful homes in Naples."

Curiously she asked, "Is this the same friend whose jet we arrived on not so long ago?"

He smiled. "It is." Pausing he broke more news to her. "I'll join you for a bit and then I need to head out to take care of a few errands. Your cooking will take awhile so there is plenty of time. I'll be back before you know it and then we will all have dinner together. They have a beautiful view from their own veranda." Seeing her doubtful look, he kissed the top of her hand. "You will love it. Prince will stay with you too."

Shifting her gaze to Prince she thought about how he had blended into the crowds of people as they walked the promenade, walking patiently beside Will, his leash and service dog harness warning people not to approach him. In her head, she heard Will asking *do you trust me Sam?* Knowing she did, she decided to go with his plan.

"That sounds lovely. I would love to have an authentic lesson in cooking pasta." she said.

He squeezed her hand he was holding and nodded.

Soon they were in the car, headed up into the hills. Sam was in awe as they pulled into the circle drive of a beautiful villa. Taking in the light stucco, the many arches, and abundance of greenery, she followed Will to the massive wood door. Taking her sunglasses off to look at him, she could feel her anticipation that it was going to be a special afternoon. Taking his hand in hers she squeezed it and said "Thank you!" softly as the door swung open.

A lovely older couple greeted each of them with a warm embrace and "Buonasera!'

Sam watched Will in amazement as they all broke into a rapid conversation in Italian. Watching his body language, she could see he knew the couple very well and was genuinely happy to see them. Suddenly the woman turned to Sam, apologizing profusely.

"Scuzi Sam! So rude of us to ignore you Belladonna!" the woman said, taking both her hands. "Come in please!"

Taking her by the elbow, Will led her deep into the house. She was stunned by the beautiful view outside the open veranda doors, before moving into the spacious kitchen with buttery yellow walls and red accents in between. Sam marveled at how their home was a perfect blend of elegance and refined practicality.

"Sam, these are friends of mine and your hosts for the afternoon, Elisa and Mauricio." Will said, finally officially introducing them to her.

Mauricio graciously led them to a large table, a spread of cheeses, cured meats, and local produce laid out. Handing out glasses of wine, he raised his glass in a toast to their small group with a simple *salute!* They filled plates and moved out onto the veranda, enjoying the view and the late afternoon sun. It was Sam who noticed the young woman walk in first.

Following her gaze, she watched as Will got up first to greet her.

Mauricio and Elisa were immediately on their feet, greeting her warmly with hugs and *"Ciao!"* Turning to Sam, they introduced her as their granddaughter, Aria. She greeted Sam coolly, before turning back to them. She sighed heavily as her grandmother seemed to admonish her in Italian, before removing the cap on her head and her sunglasses. As her long hair fell behind her Sam was startled to realize it was the same woman who had sat in the car outside her loft for two days.

Trying to keep all her questions at bay, she focused on Will as he announced Aria would be joining her for their cooking lesson. Turning to study the young woman, she realized Aria had no idea she had seen her with Will outside her loft. Abruptly Elisa bustled inside, beckoning for the rest of them to follow, Will pulled Sam to the back of the group, turning her to face him, his look concerned.

"How are you feeling about this? Are you okay if I leave to go take care of some errands?" he asked quietly.

Nodding she assured him she was all good. "Of course. Go and do whatever is so important you need to do." Realizing her tone was a little sharp, she added softly. "Elisa and Mauricio are lovely. I'm looking forward to cooking with them."

She was shocked when he leaned in to kiss her on the cheek. "Enjoy." He cruised through the kitchen also leaning in to give Elisa a kiss on the cheek with a "Grazie Nonna. I'll be back soon." Sipping from her wine glass, she stared after Will. Her Italian was very limited, but she was certain he had just called Elisa grandmother. It cut her emotionally to realize yet again how little she actually knew about Will. Were these friends of his or were they family?

As Elisa handed her an apron, she shook her mood, determined to stay in the moment and enjoy her afternoon. She quickly learned it was Mauricio's job to keep the wine flowing and fetch the things Elisa needed.

She laughed often as the banter between them and their many stories made the time fly by. Aria was quiet, her actions reserved and Sam caught her staring at her more than once. She worked to ignore her probing eyes and not think about the many questions she wanted to ask her.

Sam was relieved to find Elisa had endless patience with her as she struggled to keep up with the process of making the dough before rolling it out into large sheets. Her noodles weren't perfect, but they quickly became more uniform as she cut the dough into fettuccine. They created a sauce from scratch, adding large ripe tomatoes, basil, garlic, and other spices to a large pot. Once the sauce sat simmering they moved onto making ravioli, Sam trying her best to squeeze in just the right amount of filling. Soon a large pot of water sat boiling, the pasta waiting to be cooked.

The kitchen smelled amazing and Sam wasn't sure if it was the wine or the people, but she was truly enjoying herself. She realized she hadn't had fun cooking like this since she and her grandmother had spent time in her kitchen. Shyly she shared a few stories about cooking with her own grandmother, informing Elisa she had her to thank for the minimal talent she brought to her kitchen today. Seeing Sam get a little emotional, she hugged her before raising her glass in a toast. "To our nonna's."

Having finished with their cooking, Elisa shooed the two young women back out to the veranda, promising they would join them as soon as the kitchen got put back together and the pasta was ready to be plated. Finding herself alone with Aria, she cringed inwardly at the sudden turn in temperature. Checking her phone, she texted Will to see if he was on his way back yet, trying not to feel anxious about how long he had been gone.

Breaking the awkward silence between them, Aria spoke first. "So. You are the dog groomer? The only other person Will trusts to care for Prince? Si?"

Covering her surprise that Aria knew who she was, Sam nodded slowly. "I am and I guess so. Prince is a special dog for sure." Hearing her say his name, Prince raised his head to look at her before turning to stretch out on his side, appreciating the terra cotta tiles warmed by the sun shining down on all of them.

Searching for which question to ask Aria first, she realized she had the disadvantage as Will had told her nothing about her. "So. How do you know Will?"

Her expression never changed as she shared. "He saved my life when I was a teenager."

Expecting anything but that, Sam could only repeat her statement. "He saved your life?"

She nodded, adding a simple, "Si."

Not knowing what to say, Sam tried to discreetly check her phone. "He'll be back any minute. Do not worry. He cares about you, but you, you are in love with him. Si?" Aria asked matter-of-factly.

Startled, she didn't know what to say. She knew she was crazy about Will, but was she in love? Taking her silence for a yes, Aria continued. "You must realize he will never allow himself to fall in love."

Not able to hide her surprise this time, Sam had to ask, "Why do you say that?"

She shrugged, seeming to think it was obvious. "He is a tortured soul, who will never forgive himself long enough to be happy let alone loved."

Feeling herself tense up, Sam decided it was time to move to a less personal conversation. And where in the hell was the tortured soul anyway!

Finding her voice, she shared her own opinion. "People can change. And everyone deserves a chance to find happiness."

Cocking her head to one side, she could see Aria was sizing her up. "People do not change. But perhaps you will be the one to help Will heal."

She was relieved to suddenly hear Will's voice, the chatter in the kitchen becoming louder. Relieved to have him finally join them, she met his gaze head on, pushing her conversation with Aria away. Greeting Prince first, he then casually pulled out a chair beside her.

"It smells fantastic in there. I assume the cooking lesson was a success?" Glancing at Aria, he turned his attention to Sam with a smile.

Nodding, Sam could be nothing but honest. "It was a fabulous afternoon. Mauricio and Elisa are the perfect hosts. I'm looking forward to trying our pastas."

Just at that moment, their hosts came out carrying large trays of pasta, sauces, and bread with olive oil. "Mangiamo! Buon appetito!"

It wasn't long before they sat around the long table, enjoying plates piled high with pasta and another bottle of wine was opened. Despite the awkwardness Aria brought to the table, Sam enjoyed her food and the company, the beautiful sunset over the Bay of Naples icing on the cake.

She was touched when Will leaned into her and said, "Your grandmother would be proud."

Nodding at him, she smiled. "Elisa reminds me of her for sure. We even toasted to all the nonnas."

Their group was settled in, the full moon shining over the sea, when Elisa stood and asked Sam to help her clear the table. Will immediately stood to help but was quickly shooed away. Sam gathered plates with Elisa, following her into the kitchen, prepared for dish duty. Seeing her pull up her sleeves, Elisa shook her head.

Taking both her hands in hers, Elisa's look was serious. Sam watched as she searched for the words in English, clearly wanting to convey something important to her.

"I do not want you to worry about what Aria said to you. She is young and struggles to find her place. But in the ten years we have known Will, he has never brought someone to meet us, even for cooking together. You are special to him even if he neglects to tell you so." She paused, looking down at their hands, her gaze teary when she looked back up. "Please do not give up on him Sam. Make him let you in. He is a good man and deserves to be happy. You are the one to show him the way."

Sam nodded, touched by her words and equally emotional. "I will try my best." she said, squeezing her hands.

Suddenly they both jumped as Will came to join them. "Is everything okay in here?" he asked tentatively.

Speaking Italian, they shared a brief exchange before hugging, the evening clearly coming to a close. Before she knew it, they were in the car headed back to their hotel. Sam was full of pasta and wine and could not wait to close her eyes and succumb to her exhaustion. Her hand lay on the seat between them, when Will picked it up and squeezed it.

"How was your first day in Italy?" he asked, his voice warm.

Resting her head, she turned to smile at Will. "It was a perfect day. Just so you know, I have so many questions for you, but I'm too tired to focus on them right now."

Returning her smile, he nodded. "I know. Save them for tomorrow." He picked up her hand and kissed it before adding, "I'm glad you had a good day. Tomorrow will be full of even more adventures."

She smiled sleepily, her full day catching up to her. "I can't wait."

It was a struggle but Will got Sam up to their room and into bed just before she crashed for real. He kissed her gently on her forehead before going to their balcony. He was curious what she and Elisa had talked about in the kitchen, but he could imagine. He knew Aria would be aloof, particularly with Sam, but she usually was regardless of who she was around. He was pleased Sam had had such a perfect day and couldn't wait for her to find what surprises he had in store for her birthday. He could only imagine she would be delighted, a memorable birthday ahead of her for sure. But first, tomorrow, knowing the day was full of more promising adventures to come.

CHAPTER SEVENTEEN

Day before Sam's birthday

Sam was curious what Will had in store for them today. Her head lay on his shoulder, her leg draped over his as she struggled to be motivated to get out their luxurious bed. Turning to look at him she decided it was time.

"So what should I dress for today? What plans do you have for us?" she asked, her eyes on his.

"We are taking a day trip to the Isle of Capri by boat. We'll be gone most of the day. After that, we can have dinner on our veranda and watch the sun set." He said, his finger slowly running up and down her arm.

She kissed his chest before pushing away, moving to sit up. "That sounds amazing! Will we be able to swim in the sea?" she asked excitedly.

Smiling at her enthusiasm, he teased her, "How does a city girl like you know how to swim in the sea?"

Flipping her hair, she tried to look superior. "I'll have you know I was on the swim team every summer. And my family always spent a week at the beach during the summer. So don't worry about me, I can hold my own in the water."

Laughing he said, "I should have known."

Frowning at him, she asked, "What do you mean by that?"

Leaning over to kiss her on the cheek before he threw off the covers, he responded with, "I mean you never cease to amaze me."

Within the hour they were dressed and standing on a gorgeous private boat, their skipper having given a short tour, pointing out a lavish spread of cheeses, meats, and fresh bread along with a variety of drinks. There was a stack of plush white towels available, promising of things to come. Sam was dressed in a modest black two piece suit with a white lacy floral cover up dress, her hat firmly on her head. Will was dressed the most casual she had ever seen him, with black swim trunks and a white shirt he had left open. Trying hard not to stare at his tanned torso, she smiled to herself to think he was all hers for yet another day.

The boat was sleek and beautiful on the outside, the Italian flag blowing in the wind off the back, the deep blue water churning below. On the deck of the boat there was a long deep leather seat positioned along the front and a comfy daybed at the back, the boat easily accommodating a group or an intimate couple. Leaving Mergelina, Sam had wanted to take it all in, positioning herself at the front of the boat, holding onto her hat just in case. Now she and Will each had a glass of prosecco while they laid sprawled out on the daybed at the back of the boat.

Seeing Sam eye him, he raised his eyebrow. "Everything good?"

She was thankful for her shades to cover her expression as she raised her glass to him. "Yep! Cheers to a beautiful day with you Will."

Raising his glass to hers, he paused briefly before prodding her. "Go ahead. What do you want to know?"

She tilted her head at him, thinking about where she wanted to start. "Meeting and cooking with Elisa and Mauricio yesterday was a fabulous experience, but tell me about Aria. She told me you saved her life when she was a teenager. Which couldn't have been that long ago."

Looking away for a minute, Will wondered how much Aria had shared and how deep this conversation might go. Taking another sip, he tried stalling, not sure what to say. "She told you that huh?"

Nodding, Sam said "Among other things. Now spill."

"The Buono's are very wealthy and ten years ago they hired me to find Aria after she was kidnapped for a hefty ransom. I had just left the Navy and was floating around Naples trying to figure out what I wanted to do next." He shrugged as if the rest were common knowledge. "Fortunately for all of us, I was able to locate and save Aria, returning her to them mostly in one piece. They were very grateful and not only paid me a handsome reward, but also took me into their family. Anytime I'm in Italy, I try to stop by."

She raised a brow. "Are you in Italy often?"

"Sometimes work takes me there. Thanks to the Buono's, I've made many professional acquaintances over the years, some who have become good friends. What else did Aria say?" He was afraid to ask, but decided it was better to rip off the bandaid and get it all out there.

"She said you're a tortured soul and will never allow yourself to be happy." Sam paused, swallowing hard. "Or loved."

She heard his sharp inhale, knowing this was hard to hear about yourself, regardless if it was true or not. Looking out over the water, he asked quietly. "What did you say? Did you agree with her?"

Realizing this could be a pivotal point in their relationship, Sam got up and went to him, putting her arms around his neck as she settled into his lap. Pulling her shades up, she ignored his stiffness, cupping his face with her free hand, forcing him to look at her.

"Of course not. I told her people can change and everyone deserves a chance to be happy." Her voice was soft as she added, "And loved."

She could visibly feel him relax but was startled when he buried his head in her shoulder. Pulling back from her, she could see the pain in his eyes. "Sam, I'm not the man you think I am and definitely not the man you need. You deserve to have only the best."

She put her finger on his lips, shushing him. "Tortured soul or not, you don't get to decide what I want. I'm a grown woman and I make my own choices. And I choose you. You are a good man Will Shaw. You stand up for what you believe is right even if that means taking questionable actions to make the world a better place. I believe in you and you should too."

He could see she was becoming emotional, wanting him to see what she saw. He pulled her close, her head resting on his shoulder, his hand on her waist. He sighed deeply wanting nothing more than to give into his own feelings for her. Taking the easy way out, he kissed the top of her head before saying "I don't know what I did to deserve you, but I am grateful for every minute we get to spend together."

They both turned as the skipper coughed, discreetly interrupting them. "Sorry to interrupt folks but I thought you might like to swim before we explore the grotto and get into Capri. That way you'll have time to dry off. If you wish to do so."

Climbing off Will's lap, Sam nodded at him. "That sounds perfect, thank you."

"Of course. Let me know if you need anything else." he said.

Turning back to Will, she threw her hat at him before pulling her dress over her head. She laughed when Will's arm snaked around her waist and pulled her back to him. Straddling him, she could feel he was hard for her and relished in kissing him deeply. Suddenly she was headed to the back of the boat, ready to jump in the warm deep blue sea. "Last one in is a rotten egg!" she teased.

He stood up, making a show of taking off his shirt before tossing it back onto the daybed beside her dress and hat. Despite herself, she stood and enjoyed the show, feeling her skin become heated. Suddenly he was beside her picking her up, shrieking as her arms instinctively went around his neck. "Unless we go in together." he said just before jumping into the sea, still holding her as they hit the water together.

The water was glorious, washing away their serious conversation as they lounged on the pool noodles the skipper had tossed out to them. The taste of salt water on their lips didn't phase them as they floated face to face, their lips connecting every so often, Sam unable to stop smiling.

Finally having their fill, Will waved Sam up the ladder first, enjoying his view as she moved in front of him.

She watched as he brought her a towel, not handing it to her but wrapping it around her before drying her off, lingering longer on some of his favorite parts of her before pulling her close and kissing her. "You drive me wild Sam. I've never been so crazy about someone. Ever."

She let it sink in, enjoying Will's openness with her, something she had waited months for. "The feeling is mutual." She said, pulling him down for another kiss before pushing him away with a smile. "I do want to get out of this wet suit."

Smiling broadly, he looked around before saying, "I'm here for it. Please feel free. That is if you're brave enough to do it right here." he challenged her.

Thanks to her brother's endless teasing growing up, she had never been good at walking away from a challenge. Pushing him onto the daybed, she deliberately leaned her chest into his face as she reached around him to pick up her bag. Making a show of digging around in her bag, she finally pulled out a floral slip dress. Turning to make sure the skipper was occupied with the boat, she slipped the dress over her head before unhooking her swim top. Throwing it at him, she tried not to laugh when it hit him in the face, her show clearly making him come undone. Holding the dress at her waist, she turned her back to him before shimming out of her bottoms, slowly letting her dress fall to her knees. With her back still to him, she asked sweetly, "Could you tie the bow at the back for me please?"

She squealed as he grabbed her by the waist with one hand before slipping his other hand under her dress, squeezing her ass. "You're lucky I'm a gentleman but you will pay for that later." he said in her ear.

Laughing she reached into her bag and pulled out a lacy thong, holding it by one finger. "Fine. I'll go put this on in the bathroom." Hearing him growl at her, she leaned in to kiss him before adding, "And don't make threats you won't keep."

"Make no mistake, that was a promise." He called out as she headed down below to the bathroom, to pull herself together. Looking in the mirror, she couldn't help but notice she was glowing, making her wonder if it was the sun or the prosecco or knowing it was her best birthday yet. Or maybe, like Aria said, she was in love afterall.

After exploring the Grotto, their skipper had pulled into a marina on Capri, setting an alarm on his watch when Will said they would be back within three hours. They had rented colorful scooters to explore the small town and enjoy the sights. As their scooters climbed the hills, her dress flowing behind her, Will checked behind him every so often to make sure she was still there. They now sat dining al fresco, their view stunning as the sea sparkled below them, the Faraglioni Rocks close by as they rose from the sea, seeming to greet them personally. After a leisurely lunch of fresh seafood and limoncello, they were ready to head back to the marina.

They were almost back down to the water when suddenly another scooter cut Sam off from Will, his unexpected appearance causing her to swerve to avoid a collision. Cussing like a sailor, she found herself headed down a side street. Dodging pedestrians, she noticed him make a quick u-turn and seemed to be headed back to her. Swiftly she turned down another street, trying to keep her wits about her and make it back to the main street. She knew Will would soon realize she was not behind him, but had no way to know the best way to find her way back to him. Realizing how vulnerable she was, she buckled down and focused on the road ahead, demanding the scooter move as fast as it possibly could even as she dodged people and large tour buses.

Finally finding her way back to the main road, she realized she had just passed Will who was headed in the opposite direction. She nodded as he pointed for her to keep going, realizing she could see the water and knowing the marina was close by. Arriving back where they had rented the scooters, she quickly handed the key back to the person in charge, saying "Grazi!" Suddenly Will was beside her, his hand on her elbow, hustling her to their boat. She smiled in relief to see their skipper there, clearly ready for departure. He nodded at Will as he spoke in Italian, prepared to head out.

Taking her hand, Will led Sam down into the boat, before turning to her. "Are you okay? What happened?"

Rolling her eyes, Sam was casual about her mishap. "The guy startled me and made me swerve when he came off a side street. But I found my way back to the main street and you can see I'm fine."

Sizing her up to see for himself, he suddenly pulled her in close. "You scared me." Pulling back, he looked into her face worriedly. "Did you recognize the man on the scooter?"

"What? No. Why would I recognize him? I'm sure it was just a fluke of being in the wrong place at the right time." She studied him, suddenly flashing back to the goons that had been chasing them in New York. Were they still in danger?

"Are you worried about our safety here in Italy? Be honest with me Will!" she asked, searching his face.

Releasing her, he shook his head. "Of course not. I'm just making sure it was a random incident and you're okay."

She watched him closely for signs of stretched truths. "If there's something you need to tell me Will, now seems like a good time to do it."

He laughed, sounding nervous to Sam, but shook his head before he said, "I'm just being cautious so you can put your fishing pole away, Castle."

Still not sure, she decided to let it go. Collecting her bag, she pulled out her sunscreen. "Fine. I'm going to use the facilities and reapply my sunscreen and then I'll be up." Nodding, he watched her close the bathroom door behind her.

She splashed cold water on her face, finally giving into her feelings. It had been scary and she had felt like he was coming for her, but her voice of reason asked what could possibly be the point of that? She could tell Will was holding out on her and that didn't make her feel any better. It had been a really great day so far and she shook off her worries, determined not to let her day get ruined.

Finding Will sprawled out on the daybed, she smiled when he patted the spot beside him. Joining him, she turned to face him, quick to notice his serious look. Holding out his hand, he asked for her phone. Without saying anything, she handed it to him, watching as he put a new number into her contacts.

Satisfied he handed it back to her. "I put Elisa's number in your phone. Just in case anything crazy were to happen, you have someone you know and can reach out to now. Okay?"

Turning to put her phone back in her bag, she tried to collect herself.

"I want to know why you're worried Will. I can protect myself better if I know what I'm up against." she said, her gaze unwavering, giving him no way out.

She resisted when he tried to pull her close, showing him she wouldn't be pacified. There was too much at stake.

Squeezing her hand tightly, she could hear the emotion in his voice. "If you think I'm tortured now, you have no idea what would happen if something happened to you. I can't let anything happen to you. I won't. Of all the people I've had to save or protect over the years, nothing has prepared me for my feelings for you. I don't just want to keep you safe though Sam, I want to give you the world. Everything and anything that brings you joy and happiness, I want to give to you."

Relenting, she put her hand to his face, her eyes full of tears. "I know Will. I feel the same way. When I'm around you, I finally feel whole. You're my someone. I love you Will. So much." she was crawling into his lap, pressing herself to him, suddenly desperate for him to hold her. She didn't know she was going to say those three big words, they had just come out.

Will squeezed her tight, burying his head in her hair. Here they were in one of the most beautiful places in the world and the woman he loved, actually loved him back. He should feel elated, but he couldn't shake his worry. He took her face in his hands to make his own declaration.

"I love you too Sam. I have for years." He kissed her gently, before hugging her to him again.

Suddenly the skipper cut the motor as they started to approach the port in Naples. Together they watched, taking in their beautiful surroundings from the water as he eased them into their designated slip at the dock.

Checking his watch, Will tipped the skipper before escorting Sam off the boat. "It was a lovely day, grazi!" she said to him as they left.

Sitting in the taxi, headed back to their hotel, Sam wondered if there was any way she had time to get a nap in. Unlocking the door to their suite, she headed for their bed after throwing her bag on the settee.

Eyeing her wickedly, Will let her get her shoes off before taking her by the hand to pull her to him. "Not so fast. I believe you owe me and I'm here to collect."

She laughed, not too tired to face the music. "That's fair. What did you have in mind?"

Pulling her dress over her head, he announced they would start in the shower and then make their way back to the bed. Putting her arms around his neck, she got up on tiptoe to whisper in his ear. "Your wish is my command."

Watching her sashay to the bathroom, he was all smiles as he followed her, one very happy man.

CHAPTER EIGHTEEN

She woke with a start, feeling the room was empty, but called out his name anyway. When Prince appeared before her, she was grateful for his presence, his eyes and ears alert on her. Will had left her in bed to nap, well earned after she had made sure he was more than satisfied she had worked off her debt from teasing him on the boat earlier. He had left to get pizza and wine, promising to be back within two hours so they could sit on their balcony and enjoy it as the sun set over the sea. Reaching for her phone to check the time, she inhaled sharply upon seeing he was well past his two hour window. Finding no messages from him either, her heart pounded faster as she quickly fired off a simple text: *where are you?* Getting out of bed, she pulled a white linen dress over herself before going out on their veranda, Prince following closely behind her.

Oblivious to the beautiful evening unfolding before her, she searched the street below their hotel for his familiar frame. Checking her phone again, she cursed like a sailor upon finding nothing there, her stomach starting to hurt. She couldn't help but think of the night not that long ago that he had failed to return to pick up Prince and she had eventually gone to the police. She cringed at the thought of going to the polizia here in Italy. Clenching the balcony, she wondered what was a reasonable amount of time before allowing herself to completely freak out.

Shaking her head, she started the breathing technique her therapist had taught her, needing to calm herself before she jumped to a worse case scenario. Inhaling slowly for four counts, she then held her breath four counts before exhaling slowly for four more counts. She stood taking in the scenery below her as she repeated her deliberate breathing until she felt her panic subside. Bending down to Prince, she gave him a quick squeeze before asking him, *what would Will do?* Smiling triumphantly, she picked up her phone, ignoring the lack of a message from Will and instead scrolled through her contacts until she came to Elisa's number.

Going to sit in one of the chaises on the veranda, she started to mentally make her plan of action. First she texted Will again, her tone more urgent. *I need to hear from you NOW! Let me know you're okay!* Knowing he was almost three hours overdue, she gave herself ten minutes as a reasonable amount of time she would force herself to wait before she took action. Last, if Will failed to show up before the window she had given him expired, she would phone Elisa and ask her to go to the polizia with her. Reaching for Prince, she absently stroked his head, hating to need a worst case plan of action, and yet it was comforting to know what would come next.

As darkness settled over the city, she held her phone in her hand focused on the minutes ticking by. Her brain tried to reassure her, reminding her to focus on the things she could control. Her heart however was sick with worry and somehow she knew it was fate Will had put Elisa's number in her phone just hours ago. The thought he knew she would need to use it sooner or later only confirmed her suspicions he was holding out on her. As her ten minutes expired, she checked again for a message she knew wasn't there before making the call. She was grateful and relieved to hear Elisa's voice on the other end.

"Pronto!" she answered.

"Ciao Elisa, it's Sam, Will's friend." she said, trying to clear the emotion from her voice.

"Awww Sam. Tutto bene?" she asked warmly.

Her heart was pounding again as she answered, "I'm not sure. Is Will there by any chance?"

"No mi dispiace. Why is he not with you Bella?"

Hearing the concern in her voice, Sam laid it out for her praying her broken Italian would translate to understanding. "Will went out for pizza e vino quattro ore fa. I'm worried something has happened." Hearing the break in her own voice, she rushed out, "He told me to call you if I ever needed help. Elisa per favore can you help me?"

Elisa quickly reassured Sam she had done the right thing in calling her, informing her she would have Mauricio contact friends to help look for him and also send Aria over to keep her company. Not knowing how to say it in Italian, she wasn't able to assure her that wasn't necessary. Instead she thanked her with many grazies before signing off with ciao. She headed back to the veranda to wait, her heart hoping and praying that Will would arrive before Aria did.

Within thirty minutes there was a discreet knock at her door. She went to it, checking the eye hole before opening it, not surprised to see Aria standing there. Opening the door, the two women eyed each other, before Sam stepped aside, motioning for her to come in.

"Thank you for coming. I know it's getting late." she said, just now realizing how dark the suite was.

Aria scoffed at her. "You think this is late? I thought you Americans like to party until the wee hours."

Biting her tongue, she kept her answer simple. "Some do, you're right. And some of us have to work early and choose sleep over a good time."

Sizing her up, Aria had a smirk on her face as she amended Sam's statement for her. "Unless Will is the good time keeping you up. Si? His tongue can be very persuasive in more ways than one."

Feeling her cheeks grow warm and realizing she was fishing, Sam searched for the words to shut her down without offending her.

"I'm not sure who you've been talking to, but yes, Will can be very persuasive in lots of ways. Can I get you a sparkling water?" she asked before moving away to get her own.

Having noticed her face cloud over, Sam could only hope she got her point. *We aren't having that conversation.*

Sullenly Aria responded with a curt, "No thank you."

Pausing to open her water bottle, Sam was quick to let Aria know she did not have to stay. Shrugging, she responded in her halting English. "I do what is asked of me. If Nonna wants me to be here, this is where I'll be. Besides, this isn't the first time Will has gotten himself into some problema."

Annoyed to give her statement a second thought, she couldn't help but ask for clarification. "What do you mean?"

Turning away from Sam, she went to stand by the french doors to the veranda. "Naples is a busy city full of beautiful women and power-ful men. In Will's line of work, he often finds himself in –how do you say? Precarious? Precarious situations. Do not worry though. He is very resourceful and always turns up. Sooner or later."

Trying to not put much stock in her words, she moved to join Aria at the doors before pushing past her to go out onto the veranda and into the night air, the city full of twinkling lights up and down the hills. "I can only imagine." She turned back to face Aria head on before con-tinuing. "There have been a few scrapes in New York too. But that's not why you were in New York is it?" Sam cocked her head to one side, try-ing to hide her own smirk. She could see she had startled Aria to know such information.

"Will told you I was in New York?" she asked.

"Does it matter how I know?" Sam volleyed back.

Aria came to stand beside her, studying her. "You saw us. Will doesn't share about his personal life. Or always answer his phone and I do not like to be ignored. There was no other way to get his attention, but he was not that hard to find."

Changing the topic, Sam moved on. "I bet you're a resourceful girl. Si? If you were to look for Will now, where would you check first?" she asked, her gaze steady on Aria, enjoying an opportunity to call her on her bluff.

Her voice was more brittle as she answered the challenge. "Like I said, many beautiful women and powerful men. He could be anywhere and will be found when he's ready to be found."

They both jumped as Sam's phone pinged, indicating a text message. She checked it quickly, relieved to see it was from Will. *Sorry something came up. I'll be back in ten.*

Within minutes they heard the beep as he swiped his card, Aria beating Sam to the door. She rushed to him, hugging him dramatically and speaking rapid Italian in his face.

Looking from Aria to Sam, his voice was reserved as he spoke in English. "Aria what are you doing here?"

She checked her nails, before swinging her gaze from Will to Sam. "Nonna asked me to come and babysit your girlfriend. It's so cute how she worries about you."

Feeling her hackles rise, Sam bit her tongue yet again, meeting Will's gaze over Aria's head. "You did the right thing by calling Elisa." Speaking in Italian he turned back to Aria, clearly letting her know she was free to go.

As Aria opened the door, clearly not happy to be dismissed, Sam stepped forward. "Tell Elisa grazie per favore."

Pausing to roll her eyes at her, Aria answered, "Tell her yourself." before giving Will one last glance and an abrupt "Ciao."

As soon as the door closed behind her, Will went to Sam. "I'm sorry I worried you. I got mugged coming out of a store and things took a turn for the worse."

She put her hand to his head gently, not surprised to see his slight wince when she touched the cut on his head.

"You need to get that taken care of." she said.

Taking her hand, he kissed her palm, his eyes daring her to look away from him. "My head is nothing. What I need is a quick shower and it will be fine. Then you and I will have a conversation over pizza and wine with that beautiful view so I can make everything fine with us too. I know you're mad Sam. I can see it in your face."

Shaking her head, she tried to deny it. "I'm not mad. I was worried."

Not letting her off the hook, Will amended her statement. "You were worried, but now that you see I'm in one piece, you're mad. I can only imagine the conversation between you and Aria."

Stepping back from him, she asked, "You do know she has a crush on you? Which makes me *not* her favorite person."

Smiling, he shook his head. "She doesn't have a crush on me. She just likes to stir the pot and see what rises to the surface."

Recalling her comment about his tongue, Sam insisted. "No, the girl has a crush on you."

"No, she doesn't. She can't because she's my cousin." Seeing the shock on Sam's face, he hastily explained. "Her mother was my mother's younger sister. She's young and impulsive and when she gets bored, she likes to play people."

Staring at Will, she had no idea what to say. How had she come half way around the world with a complete stranger? Thankfully a knock at the door distracted Will while she took a moment to breathe. Inhale four deep breaths, hold four, breath out four. When he turned back to her, she abruptly took the pizza from him.

"Go shower. I'll be on the veranda." Turning her back to him, she walked away, putting the pizza down while grabbing the wine as she passed by it. Pouring herself a glass, she stood at the balcony, taking it all in. How could anyone be mad at someone who had brought her to such a beautiful place. She knew what Will said about Aria made perfect sense and she hated like hell the words she had woven together on Sam's behalf were unraveling her. Sipping her wine, she embraced the warmth it was spreading into her empty stomach while struggling to know where she wanted Will to begin when he came out. He didn't make her wait long, the smell of fresh pizza mixed with a freshly scrubbed Will making her head swim. Or maybe it was the sight of him in shorts and an unbuttoned white shirt with wet curly hair that was her undoing.

Smiling, he handed her a slice of pizza, refilling her wine glass before jumping into their conversation. "What do you want to know first?"

"Everything. If Aria's mother was your mom's sister, then Elisa really is your Nonna. Right? Why did you let me believe you've only known them since Aria was kidnapped?"

His voice became grave as he sat down on the chaise beside hers. "As you know, I was twelve when my parents were killed. I always knew my parents met in Rome when my father was working at the American Embassy and my mother was a student at one of the universities. He spoke at one of her international studies classes and they fell in love. I always assumed they were both American but what I didn't know is that she was born in Italy and became estranged from her family when they married and moved to New York. Elisa and Maurico were hurt, feeling like she turned her back on them. Very rarely did I hear her mention them and it was always in a vague, accidental context." She was surprised when he took her glass to have a sip of her wine making her realize this was painful for him to talk about. She could only imagine how he had perfected keeping it compartmentalized over the years in a place where he didn't have to feel his loss.

"When I went to college, I wanted to follow in their footsteps and pursued a degree in International Relations. After graduation I was lost without the structure so I decided to join the Navy. Because I was fluent in Italian, I was eventually assigned to the base here in Naples. At some point, I grew bored with military life and was released from active duty. I had been here for a while and had many contacts. One day, Elisa and Maurico reached out to me for help in finding their granddaughter Ariel. It was fate that brought us together, but it was Elisa who realized I was her daughter's son. After Aria was returned home, she showed me a picture of my mother. It was life changing to learn you have a family you never knew about."

It suddenly registered with her that he was letting her see his vulnerable side. She reached out to squeeze his hand. "It must have been so emotional for you. For all of you."

He stood up, walking to look out at the sea. "At first I was angry and bitter. How could they turn their back on their daughter or their grandson? But it turned out my mother had never told them she had a child. Meeting me made them realize how much time they had wasted, time that none of us could ever get back. So many regrets. They were persistent in getting to know me and we finally reached a place where we can be together and enjoy our time without always having one foot in the past. I finally forgave them and that allowed them to forgive themselves."

Following him to the balcony, her voice was soft as she put her hand on his back. "Thank you for sharing that with me. It means a lot to me that you trust me to know." She was stunned to learn his family history, but her bigger concern was the here and now."

"Tell me why you were so late, tell me about being mugged." When he turned to look at her, she added, "And I want to know the truth."

Cringing inwardly, he took a deep breath and began verbally laying his cards on the table. All of his cards. "Actually it was more of being taken hostage than a mugging." Seeing her shocked expression, he knew he needed to go back to the beginning, explain why they would think he had something they wanted as well as why he didn't have it.

"I'm going to need to start at the beginning." He waited for that to sink in, bracing himself for what was sure to come. "From the very beginning, I knew who you were when I walked into *Paws for a Cause* the first time." Hearing her inhale sharply, he gave her a moment. "I've been searching for who killed Jordan for the past six years and everything I found gave me concern for your safety. I couldn't let anything happen to you, so I inserted myself into your life."

Feeling sick to her stomach, her voice was a whisper. "Why couldn't you let anything happen to me?"

Struggling to say what needed to be said, his voice was equally quiet. "Not only was your brother my best friend, your family was like a second family to me at a time when I really needed it. Being at your house got me through some of my darkest days. I would die before I would let your family survive another loss."

He winced to see the look of hurt on her face, her eyes suddenly flashing. Waving her arms around she asked loudly, "So *all this* is about being Jordan's little sister?! Because you *owe* my family?! Fuck you Will!"

When she turned to walk away, he grabbed her arm, bringing her back to him and forcing her to look at him. "You want to know everything so let me *tell you everything* Sam."

She focused on his chin, not able to meet his eyes. Afraid to let her go, he started talking, trying to make her understand. "In the beginning, *only in the beginning,* that's what I told myself to justify my actions. But the truth is, the places I've been, the things I've done in the name of justice left me drifting and empty. I needed a change, to feel something real, something I could hold onto. Coming home to you was the only thing that gave me hope."

Hearing Prince whine, sensing the unrest between them, they both turned to look at him. "Prince was my way into your life and I latched onto it with both hands."

She was listening, but still hurt. "Is Prince really even your dog?" she mumbled. Seeing the hurt in his eyes, she quickly retracted it. "Sorry. Obviously he is. This is just a lot to process."

Nodding, he pressed on. "What I told you about how I got Prince is all true. He *was* my way into your daily routines, but as you know you provide something special for him and therefore, me. As I got to know you better, my reason for protecting you shifted."

Still struggling to look at him, she waited, using everything she had not to let him see tears in her eyes. "You better tell me the fucking truth Will."

Releasing one of her arms, he used his hand to put it under her chin and force her to look at him. "I never forgot the night of your seventeenth birthday Sam. Singing that song to me, dancing around, you were so full of life. But when I kissed you, everything changed for me. I never forgot that night. I needed to feel something real again. Sam, you are so real. You fill me up in ways I couldn't have even imagined."

Searching his face, she could see he was putting it all out there, the tenderness, the love in his expression but also the desperation for her to believe him. With sudden clarity she realized this was about saving himself as much as saving her.

"These past three years with you have been a gift for me and I've treasured every minute of it. I fought to keep you at a distance in the beginning, telling myself it was necessary to keep you safe. But then, then I fell in love with you. *I've never cared for anyone like I care for you Sam. I've never wanted to share the things I want to share with you. I love you.*"

She could feel the sting of tears, but still needed to know more. "I love you too Will. You know that. But why would you think I'm in danger? Why we are in danger? I need you to help me understand."

Nodding, he released her and turned back to the balcony. "When Granny died and I had to clean out her house, I found a box my parents had left in the attic, full of mementos of their life together. I touched everything in that box, soaking them up again, remembering how much they loved each other, how much they loved me. At the bottom of the box was a little silk bag full of my baby teeth of all things." He turned back to her, his next statement heavy. "And a SD card. I assumed it had pictures on it and put it into my laptop. But they weren't pictures. It was encrypted and I had no idea what any of it meant. Or why my parents would have it. But, as you know, no one was around for me to ask, to clarify for me. So I gave it to Jordan, to see if he could figure it out." He paused, taking a deep breath before making his next statement.

"Jordan thought it was a list of some sort, a list that revealed important people's names." He paused again, watching Sam.

"What people's names?" she asked breathlessly.

His voice was low as he leaned into her. "Agents Sam, secret agents from around the world." Her eyes were wide as he went on. "Jordan became obsessed with it and what to do with it. I wanted to destroy it, act like we never found it. At this point my parents had been gone for more than a decade. It was old news. We burned it together one night, but it fueled Jordan even more to create a program that could keep our country's and our allies' secrets safe. I warned him he was playing with fire, but he was convinced he could be discreet, no one would know until he had it ready and he could take it to the right people."

Will turned to look at her head on, before sharing the next bit of the story. "When Spenser showed up at your dinner table, Jordan worried he was using you as a way to him. It killed him to see the two of you together. Over the years, I've learned who the players are, Spencer and Marco included, but I don't know why they believe the SD card is still out there. Somehow it seems they still want it after all these years.

Sam felt herself go very still, the bile rising in her stomach. Suddenly she was having a flashback to the day of Jordan's funeral. Broken-hearted she had wandered into Jordan's room, desperate to feel his presence. She remembered feeling like someone had been there, his room an extra layer of dishevelment. Her mom had waved the notion away, closing the door behind them. She thought of the notebook she had found in his sock drawer. Was the page missing important? *Had Jordan invented a program people were after?* Thinking of the number she had found in his letterman's jacket, she suddenly wondered if it was a combination to a lock box. Was this what he had been killed over? She thought she was going to be sick.

"What? What is it?" Will asked, reaching out to her.

"I think he actually might have." she whispered.

"What do you mean?" he asked sharply.

"Someone broke into our house the day of his funeral, but only his room had been touched. When my mom cleaned out his room, I found a notebook in his sock drawer with all kinds of equations I assumed were technology gibberish, but there was one page obviously ripped out. Also, one day when I was wearing his letterman's jacket, I found a piece of paper in the pocket with a number written on it. What if it's a combination for a lock box?"

She could see from his face he didn't think she was crazy, but was taking her seriously. They stood together looking over the sea, their thoughts flying around like a rollercoaster that had suddenly gone off the tracks and was doomed to crash.

"What did you do with the note?" he asked her quietly.

Sheepishly she realized she would have to confess about her suspect's board hiding in her closet. "I made a board and it's pinned to it. Hiding at the back of my closet."

"You don't happen to have the number memorized do you?" he asked hopefully.

Shaking her head, she asked sharply. "What would it matter? We're not in New York and besides, I have no idea where this lock box could be located."

Taking her by the shoulders, his voice was ragged. "Think hard Sam. Where would Jordan think was a safe place to store something he didn't want found by the wrong people?"

She closed her eyes, trying to fathom this was actually the conversation they were having. She had been asking to know the details for months and now she understood why Will had protected her from knowing everything. The hard cold truth was shattering for a number of reasons. He could see she was scared when she mumbled to him, her voice small, "I don't know. We were both living our own lives at that point. It could have been anywhere."

He pulled her to him, wishing like hell he hadn't told her. "It's okay. We'll figure it out when we get back to New York. It's getting late. We need to get some sleep so we're ready for your birthday tomorrow."

Her eyes filled with tears. "It's the Tower card Will. It's happening just like she said it would."

Giving her a firm little shake, Will shook his head. "There's nothing we can do from here and we're not going to let some card ruin your birthday. We're going to put this on hold and celebrate you tomorrow and being in Italy on your birthday." Seeing her look of doubt, he added, "Isn't that what Jordan would want you to do?"

She could hear him in her head. *I didn't lose my life for you not to live yours.* Nodding, she hugged Will to her tightly. "You're right. Everything will feel better in the morning. Let's get some sleep."

Within minutes they were in bed, Sam curled up against Will, thankful for the warmth of him. It was comforting to know Prince was on the floor beside her. Kissing the top of her head, Will gave her a small squeeze. "Get some sleep. I have some special surprises planned for your birthday. It will all be fine. I promise." She trusted Will and she was going to choose to believe him when he promised everything would be fine. What other choice did she have?

CHAPTER NINETEEN

Happy birthday Sam

Hearing her alarm go off, she reflexively moaned. Hitting the appropriate button, she rolled over reaching for Will before checking the time on her phone, knowing she had given herself ten minutes until she needed to make this year's wish. Finding the bed empty, she sat up to take in her surroundings, noting some daylight peeking past the heavy black out drapes. Realizing the veranda door was ajar, she went to find her robe before going out to find Will. Tying her belt around her, she kept last night's conversation pushed to the back of her mind, choosing to focus on the beautiful day ahead of her.

"Morning." she said, stepping out into the early morning, the sea sparkling below her. She was quick to notice a round table had been set up with an assortment of breakfast foods the Italians were well known for. There was a vase with a beautiful arrangement of flowers and a long white box. She was curious, but had to focus on the business at hand first.

Coming out of his chair, Will moved to greet her. "Good morning birthday girl!" He leaned in to kiss her on the cheek before breathing into her ear, "Happy birthday."

She smiled as he handed her a cup of coffee, grateful for the physical distraction while she mentally reconsidered this year's wish. Going to the balcony, she looked out over the Bay of Naples in pure awe, the beauty breathtaking. Noting it was time, she closed her eyes and put her wish out to the universe, desperately hoping with all her heart it would find its way back to them. Glancing at Will shyly, she raised her cup of coffee to him before taking a sip.

Turning to admire the table, she realized she was starving, having never really had dinner last night. "This table looks lovely." she said as he pulled out a chair for her. He was quick to notice she became focused on the long white box, tied beautifully with a floral bow. With his encouragement she opened it, stunned to find a diamond necklace inside. Her eyes flew to Will's before she got up to go to him.

"It's absolutely beautiful!" she gushed.

He hugged her to him, before telling her, "Like you Sam, inside and out. Happy birthday."

Settling into their breakfast he announced she would need it to go with the dress she would be wearing tonight. She paused her fork, "Tonight? I don't have any dresses fancy enough to do those diamonds justice." she said worriedly.

"Don't worry. You will but you just have to wait for it." She could feel his anticipation and her smile was everything he had hoped for.

"I can't wait to see." she said softly, her eyes warm on his.

They were finishing their coffee, enjoying the view when Sam informed Will she needed to go for her run. Nodding at her, he took her hand before saying, "I know. We're all going to go."

They were out for their run in no time, Prince happy to have both of them with him. They moved quickly along the promenade they had walked along on their first day, Will letting Sam set the pace. He could feel her demons chasing her by her brutal pace, but knew from other birthdays, she always pushed herself hard on this day in particular. Having set her timer, he knew she would finish the first half in thirty minutes, but half way through he sensed a shift in her pace as she slowed it down, taking in her surroundings. Finally she stopped, hands on her knees catching her breath. Handing her their water bottle, she drank eagerly from it before turning to enjoy their view of the sea.

"Are you okay?" he asked, his hand on the small of her back.

"I am. It's a beautiful day in a beautiful place." she said, turning to him before adding, "With a beautiful man. It's a great day to let some demons go and just celebrate being alive."

Smiling at her, he put his arm around her shoulders, pulling her in for a side hug. "Absolutely. Are you ready to head back?"

Taking one last sip, she nodded. "Yep, but let's walk. I want to savor being here. With you." she said, taking his hand with her free one.

They moved slowly along the promenade, Will indulging her when she wanted to stop at a cafe to sit and have coffee. He was relieved to see Maurico's people were tailing them as promised, keeping a respectful distance, but close enough to intervene if necessary. When Sam got up to use the facilities, he nodded to the woman who followed behind her, his gut clenched to think she was the only one to have eyes on Sam for the moment. He wanted to assume he was being over protective, but knew the minute he let his guard down, they would pounce. It was clear they weren't finding what they wanted and sooner or later, they would want to hear it from the horse's mouth.

They returned to their suite to find lunch served on the veranda, a lovely spread of pasta, eggplant parmesan, and Caprese salad. Amused, he watched her as she ate heartily, her run having burned off her breakfast. Suddenly she paused her fork to ask, "Um, how tight is this dress going to be that I'm wearing tonight?"

He laughed at the look on her face, her question quite serious. "Oh don't worry, I have a plan for working off this lunch. When your food has had time to digest."

Leaning back in her chair she smiled wickedly. "I can only imagine. What does the rest of our day look like? After that?"

Watching her closely, he made an offer. "Elisa and Maurico have invited us to join them poolside for the afternoon. Or we could hang here at the pool. Or just lounge about and be lazy."

Raising her eyebrows at him, she made an observation. "Wow! It must be my birthday for you to lounge about. I think I would love to see that for myself. We can go to their house, if you like. Or sitting by the pool with this view sounds nice. Seems like a win-win either way. You choose."

Pushing her chair back, she announced it was time for a shower. When Will moved to join her, she waved him off. "It's a quick rinse and I'll be right out. "

Her quick rinse turned into a good twenty minutes of letting the hot water wash away her worries. She had noticed the woman earlier when they sat down at the cafe, confirming for her they were being followed. She knew if she was smart enough to realize it, then Will had to be the reason they were there. She had tried to feel appreciative that the woman had followed her into the bathroom for her own safety, pretending to be oblivious to Sam as she powdered her nose and touched up her lipstick. She told herself Will was being overprotective, that everything was fine, but it took another ten minutes before her body was ready to believe what her brain was trying to sell her.

Going to the french doors, she stood dressed in her robe, freshly scrubbed. Will was quick to notice her, coming inside to join her. Walking to stand beside the bed, she opened her robe to him, revealing her nakedness underneath, pausing deliberately before letting it fall to the floor. She watched as his eyes grew dark.

"Let this birthday celebration get started." she said wickedly.

Nodding his agreement, he pulled off his own clothes. She felt her body go up in flames as he pulled her to him, his lips everywhere all at once. Wrapping her legs around him, she squealed when he tossed her onto the bed. She took in his nakedness, her vagina screaming for his attention.

"What would you like me to do first, birthday girl?" he asked softly. Saying nothing, she made her invitation obvious. Quickly he was down on his knees, starting with light kisses along her inner thighs before using his tongue to make her crazy, slowly working his way around her hot spots he knew so well. She moaned softly as he slowly moved inside her, the pleasure causing her to catch her breath. Moaning his name, his lip curled in satisfaction as she started to pant, knowing she was close. Closing her eyes she took it all in, knowing it was a birthday win for sure.

It wasn't long before they lay spooning, Sam snoring softly as she slept in Will's embrace. He was looking forward to tonight, hoping it would be as special for Sam as he imagined it should be. Gently he extracted himself from her, putting his pillow at her back before going to sit on the veranda and double check everything was in place for the night. She had been asleep for an hour, when he went back to join her, feeling his own fatigue setting in. Setting his alarm, he peeked at Prince over the side of the bed, offering a "good boy Prince" before closing his eyes and finally letting himself sleep.

She woke them both, realizing it was late in the afternoon. "I think we might have missed the pool party." she told him, her voice deep after sleeping hard.

"Not a problem." he said, pulling her to him. He knew neither one of them had slept very well last night and he didn't want anyone drifting off tonight. Getting out of bed, he brought her robe to her before putting his long awaited plan in motion.

"You have two hours until you need to be ready. I have several surprises for you." Checking his watch, he added with a big grin, "In thirty minutes a friend of mine will be here to do your hair and makeup."

His anticipation was contagious and Sam's smile was big as she got out of bed to thank him. Suddenly it occurred to her, "How do I know what I need to wear if I don't know where we're going?"

She watched curiously as Will went to retrieve a large white box tied with a pretty red bow. Bringing it to her, he said, "I'm glad you asked. Go ahead, open it."

Intrigued, she moved to open it, the lid snug and covering tissue paper. Pulling the tissue paper aside, she gasped to see a red dress underneath. Pulling it out, she was stunned to see it was the red dress Julia Roberts had worn in her favorite movie.

"Oh Will it's so gorgeous! I can't believe you did this for me!" she said, her voice almost a whisper. Looking up at him, she realized she had never seen him look happier.

"There's more." He took the dress from her, pointing into the box. Finding long white gloves, she was speechless.

"Happy birthday Sam." he said softly, leaning in to kiss her on her cheek.

As he pulled away from her, she searched his face. She was stunned by his generosity, but even more how much thoughtfulness had gone into his gift.

"This is too much Will. I don't know what to say." she finally managed.

"Well the dress is on loan, but the necklace and gloves are yours to keep. And the memories you will take home with you. Those are yours to keep forever, here and here." He made the last statement, gently touching her temple before laying his hand on her heart.

She wondered if he could feel how fast it was beating as she brought his face to hers, realizing more than anything she would remember how his lips felt on hers right at this moment, their tenderness almost enough to bring her to tears.

Releasing him suddenly, he laughed when she hurried to the bathroom. "First I need to brush my teeth and then I need to text Riley. She is not going to believe you did this!" She squealed with excitement before heading into the bathroom.

Will had discreetly moved to their veranda, sipping scotch as he worked from his laptop, giving her space to do her thing.

Giving the feel this was a special day, a bottle of champagne sat chilling for the girls to share. When Will introduced Bianca to Sam, she was quick to realize she was American, piquing her interest in how they knew each other. She immediately won Sam's trust as she made light conversation while finding out her likes and dislikes. Sam didn't hold back, letting her know she wanted to look beautiful but not plastic. She knew makeup could be used to enhance her looks, but she didn't want it caked on to the point you couldn't see the real her. It was important to Sam that she still looked like herself tonight. Uncertain about what to do with her hair, she texted Riley who suggested she ask Bianca to give her an updo but to leave some down so she could still feel hair on the back of her neck.

Curious how much Bianca knew about her, Sam decided to ask a few questions of her own. "So how do you and Will know each other?"

Startled, Bianca paused her hot iron. "Wait. He told you nothing about me?" Sam wasn't sure what to think when she laughed at the idea. "Of course he didn't. We went through RTC together. Boot camp for you civilians. We were stationed in different places afterwards but somehow eventually ended up stationed in Italy together."

Sam thought about it, her curiosity getting the better of her. "Did you two go out?"

Bianca laughed. "Go out or sleep together? Will doesn't date, but yes we did sleep together. One time. After way too many drinks and he couldn't apologize enough. Honestly, I was a little shocked when Will reached out to me with this request. I mean don't get me wrong, we're still friends. I left the navy shortly after he did, but this is what I do now. I work in a salon for one of the luxury hotels. Women come here to be pampered and I'm here for it."

It hit Sam like a ton of bricks, realizing Bianca had a crush on Will, one that she had filed away under fails. "You liked him more than a friend."

She paused again, Sam's directness catching her off guard. "Yep. But Will wasn't looking for a relationship."

Afraid to hear her answer, she asked anyway. "Because he's a tortured soul?"

Considering the term, Bianca wasn't quick to dismiss her theory. "Not exactly. He was always about the job. It was in everyone's best interests that he stayed focused and kept emotions out of the equation. He's really good at keeping his cool because he does that so well, freeing him up to think through every situation with clarity, especially when it's life or death.

Thinking about what she said, Sam pressed on. "Has he ever killed someone?" She cringed mentally, waiting to hear her answer.

Surprised by her question, Bianca chose her words carefully before coming around to look Sam in the eyes. "Will has had to make tough choices and do things the rest of us couldn't. But if you ask me, he's a god damn hero, because he's also saved ten times that many people from evil. He keeps his cool, but in the end, he beats himself up for not creating a different option. He feels the weight of what he's done after the fact.

Nodding, Sam could only imagine, but definitely knew what Bianca meant. She hated to think it, but Aria's description of him as a tortured soul seemed pretty accurate after all.

Having returned to curling her hair, Bianca came back around to face her. "Sam, I've never known Will to care about anyone's happiness, let alone how much he wants to make you happy. If anyone can help him understand what a good man he is, it's you. I don't really know you, but he deserves to be happy and I'm rooting for you two all the way."

She nodded, not able to talk over the lump in her throat. When it came to Will, she was definitely getting the same message. He was a great guy, but came with lots of baggage. Then again, Sam told herself, who didn't?

Having decided to wear her hair up, she loved how Bianca had left her some loose curls long in the back. Finally finishing her make-up, she helped her into the dress before handing her the long white gloves. Stepping back to look at her, Bianca nodded her approval.

"I've known Will a long time and I've never known him to spoil someone like he's spoiling you. I hope you have a lovely night." Giving her a hug, she stepped out onto the Veranda, speaking in Italian with Will, her voice animated, his responses quiet but appreciative. Picking up her bag, she left discreetly, tossing a "Ciao!" over her shoulder before closing the door behind her.

Waiting for Will to come in, she thought about Vivian standing before Edward, waiting for his approval, and suddenly understood her nervousness. Smoothing down her dress, she was surprised to see Will in a tux, having not even thought about what he would be wearing. Seeing him with a bow tie, his hair all slicked down, took her breath away, making her loins ache for him. "You look so handsome!" she breathed out.

"And you look absolutely stunning Sam." Will said as he took in her creamy shoulders, the sweetheart neckline plunging into her cleavage, the bodice highlighting her curves before falling away into a dramatic train. He brought the necklace to her, taking it out of the box, his eyes dark as he moved behind her to put it around her neck. His breath was warm as he leaned into her. "Happy birthday."

She shivered in anticipation of things to come as he kissed her neck, his lips light before moving to her bare shoulders, his hands warm on her arms. Sighing, he moved beside her, holding his arm out to her. "If we don't go right now, we'll never make it to dinner."

She laughed, taking his arm, knowing he had a point.

The car whisked them away, heading up into the hills, the ristorante giving them an excellent view from their table, breathtaking as the sun set over the sea. Will ordered a variety of pastas and seafoods, wanting her to experience a variety of flavors. Their service was impeccable, their server keeping her champagne flute full.

Before long they were back in the car headed to her last birthday surprise. She was delighted when she found them in front of the Teatro id San Carlo, the oldest opera house in Europe. She had felt somewhat overdressed for dinner, but here found other couples dressed to the nines just as she and Will were. She had never been to the opera and knowing it would be in Italian, wasn't sure what to expect. Still, it was on her bucket list and she had planned to go with her travel group if she had gone to Rome. She was even more delighted when Will told her they were seeing Verdi's La traviata. It couldn't have been more perfect and she had to wonder if Will realized that was the opera Edward had taken Vivian to see in Pretty Woman.

Sam was unprepared for the near three hours the opera would last, assuming they were half way through at the first intermission. She was thankful for her nap this afternoon, but soon found herself swept away by the romance and heartbreak of Violetta and Alfredo's story. Despite being unable to understand what the actors were saying, she could feel their words, the music moving her as well. Will watched her as she was moved to tears more than once, taking her hand and squeezing it.

Sitting in the car, headed back to their hotel, she was quiet, the opera draining her while she continued to process it, their tragedy feeling almost contagious as she pushed away thoughts of the damn Tower card. Reaching for her hand, Will picked it up to kiss it before asking if she was okay.

Shaking off her feelings of trepidation, she smiled at him before sliding over to snuggle into his shoulder. "It's been such a beautiful evening. Thank you Will for making my birthday so memorable. Dinner, the opera, this dress, it's all been so special. I will never forget this day."

Feeling him kiss the top of her head made her smile. "Don't forget, there's still cake waiting for us." he said into her hair.

The thought of cake brightened her mood. "Perfect! I need to double down on my wish this year."

He laughed, shaking his head. "I keep telling you, I'm here to make you happy, just say the word."

She touched his cheek, her eyes warm on his. "You make me so happy Will." She could only wish for it to last forever.

CHAPTER TWENTY

They lay in bed wrapped around each other, their room dark and quiet. Will woke up with a start having heard Prince's low growl. Disengaging himself from Sam, he looked to see where Prince was focused. Watching him army crawl to the door, Will was out of the bed instantly, locating a heavy vase and ready for the intruder. He was soon rewarded when the man went down with a thud. Quickly he zip tied his hands and feet, his adrenaline pumping as he stood over the man dressed in black, his hood still over his face. Cautiously he removed the man's hood.

"What's happening?" Sam asked, sitting up in bed. Realizing Will was standing over someone, she was quickly beside him. "Oh my god!" she whispered, her face white. She went to turn on a low table light, her hands shaking. Prince stood by watching the three of them, his eyes and ears on alert.

Watching her, Will nodded grimly. "You know who this is."

She nodded in disbelief. "Is he? Is he dead?"

Shaking his head, he reassured her. "Not even close. You need to get dressed."

Quickly she threw some shorts on with a t-shirt keeping one eye on the man. Grabbing her running shoes, she brought Will his.

"Are you sure he's not dead?" she asked, needing confirmation.

"He's just knocked out from the vase I hit him over the head with. He'll come around."

Before long they both stood watching him as he shook it off before he struggled to sit up despite his zip ties.

Turning to his captors, he said with a wicked grin. "Hello Sam. Surprised to see me?"

"What the hell are you doing here?" she spit out.

"Isn't it obvious? I've missed you. You and your sweet ass." Turning to Will he added, "She's pretty good in bed isn't she? You're welcome."

She could feel Will's controlled rage beside her and quickly jumped in. "Shut up Spencer! Again, what are you doing here?" she said, trying to control her own rage. And fear.

His face became hard, his demeanor doing a three-sixty. "We have some unfinished business, don't we Shaw?"

Will appeared unruffled, but narrowed his eyes at the man. "If you mean having the authorities come to haul your sorry ass away, yes we do."

"You know you've got nothing on me. Picking a lock will never keep me in. But if you want me to go away, you know what I'm here for."

"If you couldn't find it in New York why would you think you can find it here?" Will kept his voice even, but Sam could feel his tension as she stood beside him.

Suddenly the intruder swung his attention back to Sam. "Does she know the whole story yet? How you and Cooper took property that didn't belong to you?" Sam clenched her fists to her sides, trying to ignore him. "Playing the boyfriend role was such a bore until I got you into bed."

"Shut up Spencer!" her voice was trembling, but he went on.

"Now Cooper on the other hand was a bigger pain in my side. He left me no choice but to take him out of the equation. Sorry, not sorry." he sneered at her.

Will was about to hit him again, when suddenly Sam ran out the door. She could hear Spencer laughing behind her as she ran for the stairs. Calling her name, Will followed her taking the stairs two at a time, but she wouldn't stop for him.

"Sam stop! This isn't going to help the situation. Sam!" As she came to a landing, he grabbed her arm, making her stop. Seeing her face, he pulled her to him as she sobbed into his shoulder. Prince had followed them, watching them, his eyes alert.

"I hate him! I hate him so much! It makes my skin crawl to think I got into bed with him. But for him to be so callous about killing Jordan! I hate him and I want him to pay!" her voice was loud as it echoed in the stairwell.

Taking her by the shoulders, Will gave her a little shake. "I know. But we've got to stay calm or he's going to win. We have to keep our emotions out of it to beat him at his own game. Understand?" His voice was firm but gentle as he wiped away her tears.

Nodding at him, he took her hand and she let him lead her back to their room. But when they got there, he was gone, their door left wide open.

Sam had never seen Will so angry, even though she knew he had every reason to be. It was her fault they had left him alone long enough to escape and she knew it. She had apologized, but he said very little, his silence killing her. Not sure of what else to do, she headed to the bathroom to collect herself. She stopped at the door when he finally spoke, turning to look at him.

"We're sitting ducks here and will need to leave soon. Pack your things but we will need to travel light, so backpacks only. We will get the rest later. Be ready to move in ten."

She nodded at him, but he wasn't looking at her. Turning back to the bathroom, she noticed the red dress lying across the chair where Will had carefully placed it after getting her out of it when they got back to their suite last night. After making one more wish over cake, Will had made sweet love to her, his attention less hungry and more tender, the result the same for both of them in the end. It was shocking how quickly things could change. Going to pick the dress up, she returned it to the box carefully, grateful she would always have the memory of last night regardless of what happened here and now.

She left him to his packing, closing the bathroom door behind her. She stared at herself in the mirror, giving herself a mental pep talk. She started collecting her toiletries, packing them back into the small bag Riley had filled for her just days ago. Abruptly she realized someone was in the room watching her. Slowly she turned to face him, kicking herself for not realizing he had been behind the door when she closed it.

"Hello again Sam. You didn't really believe you would get rid of me that fast did you?" He turned to lock the bathroom door before he started walking towards her, his look smug.

"You're looking for something that doesn't exist anymore!" She said, holding her ground.

"You always were a terrible liar Sam. Maybe you don't think it exists, but I know for a fact, someone tried to activate the card just a couple of days ago, from here, in Naples." He could see she was shocked by this news.

"That can't be true! They destroyed the card years ago." she exclaimed, her heart pounding loudly.

Putting his finger under her chin, he tilted her face up to him. "Did they Sam? Were you there?"

She swatted his hand away, shaking her head. "You already know I wasn't there, but I believe Will."

"Why Sam? Because he makes your panties wet? As I recall, you used to do that when I touched you. Remember?" As he reached for her, she jerked her knee to his groin with all her strength, but he anticipated her move and turned sideways while grabbing her by the hair at the same time, using it to jerk her to him tightly before putting a gun under her chin.

She cried out in pain, making him sneer at her. "You're going to be a good little girl Sam or this could get a lot uglier than is necessary. You're going to do what I say or your precious Will will be eating my gun for breakfast. Got it?"

They both turned as Will knocked on the door. "Sam? Are you okay in there?"

"Answer him!" Spencer hissed in her ear. "Everything's good."

Trying to calm her nerves, she struggled to find her voice. "Everything's good. Just packing my tampons."

His breath was hot on her cheek as he murmured in her ear, "Good girl Sam. You always did like to please me."

Trying to distract him, Sam went a different route. "That's because I thought you really cared about me. I thought you were the one. I chose you over Jordan, remember? We used to have so much fun together." Trying to keep the disgust out of her voice, she turned into him slightly.

She could see he was sizing her up and slowly she raised her hand to his, moving the gun away from her chin. "Didn't we?"

He still had a handful of her hair, but she could feel him loosen his grip ever so slightly. "You said you missed me Spencer. Were you lying to me too, like Will did about the card?"

Releasing her hair, he put his free hand on her ass, pulling her to him, pressing himself into her. "You've filled out nicely Sam. Not a little girl anymore are you?" She braced herself as he bent down to smell her neck.

Suddenly the bathroom door burst open as Will kicked it in, a gun in his hand, pointed at them. Spencer quickly resumed his position of his gun under her chin, his other hand wrapped in her hair, holding her in front of him.

"Look Sam, your hero is here to save you." Spencer sneered. "Too bad for him I hold all the cards. You're not going to let her get hurt are you Shaw? I've wasted enough time here. Put the gun down or she gets it first."

Sam watched his face, trying his best to keep it stony. *He's really good at keeping his emotions out of it.* She racked her brain trying to think of something she could do to help.

"Don't give him the gun Will. He's going to kill us anyway. He wants the card but we don't have it."

"Shut up!" Spencer snarled.

She couldn't help herself and kept going. "I told him you and Jordan destroyed it years ago but he said someone activated the card a few days ago from here, in Naples. He thinks we're lying to him and that we do know where it is."

"Shut up!" Spencer screamed in her ear. "Put the gun down Shaw NOW!" Suddenly he released her hair and held the gun to her head, his arm around her neck. "I don't need both of you. You know I don't!"

Reluctantly Will put the gun down on the bathroom floor. As soon as he did so, Spencer shoved Sam toward him, while moving the gun close enough for him to pick it up. Quickly Will moved Sam behind him as they all moved out of the bathroom. Prince started a low growl but Will told him to stay.

"If your flea bag even looks like he's going to jump me, I'll shoot him, no problem. Get your zip ties Shaw, hands behind her back. And make it tight!"

Going to the door, they were surprised when Spencer opened it to a woman. Sam shook her head in confusion realizing it was the same woman who had followed her into the bathroom yesterday.

"Did you bring it?" When she nodded, they switched guns, Spencer pointing the new gun at Prince.

"NO!" Sam screamed.

Putting his hand on her shoulder, Will tried to calm her. "It's a tranquilizer gun. He'll sleep it off and be fine." He reassured her.

"Fine might be optimistic, but he's coming with us. If you don't want him dead, you'll carry him out. I'm just making sure we have all the things you hold most dear available for our negotiations. It's going to be fun, you'll see."

Spencer checked the hall before they left the room, the group headed to the stairwell, walking in single file. No one spoke, their faces grim as they descended the flights of stairs from the fifth floor. Sam made mental notes of the white van they were forced into the back of, Will gently laying Prince down on the floor before helping her to sit down. They turned to their captors in surprise when they threw in a small hissing object and Spencer snickered "Sweet dreams!" before slamming the door shut and locking it. Quickly Will pulled Sam to him, the last thing she heard coming from him. *Just remember I love you.* Then it was lights out.

Her head was groggy and she struggled to know where she was. She kept still, letting her body acclimate. She could feel a sway and decided she must be on water. Slowly she opened her eyes, finding Prince nearby, his body limp. Fearfully she said his name, very much relieved when he came to her, licking her face and hands. She realized her hands were still zip tied, but now she was secured to a pole in the room, clearly in the hull of a yacht. She could see through the port holes it was daytime, but had no idea how long she had been out. She looked around for Will, becoming frantic when she did not see him.

Suddenly the door burst open, causing Prince to growl. Not able to reach for him, she gave him her firmest "Stay!" while two men dumped Will's body beside them. She tried to move closer to him, but her zip ties held her fast. Turning to Prince, she urged him to go to Will. Licking his face first, Prince then did the only thing he could and laid next to Will, his head on his leg.

Sitting there with the two of them, she tried to think. She could remember the white van, but she had to assume it was long gone. She remembered the sudden fizzing fog and Will's last words to her.

Looking at Will she hoped he could hear her when she said softly, "Just remember I love you Will."

She had no idea how much time passed before Will finally started to stir. Prince came to his feet, excited to see him move just as much as Sam was. She watched as he struggled to sit up before realizing his left arm was swinging strangely. She felt stupid asking him if he was okay when clearly he was not. She ached to go to him, but had no choice but to wait for him to find her. When his eyes finally fell on her all she could get out was, "Hi."

He could only give her a weak "Hi yourself."

"I'm sorry Will. Whatever they did to you, I'm so sorry. I would come to you, but clearly I'm the biggest threat in the room since I'm the one zip tied."

He smiled weakly, his feeble "Clearly." giving her hope they might get out of this hell hole. "Just give me a minute," he added softly.

Sam watched in horrified amazement as Will moved to lay flat on his back, slowly going through the motions of getting his dislocated shoulder back to where it should be. She hated seeing him hurt like this, but it wasn't the first time his grit and focus had moved her to tears. Not able to think of anything inspiring to say, she just watched him as he lay on the floor, waiting for his pain to subside.

Prince stayed by his side, watching Will anxiously as he used his good side to scoot closer to Sam. The effort to reach her was obvious and she hated like hell she couldn't put her arms around him and hold him to her. She was grateful when he laid his head in her lap, knowing it was the best they could do for now. Prince lay his head on Will's leg gently, his eyes watching the two of them. She could see it in his eyes he wished he could help Will as much as she did, but neither of them knew what to do.

"I'm going to get you out of this Sam. I know it looks bad, but I promise I will get you out of this." Will said, his determination convincing for both of them.

"You mean us. You're going to get us out of this. I know you will, but you need to let me help. What can I do?" Sam asked, her voice firm.

Slowly he sat up, pulling her to him. She leaned into him, burrowing her head into his shoulder, inhaling his smells in sweet relief. "After all the shit they did to you, do they still believe you have the card?" she asked, her voice both offended and fearful.

"It doesn't matter. I told them I want to see their boss, that I need to speak with him in person." Will said. "But they may come for you before that happens."

It killed him to see her look up at him fearfully. "What do you mean? I don't know anything!"

"I know baby girl. I told them that and you'll tell them that. And if it gets hard, I want you to remember how strong you are. Nothing could be harder than the emotional pain of losing Jordan."

She nodded to him before laying her head back on his shoulder. She told herself not to cry. There were no tissues, there was no free hand to wipe her nose, there was no room for tears.

Kissing the top of her head, Will added softly. "I'm sorry I got you messed up in this. I tried to protect you, but I'm not going to lie, I got distracted from the job."

She gave a short laugh. "Who me?"

"Yes you." He gave a sigh using his good arm to pull her to him even tighter. "It's always been you Sam."

She looked up at him. "Are you saying that I'm your Vivian?"

He smiled. "Yes, but this is real life. And at the moment we're fighting for ours. And you have no idea how much I regret that."

"I wouldn't change a thing Will. I've lived more life in these three years with you than all my other years. I regret nothing. Except these damn zip ties!" she said vehemently.

They sat in silence, the three of them huddled together. Somewhere along the way she dozed off until Prince's low growl woke her in alarm. She felt Will shift away from her, his body tense and alert.

Without saying a word, a man came in and dumped a box, before closing the door abruptly behind him. Prince beat Will to the box, the two of them exploring its contents. "Well? Is there a get out of jail free card? What the hell is it?" Sam demanded to know.

Turning to her, Will held up water bottles. "There are sandwiches too. Are you hungry?"

She didn't pause to think about his question but nodded to him. He was surprised to find a bowl for Prince, which he used to pour some water for him. Pulling out one of the subs, he was even more surprised to find a small pair of scissors in the bottom of the box. He paused, realizing his request to see the boss must have been passed along and could only assume he would be leaving again soon. Going to cut the zip ties off Sam, he gave her a minute to massage her wrists before handing her a water bottle. She drank from it greedily, before taking the sub sandwich Will held out to her. He watched as Sam and Prince devoured their sandwiches, letting her finish before he started to prepare her for what was to come.

He had a plan but it was going to be hard, especially on her. He wanted to lay it all out there for her, but knew their chance for success would be better the more authentic her reactions were. When he told her she was strong, he meant it. What was sure to come would test them all, but he reminded himself if they were ever to have a happily ever after, this was their best chance. The thought of telling her good-bye ripped his heart out, but he had no choice. He would sacrifice his life for hers any day of the week, but hated that the day would be today. But first, his meeting needed to go well. He wouldn't have it any other way.

CHAPTER TWENTY-ONE

Knowing they would want to move once darkness fell, he was both afraid and ready for this meeting with the boss, his last chance to activate his plan and lay this case to rest. He was relieved they had not come for her and he could only assume their boss had seen to that. Picking up her hand, he kissed it before preparing her that he would be leaving her anytime now.

Reassuring her it was going to be okay, she nodded, keeping her face brave and trying her best not to be emotional.

They both turned to the door expectantly when Prince gave a low growl, bracing themselves for what may come. Throwing the door open, a man with a gun directed his attention at Will before barking out, "Let's go." When Will approached him, he held cuffs out, motioning for him to turn around.

Facing Sam, he gave a small smile before he mouthed "I love you." The room felt cold and empty without Will's presence and Sam was grateful to have Prince laying beside her, both of them watching the door, waiting for who knew how long until Will returned.

With a black bag over his head, he was ushered into a car before speeding away from the harbor. He could feel the car ascending into the hills, the route feeling familiar and only fanning his determination to find a way out of this growing with every minute it took to arrive at their destination. Since his harsh realization of who was behind Jordan's death, he had rehearsed their conversation a hundred times in his head, well aware it could go sideways at any given minute.

His senses were working overtime as he tracked entering a large house before coming into a room and being shoved into a chair. He took a deep breath when the black bag was removed, letting his eyes adjust to the dimly lit room. He sat across from a massive desk, the wing back leather chair turned away from him. He was not surprised it was a room he was quite familiar with.

His stomach somersaulted to hear the familiar voice demand they be left alone. As the chair turned toward him, he realized decades of family history was about to come to a head.

Nodding at him, the older man asked kindly, "I understand you wanted to see me?"

Taken aback by his casual demeanor, it was clear to Will neither of them was surprised to see the other. "That's right. I wanted to see for myself it was you. Thank you for seeing me Mauricio."

He nodded graciously to him. "It seemed only fair since one could argue I owe you a favor for saving my granddaughter."

"All the love for Aria and not your own grandson?" he asked.

Will watched as the older man got out of his chair and came to lean against the front of his desk before speaking. "I was there when Aria was born. Your mother chose to turn her back on her family. Not only did she desert us, she kept you from us. Her mother may have forgiven her, but I am less quick to forgive. Family is everything. Hence why I honored your request."

"You knew I knew who you were?" Will asked.

Smiling the old man was quick to confirm. "I'm not surprised considering you have my blood running through you. Intelligence and instincts run deep in the men in this family."

Will was quick to cut to the chase, wanting to clarify some things, but needing to not piss the old man off. That could be deadly for all of them. "My mother found out, didn't she? She learned your money is earned on the backs of innocent victims and wanted no part of it?"

Seeing Mauricio's eyes narrow, Will took a mental step back. "She thought she knew something about my business, but she was quick to judge and never came to me to learn the truth. She trusted a plastic card to turn her back on people who gave her life and loved her."

Will thought it over before asking the obvious. "What is the truth you would have wanted her to know?"

Seeing his eyes flicker to the door, Will was curious when he leaned toward him. "Sometimes things are not as they appear. Sometimes we do questionable things for the greater good of humanity. Sacrifices are made."

In an instant Will understood. He had lived the last decade on that very principle. But he was ready to be done. He needed to close this chapter and move on with his life, a peaceful life that included Sam and Prince in a particular brownstone in New York.

Will's voice was low as he spoke. "You're willing to sacrifice us in return for your true identity continuing to be classified information."

Smiling, he nodded at Will. "Aww my intelligence and instincts do serve you well I see."

Will wanted to be offended to be discarded so casually, yet he could see Mauricio was between a rock and a hard place, much as he was. "What if I have a way to change the narrative? One where we can all keep our status quo?"

"I'm listening." the old man said, folding his arms across his chest, his look intent on what Will had to say.

"I have a contact in the states. If he does not get confirmation that Sam and Prince are alive and well in the next twenty-four hours, he has an envelope ready to be delivered to the person who could take you and your operation down. We would both lose everything we hold most dear to us."

"And how do you propose I can avoid this delivery?" he asked.

"I want them released immediately, that you personally guarantee their safety and get them on your jet headed back to New York. That's non-negotiable."

"Is that all?" he asked, impressed with the ballsyness of his grandson.

"I know you're planning on blowing up the yacht. I saw the explosives. I assume that is going to be your way to dispose of us. I want to be alone with Spencer, in the hull before it explodes."

He could not mistake the hard edge to his grandson's voice. "You also hold grudges I see."

"He killed my best friend and destroyed a beautiful family."

The old man nodded. "I will agree to both things, but I have yet to hear the plan for yourself. I need to make an example out of you Will. Otherwise, this is all questionable at best."

Will swallowed hard. "I know. Once Sam and Prince are safely off the boat, blow it up. I need to let this life go. I can't do it anymore. I'll be your sacrifice. But this means Sam is left alone, no one is following her or keeping tabs on her. She is free to live her life in peace."

Mauricio thought of Elisa and how devastated she would be to lose Will when they were finally a family again. It would kill her to know he was the one behind Will and Sam's deaths. "If you're dead, how will you know if our agreement will be honored? And how will she feel living her life without you? Clearly she is in love with you." Mauricio asked, his look bordering on compassion.

His eyes narrowed at his grandfather. "I'm trusting you to be a man of your word. Let me worry about Sam. One last detail. When your men can only find one body in the ocean, you will support the assumption I was blown to pieces."

He raised his eyebrows in surprise. "So who's body will we find in the ocean?"

Will's voice was grim. "Spencer's."

The old man was proud to sit across from this young man. It was bittersweet to end their relationship in such a way, knowing he was asking him to let him go. Forever. He thought of how painful it had been to let his daughter go, realizing she had found out about his life as an agent, yet didn't show him the respect of talking to him about it. He had been devastated when she died, leaving their estranged relationship irreparable. He could only assume Will did not realize his parents had died at the hands of his enemies, and he could see no reason to share that with him now.

Trying to seal the deal, he added one more piece of information strictly for Mauricio's benefit. "Spencer said the card had been activated here in Italy just a few days ago. You know it's not the one my mother had and you know it wasn't us that activated it."

Studying each other, Will added grimly. "You have a mole in one of your organizations, but I'm not sure if it's the good side or the bad."

Will watched as the old man walked around back to the other side of his desk. For the first time, he noticed Mauricio's years, the toll this job was taking on him at a time when he should be enjoying the fruits of his labor, not blowing them up. He held his breath, waiting for an answer.

Finally he spoke, ignoring Will's observations of his organization."Do you really have this documentation you speak of?" he asked.

Will faced him squarely. "Are you willing to risk finding that out the hard way? You need to focus on selling that I do. Whatever you tell your goons, they will have to believe and follow through on."

For the first time, Will worried his plan would fall through, that the old man would deny him his second chance. He could see him thinking hard about it, walking around his desk, back to him.

"You have a deal. When you return to the yacht, Sam and your dog will be released. I will fly them both home on the same jet you arrived here on when she's ready. She will be free to live her life without looking over her shoulder. The yacht will have a bomb on it with a timer so your time with Spencer will be limited. Whatever comes of that, you will go down with the boat. Gone. Forever. Do I have the details correct?"

Will nodded, his relief evident. He stood awkwardly with his hands still cuffed behind him. "Thank you. I wish you and Elisa well always." It hurt him to be standing there, saying an awkward good-bye to the only family he had left.

Placing his hand on his shoulder, his grandfather squeezed it before telling him. "We will miss you, my grandson. Ti vogliamo bene. I hope it all works out for all of you the way you're thinking it will."

Will stared at him hard. Maybe he truly did care about him. "Grazie Nonno."

As Will turned toward the door, Mauricio called out. "She will not let you go easily. You will have to be convincing."

He didn't bother to hide his regret as he turned back to him. "I know."

Finally he was back in the car, descending to the harbor, more than ready to get the next part over with, as difficult as it would be. He thought about his conversation with his grandfather, even more convinced what needed to be done would be done, for better or worse. There was no other way out and he should know, he'd been working on it for weeks now, fine tuning it and trying to anticipate any possible deviation. He had been purposeful in bringing Sam here, knowing their chances of coming out alive were better. Just like he was, Elisa and Mauricio had been quite charmed by Sam and he had played that hand hard once he realized Maricio's part in all this.

Despite his age, his grandfather still commanded having the last word. When he had informed his goons of the change in plans, he had been surprised to hear one of them dare to question him. He had watched as Mauricio pulled out a gun from behind his back before shooting the man deliberately in the foot. Glancing around their small group, he was quick to announce intimidatingly. "Now you have other things to worry about." The man's howls ceased abruptly, afraid he would be shot again.

He could see where he was a chip off the old man, which seemed crazy considering he had not known him at all until the last decade. His granny had been the influence over him and the last word as he grew into his awkward teenage years and then adulthood. He regretted to think once again, he would have no family to speak of. The thought of having a family with Sam one day gave him the determination to see his plan through, confident it should work. He had lived enough life though to know nothing is for certain and that was the hardest part.

CHAPTER TWENTY-TWO

With sweet relief Sam and Prince welcomed him back, however short lived as it was. She could see from his face something serious was going down even as she didn't realize he was about to do the hardest thing he had ever had to do. He was going to tell her good-bye. It was going to be almost as hard to tell Prince good-bye, but he was grateful Sam would have him with her, to take care of her, to be there for her, to love her.

"How did your meeting go?" she asked, her voice worried but hopeful.

"Everything is in place. He agreed to what I asked of him." Will answered, stalling for the inevitable.

Cautiously her face brightened. "That's good right?"

He nodded, choosing his words carefully. "You and Prince will be getting off the yacht in a matter of minutes. You will fly home on the same private jet we came here on."

She became focused on his first three words, *you and Prince*. "And you're coming with us, right?" she asked tentatively.

Shaking his head, he denied her the hope she was desperate for. "I have to stay. There are loose ends to finish up and it's part of our agreement. Someone has to go down and it's only right it's me."

"Bullshit!" she said, her voice going up an octave. "If you're staying, we're staying."

Putting his hands on her arms, he looked her firmly in the eyes. "No, you're not. You're going to get off this boat and I'm staying. It's the only way this can work."

She was shaking her head, the concept not acceptable. "You can't tell me what to do. If you're staying, then I'm staying. Besides, we both know Mauricio will find us and use his men to rescue us. All of us."

He had known she wouldn't just ride out into the sunset, but started to worry she wouldn't do what he asked at all. "Sam, you're not staying. I need you to trust me and to do as I ask. When they show up, you're going with them to get off the boat so I can wrap up this unfinished business once and for all."

"I can wrap up with you. He was my brother before he was your best friend!" She was just short of yelling, her face devastated as she realized she was going to have to tell him good-bye.

He pulled her to him, his voice muffled in her hair. "Sam, this is going to be hard for both of us, but it's the only way. I need you to get off this boat if I have to throw you off of it myself. I need you to be strong."

He pulled back from her, checking to see if she was understanding him. Seeing the tears streaming down her face almost broke his resolve to get her off the damn boat.

Her voice was small. 'I can't tell you good-bye Will. I love you! Please let us stay with you. I'd rather die with you than live without you!"

He was shaking his head. "This isn't good-bye. I need you to trust me. Can you please trust me? It's all going to be okay. I'll find my way back to you."

Seeing her look of fear, he gave her a slight shake. "I promise. I'll find my way back to you." He repeated. "Just remember, I love you. I always have and I always will. Until the end of time."

She clung to him, her heartache tearing him apart. For the first time in a long time, tears came to his eyes. Would he be able to make her go?

Suddenly the door swung open. Their sorry group turned to them, oblivious to the guns and their hostile demeanor, focused on what their presence there meant. Two men walked in followed by Spencer, his look smug.

"Break it up. Time to say good-bye Sam, oh boohoo! And I guess the mangy mutt goes with you. Then Shaw and I have a score to settle." His voice became brittle at the end, his hostility unmistakable.

Will gave her one more hug before turning to Prince. He hugged him too before telling him to take good care of Sam, softly adding as an afterthought, "I'll see you soon ole boy."

Standing before him, knowing it was time to go, she couldn't get her feet to move. Will went to her, taking her face in both hands and kissed her tenderly, but fiercely. "It's going to be okay. Sooner or later. I promise."

"The clock is ticking Shaw and I don't want to be on a sinking ship any longer than I have to be. Let's go Sam. Now or never!" Spencer dictated.

Reluctantly, Sam and Prince walked out, the two other goons escorting them to the deck of the yacht. Sobbing all the way up, Prince felt her heartbreak and stuck close to her. Turning to them, she asked how they were to get to the small motor boat anchored close by. Their smiles were hateful as one answered, "Jump."

Pushing the gun into her back, one announced. "There's a bomb on the boat and it's time to go. Jump already or we'll jump without you!"

"There's a bomb on the boat?" Sam asked fearfully. Suddenly she turned to head back the way they had come. "Will! I have to get Will!"

Prince growled as one of the goons stepped in her path. "It's our job to get you and the damn dog off the boat *before it blows!* So let's go bitch! I'm not getting blown up for your sorry ass!"

As the other goon grabbed her by the arm, he led her to the edge of the bow, the motorboat waiting for them. She cringed as he yelled, "Let's go!"

Suddenly Prince gave her a push just as there was a loud explosion behind them, debris flying everywhere around them. Screaming, Sam hit the water, quickly turning to see the yacht going up in an inferno. "Noooooo!" she screamed from the water. Struggling to stay afloat, she was oblivious to the boat nearby, focused on Will and knowing he was down in the hull of the yacht. As debris settled around her, she felt her arms and legs stop treading water, letting herself start to sink into the sea. She didn't fight it, her body going limp, ignoring her lungs as they screamed for air. Closing her eyes, she could only think of her loved ones.

Remember I love you.

I'll find my way back to you. I promise.

I didn't die just for you not to live your life.

Happy birthday Auntie Sami!

Suddenly she felt a nudge, pushing her back to the surface. Realizing it was Prince, she let him push her before choosing to take action to move to the top of the water, choosing to live. She could hear the motor boat in the distance while debris burned all around her. Grateful for Prince swimming beside her, she followed him to shore before she collapsed on the beach in exhaustion. She watched in horror as the yacht she had just been on ceased to exist. She hugged Prince to her, his whines piercing her broken heart.

As sirens came into her hearing, she realized her head was bleeding. Feeling dizzy, she lay her head on Prince, her sobs unmistakable. Her last thought was that Will would find his way to safety. Comforting herself, she told herself he had to. Afterall, he had promised her it would all be okay and she was going to hold him to it.

HOW THEY GOT THEIR HAPPY ENDING

CHAPTER TWENTY-THREE

Sam's birthday a year later

Sunday mornings were always tough for Sam, the day of rest allowing her thoughts to crowd in, forcing her to deal with her tormented heart. She still held onto the fact that Will would find his way back to her, but it was getting harder the longer it had been since that fateful day almost a year ago. Her trip to Italy had been a dream come true, experiencing the beauty of Naples and basking in the love she and Will had finally allowed themselves to feel. God she missed him, especially when she was in bed, remembering their bodies wrapped around each other. She had never felt safer or more loved than when he held her in his arms. She rolled over, finding Prince watching her, his head on his paws.

She greeted him the way she did every morning, rubbing his ears before she kissed him on the top of his head. "You're such a good boy Prince. What would I do without you?"

Wrestling the sheets off of her, she got up to go make her coffee and feed him, appreciating that he would wait his turn patiently. As her Keurig worked its magic, she pushed away the thought of the explosion, waking up in the hospital, and flying home without Will. She was grateful to Riley, who had flown to Italy to be by her side, providing reinforcements for Prince, who had refused to leave her, growling at anyone who tried to make him leave her. She appreciated that the hospital staff had shown them both compassion, allowing them to stay together.

Coming home without Will had been traumatic and she knew she was making allowances for Prince that he would never have agreed to. Their first night back in her loft, she had been unable to sleep until she had patted the empty bed beside her, desperate for Prince to be closer than the floor. That night she had laid her head on him and cried herself to sleep. He had slept beside her ever since and eventually she hadn't had to cry herself to sleep.

Riley and her family had been her lifeline, checking on her almost everyday in one way or another. Riley and her mom took turns bringing lunch to her, making sure she ate, needing to lay eyes on her to see for themselves how she was doing. Some days were better than others, but they all knew from losing Jorden, that was part of it. There was no way to avoid the pain, but to move through it one day at a time, doing the best you could.

Paws for a Cause was also her salvation. She extended her hours to Saturdays, grateful for the distraction her four legged friends provided her, their antics bringing smiles and laughter to her most days. Some of her customers were aware of her loss and tried their best to be there for her without overstepping the professional relationship they shared with Sam. One of her customers, a veterinarian himself, had brought her a copy of *Animal Wellness Magazine,* encouraging her to write an article about her holistic approach of adding touch therapy or massages to her grooming services.

As Prince ate heartily, she sipped her coffee, watching her neighborhood from her window. As she did everyday, she mentally made a list of five things she would get done today starting with final edits for her article before she would finally take the plunge and hit submit. She needed to shower too, knowing she was expected at her parent's home for birthday dinner. She sighed, just as happy to skip it, but knowing it would be good for her to go and embrace having made it through this hellish year. Tomorrow was actually her birthday, but she had promised to meet Rachel and Jen for dinner at Charlie's after work.

She had learned her lesson, shutting down about Jordan when he had died, and this time she surrounded herself with people who had known Will and would embrace her occasional stories about him. Her head tried to tell her grieving him was expected, but her heart refused to believe he wasn't coming back to her. Riley was the only one she had confided this certainty too and it had killed her to see the sympathy in Riley's eyes, knowing she didn't believe her. It wasn't lost on her she was the epitome of living with one foot in the past and one tentatively in the future.

She went to her kitchen, pulling out the drawer that held her ray of hope, her lifeline that Will was still out there, that he would find his way back to her like he had promised. The card had come with a beautiful arrangement of flowers and simply said, *He will be found when he's ready.* She had caught her breath, remembering a conversation with Aria the day before the explosion. Did she know where he was? Tears had filled her eyes that day, needing this little sliver of hope to keep her moving forward. She had shown it only to Prince, telling him his daddy could come home to them any day now. That had been months ago, and Sam was growing weary of believing in something that was starting to feel highly unlikely.

Before Sam had flown home from Naples, Elisa had come to see her at the hospital. She had been devastated, holding Sam to her as they cried together, their lives now connected forever over their mutual love for Will. She reached out to Sam regularly to check on her as they marked each monthly anniversary. After getting the card and flowers, Sam had asked about Aria, curious if she knew anything about her special delivery. She didn't know how to contact Aria and something told her to keep the card to herself.

Settling into her couch, she pulled her laptop to her, ready to reread her article one last time. She was annoyed to find the battery was basically dead and realized her charger was downstairs in *Paws for a Cause*. Pulling on some jeans and a t-shirt, she padded down the stairs to retrieve it. About to head back up, she was startled when there was a knock on her door. She looked at Prince expecting his usual low growl, but instead he stood at attention, wagging his tail.

"Really Prince? I must be making you soft. What would your daddy say about that?" she asked him, getting her key, prepared to unlock the deadbolt to her door if warranted.

Shaking her head at the stranger, she announced loudly she was closed. Holding a newspaper up, he explained he was interested in the loft she had listed for rent. Nodding she unlocked the door, stepping aside for him to enter. They were both shocked when Prince made a dash to him, putting his paws on the man's chest, his tail wagging furiously, whining an excited greeting.

"Prince! Sit!" she said sharply to the German Shepherd. "I'm so sorry! He never does this!" she said, bending down to take him by his collar and move him away from the man.

Pushing his shades up, he laughed. "It's all good. I had a dog once." She watched him as something clearly dawned on him and changed his expression. He repeated softly to himself *I had a dog once* before quickly shutting it down.

Turning to face her head on, he held up the paper, her ad circled in black ink. "About the loft. Have you rented it out yet?"

She was dumbfounded to look at him. He looked like Will, but was clean shaven and had a large scar over his left eye. "No, it's still available. What did you say your name is?" she asked.

"William. William Shaw." he said, holding his hand out to her to shake.

Seeing the color drain from her face, he paused his hand before dropping it back to his side.

"Do you know me?" he asked tentatively.

Finding her voice, Sam stammered out. "You look like someone I used to know. Do you know me?" she asked, her heart in her mouth.

She nearly fell to her knees when he put his hand up to rub the back of his head. "Actually I don't. But maybe I did once upon a time. You would think I would remember a girl as pretty as you, but I don't. I'm sorry."

She could see he was struggling as much as she was. "It's okay." she said softly.

Grateful to her for letting him off the hook, he felt compelled to give her a brief explanation. "I was in an accident and I'm still suffering from amnesia."

She tried to look away, but couldn't. "I see. That must be hard."

He shrugged. "It's been almost a year, so I've gotten used to it. I was pretty badly injured so my recovery has been slow." Looking at her, he said quietly. "You're the first person to seem like they know me. It's more unnerving than I imagined it would be. I take it we were friends?"

Letting Prince go, she nodded. "Something like that. You were my brother's best friend."

He paused briefly, taking it in as quickly as he let it go. "So can I see the loft? Or would this be weird?" When she didn't respond he pressed on. "I just feel really drawn to this neighborhood, this building even and I'm hoping to be able to continue recovering my memories from a place like yours." He was looking at her expectantly and suddenly she smiled, taking his breath away.

"It wouldn't be weird at all." She lied. "Let's go take a look and see if the space will work for you."

She went to her desk to retrieve the key before leading him to the stairs, the potential loft right above hers. Swinging the door open to him, she stepped aside to let him take in the space for himself. Going to the large window, he looked out over the neighborhood before turning to her thoughtfully. "I've spent time in this building haven't I?"

She could only nod, her voice failing her again. They both laughed when Prince gave a short, but friendly bark, answering for her.

Going to him, he bent down to rub his ears and under his chin. "That must be why you know me so well! What's his name?" he asked, looking up at her, his eyes warm.

"Prince." she answered.

"Well Prince, it's going to be good to get to know you again." He turned to Sam. "I'll take it. Just let me know when I can move in. I don't really have much. Just clothes and a picture of my parents someone left for me at the hospital. I guess I'll need to get new furniture. Live like a grown-up, not some college kid." He said with a smile.

Sam's head was swimming. Was this really happening? Had Will found his way back to her somehow after all these months? She worked hard to keep the emotion out of her voice as they headed back downstairs, focusing on procedural things instead such as filling out the lease, paying first months rent and deposit etc.

They were finishing up, Will ready to begin his lease immediately when his face became serious. "There's just one more thing. My doctor says my amnesia is most likely dissociative, causing my mind to block traumatic memories as well as any good memories I had. I'm not trying to go back, but I want to keep moving forward. I want to find my old memories organically, not look at photos or have someone tell them to me. Does that make sense?"

Nodding, Sam hedged her own revelation. "I get that. I happen to know your stuff is still in storage. And when I say stuff, I mean furniture and clothes. Not really any personal mementos, no knick knacks. Do you want your old stuff?"

She watched his face as he thought it over. Finally he took a deep breath and answered with a shrug. "Sure. Can you give me the address?"

Finding a post-it on her desk, she quickly jotted it down before handing it to him. "Let me know if you need anything else. You know where to find me."

As he turned to go, she called out to him. "And Will. Welcome back to the neighborhood." She said, giving him a big smile.

Returning her smile, he said softly. "Thanks. It feels good to be here."

She got to her parents home early, wanting to steal her sister away for a quick walk around the block before dinner. She was busting to tell someone her news, still finding it hard to believe. Riley was astonished to see Sam greet her children with more energy and warmth than she had in a long time. She agreed curiously when Sam requested she join her for a walk around the block.

Looking at her eager face, she couldn't help but smile. "What's up? Did you win the lottery?"

"Better than that!" she said excitedly. Linking her arm through Riley's, she was all smiles as she announced "Will's back!"

Riley stopped dead in her tracks. "What?! How is that possible?"

Pulling her along, Sam spilled how he had stopped in to inquire about the loft open for renting. She shared how Prince had gone nuts over him, how he looked different with his beard gone and a large scar over one eye.

"So just like that you're back together?" Riley asked, still stunned by this news.

Here Sam faltered, hesitating as to how to best explain it. "Not exactly. He's suffering from amnesia and doesn't remember me. Or Prince."

Again Riley stopped. "Amnesia? That has to hurt Sam."

Turning to her big sister, she suddenly let her emotions run free. Nodding at her, she agreed. "It was shocking and disappointing. He suffered serious injuries including one to the head I guess."

"So did you *tell him* who you were?" she asked gently.

She shook her head miserably. "I can't. He let me know he's not living in the past but only moving forward. He wants to find his memories in his own way, at his own pace. No pictures, no stories."

"Oh Sam. I'm happy that you have him back, but that's going to be so hard to ignore the history you two have." Riley was sympathetic, hugging her little sister, knowing this news was a double-edged sword.

"I just want to wrap my arms around him and tell him how much I missed him, but I can't. I want to honor his wishes." Her eyes were full of tears. "He found his way back to me physically, I just have to believe he will emotionally too. Even if it's different, it's better than nothing at all. Right?"

"Right! Keep your faith Sam. What's meant to be, will be. If anyone has the patience for this, it's you." Squeezing her hands, she suddenly said, "Oh my god Sam he found his way back to you! It's all going to work out."

Nodding furiously, she agreed. "Just like he promised. I just have to trust him that it will all be okay." Heading into her parents home with Riley, she realized she had no other choice but to believe her own words and trust him.

CHAPTER TWENTY-FOUR

Not in a million years could anything have prepared Sam for how hard this would be. She thought the friend zone had been frustrating, but now it almost felt like they were strangers again. Maybe because they were. It had been a month since he moved in and she saw him almost daily, always working hard to keep their conversation light and impersonal, per his request. Her emotions were a rollercoaster, ranging from the joy of a smile he would bring to her face with something he said to absolute despair at the thought they would never lay in bed naked together again. To go from such an intimate loving relationship to near strangers was a new personal low for her and she worried she had made a mistake letting him be so close, his presence in her face and yet off the table.

She tried to focus on work and found herself at Charlie's most nights, needing not to be home and hear him moving around above her loft, obsessing about what he might be doing. One night, after a long day, she was dismayed to find Will already sitting at the bar. She realized with a jerk he was even in his usual spot, the barstool beside him open like always. She almost turned to run, but Frankie had spotted her and waved her over.

Pouring her usual glass of Pinot Grigio, Sam thanked Frankie. Having exchanged greetings with Will she ordered her pimento cheeseburger and added a shot of tequila as an afterthought. She ignored both of them questioning her life choices, squeezing her lime before throwing it back. Watching her, Will asked sympathetically. "Tough day?"

Nodding, Sam kept her thoughts to herself. *Tough day, tough month, tough year.* "One of my clients got diagnosed with cancer and it's a little triggering because I had another client with cancer. He didn't make it."

She stiffened slightly to suddenly feel Will's hand on her back. "I'm sorry to hear that. I know how much you love your pups. That's got to be tough."

Taking a sip of her wine for courage, she looked at him. "It really is. I feel like I'm the fun aunt, they're all my kids. I get attached."

"I get it. I can tell you have a big heart. How long have you had Prince?" he suddenly asked.

She froze, unsure of what to say. "A friend gave him to me." she finally mumbled.

He was quiet before finally asking. "He was mine, wasn't he? That's how we met? Through *Paws for a Cause?*"

She nodded numbly, not sure how much he wanted her to say. It seemed pointless to remind him he had known her years ago as her brother's best friend, but yes, that was how they had reconnected years later. And boy had they connected. God she missed him so much even as he sat right in front of her.

"I can tell he adores you. I'm glad you have each other." he said, putting his hand over hers.

Instantly she was on fire and it annoyed her to no end to think he didn't feel the heat between them. Actually, check that, it hurt like hell.

Signaling to Frankie for another shot, she was shocked when Will added, "Make that two!"

He watched her curiously as she squeezed her lime into her shot before turning towards him. "Cheers!" she said with false bravado.

She watched him throw his back, shaking his head before turning back to her. "I don't really drink, but I feel like we've done that before."

Her heart stopped, not sure if he was asking her a question or making a statement. Not even thinking about it, she instantly regretted her flip answer. "Yep, we have and yeah you just drink beer, two at the most."

Giving him side-eye, she could feel his eyes on her. "I know we're not strangers Sam. I can feel it. It's okay to share."

For the first time in a month she felt hope. "Yeah?" she asked cautiously. "I wasn't sure if you were cool with that."

"I don't want a trip down memory lane, but we're in the moment. I need this as much as you do." His voice was quiet, his look melting her.

Instantly she regretted her shots mixed with her near empty glass of wine, struggling greatly to keep her emotions in check. "Okay." she said with a smile. Thankfully Frankie chose that minute to set two plates of food down in front of the two of them. She couldn't help but notice he had ordered a pimento cheeseburger and fries too. She sighed, realizing how good it felt to be like their old selves just for a minute, even if they were far from it.

A couple of hours passed, Sam sipping her second glass of wine, taking her time and skipping the urge for more shots. They talked about a variety of things, before Sam asked innocently, "So what do you like to do for fun? Besides cheeseburgers and tequila shots?"

"I'm not sure. I'm open to suggestions. What do you like to do?" he asked, his curiosity sincere.

"Well. I work six days a week. I live for getting to this particular barstool before anyone else, and I love to hang out with my family and friends when I get the chance. They're all about their kids, so it's more when they can fit me in."

He was watching her. "But what are your interests? Don't people like doing stuff by themselves too?" Seeing her eye him skeptically, he clarified. "You know books, music, movies, sports. Take your pick."

Her face suddenly brightened. "Actually I have quite the record collection and, thanks to my grandmother, quite a collection of books.

Although I personally struggle to sit still long enough to read three hundred pages." She added as an afterthought, "And I live for my runs. Prince loves to go with me. It's how we usually start our day, followed by a strong cup of coffee."

He was nodding at her. "I've noticed you guys head out in the mornings. You get an early start."

She was startled to hear this and on impulse invited him. "You're welcome to join us if that ever seems like something you want to do." She kept it to herself how she had thought he was creeping on her before he had come into *Paws for a Cause*, eventually realizing he actually lived in her neighborhood.

"I'm not sure you want me to take you up on that. Running seems like a lot of effort. I might not be any good and I would hate to hold you back. You seem pretty serious about it." She tried to keep her smile to herself, enjoying that he was aware of her and her routines too. "What kind of music do you like to listen to?"

She stared at him recalling an invitation years ago he had declined. "Do you mean when I run? Or my record collection?"

He smiled, her heart skipping a beat when he clarified. "Your record collection. I would love to check it out sometime. I seem to be in the market for some new hobbies."

She checked in with Frankie, knowing she looked busy drying a glass, but clearly aware of their conversation. Glancing at Sam, she gave her an encouraging nod. "Do you mean like now? Or another night?" she asked cautiously.

"How about now? Unless it's getting too late?" he added hastily. In no time their bill was paid and they were walking home together. Sam closed her eyes, reminded of the many times they had done this in the past. It felt the same and yet different, but maybe it would be okay.

Prince was excited to see them both, making a fuss over Will as only a dog can get away with. She hated to admit it, but she wished she could throw herself at Will too and get some attention herself. One step at a time she told herself.

Turning to him, she offered something to drink. When he declined, she went to fill her water bottle. Standing at the sink, she watched him as he explored her shelves, pausing to take in the many photos that were mixed in with her grandmother's extensive book collection. Finally he turned to her.

She could see the emotion on his face. "You're lucky to have all this family, all these memories. What happened to Jordan?"

She was startled to hear him say his name. Had she said it somewhere along the way without realizing it? Or were the photos triggering a memory of him? Seeing her face, he clarified for her.

"You said his name earlier when you were talking about your family. I assumed he was your brother, the one that was my best friend growing up. I could tell by your voice something happened to him. But we don't have to talk about it if you don't want to." His eyes were warm on hers.

"He was killed when his car exploded seven years ago." Her voice was low, her explanation brief. Shaking it off she went to retrieve her wine crate of albums.

They sat on the floor, the three of them, the crate in the middle. She had turned it towards Will, inviting him to look through and see if there was anything he wanted to listen to. "Do you actually listen to these?"

She shrugged. "I go in cycles. They become part of my routines and I listen to certain albums over and over. Then I'll move back to my playlists on my phone."

He nodded, seeming to understand. "You have a lot of Imagine Dragons. These were Jordan's, weren't they?"

She held her breath, her voice quiet. "They were. He was obsessed."

Holding out *Night Visions* to her, he asked her to play it. Quickly she got up to go put it on her record player. "Can you skip to *Demons*?"

They sat in silence, listening to the words together. Sam tried not to stare at him, but she could see he was somewhere else, far away from her. The mood was broken when the next song came on, but she waited for him to speak first.

"Do you have any beer?" he asked suddenly.

"I'm not sure." she said, jumping up to check. She was shocked to find one lonely Budweiser at the bottom, all the way at the back of her fridge.

Handing it to him, she apologized. "It's been there for a while. Does beer go bad?"

He looked at her, thinking about her statement. "What's a while?"

She couldn't look at him directly. "It's been more than a year." she stammered out.

"Do you have any tequila?" he asked, handing the beer back to her.

"Only the best tequila." she said, getting her bottle of Don Julio and two shot glasses. Pouring them each a cautious amount, she handed Will his shot, tapping her glass to his before throwing it back.

She cringed, having no limes in her loft to soften the bite. She took his glass from him, setting them and the bottle on her coffee table. Turning to him, she wanted to say something helpful or witty or anything that could bring him back to her.

"This music takes me back. Jordan and I had a lot of good times growing up, didn't we?" Will finally said, his eyes on the record album he had picked up.

Nodding, Sam was somber. "You did. You were the brother he always wanted."

He turned to her, his face still deep in thought. "Jordan had so many friends. I never could understand why he picked me to be his best friend."

On impulse Sam took his hand. "You were a great kid! My whole family loved you."

His look on her became intense. "Except for you. Jordan always told me he was your hero and you weren't very good at sharing."

Sam stared at him, shocked by his admission. She never had given him the time of day, always dismissive of his presence in their house. Was that really the reason why? She was jealous of what Will shared with Jordan. "Huh. I never thought of it like that before. I guess I was a bigger brat than I remember." she joked.

Suddenly her face turned serious again. "He was my hero though. My whole family is actually. It hurt like hell when we lost him."

She had forgotten she was holding his hand, until he squeezed it. "I know."

She looked at him, feeling the heat in her hand, but also his look. "Do you remember being in my house? My family?" she asked, crossing her fingers.

"It's more of a feeling than specific things. I know your family was very good to me. That must be why I feel so drawn to you." he shared.

She tried to keep her face neutral, not wanting him to see her hurt. As the record came to an end, she jumped up. "That makes sense. It's getting late. I have a long day tomorrow."

Putting the album back in its jacket, she moved to put it back with the other records. She stopped in dismay to see he had found *Luna Sea* by Firefall.

"You have a lot of seventies soft rock in here. Maybe next time we can listen to this one? I feel like I know it too." He said, holding it out to her.

Taking it from him she tried not to snatch it, telling herself to just breathe. "Sure." she said, walking him to her door, Prince following them.

He paused before opening her door, his look intense. "Thanks for a great night Sam. It's good to finally feel connected to something, to someone. I needed it more than you know. I appreciate how patient you're being with me. Don't give up on me, okay? I'll get there."

She willed herself to not cry, to hold her tears. "I'm glad to help." Seeing him watching her, she said what she knew he needed to hear. "And don't worry. I could never give up on you Will." *Because I love you.*

She was shocked when he leaned in and kissed the top of her head.

'Thank you. I'll see you later. Night Prince." and he was gone.

Closing her door, she leaned against it before letting herself slide down it to the floor. Sitting with her head in her hands, she let it all out, her sobs racking her body. Prince came to lay beside her, his head in her lap, whining softly. She didn't have to explain it to him and doubted if she could, but she knew Prince got it. It didn't help, but it was something.

Reluctantly she got up in search of a tissue. Flipping the bathroom light on, she looked at herself hard in the mirror. Was she being a brat now, all these years later? Prince woofed softly beside her, clearly disagreeing with her. Turning to him and his watchful eyes, she bent down to kiss him on the head like she often did. "Thanks Prince. I needed that."

Standing up, she was struck by an epiphany. She had just received a kiss to her head just as she had given one to Prince. Her smile grew slowly as she realized both had been given with *love.* Somewhere in there, down deep Will still loved her. She thought about Elisa asking her not to give up on him when they had stood together in her kitchen that day.

She thought about Will thanking her for making a connection with her tonight, how much he had needed it. She thought about how sad he had looked while perusing her family photos. She was suddenly struck by how lonely Will must be, trying to find himself. On some level it had to be scary to think of what and when the trauma in his life might rear its ugly head. But at the same time, would he be able to find his memories and who he was without activating the bad things too? She knew Will had had a lot of hard things happen in his life but had never really thought about the toll it had taken on him.

"I am a brat!" she told herself in the mirror. She had been acting like this had happened to her, like how would she ever get through it?

The truth was it had happened to both of them and it was fucking hard, but denying it didn't serve either one of them well. She needed to give herself grace, but also think about how she could help Will find himself. She needed a plan and knew just the right person to help her. Riley!

CHAPTER TWENTY-FIVE

Her loft smelled amazing, the tomato sauce simmering on low, the smell of garlic and onions unmistakable. Her bucatini bubbled in its pot while the garlic bread was sliced and slathered with garlic butter, ready to be toasted in the oven. She checked her watch, going to the window to see if Will was headed back from the gym yet, nervous to intercept him but having faith in round one of the plan she had hatched with Riley a few days ago. She could hear Riley in her head. *Be patient, let him come to you.* She grimaced at the thought, knowing it wasn't her strong suit.

Busy giving her sauce a quick stir, she jumped when there was a knock at her door. Peeking through her peep hole, she was surprised to see Will standing before her.

Opening her door with a smile, she asked, "Hey! What's up?"

Dramatically Will took a deep breath, his eyes closed, a smile on his face. "I don't know what you're cooking in there but I think it's only fair to warn you that your table will need to be set for two!" Suddenly his face changed. "Unless this is date night for you? I wouldn't want to interrupt that."

"Aww that's funny you think I have time for dating! Actually with the cool weather, I was craving comfort food and decided to cook for myself. I would be happy to have you join me." She cocked her head to one side, fairly certain of his response.

It took her breath away to watch his face light up. "Yeah? Great! Let me shower and I'll be back down in ten."

"No rush, the bread still needs to be toasted!" She called after him, watching him take the steps two at a time.

True to his word, he was back at her door in ten minutes. She called out "It's open!" when he knocked, letting Prince be the welcoming committee. Putting the bread in the oven, she turned to him expectantly.

She had forgotten how good he looked when his curly hair was wet or how good he could smell fresh out of the shower.

Seeing her look, he offered. "I found some new products I thought I would give a try." She nearly came undone when he came to lean into her. "What do you think? How do I smell?"

She kept her voice light. "Very nice." She was stunned to realize it was what he had always worn. Before.

Soon they were seated at her table with hot steaming plates of pasta, the bread crusty on the outside but warm and buttery in the middle, the caesar salad crisp. She kept the conversation going, sharing the latest shenanigans of her four legged clients.

She was rewarded with smiles but was taken aback when his look turned serious. "I really appreciate you letting me crash dinner Sam. It's been a minute since I had a home cooked meal. Not that I gave you much of a choice." he added with a depreciating laugh.

Nodding she responded with "Of course. To be honest, I was thinking about inviting you for dinner, but, but I didn't want to overstep." Seeing the look he was giving her, she added lightly. "Clearly I cooked enough for an army, so I'm happy to share it with someone."

His stare made her squirm, not sure how to read it. She was thankful when he moved on. "Where did you learn to cook like this?" he asked.

She paused to collect herself, hoping he would ask, but not expecting it to trigger her. *From our Italian grandmothers.*

"From my grandmother. When she got cancer, I moved in to help take care of her. I was never much of a cook so we spent time together here, in her kitchen while she taught me all her secrets for success. She was Italian and quite the cook."

He was watching her, thinking about her story. "It must have been hard to lose her, but it's special that you have these recipes you shared with her. Did she use any secret ingredients?"

She hesitated before looking at him with a small smile. "Love. Sounds corny, I know, but that's what she always told me."

Nodding, Will looked thoughtful. "I think my granny used to say that too." The revelation struck them both at the same time. "So I had a granny?" he asked, looking to her for confirmation. When she nodded he added, "I don't think she was a great cook though." He shrugged, not getting hung up on it. Following his lead, she let it go too.

They had cleaned up, their bellies full, but she could tell Prince needed to go out. Apologizing, she told Will she would be right back if he wanted to stick around. Instead, he suggested they all go for a walk, mentioning a cool diner he had found nearby a week ago.

"I've heard they have a great bakery. How about I buy dessert since you cooked that great meal? Coconut cake's on their menu and for some reason I feel the need to try it. Do you like coconut?"

Pulling her coat tighter around herself, she could only say, "I love coconut." Realizing her favorite server would be behind the counter, she prepared herself that this could get interesting.

As expected, Rosie greeted them loudly. "Sam! Back so soon luv? How was your pasta? Oooh is this the young man you cooked for?" She turned to Will, focused on him like a moth to a flame. "How'd she do hon? Did she do her nana proud?"

She gave Will credit, watching him speak up, not missing a beat. "Absolutely Nana would have been proud. It was so good that we needed a walk and here we are, ready for dessert. We'll take two pieces of your coconut cake, to go please."

"Sure thing hon. Let me get that for you two."

They were headed home in no time, Will walking Prince and Sam carrying the sack full of their sweet treat. She waited, letting him get to it when he was ready.

"I should have known you'd been there before." he said ruefully.

She nodded, "Yeah Empire is kind of the neighborhood jewel. I get take out from there at least once a week. Everything they have is good."

"So, have I had this coconut cake before?" he asked bluntly.

She paused just briefly, focused on the sidewalk. "Actually yes, a bite. A couple of times you got it for me on my birthday. Like I said, I love coconut." She kept it to herself that he had never been one to eat sweets. Or that she ate it only on her birthday.

"I take it we hung out a lot?" he asked, his eyes on her.

She smiled, keeping her answer brief. "Something like that." It felt natural for them to walk into her loft together, Will going to hang up Prince's leash while she got out forks and poured herself a glass of milk. Together they sat on the couch, their anticipation great. She took equal parts caramelized fruit with a bite of cake, showing Will how it was done.

Savoring hers, she watched his face knowing he was not having the same feeling of happy taste buds. "Well? What do you think?" she asked, having a pretty good idea of what he would say.

Putting the plate down, he drank heartily from his water bottle. "It's not that it tastes bad, I'm just not big on sweets."

She laughed, not able to help herself. "That's exactly what you said the first time you tried it."

He smiled at her wryly. "Well thanks for letting me rediscover that for myself."

She smiled at him, her voice teasing. "No problem. It just means more cake for me! It's great cold for breakfast too."

Startled, he asked in disbelief. "You put that in your body after a run?"

Still teasing him, she shook her head. "Tsk, tsk, this is a judge free zone! You're the one who wanted cake after eating two plates of pasta! Did I shame you for that or support you whole-heartedly?"

He laughed at her, his smile lopsided. "You're right. You were all in. But you gotta make sure if I'm about to do something stupid, you call me on it. Deal?"

"I don't know. Stupid can be fun. If it's the right kind of stupid." She smiled at him wickedly, not letting him off the hook.

He shook his head at her. "You always were such a smartass."

Her breath caught. Was he remembering her? Seeing her face, he picked up her hand and squeezed it. Suddenly he stood up, headed to her door. "I have an early morning. I'm going to try going for a run. So if you see me and I don't see you, just know I'm focused on my breathing. Okay?"

She nodded with a small smile. "Got it."

He was almost out her door when he turned back. "Hey Sam. Did we date? Or just hang out?"

She could tell he really wanted to know. "We never went on a date. We went places together, but it was pretty casual."

He put his hand to his head, rubbing the back of it like he did when he was thinking. "Is it because you were Jordan's little sister? Did Jordan not want me to go out with you?"

She was shaking her head, not sure what he wanted to hear. "First of all, Jordan was never the boss of me. Second, I was a teenager when you moved away. Jordan was gone when we reconnected."

"I moved away? Why?" he asked, his look earnest.

She held her breath, hoping she was doing the right thing in telling him. "You joined the Navy." *After one epic kiss on my seventeenth birthday.*

He nodded, not seeming to be surprised. "So would you want to go out on a date? With me? Next week?" he asked, his voice tentative, like he was worried she might say no.

"I would love to, but Thanksgiving is next week. Why don't you come with me to my family Thanksgiving?" she asked. She didn't have the heart to tell him she would be spending most of the long weekend with her family as they rolled Thanksgiving into the Christmas season.

He was shaking his head. "No, sorry, I'm not ready for that. How about we go out the week after?"

Nodding, she announced, "It's a date! Just let me know when and where."

Shaking his head, he let her know he wanted to surprise her, but to plan on the first Saturday in December. Having said good-night, she texted Riley. *Cooking dinner went well! We're going on a date after Thanksgiving."*

Getting ready for bed, she was grateful for their evening together. She felt like he learned some things about himself and even them for that matter. She was curious to see what he would plan for a first date. Laying in bed, she realized she and Will had jumped from being professional friends to sleeping together, although to be fair, that jump had literally taken years to solidify. Maybe this would be a good thing, starting from the beginning and taking time to date. She sighed, ready to end her day as she always did, counting five things she was grateful for today. Her piece of coconut cake was up there, along with not messing up her bucatini and Will asking her out on a date. She was asleep before she could get to five things, her heart already full.

Thanksgiving morning, Sam had texted Will to see if Prince could hang with him for a few days. She hated the idea of him being alone and knew that Prince was always good company. Even though Will had declined to join her family for Thanksgiving, she had fixed him a plate and brought it to him late that night, having promised him all the fixings. He had been more than appreciative and when he patted his black leather couch for her to join him, she had willingly done so. He was just finishing up Home Alone and was about to start Home Alone 2:

Lost in New York, telling her he couldn't remember ever seeing either of the movies. As they watched the movie, he had made a mental note of her reaction to The Plaza Hotel, still struggling to figure out a perfect date night.

A week later, it was finally date night and Sam had ripped every dress out of her closet, unable to make a decision about what to wear. In desperation she facetimed Riley who didn't hesitate to remind her of the green sweater dress she had gotten her a few Christmases back, telling her that it would be perfect paired with her tall boots. Sam knew the one she meant, but worried about how it fit her. Finally exasperated with her flimsy excuses why not to wear it, Riley came right out and told her it was okay to wear something that hugged her curves and made her look like a woman. In fact, it might just be what the doctor ordered. Her last piece of advice was not to throw herself at him, but let him come to her.

Following Riley's suggestion, Sam pulled out the dress knowing she had already tried it on multiple times, struggling with how to keep her cleavage contained in the wrap around dress. Looking in the mirror she realized she would have relished wearing this for the old Will, but things were different now and she didn't know if she would survive just a kiss on the top of her head at the end of the night when she looked like this. Sighing heavily, she started her playlist, while she got her makeup on and did her hair. She finished her last curl just as she heard Prince go to the door, announcing Will's arrival before he even knocked.

She had been so focused on what she was going to wear that she hadn't given much thought to what Will would be wearing, finding herself unprepared for how good he looked in his sports jacket over a white button up shirt. As they both stood taking in the other, she realized his attraction to her still ran deep.

Giving him a big smile, she started with "Hi."

She could see she had his full attention as he struggled to find words. "Wow Sam. You look stunning!" She could feel the old Will come out as his eyes moved over her, taking in her curves, pausing at her cleavage, before finally resting on her lips.

"Thank you. You look pretty good yourself. Shall we go?" she asked, putting her arms through her cape and pulling the fur collar up around her.

In no time their Uber had deposited them in front of The Plaza Hotel. Stopped on the steps by the doorman, Will was quick to announce they had reservations for drinks in the Champagne Bar. After finding his name on the list, he was happy to go and open the door for them.

Letting her take it all in, he watched as she soaked up the glamorous ambience, even more glitzy with the holiday decor. Putting his hand on her elbow, he guided her to the left, where they found themselves quickly escorted up an ornate staircase, seated at a table for two overlooking the gorgeous lower level.

Turning to Will, Sam was all smiles. "I've always wanted to come here! Every year when I watch Home Alone 2, I tell myself I need to come here!"

Will was smiling too, clearly pleased with himself. "I know."

She paused. "You know? How?"

"When we were watching the movie Thanksgiving night. I could tell. Order anything you want to drink. And eat. I hope you don't mind, this is where we're having dinner too, but it's not our final destination."

Ordering a French 75, she deferred to Will whether to order an appetizer or not, although in the end, they ordered truffle fries and The Plaza Wagyu burgers. Sam was trying to play it cool, but had to admit it felt pretty good to be wined and dined in so much style.

It was a quick Uber ride to their next destination, a large church on the upper east side with gorgeous stained glass windows. Sam was in awe as they walked into an intimate room, seemingly lit by hundreds of candles.

"What is this place?" she asked.

"We're here for a Candlelight Concert. Tonight a string quartet will play songs for us from Imagine Dragons and Coldplay. How does that sound?" he asked her.

"That sounds amazing!" she said, taking his arm and hugging it towards her. "You're spoiling me Will!"

Finding their seats, she shimmied out of her cape, before hurriedly readjusting the top of her dress. "I'm enjoying the view, don't adjust on my account." Will said, leaning into her ear.

Laughing, she said, "Wow. That seems familiar!" Too late, she wished she could take it back.

Will's eyes were intense on her. "So that's how we hung out."

She nudged him with a small smile. "There was more to it than that. It was complicated."

Thankfully the house lights went down, and the musicians were introducing themselves. Sam was immediately hooked as they chose to start with Coldplay's Clocks. She was touched by the quartet's rendition of songs she knew and loved, the glow of the candles making it that much more special. She could feel herself relaxing, letting the agony of the past year get swept away for the night. Glancing at Will, she could only hope he felt it too. Instinctively she laid her head on his shoulder, smiling when he found her hand and brought it to his lips, kissing it lightly.

Too soon they were standing at her door, having to face getting back to reality. Hearing Prince breathing under her door, she quickly turned to unlock it. Having left only one small lamp on, the room was dim as she closed her door behind them.Turning back to Will, she felt the heat rise as he moved in very close to her, his arm on the door over her head.

"Did you have a good first date Sam?" he asked, his eyes focused on her lips. She nodded, her heart pounding so hard she was sure he could hear it.

"It was a magical night. Thank you Will. You outdid yourself." she said, reflexively moving her hands to his hips.

He smiled, taking her chin in his free hand. "Can I kiss you Sam?"

She could only nod, closing her eyes as his lips slowly descended on hers. His lips were hungry for her, sweeping her mouth urgently, until abruptly he stopped and pulled away to look at her. Taking her face in both hands, he brought his lips back to hers but this time with such sweet tenderness, that tears came to her eyes. God how she had missed his lips on hers. This time when he released her, he quickly pulled her into him, burying his head in her shoulder and hugging her fiercely. She could feel he was hard against her, but didn't move, afraid she would scare him away. *Let him come to you.*

Moaning he finally pulled away, taking her hands in his. "God, you know I want you so much. There's nothing I want more than to untie this dress and get you out of it." Even as he said it, he was tracing the V of her neckline, letting his finger linger between her breasts.

Still, she could feel him shifting away from her. "But." she said.

"But, I feel like our relationship before was mostly about sex. I can only imagine it was really good sex. I don't want to mess this up for either of us this time. You said it was complicated and I don't want us to be like that. I care about you so much and I can't lose anything else in my life. I want to do this right and build something that will last. Forever." He had leaned his forehead into hers, his voice emotional.

"Can you please keep being patient with me Sam?" he asked.

She wanted to promise yes, but her body was screaming NO! I need you now! All she could do was nod, not able to find her voice. He kissed her on the cheek, kissed her hand, and was gone.

She didn't know what to do. She knew what he said made sense. He was right, their relationship had started on a strong attraction neither of them had been able to resist. Tonight had been a beautiful night and she was going to have to accept it for what it was. She reminded herself, he hadn't rejected her, he just needed more time. Untying her own damn dress, she threw it in the chair nearby, before climbing into bed. Closing her eyes, she imagined him in bed with her, their bodies wrapped around each other.

Sweet dreams Sam, sweet dreams.

CHAPTER TWENTY-SIX

Checking her weather app one more time, Sam smiled to herself to see the winter storm warning posted. Heavy snow was likely to start after midnight with gusty winds lending itself to white out conditions, followed by dangerously cold temps. She wasn't much of a winter weather lover, but she did love the thought of having a few days all cozy and hunkered down in her loft. The true indicator of how bad the storm would be was predicted by the number of messages her family members had bestowed upon her in the past thirty minutes.

"Hey Peanut, it's dad. Make sure you have batteries and extra water and flashlights ready to go. Keep your phone charged. Never know when the city might lose power. Love ya kiddo! Be safe!"

"Hey Sam, it's mom. Why don't you just come home for a couple of days so you're not all alone during the storm. We can watch movies and make chocolate chip cookies. It'll be fun. Let me know. Love you!"

She saved Riley's text for last, knowing it would be the best choice of the three. "Hey Sami! I'm sure the folks have already reached out, so here's plan C. Come hang out with us for a couple of days. I will pay you in wine to play with the twins! C'mon! You know you want to! Hit me back."

Smiling ear to ear, Sam felt lucky to have a family who loved her so much. All the same, thank you, no thank you. Having texted them all back with hearts and kissy emoji's, she picked up her phone when it pinged again.

"Is this storm for real? Should we go get stuff? Dog food? I'll prolly head out in ten if you want to go together."

Now this was a text she could get behind, thank you very much Will. "Sounds good. I'll be ready."

Will looked like a deer in the headlights as they moved through Target, filling her cart up with enough goodies to survive three blizzards. "Is the whole fricken neighborhood here or what?" he asked grumpily.

Sam moved through the crowd like a professional, smiling pleasantly while her eyes said stay out of my way. She had made a beeline for the books first, excited to find the last copy of Taylor Jenkins Reid's *Atmosphere*. Will followed along behind her, occasionally throwing his own things in the cart. She checked her list, having also secured the last bag of chocolate chips. Satisfied they had everything they would need to survive the storm, she headed for the checkout.

"You look a little too excited to be standing in this line." Will said.

Shrugging, she informed him, "I don't mind. It's worth it to have a free three day weekend. My clients are rescheduled and I've got nothing planned but reading my book and baking cookies." Suddenly she remembered. "Oh shoot! I need more wine! I'll be right back! Stay in line with the cart."

Taking a firm grip on the cart handle, he focused on moving with the line, slowly but surely. He was relieved when Sam finally returned, carrying her wine like they were trophies.

"Sorry! I saw Frankie in the wine aisle and we were chatting. I got all my favorites. We are in great shape for this storm!"

Having finally reached the cashier, Sam went to pull her debit card out of her back pocket, before realizing the cashier had already swiped Will's card. He shrugged when she said she would Venmo him, curious if he even knew what that was. Carefully she secured the wine in her oversized bag she had brought, cushioning it with toilet paper, her book and the chocolate chips.

Somewhat amused, Will couldn't help but ask, "Wow, you really protect your favorites don't you?"

It had been a chore, but they had managed to lug all the sacks home stopping only one time for Sam to shift her wine bag to her other shoulder. Now the bags sat all over her table, as she pulled out stuff to put away. Handing Will his bag, she announced she would be ready to head out in twenty minutes.

"Head out where?" he asked worriedly.

"It's Thursday. We always go to Charlie's on Thursday nights! Last chance to be around other people for a few days!"

"But you just bought all this food. And you have plenty of wine, even for you." he argued.

"Hey! Judge free zone remember? All this is for the storm starting later tonight. So burgers and fries like usual?" she asked, clearly expecting a yes.

He relented. "Alright, let me go put this stuff away and I'll be back."

She couldn't help but smile to herself. She really did love a good New York City winter storm and being snowed in with Will seemed like endless possibilities. Seeing Prince watching her, she rubbed his ears before kissing him on the top of his head. "That's right Prince, there will be plenty of snuggles for all of us!"

It had been a couple of months since they had casually made an unspoken agreement to meet for dinner at Charlie's on Thursday nights. Sam looked forward to it and saw it as the beginning of the impending weekend. She was slowly phasing out clients coming in on Saturdays and credited that to being in a better place mentally and emotionally. Things were different, but also in some ways the same, and she found herself grateful just to have Will in her life. She knew it was fate he had walked into her building looking for a place to live that day.

Tonight their cheeseburgers had been devoured hours ago and Sam was unexpectedly on her third glass of wine. "What's with you tonight?" Will asked, not sure what to think.

Frankie shook her head. "Our girl Sam gets downright giddy over a blizzard while the rest of us cringe and hate on winter."

"Hey!" Sam said offended. "You know I'm not a fan of winter and giddy is a very strong word to throw around like that. I'm just a girl who enjoys being stuck at home for a few days with no plans."

The bar was so slow Frankie was nursing her own drink tonight and she raised it to Sam's wine glass expectantly. "I'll drink to that! Cheers!"

Knowing she and Will would be some of the few brave enough to come out given the upcoming blizzard, she had brought two decks of cards with her to the bar. She and Frankie were in the middle of playing a competitive game of ¾₁₃, Will caught in the crossfire as he learned how to play the hard way. The last two rounds were long and grueling but in the end, Sam held on to win the game and Will ended up paying the tab. Standing up, he moved to pull Sam off her barstool.

"I demand a rematch, but now it's time to head home and let Frankie close up." Turning to her, he asked if there was anything they could do to help.

Waving him off, Frankie thanked him, but said it would all keep. "Just get our girl here home safely."

Reaching over the bar, Sam hugged her, telling her to get home safe too. Throwing her coat on, she headed for the door, curious to see if the snow had started yet, although her app said no. She was delighted to walk out and find big fat flakes falling lazily from the sky, the ground already dusted with white. "Yay! It's coming!" she yelled out.

Grabbing her arm, Will pulled her to him, shushing her at the same time. He knew it was after midnight and some people might not appreciate the weather update.

"Okay, okay, but those people sleeping are missing out! Look how beautiful it is!" she said, spinning herself around, her arms spread wide, her head tilted up to the sky. It was early February and yet lots of neighbors still had holiday lights up, making the night feel even more beautiful and cozy.

Catching Will watching her with some amusement, she paused. "You see it right? How beautiful it is?"

He nodded, his expression giving her a sudden heat flash despite the freezing weather. "Oh I see it."

Coming close to him, she disagreed. "How can you see it if you're not looking in the right place?"

"What's it matter where I'm looking as long as I see it?" he asked her.

She laughed, taking his face in her hands and turning his head up to the sky. "I'm talking about how beautiful the snow is!"

Humoring her, Will watched as the big fat flakes swirled and twirled as they fell down around them. "I see it." he said, realizing she did have a point. Pulling her to him, they stood together looking up and watching it snow.

Feeling her shiver beside him, he pulled her around, heading them both in the direction of their brownstone. "Time to go home Sam."

Leaning into him, she said softly. "I like the sound of that."

Pulling her even tighter to him, he smiled, feeling a little giddy himself about the possibilities ahead of them in the name of a winter storm.

The smell of bacon and eggs woke her, as a cup of coffee magically appeared before her. Realizing she was on her couch, she looked up at Will with confusion. "Good morning sunshine." he said softly, positioning himself on the edge of the couch.

Sitting up, she took the cup of coffee from him with a grateful smile. "So, I crashed on the couch last night?"

Nodding, he amended her statement. "We crashed on the couch. But not until after a good twenty minutes of giggles over Castle."

Blowing on her coffee, she acted offended. "What? The guy is funny!"

Raising an eyebrow, Will answered dryly. "If you say so."

Looking toward the kitchen, she got to her point. "So will that bacon and eggs walk itself over here or should I move myself off the couch and make my way there?"

"I forgot you're not a morning person." Will said with a laugh. "Stay put and I'll bring it to you."

She watched him, her heart hammering already so early in the day. Did he really remember that about her or was he just making conversation? She was delighted when he handed her a bacon, egg, and cheese sandwich, the biscuit promising of things to come.

"Not exactly the diner's, but I did use one of their biscuits. I went by there yesterday and bought a dozen. I know how you live for breakfast."

"You are too kind!" Taking a big bite, her face was pure joy. "Oh my god, it's so much better with bacon!"

Sitting at the end of the couch, he watched her as she inhaled it. "Aren't you going to have one?" she asked around her last bite?"

"I ate with Prince. I'm good." he said.

"Prince!" Hearing his name he was obliged to come see her, hopeful for any crumbs she had left behind. "I need to take him out." she said, kicking the covers off of herself.

"I already did," he said casually.

She paused, thinking about that. "Wait. You really did crash here last night?"

Nodding, he asked, "Is that a problem? Your head was in my lap and you just looked so cozy all tucked in. I hated to wake you."

"Not a problem at all. I just feel bad you slept on one end of my couch." she said, trying to get past her head in his lap.

"I've slept in a lot worse places I'm sure," he said.

She could imagine. Moving on she asked him what his plan was for the day. "I have some work to do, but I'm pretty wide open. How about you?"

She studied him, finding herself wondering what he meant by work. Not able to resist, she heard herself. "So what does work mean for you?"

He shrugged, keeping his answer simple. "I read books and write reviews and people pay me for it."

She frowned, thinking about what he'd said. "You mean on Instagram? You're on social media?"

He nodded. "Under a pen name. I like helping Indie authors grow their fans and sell their books."

Loving how innocent this was compared to his last job, she embraced his news. "That's cool. Especially if you can pay your bills reading books."

Pausing, he clarified for her. "Apparantly money is not a thing for me. I was surprised when Aria went through my bank accounts and investments with me. I like helping people more than money, so I read and write. How about you? Are you starting your new book today?"

This time she really did get up, headed toward the bathroom. "Yes. right after I brush my teeth. But the day is young and I'm down for any-thing. You're welcome to hang with me and Prince. Come and go as you please."

She took her time in the bathroom, freshening up and thankful she had the presence of mind to put on a comfy sweatshirt over her leggings last night. She brushed her hair into a ponytail but drew the line on putting any makeup on. Opening the door, she really wasn't sure if Will would still be there or not. She was happy to find him in the kitchen, cleaning up.

She watched as he assembled the rest of the bacon and eggs with cheese into more biscuits for breakfast sandwiches. "What are you going to do with the other biscuits?" she asked curiously.

"I'm saving those for biscuits and gravy tomorrow morning. Sound good?" he asked knowingly.

"Yes please!" she said with a big smile. She wasn't sure which sounded more promising, his plan to be here in the morning or the B's&G's.

Having put everything away, he went to the bar, bringing her a pile of mail. "In your excitement for the blizzard, you forgot to get your mail yesterday. I hope you don't mind that I grabbed it when I took Prince out earlier."

"Thanks." she said absently flipping through. Suddenly she stopped, pulling out one of the envelopes. Ripping it open she quickly scanned the letter before gasping over the check in her hand.

"Everything okay?" Will asked curiously.

"My article I wrote actually is getting published AND they're paying me! I got an email a month ago, but it seemed unlikely it was for real. I can't believe it!" she said excitedly.

Coming to stand beside her, he was happy to take in her check she proudly displayed for him. "Congrats. When did you submit an article? What publication?"

"*Animal Wellness Magazine* and it was last August. One of my clients is a veterinarian and recommended I write an article about using massage therapy to help manage pain and improve mobility for dogs. Speaking of, Prince come. Let's do your therapy."

Will watched as Prince trotted to her, giving her his back half, clearly excited for what he knew was to come as his tail fanned her face. Kneeling beside him, Sam used the flat of her hand first to rub firmly along his lower back and hips. Then she used her finger tips in a circular motion along the same area.

Watching her with Prince, Will was overcome with emotion. The love she was putting into the smallest of gestures meant everything to him and to Prince. Glancing up at him, Sam was caught off guard by what she saw in his face.

"Are you okay?" she asked.

Nodding, he knelt down on the other side of Prince. "Can you show me how to do it?"

"Of course." Taking his hand, she flattened it before guiding him over the same areas she had just covered. "The trick is to be firm enough he feels it, but not so firm it's painful. The goal is that the massage keeps his hips loose and not all tight with pain. In my opinion, this is a much healthier way to manage his hip dysplasia than using medications. He just needs it done regularly. It's a habit."

She sat back watching Will with his dog. "That's it." She said, encouraging him. When Prince turned his head to look at her, she knew he was ready to be done. "Good boy Prince." She laughed when he came to lick her in the face, knowing it was his way to thank her. They watched as he walked away, climbing into his bed at one end of the couch.

Standing up first, Will held his hand out to her, pulling her to her feet.

"Thank you Sam. It may seem like such a little thing, but it means so much. To him and to me."

"You're welcome." she said, struggling to break their gaze.

"What's next on your agenda?" he finally asked.

"I'm going to read for a while. How about you?" She tried not to look too eager when she made her offer. "I'm happy to share the couch with you."

Nodding he told her he would be right back. She smiled when Prince jumped up to follow him out. They were back in no time, finding Sam already settled into one end of the couch. They sat sharing the middle space of the couch, a thick fleece over their legs, reading the hours away. Sam couldn't help but steel glances at Will every so often, caught off guard with how unusual it was to see him so relaxed.

And so their day went, peaceful and relaxed and for a while, Sam embraced it all. They made grilled cheese for lunch before returning to the couch. It was getting late in the day when Sam started to feel restless, torn between making cookies and getting a workout in. Closing her book, she got up to look out her window, hoping to feel inspired to do either.

"Taking a break from reading?" Will asked, coming to stand beside her.

"I need to work out. I'm going to change and throw some punches on my bag. Want to join me?" she asked hopefully, pointing it out in the corner of the room. It was always a better workout when she could get someone to hold her bag.

"Better yet, why don't I spar with you. I'll go and get my gloves." he offered her.

"That would be great." she said, remembering a particular night in the park, just a small piece of their history together.

In no time, she was a hot sweaty mess trying to keep pace throwing punches at Will or working even harder to block his. She wondered if he remembered doing this with her before and how it had ended with him pinning her on the ground.

"We've done this before, haven't we?" he asked.

She nodded, breathing hard trying to bob and weave her way around his punches, staying in motion and getting better at predicting them.

"It's the night you fell and dislocated your shoulder, right?" he said.

Stunned he remembered that, she stopped cold just as he threw a left hook, landing squarely on her jaw. Unprepared she literally took it on the chin. She would have fallen had Will not grabbed her. "Jeez Sam, I'm so sorry! Why didn't you bob?"

His concern was obvious, as she held her jaw. "You remembered something about us!"

Suddenly he started to laugh. "It's not funny, I'm so sorry, but your expression! Are you okay?"

Punching him in the shoulder, she defended herself. "You caught me off guard. You know I was kicking your butt until you said that."

Letting go of her, he threw his gloves to the floor before bringing her in for a hug. "I really am sorry about that." Pushing her away far enough to look at her, he added. "And you should know, the more time I spend with you, the more I remember about us."

"Really?" she breathed out.

He was smiling at her, but his eyes were focused on her lips. "Really. Do you need an ice pack?"

"Hmmm, that would be the practical solution. But it seems like that would be letting you off easy." she said wickedly.

"I'm here to right my wrong. What can I do?" he asked, playing along.

Tossing her gloves under her bag, she laid it out for him. "Well I'm going to go shower. But you can make yourself useful by starting dinner. And later you owe me a game of 3/13. Deal?"

Giving her a slow nod, he agreed. "If that's all it takes, sure. Enjoy your shower and I'll start dinner." *If that's all it takes.*

"Great thanks!" she said, heading to the bathroom.

It was a good thirty minutes before she emerged, her hair in wet wavy curls down her back, having thrown on a new pair of leggings with another oversized sweatshirt. She hated to admit it, but she had put just a touch of makeup on, trying to keep a natural low key glow up. The smell of garlic and butter was unmistakable as she joined Will in the kitchen, finding a glass of red wine poured and waiting for her.

Offering her a frozen bag of corn for her jaw, he informed her of his progress with dinner. "Steaks are in the oven finishing. Potatoes are five minutes away and salad is good to go. How was your shower?"

Taking a sip of her wine, she answered him blissfully. "Good! Life is good!" she said, surprising them both.

Raising his beer to her wine glass, he agreed. "I'll drink to that."

The steaks were perfect, seared with flavor, but still juicy and tender on the inside. They were soon deep into 3/13, finding out just how competitive the other could be. Their score was within thirty points when Sam announced, "The loser has to give the winner a massage. Deal?"

Looking at her incredulously, Will agreed. "Aren't I kicking your butt right now?"

She shrugged. "We have two more rounds. It's still anyone's game.

Smiling, he agreed. "Deal. I could use a massage."

Sam wasn't worried about it, seeing it as a win-win either way. She just needed a good excuse to put her hands on him, even if it was limited to his upper half versus his lower. *Let him come to you.*

Losing in the end, she offered him fresh baked cookies in lieu of a massage, but he wasn't about to let her off the hook. Sitting on the couch, she pointed to the floor, ready to make good on their bet. Thank god there was a hoodie between her fingers and his flesh, the thought of her skin touching his enough to fuel a small inferno. Having set a timer on her phone, she was both relieved and disappointed when it went off. Turning around to face her, she savored his close proximity, hopeful it would lead to something more. Instead he asked her if she wanted to go out in the snow for Prince's last call. Nodding, she got up to go find her coat and boots, Prince waiting by the door for the two of them.

The storm had passed and it took Sam's breath away to see the moon shine down brightly on the snow. A plow had been down their street and they walked casually with Prince down the middle of it, the bitter cold air refreshing after being inside all day. Bundled up against the cold, they walked companionably in silence, each of them lost in thought. It wasn't long before they found themselves back in front of Sam's building, Will pausing her before going up the steps.

"Sam, wait." he said, his hand on her arm.

Turning to him expectantly, she asked, "What is it?"

"Can I kiss you?" he asked, getting straight to the point.

Turning to face him, she pulled her scarf down before lifting her face to his. "Always."

She reveled in his hands on her face as he pressed his warm lips against hers, ever so gently, careful of her newly bruised jaw.

As he pulled away, she wondered if he remembered the first time he had kissed her, not even realizing it had come out her mouth.

"It was your seventeenth birthday. And tequila was involved as I recall." he said, not having to even pause and think about it.

She smiled. "That would be a yes and a yes again."

Heading up the steps, Prince on his heels, she was happy to follow both of them inside.

They sat close together, snuggled under a blanket on the couch again, Prince laying at their feet, their hot chocolate sitting on the coffee table in front of them. Starting another episode of Castle, Sam knew it was getting late and could feel herself getting sleepy. Without even realizing it, she leaned her head on Will's shoulder, sighing heavily.

"You should get to bed Sam." Will said quietly after seeing her eyes droop.

Shaking her head, she declined. "I'm awake. I'm just listening. I want to stay right where I am."

Smiling Will got up to go get her a real pillow and another blanket. When he came back he stood over her, watching her before telling her to scoot down. Looking up at him sleepily she mumbled. "Don't leave. I want you to stay. Okay?"

He nodded, his heart in his throat. "Okay baby girl, I"m staying, but I want you to stretch out on the couch. So scoot down."

She did as she was told, finding her head on a pillow, back in Will's lap, his feet up on her coffee table. She drifted off quickly, her face serene and looking like she was seventeen again with her ponytail and no makeup. He could stare at her all night, but eventually found an old western to watch, falling asleep soon enough with his own handsome face relaxed and happy. He dismissed his last thought, wondering how long could it last?

CHAPTER TWENTY-SEVEN

Sam was suddenly jolted awake by Will twitching beside her, crying out in distress. Sitting up quickly, she put her hand on his arm to try to wake him. When he didn't respond, she knelt down in front of him, putting both hands on his arms, shaking him gently while saying his name. Finally, he came too, his breathing rapid, his look still distressed. Becoming focused on her face, he crumpled with relief, pulling her to him.

"Sam! Thank God! I was so afraid I'd lost you!" he said, his voice emotional.

Feeling tears come to her eyes, Sam pulled back from his embrace wanting to look him in the face. "I'm here Will. I'm okay, you're okay. We're both safe. You had a bad dream."

He focused on her, taking her words in, slowing his breathing. "I have this dream sometimes. Sorry I woke you."

"Do you want to tell me about the dream? It might help?" she said gently, wondering if it was the same dream she had for weeks after returning home from Italy.

He shook his head, looking around. "I need some water."

Getting up, she went to get him his water bottle. He took it from her, gulping it down like it was the oxygen he needed to keep breathing.

She could see he was back to normal physically and sat back down beside him, taking his hand. Prince, who had been watching him with his own anxious look, came to rest his head on Will's knee.

Smiling, he rubbed Prince's head before mumbling he was fine. Sam found herself bent on making this an opportunity for both of them to grow and spoke up. "I've had that dream." she said softly.

He glanced at her sharply. "What dream?"

"Where we're on the yacht and it blows up. I'm in the water, screaming your name because I'm terrified you didn't make it off in time." Her heart was racing just thinking about it, her anguish written all over her face.

Will nodded grimly. "That's the one." Pulling Sam to him, she realized it was more of a rhetorical question he was asking. "So that really did happen to us?"

She nodded, struggling to speak. "You were adamant Prince and I had to get off the boat. It broke my heart to leave you. I thought I had lost you when the boat exploded. Prince was the one who saved me. He pushed me back to the surface and we swam together back to shore. I woke up in a hospital bed, with Prince still at my side."

Pulling her to him even tighter, his voice was low. "I don't know why we were there, but I'm so sorry that happened to you. It's haunted me to think about you being on that damn boat and there's nothing I can do to save you."

Pulling away, she shook her head. "It happened to us, Will. It was traumatic for all of us. And you're the reason Prince and I made it off the boat in one piece." she said. She wondered if he needed to know why they were there or she should just let it go.

"Why were we there Sam? What did I do?" he asked fearfully.

"No, it wasn't you! You weren't the reason we were there. It's complicated and ugly and maybe it's better to focus on that we all got out alive. You promised me you would find your way back to me and you did and that's all that matters."

She could see he was thinking about what she said. She held her breath, hoping he would let it go. It had taken a lot of time and therapy for her to let it go to the point she could move on with her life.

She let him pull her back to him, resting her head on his shoulder. He squeezed her tight before kissing the top of her head. "I don't want to go back Sam, but can I move forward without knowing where I've been? The thought keeps me awake at night."

She could see his point, but knew he had to be the one to decide that for himself. "Do you remember what happened after the explosion? You don't have to share if it's too much." She had asked herself this a hundred times, curious if Will even knew the answer.

"I don't remember, but a girl rescued me and got me to a hospital. Apparently I was in a coma for months. She was sitting there when I woke up. When I was released, I still couldn't really function so she took me to her apartment to continue healing."

When he paused, Sam asked breathlessly, "What was the girl's name?"

"Aria. She said taking care of me was the least she could do after what her family had done to me. Whatever that means."

Sam closed her eyes, *what her family had done? Was Mauricio the boss Will had insisted on seeing and making a deal with?* Thinking of the card in her kitchen drawer, she was suddenly overcome with so much gratitude for what Aria had done. "How did you end up back in New York?"

"Aria's family is loaded I guess and she flew with me on their private jet. She got us a room at The Chelsea Hotel. We went for a walk, looking for a place for me to live. You were the first place she wanted me to see. She could see it on my face that it felt right. After signing I went back to the hotel, but she was gone." His voice sounded puzzled, clearly not sure what had happened to her.

"What?" Sam asked fearfully. Did he fall for her?

"She left me a note. *Have a good life Will. Be happy.* That's all she said. I wouldn't have made it without her, but I got the feeling she knew I belonged here. With you and Prince."

Sam let it all soak in, processing what he had shared. It answered some of her questions while creating so many more. Had Sam and Will been in the same hospital? Did Aria not tell Elisa and Mauricio Will was alive because Mauricio was responsible? And how did she know that? Was part of the deal he'd made with him that he would evaporate off the map? She knew what she thought, but kept it all to herself. Pulling away from him she stood up, holding her hand out to him.

"Let's go to bed for real. There's plenty of time before the sun comes up." Seeing his hesitation, she added softly, "I need you to hold me Will and I need to hold you."

He followed her, bringing the blankets with them, not even getting under the covers. They lay together, fully dressed, wrapped around each other, both of them sleeping deeply for the first time in a long time. Tonight seemed like a major breakthrough and it felt like enough, promising of more days ahead together. What more could she ask for?

It was day two of their blizzard shut in and Sam was looking forward to another day with Will. She could feel something had shifted last night, and she was curious what today would bring. Her apartment was dark save for a lamp here or there, the weather outside her window dreary and bitterly cold. She appreciated Will had been up early to take Prince out as well make her biscuits and gravy as he had promised. As she brought her plate to the sink, she saw Will go to the drawer and pull out her card from Aria all those months ago. She watched him, wondering how he had found it and why he had pulled it out.

Tossing it on the bar between them he asked, "I was looking for your pot holders and discovered this. Where did it come from?"

"Someone sent it to me months ago with a bouquet of flowers." she answered cautiously.

"Who? Another guy? Or a girl?" he asked, his face hard to read.

Sam went to pick it up, curious what this was all about. "I'm not sure. As you can see, they left the card unsigned."

He shook his head. "But you have an idea of who it was, don't you?"

She nodded as it occurred to her to ask, "Do you know who it's from?"

He sighed heavily, pulling a small piece of paper out of his pocket before coming to stand in front of her. Wordlessly he held his paper to her card, the loopy handwriting on both unmistakably the same.

Sam didn't know what to say. Why was he carrying this note around with him? Looking at her he asked quietly. "So you knew Aria also? Why did she send this to you?"

She was overwhelmed with how much to tell him, trying to keep her answer simple. "Yes, I knew Aria. When I got her card, I knew it was from her because she had said that to me before. It was a lifeline for me, Will. The day I read it gave me undeniable hope that you would find your way back to me. That you were alive and I wasn't crazy." She was getting choked up, her emotions on her face.

Folding his note, he stuffed it back into the pocket of his jeans. Taking her hands, he focused on the floor as he spoke. "I'm so sorry I hurt you like that. That I was the kind of guy who would just disappear on you and make you worry about me. That's not who I want to be."

Shaking her head vehemently, she denied his words. "It wasn't your fault Will. It was complicated and I know you don't want all the details, but you have to believe me, you're a good man, then and now. We will both be indebted to Aria forever for saving you."

He finally looked her in the face, his voice somber. "I can't imagine the horrible things I did that my brain is so desperate to protect me that it won't even let me remember the good things. Like loving you."

Sam caught her breath, only able to focus on his last three words. "You remember loving me?"

He nodded. "What I'm trying to figure out is why you loved me back. Someone like me doesn't deserve happiness."

Suddenly she was angry. "Stop it right now! We are not going down this tortured soul path again. You are a good man and you deserve to be happy just as much as anyone does! Everything you ever did was to save others from evil even as you sacrificed yourself to do so. You shoved your emotions so far down, you didn't care if you put yourself in danger or not, because you thought you had nothing to lose."

She was on the verge of tears, needing him to understand. Pulling her to him he mumbled into her hair, equally emotional. "That's why I came home to you Sam. Twice. Because loving you gave me something to live for."

She felt her heart soar as he put the pieces together. She pulled away from him, smiling. "Yes! And I love you Will. We were always meant to be together. There isn't anyone else for me."

She watched his face as the reality of what she said sunk in. She could feel the shift in him, his expression lighter before his gaze became focused on her lips. Putting both hands on her face, he kissed her gently, his tongue slowly sweeping her mouth, before pulling her even closer to him.

They were out of their clothes in no time, crawling under the covers together, their hands and lips all over each other, everywhere all at once. It had been months since they had laid naked together in her bed, but they knew it wasn't just the sex, it was all the shit they had been through and that they had somehow finally managed to find their way back to each other, still deeply in love. Laying on her back, her arms wrapped around his neck, she was suddenly overwhelmed with the joy of feeling him move inside her.

He paused suddenly, "Sam? Are you okay?" he asked, using his thumbs to wipe away her tears.

She laughed softly, unaware she was crying. "I'm just so grateful to be here, on the other side of it all. That you're here, that we're here together. I love you Will."

He smiled, kissing her salty tears. "I'm right there with you. I love you too Sam."

They spent a good part of the day in bed, taking breaks from getting reacquainted with each other's bodies to being wrapped around each other, talking and enjoying the intimacy they had missed over the last year and a half. Occasionally one of them would brave leaving their warm bed to make a run for their water bottles or a snack.

As they lay snuggled under the sheets, Sam sighed, feeling the need to ask Will something. "What do you want to ask me?"

"Why do you keep Aria's note in your pocket?" she blurted out. She felt petty for asking, but her curiosity was getting the better of her.

He let her go, turning on his side. "There was nothing between us if that's what you're worried about."

She shook her head. "I know, I'm just curious I guess." Did he feel an unspoken bond between them?

He rolled back over on his back, thinking about her question. "I'm not sure, but I couldn't just throw it away. I don't remember what we went through together or why, but there was a connection. First she saved my life and then I felt like she purposefully brought me to you and I was grateful. Even though I didn't recognize you that first day, I felt an undeniable connection to you. It felt like her note was my get out of jail free card, her blessing to be free, to live the rest of my life and be happy.

"I get that. And we will take all the blessings we can get." Sam said with a smile.

Finally, they agreed it was time to get up and think about what was for dinner. Sam seasoned chicken to bake in the oven before challenging Will to sparring with her, needing to get a workout in before she baked cookies. She was full of energy, her happiness overflowing.

"Are you sure you'll be able to focus and keep your guard up this time? I need you to protect that beautiful face of yours." he teased her.

Throwing his gloves at him, she reassured him. "I've got all this energy to burn so tag, you're it!" They went at it hard, Will showing her very little mercy, enjoying a different act of physical contact for the two of them. When the oven timer went off on her chicken, Sam pulled her gloves off before going to turn it off. Joining her in the kitchen Will offered to make some pasta and green beans so she could go shower. Thanking him with a kiss on the cheek, she headed to the bathroom.

She came out of the bathroom, the dining room table set with candles, her glass of wine waiting for her. Going to the kitchen, she discovered Will had made egg noodles and a beschemel sauce to go with her chicken.

Picking one up, she slurped it up before turning to Will. "Wait. Did you make these from scratch?" When he nodded, she went to investigate his sauce still bubbling on the stove. Giving it a stir, he held out a sample for her to try. "Oh my god Will. That's so good! I can't wait for dinner!"

Finding herself most impressed with Will's pasta, she overindulged, pushing off making cookies for another day. Their evening passed quickly listening to albums and playing 3/13 before finding themselves back in bed. Curled up together, it had been the sweetest of days and they both relished in it, their happiness long overdue.

CHAPTER TWENTY-EIGHT

Happy birthday Will

It was early summer and Sam and Will were headed to her parent's home to celebrate the twins' birthday. Sam had agonized over how to approach Will about going, making a mental list of all the reasons why she thought he should go. They were walking home from Charlie's and she had paused them outside her building to take the plunge and finally ask him to join her, knowing it was just a few days away. He had let her have her say, his eyes warm on her, a small smile playing on his face. When she finally finished he had taken both her hands in his.

"Sam, I'm all in. You don't have to convince me. I love you and I know how important your family is to you. I'm happy to go. A little nervous, but happy to go."

Smiling with relief, she could only think to say thank you before jumping into his arms and hugging him.

Now before she turned the knob and walked into her family home, she squeezed his hand in hers, feeling his apprehension. They had come a little early, knowing the chaos that would ensue when Riley and her crew arrived, their birthday energy a lot when it was times two.

"Mom! Dad! We're here!" Sam called out.

"In the kitchen!" her mom responded.

As they entered her family kitchen, her mom stopped stirring to come and greet them. After hugging Sam, she turned to Will.

"Will! We're so happy you're joining us today. It's good to see you." She reached up to hug him, holding it long enough to convey she had missed him terribly and was glad to have him in their home again.

Feeling the heaviness of having Will there for the first time without Jordan, Sam asked tentatively. "Where's dad?"

Wiping her eyes quickly, her mom pointed to the back door. "He's at the grill working on burgers and hot dogs."

As Sam started to head that way, Will put his hand out to stop her. "Do you mind if I go out first? It's hard to do this with an audience."

Sam nodded. "I'm sure mom could use some help in the kitchen anyway. Right mom?" she asked, looking for support.

"Of course. You can finish frosting the cupcakes." she agreed with a smile.

The two women worked in the kitchen, making small talk while Sam worried how it was going between her dad and Will. They both jumped when her dad called out to her mom. "Susan, can you bring me more BBQ sauce please?"

She rummaged in the pantry for a minute before heading out to him. "Keep up the good work Sami. They look perfect."

Sam was dying to know how it was going and tried to hurry to finish her assignment so she could go see for herself everything was good. When her mom came back in she was quick to ask, "Everyone good out there?"

Nodding, her mom gave her a side hug. "Of course. It's so good to have Will in our home again. You two look so happy together." As she started to tear up again, Sam turned to give her a proper hug.

"These past months have been so special. Who needs cupid when a good blizzard can bring two people together." She joked.

Finishing the last cupcake, she decided it was time to join the boys in the backyard. She stood at the door for a moment, taking the two of them in, her heart full.

"How's it going out here? Riley and her crew will be here any minute." She warned them both, walking up to Will, delighted when he casually put his arm around her shoulders to pull her close to him.

Suddenly the noise level kicked up a notch as Riley, her husband, and their twins arrived. In no time they were running through the house to the backyard. "Auntie Sami!" they yelled excitedly, stopping short upon seeing Will standing there beside her. She smiled to see their different reactions.

"So you're Will? Are you really Auntie Sami's boyfriend?" Ava asked candidly. Alex on the other hand, stood shyly, giving a small wave from the safety of his sister's presence.

Will laughed before going to stand in front of them, coming down to be at their level. "Yep, I'm Will. I'm happy to meet you both. Auntie Sami has told me a lot about you both."

"Did she tell you we're going to kindergarten soon?" Ava asked.

"Today's our birthday." Alex offered.

Coming to his rescue, Sam came to offer them both birthday hugs. "Happy happy birthday you two! Nana let me frost the cupcakes so you know what that means! Lots of it on the two I saved just for you!"

"Yay!" They both cheered before turning to go back into the house to see for themselves.

Before long dinner was done, presents opened, and cupcakes demolished. They all sat around the pool, Riley giving the twins their five minute warning before they had to get out. Will let Sam know he was going to find the bathroom before they headed back to Chelsea. When she had jumped up to show him the way, he had stopped her. "I remember," he said with a small smile.

After he'd been gone for ten minutes, Sam grew worried. As she went to get up, it was her mom who stopped her this time. "Let me go Sami." She nodded at her, watching her mom go into the house.

She found him seated in the oversized chair in the twins bunk room, lost in thought. Gently she knocked on the door to get his attention. Quickly he stood up. "Sorry. I took a detour."

"It's okay. It wasn't hard to guess where you might be. Do you need more time? Or someone to talk to?" she asked him.

He smiled then. "You always were great at listening." Going over to the built-in desk he ran his finger along the edge. "It looks so different, but I still feel him here. We had so many great times together. He was the brother I never had but always wanted." Checking his emotions, he added. "I'm grateful to have these memories back, but I'm also trying to let some regrets go once and for all."

She nodded in complete understanding, her face full of emotion too. "He loved you so much, Will. He would be so happy to see you and Sam together."

Will shook his head. "I don't think so. I put her in harm's way. I hurt her and I let her get hurt. Jordan would have kicked my butt."

Putting her hand on his arm, she shook her head at him. "Nonsense. You've been put in some hard places and you survived it all Will Shaw. You've brought Sam all the love and joy we've wished for her since the day she was born. And you better believe Jordan is smiling down on you both and wishing you all the best."

They were both a little misty as he let her pull him into a fierce hug. "We love you Will and will always think of your family as a part of our family."

He pulled away from her, nodding. "I'm lucky to be here and so thankful to be part of your family."

Handing him a tissue, Susan said knowingly, "We know our girl Sam isn't always the most patient person so we better pull ourselves together before she comes looking for us."

He laughed, knowing she was right. The twins were out of the pool getting dried off, Sam helping Riley to reign them in when they found their way back to the backyard. The lingering emotions on their faces wasn't lost on her as she announced it was time to give Nana and Pop their house back. As Riley rounded her crew up to head home, Sam and Will prepared to walk out with them, their uber only five minutes out. After hugs all around, they embraced the peacefulness of the car as they headed back to Chelsea. Turning to Will, she studied him to see if he seemed worse for wear after surviving her family for the last couple of hours.

"You okay over there?" she asked gently.

Suddenly he leaned forward and gave the uber driver another address. "Can we please stop by 106 Rosewood. Just for a minute? It should be right up here on the left."

Sam watched as the driver did as requested, Will climbing out of the car to stand and look at a modest home with a large front porch. She leaned forward to reassure the driver they would only be a minute before climbing out to join Will, his face hard to read. Not knowing what to say, she stood silently beside him, holding his hand. Lost in his thoughts, he eventually put his arm around Sam and pulled her to him.

"The house looks good. Granny would be proud." he said softly.

Suddenly two young kids came running out of the house, their shrieks joyful as they ran around the front yard, a puppy chasing them. Will pulled her to him even more tightly before turning to her. "That's what I want, Sam. With you, someday."

Feeling her heart catch in her throat, she could only nod. As Will opened the door for her, she climbed back in, thanking the driver for his patience, giving the house one last look before the car pulled away.

As the long summer day came to a close, Will and Sam were headed out to walk Prince, making it last call for the night. They walked in silence a couple of minutes before she couldn't take it any longer.

"Penny for your thoughts. Are you okay?" she asked worriedly.

He gave her a smile. "It was a big day. I'm just processing it all. But, yes I'm okay." He put his arm around her, pulling her to him reassuringly.

"Thanks for going with me today. It meant a lot to all of us." she said.

"You don't have to thank me Sam. It was good to be there. I loved helping the twins celebrate their birthday. We both know how special birthdays are."

"I'm glad to hear you say that because yours is the next birthday. And I have some thoughts." she said invitingly.

"I don't need to celebrate my birthday." he said with a sigh.

She stopped him, making him turn to face her. "Bullshit! You do need to more than anyone I know. You know I'm right!" she resumed walking, not giving him a chance to argue, closing the subject once and for all. "What I need to know is what you would like to do on your birthday. To celebrate."

This time he stopped her, turning her to look at him. Putting both hands on either side of her face he kissed her hard, leaving her breathless. "Since you asked, I would like more of that, but preferably we're naked and in bed."

She smiled as they resumed their walking. "Done and done. I'll figure out the rest."

He sighed heavily, stopping her again. "I know it's my fortieth but keep it low key Sam. I don't need a lot. Just you. Understand?"

She nodded at him. "Got it."

As they turned to head back to her brownstone, Will added one more nugget. "What would you think if I bought myself a motorcycle for my birthday?"

She stopped dead in her tracks. "Yes! I think you should absolutely do that!"

He laughed at her enthusiasm before asking dryly. "So I take it, I used to have a motorcycle?"

She nodded, the thought of sitting behind him holding onto him tightly making her flush with anticipation. "You did. We rode it all over the city. So many good times."

"Great. I'll start looking tomorrow."

Will's big day was finally here. Sam had respected his wishes, but still she was excited for their low key evening ahead. She was putting the finishing touches on his gift when her phone rang. She paused, noting it was Elisa. Did she know it was Will's birthday?

"Ciao Elisa! How are you?" she asked.

Putting her on speaker phone, she was astonished as Elisa fired off rapid Italian before catching herself. She got the gist of it, understanding something bad had happened to Mauricio. Using her English, Sam listened in horror as she shared that he had been gunned down sitting outside a cafe, a random shooting. Expressing her heartfelt condolences, Sam wondered if she had been there, horrified at the thought she might have witnessed such violence. Elisa denied it, telling her Aria had been there but had just gone to the ladies room when the shooting happened.

Sam had no idea as to what to say, letting Elisa talk, first in Italian and then repeating herself in English. She asked her how Aria was taking it and was surprised to hear she had become Elisa's rock, even taking over Mauricio's business, keeping the status quo alive. Sam was desperate to let her go, her anxiety mounting the longer they talked. When Elisa thought to ask her how she was, she asked her not to worry about her but to focus on herself as she went through this difficult time.

She sat in shock absorbing the conversation. She went to google, searching for any postings regarding the shooting, but everything was in Italian. She got up, staring out her window, forcing herself to slow her breathing and not let this news ruin her day. Suddenly the roar of a motorcycle caught her attention, the driver pulling up beside a parked car. She smiled as her phone pinged. *Can you come down?* Hurriedly she hid his present under the bed before texting *On my way.*

She had forgotten how good he looked in his helmet and was touched when he handed her a helmet, having bought her one to wear too. They spent an hour going all over the city, past Bryant park, over the Brooklyn Bridge, past Will's old house, back to Chelsea. Still struggling with Elisa's news, she savored holding onto Will, the warmth and strength of him lifting her mood, allowing her to push thoughts of Mauricio away. Will had dropped her in front of her brownstone, telling her would see her at six, ready to begin his birthday celebration.

Finishing his gift, she wondered if she had gone too far, the book way too personal. She had reached out to people such as Tony and Bianca, friends who had known Will the longest, asking them to write a letter to him talking about their favorite memory of them together and why they were friends. It had been an overwhelming response from the handful of people she could reach out to, all of them more than happy to share their love for Will. She had asked for pics to share as well, wanting to put them together in the book.

Asking her mom to search old photo albums, she was curious to see how far back she could find pics of Will and Jordan together. Her tenacious search had also discovered a pic of Will and his granny at a neighborhood picnic Sam's family had hosted, maybe a year after his parents had passed. She had included one of him and Prince that she took the weekend of the blizzard, making a little paw print beside the pic.

The last page she had reserved for a few pics of them together, mostly selfies, but one really good one Riley had snapped the night of the twins' birthday party. She had vacillated on including a selfie of them in Italy and had finally printed it because it was so symbolic of all their relationship had endured since he first walked into *Pause for a Cause.* Writing her own letter to Will had been emotional, hoping with all her heart Will would know how much he was loved. Satisfied the book was perfect, she went to pull out her dress, before jumping in the shower, satisfied everything was in place for a perfect birthday celebration.

Will was on time, dressed in blue jeans and a black shirt, his sleeves rolled up, his hair still wet and curly. He seemed frozen in place when she opened her door to him wearing *the* burgundy paisley dress with the sweetheart neckline and puffy sleeves, her lariat necklace falling into her cleavage.

"Happy birthday Will." she said before taking his hand and bringing him into her loft. Turning back to him, she let him stare, his look putting her libido into overdrive.

Finally finding his voice, Sam was ecstatic to hear he remembered this night. "That dress. You've worn it before. You made your birthday wish for me to take you out of it, to feel my skin on yours."

She nodded, letting him take the lead. "We danced at Charlie's and you got mad and said I cock blocked you. I walked you home even though you were so mad at me."

Her eyes were glowing, the thought of what came next making her body hum with wanting him. "Then what happened Will?"

He moved to stand in front of her, slowly tracing the neckline of her dress, letting it linger in the dip he knew so well by now. Pressing himself into her as his mouth took over, she could feel his hardness, letting him wreck her wherever he wanted. Coming up for air, he stepped back, his expectation obvious.

"It's my birthday tonight Sam. Let's see what you've got for me."

Slowly she unsnapped her dress, enjoying his eyes on her as she exposed herself to him before letting her dress fall off, stepping out of it when it hit the floor. Using his jeans, she pulled him to her, unbuttoning his shirt before getting his jeans down and releasing him to her. Quickly they found themselves under the covers, Sam enjoying herself as she worked to drive Will crazy, giving him the happy ending he had requested for his birthday.

An hour later they had worked up quite an appetite, ready to find their clothes and go in search of food. Walking to Charlie's, she asked if he was disappointed she wasn't whisking him away to some fancy restaurant with a hundred of his closest friends. Bringing her hand he was holding to his lips, he kissed it before telling her that it had already been the perfect birthday. Being cautious, he let her go in first, half afraid a group of people might yell out *surprise!*

Relieved that there was only Frankie to greet them, they took their usual seats at the bar, quick to order burgers and fries. "Beer and wine too?" she confirmed.

Placing drinks in front of them, she made a big show of popping open a bottle of champagne before pouring three coupes, handing one to each of them before raising her own in a toast. "Happy birthday Will and to many, many more."

Glancing at Sam, he nodded with a quiet "Thank you Frankie."

As Frankie went to check on another customer, he leaned into Sam. "Tell me she's the only one who knows it's my birthday. People aren't going to start randomly showing up, right?"

She could see the anxiety in his face and was quick to assure him she had respected his wishes. Believing her, he sipped his beer before digging into the burger and fries Frankie had just put in front of him. They didn't stay long, Will letting Sam know he was ready for his birthday dessert.

As they came to her brownstone, Will stopped her, turning her to face him before pulling her close. "Thank you Sam for the best birthday I've ever had. You're stunning in this dress, but you out of this dress took my breath away even more. Dinner at Charlie's was perfect. I"m looking forward to what's next."

Reaching up to him, Sam kissed him gently, her voice soft. "You're so welcome Will. I'm glad you're having a good night. Just know, there's more to come."

As they headed up her stairs, he warned her there better not be people waiting for them in her loft. She shook her head no, laughing. As her door swung open, she caught her breath. Everywhere she looked was a lit candle, the room aglow. She walked in, not knowing what to think.

"Who did this?" she asked incredulously. Realizing Will was watching her with a big smile, not the least bit surprised, she asked in a hushed voice. "Did you do this? How? There must be a hundred candles."

"Surprise!" he said softly. She watched as he walked to her albums pulling out Sheriff. Taking it out of the dust cover, she didn't know what to think as he put on their song *When I'm With You*. Coming back to her he held his hand out to her. "Dance with me Sam."

She took his hand, letting him pull her to him, resting her head on his shoulder, while he softly sang the words to her. *I never wanted to share the things I want to share with you.* Turning her face up to his, he gently kissed her, still moving her in slow circles. "Remember when you asked me what I want for my birthday Sam?"

She nodded, the look he was giving her melting her heart. "I know I'm a work in progress, but I want you Sam. Not just in bed, but all of you, all day long, everyday. I want to know you're mine and I'm yours. I want to be the first thing you see in the morning and the last thing you see at night. You fill me up and make me whole. I'm so in love with you Sam."

He had stopped moving, wiping the tears from her cheeks. She watched as he pulled a ring from his pocket, holding it out to her. "What I want most for my birthday is for you to agree to marry me. To tell me you'll love me forever. Will you marry me Sam?"

She was nodding, struggling to find her voice. "Yes! I will love you forever and marrying you would make me the happiest girl in the world."

He put the ring on her finger before picking her up to swing her around. "I don't know what I did to deserve you, but I promise I will always do my best to make you happy!"

Setting her down, he kissed her tenderly, with so much love she felt it all the way down to her toes. "I love you so much Sam." Gently he picked her up and carried her to the bed. It was different, taking their sweet time, relishing in their commitment to love each other until the end of time. As they lay wrapped around each other, Sam suddenly had a thought.

"You know I need to call my sister. And my parents. And who lit all those candles for you? And where's Prince?" she asked, a little concerned.

Getting out of bed, he turned to her as he put his jeans back on. "Your sister already knows and she's the one who lit the candles and put Prince in my loft. And your parents already know because I asked their permission."

She sat up, letting it all sink in. What? When had he asked them? And how had Riley managed to keep this from her. How long had she known? She had to hand it to all of them, she never saw it coming.

Suddenly Prince came bounding in, Will not far behind him. She laughed when he jumped into bed with her, licking her face and sensing something big was going on. Will quickly put the kibosh on it though telling him down in no uncertain terms.

"When did you ask my parents? You went over there?" she asked, needing more information. Slipping out of his jeans, he rejoined her in bed.

"The night of the twins' birthday. That's why I wanted to go out first and why he called your mom out for more BBQ sauce. I know what progressive thinkers the women in your family are and I wanted her to be included." he was smiling, recalling their emphatic yes to his proposal.

She was touched, sure that her mom had been as well. "I'm so glad you did that, thank you. I'm sure Riley loved helping you do this tonight too. Knowing something before I do is her specialty." She acknowledged with a laugh.

"Actually, to be honest, Riley helped me pick out your ring." Seeing her look at it and back to him, he added hastily. "I needed it to be perfect! Just like you."

She leaned back into her pillows, turning her hand to admire it before turning to reassure him. "You two did very well. I love it!"

She smiled as he came to lay his head on her chest. She stroked his hair, loving that he would be so vulnerable with her. "There's one thing Sam. And if it's a deal breaker, I will find a way to handle it."

He felt her stiffen under him ever so slightly. "What's the one thing?" she asked.

"I can't do a big wedding Sam. I need it to be small and intimate, just your family and closest friends. Is that okay?" He had thought a lot about it, wanting her to have the wedding of her dreams, but the thought of a big wedding gave him anxiety for lots of reasons.

"I don't need a big wedding. Family and our closest friends sounds perfect to me. When do we want to do it? And where? Do you have a location in mind?" she asked thoughtfully.

He sat up now, ready to lay it all out for her, having been thinking about it a lot longer than she had. "What if we did it in your parent's backyard? They have a beautiful area and plenty of room for the twenty people who might show up."

Sam was smiling, loving his idea. "I love it. Now the question is when?"

"The sooner the better, but I realize there are details to put in place. I'll defer to you and your family. If I had my way, I would do it in August, the week after your birthday."

She looked at him, her expression thoughtful. "The anniversary of when you and Prince walked into *Paws for a Cause*?" she asked.

He nodded. "That day changed my life Sam. I can't even begin to tell you how much."

Pulling him to her, she said softly, "Actually, I have a pretty good idea."

Suddenly she jumped out of bed, remembering his book. He watched curiously as she pulled it out from under the bed, not having bothered to even wrap it. "I made this for you, but I had some help. You can look at it later. In private. It's pretty personal, but important stuff you need to know."

He watched her take it and put it on the bar. Coming to join her, he looked over her shoulder, wrapping his arms around her waist, his chin on her shoulder. "Can I just see one page?" he asked curiously.

Sighing Sam turned to the last page, her page. "It's a memory book. We wrote letters to you and I added photos. You can read my letter." She fled to the bathroom, giving him time to read it in private. He was waiting for her and immediately came to her, taking her face in his hands. "Thank you Sam. What you said, in your letter, means the world to me. I love you so much." Relieved, she smiled, letting him pick her up and carry her to their bed. Their bed. It had a special ring to it, just like the one on her finger.

CHAPTER TWENTY-NINE

The day before Sam's birthday

Sam was in the shower, washing away her day and all the dog hair that went with it, looking forward to meeting Jen and Rachel for dinner at Charlie's. Having shared the news of her engagement, they were excited to celebrate it and her birthday tonight. She threw on white shorts and a light pink tank, adding a ponytail and some light make-up, knowing it was way too hot to worry about it too much. Heading out the door, she noticed a flower truck stopped in front of her building. She stood to watch a large bouquet of flowers headed her way, accepting them from the delivery man.

Calling out a big thank before she took them upstairs, quickly searching for the card she assumed would be from Will. Opening the envelope, she froze to see the loopy handwriting, another card immediately coming to mind. *Congrats on getting our tortured soul to marry you. Wishing you both a good life full of all the love and happiness.*

Taking a deep breath, she knew she didn't need a name to know who they were from. Wanting to see the flowers as a sincere gesture, she chose to believe the hand-written note was a token of Aria's true affection for Will. It bothered her to wonder how she knew about their engagement. Was she keeping tabs on them? And why?

Leaving the card on the table beside the flowers, she briefly admired the beautiful arrangement before heading out the door to Charlie's. She was there in no time, the girls already seated in a booth. They ooohed and awwed over her ring, touched by all the thought Will had put into his proposal. They were happy to see Frankie come over, a big smile on her face.

"Okay girls, before you order your cheeseburgers and fries, I have a special treat for you. We have a pasta special that will blow your taste buds away. Can you do me a favor and give it a try?" She eyed them expectantly.

Sam caved first. "Sure. What kind of pasta is it?"

"The kind that is tonight's special." Frankie said with a laugh.

Having talked them all into ordering the mystery pasta, Frankie was soon back with a bottle of champagne. "This is compliments of a certain someone's fiance. His precise words were "enjoy ladies!"

They were all a bit impressed, Sam's smile the biggest. After popping the cork and pouring a glass for each of them, Jen led the toast on Sam's behalf. "To Sam, who knows how to make the most of a birthday wish and congrats on finding your happily ever after! And cheers to many more happy birthdays!"

As the champagne flowed, there were soon plates of hot heaping pasta, the smoked chicken tender, the carbonara creamy and perfectly seasoned. They requested more bread, the garlic delicious.

When Frankie came to check on them, they were enthusiastic with their compliments. "Oh my gosh it was so good! Please pass along our compliments to the chef!"

"I have a better idea." Frankie said with a mischievous grin. "Why don't you tell him yourself."

Looking in the direction she pointed, they watched curiously as Will made his way through the bar, other customers bestowing accolades upon him. Finally finding his way to them. Sam eyed him in his chef's uniform, not sure what to think.

"Surprise! What did you think of my carbonara ladies?" he asked tentatively, his gaze focused on Sam.

Rachel found her voice first. "It was fantastic Will. Sam didn't tell us she's marrying a chef! You lucky girl!"

Jen was eyeing him suspiciously. "So is this a one night stand or are you Frankie's new chef? Will there be other delectables we will need to taste test in the future?"

He smiled proudly. "Only on Tuesday nights will you be able to find my chef specials."

Noticing Sam hadn't said anything yet, he moved to sit down beside her, the girls quickly scooching around the generous leather banquet. "What did you think, Sam?" He asked quietly.

Realizing all eyes were on her, she leaned into him, her smile warm. "It was delizioso! Why didn't you tell me you were doing this tonight?"

Feeling the awkwardness of their conversation, the girls discreetly got up to go get another bottle of champagne at the bar.

"Actually, I've been doing this for the past month," he said shyly.

"How is that possible? We're together most nights. We're in *here* together on Thursday nights." She said, her look confused.

Nodding, he clarified for her. "I'm only here on Tuesday nights. I've been doing it for fun and to help Frankie out." He shrugged. "Cooking is cathartic for me, especially when I'm only feeding a crowd once a week. I'm sorry I didn't tell you. I knew you would be coming in tonight and thought it would be a fun surprise. Are we good?"

Sam had a sudden flashback to another time she had discovered what Will did to pay his bills. She realized she liked this choice much better. "I love you Will. Anything that makes you happy, I'm here for it. Of course we're good."

She leaned into him, letting him pull her in close for a hug. "I'm happy to hear that. Guess I better get back to the kitchen. I'll be out in an hour and we can walk home together. Sam was all smiles as her friends returned with another bottle, focused on Will's word choice. *Home.* She was a lucky girl.

Soon they were two empty champagne bottles deep, dinner cleared away, her small birthday cake demolished as well. It was getting late when she noticed Will headed their way.

"Ladies. How's it going? I trust you're taking good care of our birthday girl?" he asked. Will's presence signaled their celebrating was over. Headed out with a wave to Frankie, Will got Jen and Rachel into their uber before taking Sam's hand in his to walk her home.

Suddenly he stopped to check his phone as an alarm went off. Turning to Sam, he asked with a smile. "It's almost that time. Do you have your wish ready to send out to the universe?"

Taking his arm, she started walking again. "Actually I'm not making a wish this year."

He stopped them again, clearly startled by this news. "Why not?"

She laughed that his expression was so serious. Putting her arms around his neck she was happy to share why not. "Because I don't need to make my wishes anymore. Nothing I could wish for would make me any happier than I am right at this moment. I have everything I could ever want. In case you didn't get the memo, you were always what I wanted, Will."

He kissed her deeply. "Lucky for both of us, I'm all yours. This birthday and all your future birthdays. I love you Sam."

As they resumed their walking, she laid her head on his shoulder. She was one happy girl and nothing was going to ever jeopardize that again.

She was getting married in a week in her parent's backyard to the man she loved. The twins were excited to walk down the aisle behind her, Ava ready to show Alex how it was done. She had found the perfect dress, flowers and cake were ordered. Their small group of family and friends had all accepted, eager to celebrate them and their love. She had never been so happy in her entire life.

Suddenly it was hard to breathe, feeling herself falling into her old ways. Mentally she chastised herself, reminding herself grimly she was too happy. It couldn't last. What would happen to bring their happiness to a grinding halt this time? Was Aria's note a premonition or a protective blessing? Who was she to turn her back on the keeper of birthday wishes?

Checking her watch, she said out loud, "You hear that universe? He loves me!" *Please protect us and let us live happily ever after.*

Her breathing was just starting to regulate itself again as she watched Will unlock the door. Seeing her face, he brought her some water as she stood reading Aria's card over and over. "Just breathe Sam." He took the card from her before pulling her to him.

He knew she was on the verge of a panic attack, having experienced several himself after the explosion. "You're all good Sam. We've had our share of hard knocks, but now it's our turn to have our share of happiness." Stunned to know he could see her anxiety, she nodded, letting the warmth and strength of him calm her body and mind.

Feeling her relax, he pulled away from her, wanting to see her face. "Was that about me surprising you with my cooking at Charlie's? Or this note from Aria? Or thinking you didn't need to make birthday wishes anymore? Talk to me Sam."

She took his hand and led him to the couch, pulling him down beside her before snuggling into him. She chose her words carefully, not wanting to trigger anything for him.

"I don't do well with surprises. Sorry about that. It's dumb I know."

"You didn't mind when I surprised you and asked you to marry me. Tell me what it really is. I can take it Sam." His look was earnest, needing her to be honest with him.

She knew he had a point, but where to start? "At Charlie's I felt like I didn't even know you when I learned how much you love to cook, that you want to do it professionally. That was a big problem before. You never let me in. I need you to let me in. I need to know the person I"m spending my life with completely. No secrets."

He nodded. "I'm sorry I didn't tell you before. The whole thing happened so randomly. One day Frankie was freaking out when her cook didn't show up for the lunch shift, so I jumped in to help. It was hectic, but fun. The next week I approached her about how she would feel about making Tuesday's pasta night. She loved it. But if you If you hate me doing it, I don't have to." Knowing he was rambling, he stopped talking.

Sitting up, Sam turned to look at him. "I love that for you and for Frankie. I want you to do things that make you happy, that you have a passion for. Everyone needs that. I just want you to share your hopes and dreams with me." She paused, her look intent as she added on. "And your fears Will. This is a two way street, we're here for each other."

Looking over at the flowers sitting on the bar, he knew what was coming next. "How does Aria know we're engaged? Why is she keeping tabs on us?" Turning to him, she watched for his reaction. "Do you think her card is a warning or a blessing?"

He could feel her body tensing again, knowing this had been the trigger for her big feelings tonight. He wasn't sure what the relationship had been between her and Aria, but he knew Sam didn't trust her. Still, he wouldn't be sitting here with her if Aria hadn't saved his life and then brought him to her when he was finally ready.

Suddenly her eyes filled with tears. "And how did I have the audacity to think my life is going to be so perfect I don't need to make birthday wishes anymore! It all just got to me."

He pulled her into his lap, holding her tight. He realized this was the first time he could remember her falling apart in front of him, while also knowing he had held her like this before. He focused on her now and the things she had said.

"I'm going to choose to believe Aria truly wants us to be happy. It's a blessing. Why wouldn't it be? I feel like Aria is powerful in her family and for whatever reason, she's watching over us, making sure we're safe."

Sam thought about what he said, knowing what Elisa had said too. She wasn't sure how Aria had managed it, but it did appear she was now in charge, the head of her family, whatever that entailed.

She nodded. "You're right. I know how much she cares about you Will. I love that you see it as her blessing."

He took her hand in his, bringing it to his lips. "I love you Sam and I know how strong we are together. We both know how hard life can be, but we'll have each other to get us through those hard times, whatever they may be." She nodded at him, laying her head back on his shoulder.

"I also know how beautiful life can be, Sam. In a week you're going to be the most beautiful bride Brooklyn has ever seen. The joy we're going to share becoming husband and wife is endless. We're way overdue for some happiness and we're going to have it, birthday wish or not. I promise."

She sighed, keeping her last minute hail mary to herself. Putting her arms around his neck, she brought Will closer, kissing him fiercely. "I love you Will and can't wait to marry you. Let the happily ever after begin!"

She was going to choose to believe in them and their love. Why wouldn't she? When Will made a promise, she believed him, knowing he had kept the last one, finding his way back to her. Why would her birthday wishes fail her now when they had never let her down before? Yep, she still wasn't too old to believe in making wishes. Happily ever after sounded pretty good and she was going to hold on to it with both hands.

EPILOGUE

Ten months after Sam's last birthday

They sat together on the couch, Will holding their new daughter. Sam's mom and Riley had popped in to make sure they were getting all settled in and to bring them food. Now for the first time they were alone as a family of three, Sam's heart about to burst with the joy she felt seeing her husband hold their beautiful baby girl.

"This is one of the happiest days of my life." Sam said softly, taking her daughter's tiny hand, marveling when she wrapped it around her finger.

Looking over at her, she realized Will was feeling all the emotions too, even without the hormones raging through him. "I can't believe I finally have a family again. You've given me the greatest gift ever Sam. I never thought I would be a dad." Leaning over, he kissed her on the cheek. "I've always loved you and now, now I love us."

She nodded, her emotions preventing her from speaking. Will had been the happiest man in the world on their wedding day. He had been cautious but full steam ahead when Sam had encouraged him to follow his passion and open his own catering business. As her baby bump had grown bigger and bigger, she had decided it was time to close *Paws for a Cause*. Having just finished renovating their brownstone back into a home, it seemed only logical to turn her grooming space into a commercial kitchen.

His business had only been open six months, but was already booming thanks to his Tuesday night pasta nights at Charlie's. Sam was happy to work from her home office, taking on their website and social media, Riley serving as their chief consultant.

Throughout her pregnancy, Will had made sure he did everything he could to support her. Answering to all her cravings, holding her hair during morning sickness, and even giving foot rubs at the end of the day, he could not have been more attentive. Setting the nursery up had been Will's pride and joy, painting the room, putting together the crib, and running all the packages delivered up the stairs for Sam. He had sat in awe one night as she folded freshly laundered baby clothes, trying to fathom they would be responsible for someone so small.

Sighing heavily, Sam laid her head on Will's shoulder. "I love us too. We're one blessed family."

"Do you hear that Rory? We are so blessed to have you as our daughter. Welcome home sweet girl." Will crooned to her.

It had been a challenge to find the perfect name for her. Will had been torn between making her middle name after his mother or his granny, Sam deciding to leave it up to him. In the end, he had wanted to go with Jordan, not needing to explain why. Sam had hugged him tearfully, the thought of Jordan living on through their daughter bringing her much happiness. Given all they had been through, it gave them both comfort to know there would be so many angels watching over their baby girl.

They had researched names carefully, needing her name to be perfect but confident they would know when they found the right one. It had taken awhile but one night she had come across the name Aurora. When she told Will it was meant to symbolize hope and new beginnings, he had agreed it was perfect, just like she was bound to be.

Finding Aurora a mouthful, they had quickly shortened it to Rory. And now here they sat together, Will, Sam, and Rory starting a new chapter, finding their happily ever after to be everything they had ever hoped for.

They had been so focused on getting Rory inside, they had both failed to notice the expensive black compact car sitting across the street from their brownstone. Upstairs, they were enjoying their new bundle of joy when she crossed the street in her hat and shades, leaving a white package with a pink bow flapping in the breeze. She almost felt bad ringing their doorbell, disturbing their new found family bliss. Tucking her note with her loopy handwriting under the bow, she knew it said everything she wanted it to say.

Happy birthday baby Rory. Always know where your story started.

QUESTIONS FOR BOOK CLUB

1. Did you enjoy Prince or Riley more as a secondary character?

2. Have you ever had your fortune read with tarot cards? Did you feel like the Tower card did come true for Sam? Did her upheaval in Naples lead to a blessing in disguise?

3. As a reader, did you ever feel frustrated that Will and Sam struggled so much to get out of the friend zone? On a scale of 1-10, how spicy did you think the story was?

4. Do you feel like Sam and Will helped each other grow in the story or did they grow together through the things that happened to them?

5. Did you feel the story was more romantic or suspenseful, or a good blend of both.

6. When Sam turned to Pretty Woman as her self-soothing movie, did it make you think of your own comfort movie? What were your thoughts when Will worked to create a similar scene for Sam in Naples?

7. What did Sam's birthday wishes represent to you? Did they seem contrived or meaningful? Did you agree when she made her hail mary after declaring she didn't need to make wishes anymore?

8. On a scale of 1-10, how satisfying did you find the ending? Do you feel like the author left room for a sequel that you would want to read?

9. If you could ask the author one question about the story, what would it be?

10. If this book became a Hallmark movie, who would you cast in the roles of Sam and Will?

ABOUT THE AUTHOR

After forty years of inspiring young children to love reading and writing, Elaine is looking forward to retirement and taking on a new chapter, hopeful of becoming your next favorite author. Birthday Wishes is her fourth novel and after spending a year and a half writing it, she is excited to share it with you. She was inspired for this book one day when picking up her dog Winnie from the groomers. Curious as to what happens if someone fails to pick up their dog, it was the nugget she needed to be off and running writing her newest romance, building the story of Sam and Will and how their lives would intersect a decade later.

In addition to being a first grade teacher, Elaine has been married for thirty-seven years, is a proud mom to two grown daughters, and one four legged problem child named Winnie. She loves to spend time with family and friends playing games over a glass of wine and listening to music. Her hobbies include reading, writing, gardening, and traveling. She is looking forward to making a trip to Italy in the near future.

Having experienced tremendous loss in the last decade, Elaine knew how her characters felt as they worked to find their new normal and embrace happiness when it finally came their way again. She wishes you all love, joy and good health always.

Happy reading!